DOMESTICATED MAGIC

Published by Winterbourne Publishing, Western Australia.

ISBN: 978-0-9874511-7-0 (ebook) / 978-0-9874511-9-4 (print).

DOMESTICATED MAGIC

WENDY PALMER

Winterbourne
Publishing

CHAPTER 1

MATEO WAS UP WELL BEFORE THE sun to dress in the formal robes for the morning ritual, and he was not happy about it. There was a reason it had become the morning ritual rather than the dawn ritual during his tenure as Soul of Kindred Taurasi, and a reason he'd refused the full regalia even before Anika had sold most of it off.

But it was the first ritual since the news had reached the Imperial port city of Anceral that Ysthera, the Sunlit Isle, had sunk to the bottom of the sea, forever lost. Sometimes sops had to be thrown to a frightened and grieving people, no matter how much they tried to pretend to him that they were not frightened and grieving.

Anika herself had brought the silk robes over from storage, and she stayed to help Mateo dress in the layers, and painted his face with the kohl and powders, and styled his hair into an elaborate coiffure that involved a good hour, a great deal of paste, and a fair number of pinned and looped braids.

Then he did the same for her, because if the Soul had to do it, so did the Heart, except her costuming was, unfairly, very much less extravagant.

By the time they crossed the misty street to the teahouse, Mateo's bad hip was already aching from the unfamiliar stress of the dressing palaver and the unfamiliar weight that was this awful ritual costume and the unfamiliar chill of being awake and moving this wretchedly early.

It was fair to say Mattias Taurasi, Soul of Kindred Taurasi, was not in the best of moods.

Anika, on the other hand, was looking very fetching in her silks and cosmetics and was her usual buoyant self—or at least, that was the self she presented to her people, when her buoyancy was needed to keep some eighty refugees afloat.

Darius, Anika's uncle, had left the teahouse shutters closed but lit the porch lamps, a golden glow against the light mist, and lit the interior lamps, and lit the fires in the big kitchen stove and in the small ceramic stove in the near corner, which was where Mateo went to stand, angling his hip to the radiating warmth.

He didn't rub the hip. Too many of his people were already here, kneeling on their cushions, the woven fabrics making bright squares of patterned colour against the polished parquetry.

Penelope came in. She was a Taurasi elder, inky hair stranded with silver but spine ever straight. She had been Heart before Anika and before Charion, who had been lost on the day of the exile. Penelope was perfectly pleasant, a stickler for tradition, and had a way of reminding Anika and Mateo that they were both a good ten or fifteen or even twenty years too young for their roles.

'Oh, don't you look lovely,' she said to Mateo when she saw him in the regalia. 'Very ceremonial today, that makes a welcome change.'

This, of course, was to point out that he usually did not look ceremonial at all.

'You could be wearing the status markers,' she suggested, touching her throat and her earlobes to indicate the lack of jewellery in those places on Mateo.

He looked around at the others. 'They…know my status, Penelope.'

'Always in such a mood in the morning,' she said, walking off to find her cushion.

'Well, *now* I am,' he muttered, unjustly, which merely proved her point and further annoyed him.

Anika had gone behind the counter into the small kitchen workspace and was reading the esoteric marks carved into the mossy-green wax of a tabula, picked from the top of a short stack. The little boxwood-framed tablets were used for sending messages throughout the city, in preference to the far more expensive innovation of paper.

As not only their Heart but one of the few literate Taurasi, Anika dealt with the Imperials, and the Imperials had learnt to be thorough administrators. A steady stream of tablets issued from the governor's residence and its associated army of clerical scribes, as well as from friends, customers and associates of the Come-By-Chance Teahouse. Anika wielded an iron stylus to carve her own marks—acknowledgements, replies, counterpoints—and dutifully sent them back.

Shaking her head, Anika rubbed the wax clean with the flattened wedge end of the stylus and dropped the offending tabula close by the kitchen stove where she brewed her herbal teas. The wax would soften in the heat, melting away any last trace of whatever unpleasant message the surface had held. That message, it seemed, would not be receiving a response, dutiful or otherwise.

It was typical, thought Mateo in his morning gloom, that Imperials took something as beautiful as pure beeswax, golden and gently scented, and polluted it into mossy darkness with resins and soot just to make it more useful to their own narrow needs.

Eminently pragmatic, were Imperials, in language, in dress, in worship, in food, and in their longstanding overlordship across the entire landmass from Chalcadea in the west to the city-states here on the east coast.

Anika set aside the rest of the tabulae for later attention. She came around the counter to stand on the lowest step of the short flight of stairs that led up to the storage room and her own private quarters.

That lowest step acted as the metaphorical equivalent of the village dais back on Ysthera. Mateo paced over to join her. The layered robes made his walk slow and stately, which was, now he thought about it, probably half the point of the blighted things.

He looked about the young and old faces upturned attentively towards him. Almost all the adult Taurasi were here today, emerging from the traditionally prescribed three days of private mourning and the rituals that went along with that. It hardly seemed adequate to mark the passing of an entire island and its people; certainly, none of the sole surviving Ystheran Kindred could truly be finished mourning.

But they had mortgages, and children to feed. The teahouse had to re-open to customers. Kindred Taurasi had to find its strength and move on, as it had done before, Anika its steadfast guiding light and unfaltering bulwark both.

Most of the Taurasi were kneeling on their cushions now, in ragged rows. They stared silently up at Anika and Mateo, their Heart and Soul, the very last Heart and Soul in all the world. The air felt heavy, the moment too significant.

Timon wolf-whistled, then, and the anticipatory tension broke. Anika laughed and took Mateo's hand, and they bowed together to their people, and their people, kneeling, made the genuflection in return. Most did it in the moderate way that Mateo preferred, if it had to happen at all, but Penelope and her faction lowered their foreheads all the way to the floor as per the oldest tradition.

Anika sighed, seeing that. She raised her voice into oration. 'We have taken a heavy blow,' she said, and the Taurasi murmured in return. 'We have all lost family and friends, far more permanently than we ever expected. I think we all thought we would go home one day, didn't we?'

Again came the murmur of agreement.

'We suffered when we made the decision to leave the island, and we suffered on the day of the exile itself,' she went on.

The Taurasi response was louder this time, and Andrea, Timon's twin sister, called, 'Aniketa the Unconquerable!'

'Yes, yes, all right, settle down,' Anika said, waving a hand. 'We suffered then, and we suffer now. Our Sunlit Isle, gone beneath the waves well over a week ago, and none of us felt a thing.'

It felt pointed; it wasn't, of course. But Mateo bowed his head, feeling the sting all the same. He was a Soul, blessed of their sleeping goddess. Shouldn't he have felt something when Ysthera cracked and all the other Souls were lost, their web of interconnection sundered forever? Should not something in him have cried out as most of their people were crushed or drowned in cataclysm?

Anika lifted her voice now. 'Yet we are Taurasi. We are strong, and we are brave, and we are resilient, and, most importantly, we are together. We will prevail.' She raised a fist. 'Kindred Taurasi!'

'Kindred Taurasi!' came the chorus, a throbbing echo that rang through the teahouse.

'That said,' she went on, quieter. 'We suffer, but we need not suffer alone. If anyone finds themselves awake in the middle of the night, ruminating on these things, you are always welcome to talk to me. Or Mateo.' She smiled at him. 'Though not today. We all know how Teo copes with mornings.'

The grouchy face Mateo helpfully pulled, and the resultant ripple of laughter, effectively shifted the mood towards a more normal morning gathering.

'Right.' Anika clapped her hands, signalling the final switch from leader to administrator. 'We were discussing sending our children to the temple school at the bottom of the hill. Do we have more to say or are we ready to vote?'

Penelope immediately rose. 'We must vote no. Our children would be indoctrinated into Imperial customs and the Imperial language and the Imperial worship of a truly profligate number of gods.'

'Yes, that's why they strongly encourage us to send our children to the local school,' Anika said patiently. 'Please bear in mind, when I say they strongly encourage us, it is on the threshold of being a mandate. They are merely playing nice, for now.'

That was probably the waxen message she'd deliberately obliterated, then.

'One of their mandates is no magic,' Timon pointed out. 'We defy that one.'

'Not openly,' Anika said, with a glance towards the door as if an Imperial spy might be eavesdropping. 'Nevertheless, it will be our burden, to ensure we do not sacrifice our children's heritage, if we decide in favour.'

This merely triggered the Ystheran tendency to be overdramatic. 'This is how they destroy us,' Penelope declaimed, to scattered applause. 'Not with swords to our throats but with words forcibly inscribed into the impressionable clay of our children's minds!'

It was Helena's turn to stand up. She was a mother, with three children of her own and another two fostered under her care. She'd allied into Taurasi, to a man now lost, and was nervous to address the whole Kindred. She smoothed her sash as she cleared her throat. 'I'm concerned… *We're* concerned'—she waved her hand, indicating the people on the cushions around her, mostly other parents, blood and foster, a few with babes in arms—'our children will not have the skills and knowledge they need to make their way in our new world, if they don't attend a local school. If we try too hard to save our past, we may be sacrificing their future instead.'

'Why can't we teach them ourselves?' someone demanded from the crowd.

'It's not enough,' Anika said. 'If we have to do it at all, better to send them down the hill and do it properly.'

Timon, absently scratching the welter of scars on his face, said, 'We left Ysthera to preserve our way of life. This won't help.'

His sister, herself wearing a scar through her left eyebrow, said, 'There is no going back to Ysthera, Ti, not anymore, if there ever was. We must face reality.'

'I know that,' he snapped. Anika raised a soothing hand, and his hackles settled. 'Ask the children what they want.'

Lucius rose. He was an adolescent, only recently old enough to attend the morning ritual. Ystherans didn't tend towards facial or body hair but Lucius was making a try, somewhat patchy, at growing a moustache in one of the varied local fashions. Like Helena, he was uncertain about addressing the group.

Fidgeting, he said, 'It's been really difficult finding work down in the city, not having been to one of their schools. Not knowing the customs. Not being even basically literate. Numbers. We should at least know how to tell numbers.'

He sat down in a hurry, signalling the end of his contribution. Penelope, who had not sat down yet, said, 'That is why we should be trying harder to be sure all of us can be gainfully employed within the enclave itself. You could apprentice to my workshop, dear. Learn the clay.'

'Please don't call us an enclave,' Anika reminded her. 'It makes the governor twitchy.'

Andrea said, sharply, 'Some of us like working down in Anceral.'

Selia, who also worked down in the brewery, added, 'Some of us are thinking of *living* down in Anceral.'

This got some audible gasps, and the discussion rapidly became acrimonious; someone again suggested hiring local tutors rather than consigning the children to a school out of Taurasi oversight, someone else snapped that that would bring strangers too intimately into their lives, whereupon there was a chorus of pointing out that the whole teahouse did that, every afternoon, and an answering outcry that Anika was managing that well enough and how else, exactly, were they to live if they did not cater to the Ancerans?

Anika pulled a slight face at Mateo but she let the rivulets of the argument run in their diverse directions; squabbles meant the Taurasi were moving beyond the first deep bite of grief. Eventually she clapped her hands again, calling for silence.

'I am hearing that it is too soon to make the vote,' she said serenely. 'You have all made good points. I know this is contentious. I know the diverging path forwards feels momentous, given Ysthera's fate and the precariousness of our own. There is no need to rush to a decision.' She raised a finger. 'But a decision must be made.'

She nodded once, signalling the end of the morning meeting, and the start of the morning ritual.

Every Ystheran held within themselves a sacred receptacle, the *scaphosieros* in the most archaic of terminology, to hold the magic that was the last gift of their shattered goddess, transmitted by their Soul during the ritualised daily libation.

The Taurasi who had been standing knelt again. Mateo moved among them, the silk hems of his robes brushing the swept wooden floor in a soft sibilance that echoed the gentle hum of the magic rising in him like water from a wellspring. He felt the tendrils of his kith's call, a gentle tickle as if of thin roots growing through welcoming soil, seeking nourishment.

He did not need to touch them to pass on the gift, but today he did. They were tense, and fractious, and scared. Ysthera was lost, and their fate was yawning underneath them, a hungry mouth ready to swallow them into oblivion should they slip from the narrow bridge Anika led them over towards an unknown future. Mateo laid hands on bowed heads or shoulders, murmuring words that were not strictly necessary, but served a purpose nonetheless.

He was aglow with the magic, and as it flowed out to the others, the teahouse filled with delicate amber light, its hue slowly deepening, thickening, a bowl of the purest golden honey. It was a marvel that no one without Ystheran blood could perceive.

'Let's practice the shield, everyone,' Anika called.

Traditionally, only the Coterie, those few chosen to gird the Soul, formed the defensive shield, but after the day of the exile, even Penelope and her fellow conservatists saw the sense of every Taurasi having some skill at interweaving into a larger communal working. There was precedent for it, after all, back when Penelope had been Heart.

Mateo returned to Anika's side. She had already taken her fill of magic, as had the twins, the other members of the Coterie. Mateo had once supported four in his Coterie. It was taking a long time to identify a suitable Taurasi to take up the fourth place, and the fifth place that Mateo now felt able to support as well.

He pushed the magic out, the trickle becoming a gush. The Taurasi caught at it and let it flow through them. The honey aura rippled and a cascading thrum rose louder and louder as they lifted the magic shield overhead.

'Modulate,' Anika called. 'Take more if you feel you can.'

The draw on Mateo increased as the kith obeyed, and the shield thickened. Anika looked at him, and he nodded reassurance; he was fine. He would have turned off the metaphorical tap if he wasn't.

'Remember when our Soul is flooding us like this, it is up to *you* to recognise when it is too much for you.' She put a flat hand to her sternum and then squeezed it slowly closed. 'Learn what too much feels like. Your heart will stop if you get this wrong, kith of my Kindred.'

She walked among the Taurasi, watching each face, looking for signs of strain. She also nudged a few into opening themselves further to take more of the flow. Sometimes Ystherans with small receptacles—pockets, somewhat derogatorily—assumed their access to the flow was correspondingly narrow, but that was not necessarily true. Nor did a Coterie-worthy receptacle mean immunity to the dangers of overflow. That was another thing hammered into Taurasi hearts on the day they'd made it off the island.

'Look up, Kindred,' Anika called. 'Is our shield not a thing of beauty?' It was, smooth as glass, thick as honey, translucent as purest amber. 'Well done, everyone. Release.'

The shield dropped and the hum and glow of the magic faded as Mateo let it sink away, back into the endless reservoir pooled deep within him. The Taurasi were relaxed, chatting and laughing now, some already heaping up their cushions in the corner by the stove and rolling out the tables and chairs for the afternoon customers, others lingering over their bowls.

They'd be moving towards their chores or their projects or their jobs soon, soothed by the magic and by the familiar ritual that furnished it to them. Anika had been right about wearing the robes, of course. The Taurasi had begun the slow process of healing from yet another cataclysm.

Mateo had served his people well today; he had time for a burst of satisfaction about that as he offered Anika a bow and started for the door.

Then the door opened and an Imperial walked in.

CHAPTER 2

THE STRANGER WAS WHAT WAS KNOWN colloquially among the ever-blunt Imperials as an empire mongrel, one of those people with such mixed heritage it was impossible to tell which conquered nation their ancestors originally hailed from.

He was browner than both the Ystherans and the local Ancerans, and certainly the heartland Imperials, who were a very pale people from even more northern climes than this. He had light eyes, and dark hair in short curls, and an artful, if not outright vain, level of stubble that bespoke regular plucking at a barber. He wore a popular imported style of dyed long-sleeved shirt, but sported the calf-length breeches, oilskin cloak, short scabbard, and plaited leather cords about wrist and neck that Mateo associated with sailors.

That was all Mateo was capable of absorbing before his rising alarm swamped him. The man could be given some credit for hiding his double-take as he looked at Mateo and then about the teahouse, but he was still *looking about the teahouse*.

Imperial subjects were theoretically allowed to worship their own gods in private, but that was an unwritten leniency overlaid on a public law that said no foreign gods could be acknowledged within the endless bounds of the Vaeringan Empire.

The Ystherans didn't worship a god, as such—their deity was, more-or-less, lost to them, though not quite as unquestionably as their island now was—but Mateo well knew how the morning ritual would appear to Imperial eyes, especially today, he and Anika bearing their elaborate regalia and half of Kindred Taurasi caught still kneeling.

'The teahouse is closed,' he said, reflexively and with a good deal of sharpness to it, a spit in the face of an amiable smile and upheld, spread-fingered hand, the local gesture of peace.

'Door unlatched, porch lamps lit?' The man didn't say it rudely; he merely raised his eyebrows in an exaggeratedly puzzled way.

Mateo, on the other hand, was dramatically snide in reply. 'An Imperial informs us we're open, I suppose we better be, then.'

He tried to exit past the other man, who languidly put out an arm to barricade the doorway, still smiling but also watching Mateo intently. Though shorter than him, he was much broader, and the arm that blocked the doorway looked thickly muscled under the weave of the shirt, as if it regularly swung a fist, if not a sword.

Mateo experienced another spike of anxiety and simultaneously produced a bloody-minded scowl, defying not so much the stranger as the *what-if* worries that were ever-ready to swarm him.

'I wasn't insisting you must be open, friend,' the visitor said, as conspicuously patient as he had been conspicuously puzzled. He was speaking the local dialect, Imperial with a generous sprinkling of Anceran loan words; Imperial itself was a simplified, if not bastardised, version of the pure Vaer spoken in the northern heartland. 'I was just wondering how I could tell you're closed, so I know for future visits.'

'Because I told you we are,' Mateo said through gritted teeth, since the man had actually made a good point regarding the external clues.

'Understood,' the man said, to his surprise. 'But since I'm here, and it's a long way up a particularly steep hill to get here, could I perhaps speak to someone regarding a business matter?' After a moment, he added, flashing a rueful smile, 'Someone reasonable would be preferable. I can wait.'

Unable to decide whether he had justification to be huffy at this blatant slander or not, Mateo availed himself of his usual recourse, which was to call Anika, who was, of course, already coming to him, and Darius was, of course, trailing along with her, all narrowed eyes and glowering aspect and conspicuous hilt.

Anika firmly dismissed her uncle with a glance, and turned to the newcomer, repeating the gesture of the upheld open palm. 'Heilsa,' she said, the slangy local greeting that would never not sound strange to Mateo in the mouth of an Ystheran. 'Welcome to the Come-by-Chance Teahouse. I am Aniketa Taurasi. How may I assist you?'

The stranger had still been leaning casually in the doorway, blocking the way either by design or accident. He straightened to greet Anika, and Mateo slipped past, back into his sandals while the man was introducing himself as one Jonas Nebrija, and over to the lodging house.

In his small apartment, Mateo unlaced and wriggled out of the silk robes, hanging them on the back of the door for one of the younger Ystherans to collect and brush down and put back into storage. Already calmer out of the smothering robes, he changed into the Ystherans' usual working clothes, a knotweed-blue cotton tunic worn over a long-sleeved undershirt, and matching loose trousers.

He expected the Imperial to be gone by the time he'd secured the wrap-around tunic firmly closed with his favourite emerald-green sash, scrubbed his face clean of kohl and powder, tugged his braided hair out of its elaborate formal styling and bound it, still braided, into its usual bun low at his nape, and shrugged into his quilted jacket for the walk back over to the teahouse.

He toed off his sandals again by the door and went in, and stopped on the threshold.

Jonas Nebrija was not gone. Jonas Nebrija, cloak comfortably discarded because he was well and truly and horrifyingly *settled in*, sat at the small, high table set by the little ceramic stove—the table where Mateo always ate his morning meal because that allowed the stove's radiating warmth to sink into his hip before he began his daily round of chores.

Anika stood beside him, her hand on his shoulder, her face sympathetic, bending to murmur some quiet reassurance or compassionate sentiment into his ear. Even as Mateo stared in surprise, she gave him one last sympathetic squeeze and crossed towards the kitchen.

'Sit and be nice to Jonas,' she murmured as Mateo hovered, assessing exactly how alarmed he should be by this fresh turn of events.

Oh. Highly alarmed, then. Excessively, even.

Anika knew him. Without pausing, she called over her shoulder, 'Your tea is steeping, *melimou*, go sit down and I'll bring it over.'

This, unlike her first suggestion, was in the local dialect, and loud, and accompanied by a point towards the table, so he was blockaded from arguing, or about-turning and walking out of his violated sanctuary, and thus obliged to obey his Heart.

He eased onto the bench opposite Jonas Nebrija, absently pushing on his hip as he did so. Anceran-style seating was easier than getting up and down from the cushions, which was the entire purpose of his high table near the stove, but the transition from standing to sitting was still fraught.

'Oh, so *you're* Mattias,' Jonas said, in tones friendly and yet not entirely pleased.

Mateo took a moment to refuse to be impressed that the man had managed to recognise him despite the transformation out of the formal, and ridiculously dramatic, ritual attire—which made most locals decide that all Ystherans were strange and exotic—and into the workaday routine attire—which let most locals decide that all Ystherans looked alike. Mateo was taller and leaner than the other petitely rounded Ystherans, and that was an easy enough cue to mark even through the frippery.

'I'm not happy about this either,' he pointed out.

Jonas snorted a short laugh, teeth flashing square and white as he grinned, a hint of wolf to it. The teahouse lamplight gleamed off the earrings Mateo was now calm enough to notice—jet teardrops, in both lobes, properly pierced. Mateo associated that not just with sailors but with the bold privateering traders who had taken Kindred Taurasi off Ysthera.

His Soul cup was already on the table, its small gilt elegance contrasted with the larger cup—one of their locally produced efforts—sitting in front of Jonas. In lieu of anything else to fidget with, Mateo picked up his cup and turned it around and around in his fingers.

Penelope and a few other Taurasi lingering on cushions on the far side of the teahouse were beginning to glare at him over their morning bowls of millet porridge. This particular cup was over one hundred years old. There was no replacing it once it broke, not anymore. He did not particularly want to be the Soul who broke it, though it would be an apt sort of metaphor if he happened to.

Mateo put it back down, very carefully.

Jonas, appallingly, picked it up. 'Why butterflies?' he asked, holding it up to the light so that the colours glowed.

Mateo knew exactly what Jonas was asking. He braved the pang in his hip, half-stood, leaned over the table, and retrieved the cup from the man's hand, Jonas obligingly opening his fingers and allowing it to be plucked free.

Smiling, he rested his forearms on the table. 'Why butterflies, when you're Taurasi?'

He nodded to Mateo's rescued cup, and then across the room to where the last few Taurasi sipped from their own brightly decorated cups. More Kindred cups were already washed and dried and set within the niches of the pale honeycomb shelving behind the counter. A section of the hexagonal wooden alcoves was devoted to the cups of kith lost on the day of the exile, as well as older ancestors; they'd each be preserved in their discreet shrine until it came time to be ritually presented to a Taurasi child when they came of age. Lucius had just received his with shy pride.

Every cup was different, in colour and design and shape, except they all featured oxen or cows or the horns of such or abstract suggestions of the same. The very door of the Come-By-Chance was painted with a horned bull's head, though Timon had transformed its traditional simple lines into botanically-influenced curves, a nod to both the floral and herbal tisanes the teahouse purveyed, and to the feminine composition of their regular customers.

Mateo's cup, however, was festooned, quite beautifully, with butterflies of bright green, the same colour as his sash, touched with gilt on their wings and all around the rim of the cup itself, so that it glittered in the low light of the cosy teahouse.

'Very pretty,' Jonas added encouragingly.

'You are trying to imply I am effeminate for drinking from a cup ornamented with something pretty,' Mateo said, 'yet you cannot insult me, for this is my Kindred cup and therefore it is a tradition to drink from it and makes me no less of a man regardless of the social constructs of your own people.'

Jonas missed a beat and then said, 'I'm an Imperial, I don't imply things, I just say them.' He smiled at Mateo and returned to his point, puzzlingly persistent. 'Are you not Taurasi, then?'

Mateo silently tilted his cup so that Jonas could see the stylised horns painted on the bottom. 'How is it that we can assist you, honoured guest?'

Jonas raised his eyebrows at that extremely formal salutation, which Mateo had fairly laden with acid. 'I'm looking to tour your pottery workshop.'

Mateo looked over at the kitchen workspace. Anika was not in evidence; she'd be upstairs, changing out of her own ritual outfit, or outside, snipping herbs. He looked back at Jonas.

'I'm a merchant, friend,' Jonas said, eyes bright with amusement. 'As I told your wife, I'm here on behalf of a consortium interested in Ystheran artisanal products.'

Raising a firm finger in negation, Mateo said sternly, 'Anika is not my wife, and you, *friend*, are not a merchant.'

The man not only lost his battle to not smirk, he openly grinned. 'I would like a tour of the pottery workshop. I was making small talk about the ceramics on display in here first, because I was under the impression Ystherans like a bit of dancing about the bush before they get down to business. Am I wrong?'

'Am *I* wrong? You are not a merchant.'

'Why am I not a merchant?'

At which point Mateo realised that if he wanted to justify his own dudgeon, he would have to provide commentary regarding wicked smiles and strong, well-shaped bodies with swordfighter muscles, and their unlikely relation to the mercantile notables he'd encountered in Low village, the little harbour enclave—literally, the lowest point on Ysthera—where foreigners had been permitted to stay. But he could hardly tell the man he looked… Ah, that he looked like he belonged swinging a sword in the fighting pits.

He said, 'You're just not.'

'That is true,' Jonas conceded at last. 'I'm doing a favour for a family friend before I take up my new calling as a laeknir. A physician.'

'You are *not*,' Mateo said, fully indignant.

The creaking old doctors of his passing acquaintance—Anika had brought in a veritable raft of them in the first weeks of their arrival in Anceral before deciding she could do well enough by Mateo on her own—were even further from the striking figure across the table than the big-bellied merchants at the old market.

Jonas burst into atrociously loud and unrestrained laughter that briefly stopped the quiet clatter among the Taurasi still finishing their meals. 'I've undertaken training as a physician so I can work with my father,' he insisted, wiping his eyes.

'Then why do you look like you murder people for a living?' Mateo blurted.

'Honey, you are hilarious,' Jonas said. 'I didn't say I was a particularly *good* physician, did I? Maybe I *do* murder people for a living.' He held up his hand. 'But I was once a merchant. Or trader, actually, I think Ystherans would translate it. I followed in my mother's footsteps in my younger days and crewed a trading ship. Low was on our route, before it closed.'

Trader, not merchant. That made more sense. The sea traders who made it to Low were of the more piratical sort; they had to be, to run the Imperial blockade. Mateo had even recognised that the man's earrings reminded him of the dauntless crew of *Steadfast*, and yet he'd still failed to make the connection in time to stop himself being rude.

Timon came over to set a plate in front of him, its contents laid out just so: sliced figs in a fan, drizzled with honey and sprinkled with soft crumbled cheese made from the milk of their own cows.

Mateo silently gave his thanks, head dipped over folded hands. Timon mischievously patted his head and headed out, followed by a cluster of his renovation team.

Andrea was next, bringing over pucks of barley cake still warm from the ovens of the stone bakehouse. She put this plate before Mateo, but then nudged it towards the centre of the table as a nod to their guest.

Mateo gave another small seated bow. Andrea squeezed his shoulder. She and Selia, and some of the other city workers, went out the door, Andrea carrying a stack of Anika's tabulae to drop off at the local messenger office on her way to the brewery.

Jonas was swallowing another smile. 'Your people like to serve you, don't they?'

Mateo would have very much liked to deny this, but since Anika was currently carrying a tray over with his tea, not even he could bring himself to do so. Instead he repeated, flatly, 'You people.'

'I did say your people,' Jonas corrected him with nary a flicker of impatience nor annoyance.

Anika set down the tray and its two pots of tea. She had indeed taken the opportunity to change out of her ceremonial robes and wash her face. Her sash was dark blue, embroidered with paler blue flowers that matched the sky shade of the threads of her quilted jacket. She placed Mateo's brewpot in front of him. He bowed his thanks, ignoring Jonas's grin.

'It'll taste different today,' she told him. 'I'm trying crushed holly leaves.'

'Make this foreigner go away now, please,' he said in Ystheran, pouring himself a cup before she could further amuse Jonas by pouring it for him.

'He's not a foreigner,' Anika said, also in Ystheran, setting the second pot in front of Jonas and carefully tweaking its positioning to best show off the pattern of Ystheran wildflowers adorning its rounded sides. 'We're the foreigners, and he might say he's merely a trader but he presented some very impressive-looking credentials from a large merchant conglomerate. We need to ingratiate with the locals and we have accounts to pay, so stop trying to antagonise the man, be the good little refugee you're expected to be, and take him for his tour. Charm the pants off him, my sweet.'

Mateo was appalled, both by the Imperial colloquialism creeping into their language, and by the very idea. 'We both know I couldn't charm the pants off *anyone*. He could already be naked and I still wouldn't be able to charm the pants off him. He'd put his pants back *on*, Aniketa.'

They both looked at Jonas, who smiled at them, apparently unoffended by the unintelligible chatter. 'What've you got for me, then?'

Mateo had a moment of sheer horror before the man added, 'Is this the famous Ystheran spice tea?' with a nod to the brewpot Anika had placed on the table before him.

'No,' Mateo said. 'You may not have that. It is only for afternoons.'

Anika did not quite slap her forehead but she did set the heel of her hand against the centre of her brow, pressing between her eyes in silent exasperation.

'Well, it *is*,' he said. '*And* it takes one hour to serve. A *proper* hour.'

This last was because Ancerans let their hours wax and wane with the natural length of the day, recalibrating their sundials across seasons accordingly. The Taurasi, however, had brought their own time technology with them. An Ystheran water-clock, traditional in design if not in material, both tapped and simultaneously decorated the twisted copper waterpipes along the back of the kitchen workspace beside the Kindred cup alcoves.

Daylight hours measured by sundials, and the points of each hour measured by rushlights, and night bells counted out by the slow burn of candles or incense sticks in the temples, the cinnamon hour preceding the hour of sage and succeeding the clove hour: the Imperials, Mateo thought, could have saved themselves an awful lot of the time they were so intent on measuring if they'd borrowed the design of the water-clock.

Presuming Taurasi would deign to give it to them.

'An hour? You harvest and mill those spices yourselves, do you?' Jonas asked, straight-faced.

'In fact, we do,' Anika said, in the bright tones of one trying very hard to keep the conversation from devolving into disaster. She widened her eyes meaningfully at Mateo.

He folded his arms and dug in. 'There is a ritual. The ritual takes one Ystheran hour.' The Anceran women who came for the spice tea enjoyed the wait, as far as Mateo could tell. 'In the afternoon.'

'Hey, Mattias,' Jonas said, 'do you happen to know the word "obstreperous"?'

Mateo did happen to know the word "obstreperous". 'I do not know what you are implying,' he said stiffly.

'Oh, I'm certainly not *implying* it,' Jonas said.

Nikiti flung the door open and bounced in while Mateo was still scowling and Anika was still swallowing her laugh. Thirteen years old or so, Niki was dressed as the adults, in the soft blue-grey working tunic, wrapped closed with a saffron-patterned scarlet sash, but without undershirt or quilted jacket. The young ones were adapting faster to the northern climate than the older Taurasi. Niki's hair was styled into a single thin plait hanging between their shoulder blades, and the sash was tied asymmetrically somewhere between the treble-wrap and the fold-and-twist.

This was a fairly new development, and briefly unsettling, like Mateo's eyes had had trouble focussing for a moment. His own adults had most likely gone through the same short period of adjustment when he, at about Niki's age, had emerged from his home one morning having abruptly switched suffix, hairstyle and sash fastening.

Niki collected a slice of fig and a cup of herbal tea and came to where Anika still leaned. Niki gave Anika a cautious smile, returned just as cautiously, and sat down at the other end of the bench from Mateo, the better to eye the stranger at the table with open curiosity.

'Greetings from your venerable elder, you horrible child,' Mateo said in formal Ystheran.

He sipped his own tea and made a face; the tisane, mostly silphium, juniper, and rue, was bitter despite generous spoonfuls of honey into the pot, and the addition of holly had not helped.

Mateo perforce drank the brew twice a day, to stop his monthly bleed, and Anika had been tweaking her recipe for some fifteen years. She was never happier than when experimenting with new combinations of herbs in her tisanes. The last three years had mostly been dedicated to finding something to ease his stiff hip without tainting the morning ritual.

Niki took an excessive bite of fig so as to reply, 'Greetings from your humble neophyte, you horrible adult,' with full mouth. Mateo presented his sternest look and Niki stuck out a food-coated tongue in an especially disgusting gesture.

'Is this your child?' Jonas asked, turning his smile on Niki even though the little brat didn't even slightly deserve it.

Mateo considered Niki, his nose wrinkled as he took a long and pointed sip of tea. He was mostly just bemused that he looked responsible enough to be mistaken for the parent of a nascent adolescent, and also now old enough that the idea was not completely insulting. Niki considered him in return with the same expression of bemused disinclination, mocking him.

Eventually, Mateo said, 'Nikiti is the baby sibling of my heart.'

He touched his own heart, to be clear he wasn't referring to Anika, whose title was a simplistic translation but familiar these days to Ancerans. To his great surprise, his pronouncement wiped the cheeky expression off Niki's face, and his neophyte crawled along the bench to throw their arms about him.

'No hugging!' he said, failing to push the bane of his day off him. 'Have I taught you nothing? Go away, horrible child.'

'Hello,' Niki said to Jonas, arms still about Mateo. 'Heilsa. I remember you.'

'No, you don't,' said Mateo.

'He played games with us on the ship, once I felt better.'

'No, he didn't.'

Ignoring Mateo, Niki added loftily, 'I'm glad your arm's better too. The children won't remember you, because they were too young then, but *I* do.'

'You *don't*,' Mateo said, in dawning horror, since Anika was shaking her head at him in warning and Jonas did not look in any way confused.

'No, that's right. Most of your people—'

'You people.'

'I said *your* people,' Jonas said, again without a blink but this time with notable overemphasis, 'were being miserable little elves—'

'Elves!' Mateo repeated. Those were from myths from the heartland, and *fine*, they were about small, round, magical beings outside the ken of everyday people, and the popular nickname was used with nothing but affection all over the city, but *still*. 'Should we be offended?'

Anika signally failed to be offended, offering a smile instead. 'Elves, Remnants preserve us.'

Jonas smiled back at her because he knew his audience. '—and me being an unthreatening sort—'

'Hah,' Mateo said before he could help himself.

'—who positively delights in children, and who happened to be injured enough to be useless as crew, the captain delegated me to keep your young ones out from underfoot asea. You, in particular'—he lazily indicated Mateo—'were ghastly ill. That's why you don't remember me.'

'I was seasick, deathly so,' Mateo said, because that was the lie they had decided on to explain disembarking at the wrong port.

He was rubbing his hip, he realised, and stopped.

'Sure, you were seasick,' Jonas said. 'I'm a physician, I should know.' He winked at Mateo.

'We evidently all owe you a great debt of gratitude,' Anika said, not so much steering the conversation in a different direction as hoisting it into the bowl of a catapult and unleashing the arm. 'Mateo, take our honoured guest over to the pottery workshop.'

She gave him a significant look. *And charm the pants off him*, that look was meant to indicate.

'The pottery workshop is not open yet,' Mateo said.

This time she really did slap her forehead.

'Well, it *isn't*,' Mateo said. 'Go away, Niki, I'll be along for our lesson soon enough.'

'What do you teach?' Jonas asked, all innocent curiosity.

They all three blinked at him before Mateo said, 'Domestic…management?'

Niki scoffed and escaped out the door. Mateo drank off the rest of his cooling tea in a single gulp and poured the second cup, keeping his gaze on this complicated process rather than looking at Jonas.

'If it's secret Ystheran ritual stuff, you can just say that.' Jonas sounded like Mateo had amused him again.

'Goodness me, we would never keep secrets from our Imperial hosts,' Anika said brightly. 'So. A trading consortium. I take it it's not a coincidence you've come so soon after the news about Ysthera?'

'Not to be too ghoulish,' Jonas said, taking the change of topic with a graciousness Mateo would not have managed, 'but the Taurasi are now the last Ystherans in the world, so—'

'This is incorrect and based on an untrue and inaccurate assumption regarding our customs.'

Mateo ignored Anika's glare, and also ignored Jonas's smile as the man said, 'Could I possibly finish a sentence, my friend?'

He stubbornly went on, 'Kindred Taurasi is merely the last functioning *klados*—kinship group. Not every Ystheran is enamoured of the traditional structure of our society and they are permitted to leave their kith and, indeed, the island. Your city alone, in fact, contains a decent handful of expatriated Ystherans, some of whom have made their lives here for decades.'

Some of whom had been appalled and furious when the Taurasi had spilled ashore en chaotic masse, abruptly reminding the local Ystherans' neighbours of both their foreignness and their proven sorcerous ways.

Jonas twirled a finger to capture his surroundings. 'Any of them establish a wildly popular teahouse and an entire street of Kindred-staffed artisanal workshops with the potential to meet soaring demand for suddenly-rare Ystheran artisanal products?'

Mateo gave this due consideration. Most of the handful of Ystherans in the city made their living as artificers, but for a very small and dedicated clientele. If collecting genuine Ystheran artefacts was going to become a fashion, as Jonas's consortium believed, those individual artists would surely benefit, but they would not be able to meet the peak of demand. Kindred Taurasi would, by sheer weight of numbers.

Taurasi had been the smallest of the Kindreds, back on Ysthera. Mateo was not yet used to having weight of numbers.

While he was still lost in thought, Anika stepped into the breach. 'No, they indeed have not,' she said. 'You have come to the right place. We have Ystheran pottery—'

'Wrong sort of clay,' Mateo said.

'—traditional Ystheran weaving—'

'Wrong sort of fibre.'

'—Ystheran jewellery—'

'Wrong sort of gemstone.'

'—and Ystheran honey,' Anika managed to finish over him, concentrating very hard on Jonas, who was interestedly looking back and forth between them as he followed the volleys of the exchange.

'Wrong sort of flora.'

'Ystheran bees.'

'Ystheran queens,' Mateo conceded. 'But it can't be Ystheran honey if the bees aren't collecting nectar from Ystheran flora.'

'Which they are.'

'Which they're not.'

'We transplanted chestnuts, Mattias.'

'That's six trees, Aniketa. That's perhaps twenty jars of Ystheran honey per year. That's not enough to pretend to be a supplier.'

Here Jonas gently interjected. 'Might I introduce you to the concept of luxury auctions, Mattias? To wit, an annual auction for the very few jars of the very rare Ystheran chestnut honey produced that year?'

'A dark, strong, floral honey, notes of spice and wood,' Anika said. 'See? It practically sells itself.'

'Anika,' Mateo said, 'what if we want to keep it for ourselves? That's why we brought the queens and saplings with us, wasn't it? Our taste of home?'

'That was before the island sank, *melimou*,' Anika said. 'We have mortgages to pay down and children to feed and clothe and educate. That honey will be worth twice its weight in gold.'

Jonas made a small quibbling noise; he was, after all, in charge of negotiating a contract with them on behalf of his consortium and was possibly realising he'd oversold his hand.

'At least twice,' Anika added darkly. 'Go show Jonas the skeps, Teo.' She added in High Ystheran, 'And charm the pants off him.'

CHAPTER 3

MATEO STEPPED OUT INTO THE COOL morning air, pausing on the porch to slip into his sandals again. If he'd not been so flustered by Jonas's inopportunely-timed appearance, he might have spotted the man's soft leather boots, not the hobnailed marching sort, set neatly and incongruously on the rack among the sandals, and thus had warning of Anika's ambush.

Or perhaps not; Mateo was often flustered, about a wide range of things, and oblivious to many other things accordingly.

Jonas Nebrija was obviously a great deal more observant than him, and more considerate too, given he'd not only noticed the rack but had also chosen to respond appropriately, which their afternoon visitors did not. If Mateo had been about to walk into some Imperial stronghold, he'd have been too nervous to notice a cue like that.

The man, cloak retrieved from the hook by the door, slid his feet into the boots and bent to deal with the straps. This drew Mateo's attention to the man's bare and muscular calves, and his thick backside. He stepped off the porch to wait in the street, looking out over Taurasi's refuge.

Ravenser Odd was a wide but short street, sloping up towards and petering out into a narrow trail that led up the mountainside. This supposed mountain was more of a nameless woody hill with delusions of grandeur, but it rose high enough to make the evenings here long and on a continuum of miserable for the exiled denizens of the Sunlit Isle for a good stretch of the year.

On the other hand, the mornings could be wonderful.

Mateo turned, as a matter of habit, eastwards, lifting his face to the sun. Anceral tended to reek of drying fish and smoke and dung and, on holy days, burnt offerings, but up here the breeze was melodious. The streets below, a mix of beaten dirt and paved, and already beginning to throng with people and carts, fell steeply to the port. The lower city was still wreathed in the last traces of the mist that lifted early up here, and the view of the harbour was blocked by crowded city buildings, but the vista out to sea was spectacular, dazzling sunlight sparkling off gentle waves all the way to the horizon.

Three years ago, Anika had made Mateo stand right here in the sunlight and look out over this very view with the soft sea-tanged breeze in his face.

She'd said, 'This is as good as we're ever going to get here, my sweet.'

Ravenser Odd was practically derelict then. It was a long walk to the nearest marketplace, and uphill all the way back. It was a cul-de-sac with only one proper way in and out. The apartment block, locally called the insula, was grimly rundown and promised only dank, cramped accommodations a far cry from the bright cottages of their beloved mountain village. The lodging house next door, opposite the sagging bakehouse that would become the teahouse, was owned by an elderly woman who disdained foreigners and sat on the stoop to be loud about it.

And Anika had been right, of course.

Mateo blinked out of his reverie. Jonas had joined him, and was following the direction of Mateo's trance, looking out over the waves with an oddly unreadable expression.

'Do you miss your ship?' Mateo asked him.

Jonas shrugged, his smile returning. 'Not really. The life of a privateer is not as glamorous as the theatres make it sound.'

Mateo was caught by the choice of word there, which he thought *had* been a choice, not a slip. On the one hand, there was a veritable chasm between trader and privateer. On the other hand, any trading ship running the blockade to service Ysthera in defiance of the Imperial edicts was automatically labelled a privateer and a smuggler, regardless of the legality or otherwise of its usual routes. Some of the trading ships denied it; some flaunted it. The ship that had taken Taurasi off Ysthera had tended towards the latter ilk.

He asked, 'How fares *Steadfast*?'

'Oh,' Jonas said. His smile was suddenly gone again. 'Foundered, some three years ago. All hands lost. Did you not know that?'

Mateo stared at him. He was astonished, and uneasy. Anika had not told him. Anika might not have known. No, she had, or she did now—

that was what her gentle sympathy by the stove had been about. She was protecting him, to not have passed on the news; all the Taurasi tended towards too protective these days. If the timing hadn't been suspicious already, that lie of omission definitely made it so.

Steadfast, foundered some three years ago. It must have been mere months, perhaps mere weeks, after the day of the exile.

'I happened to be ashore,' Jonas added, apparently misinterpreting Mateo's signal failure to offer any sort of commiseration as scepticism regarding his survival. He rubbed his right bicep, suspiciously reminiscent of how Mateo absent-mindedly rubbed his hip. 'Recovering from an injury.'

Mateo folded both hands over his heart and bowed. 'I did not know. My deepest condolences.'

My deepest regrets. Did we bring it down on your ship?

'I don't know why I assumed any of you would know that, actually.' Jonas made a dismissive gesture Mateo had occasionally seen other locals make, flattened fingers tapped against the back of the other hand and then swept away. 'Long time past. Who's this?'

Mateo blinked at the sudden change in tone, followed the indicative nod, and sighed. 'Madam Kerling. I apologise in advance.'

The old woman was sitting on the stoop of the lodging house, cane held upright between her thick-skirted knees, basket of yarn beside her, long copper nailbinder sticking out. It was her usual perch whenever the sun was out, which was not so often that he needed to dread finding her eldritch figure guarding the portal.

And yet, dread it he did.

Mateo would be the first to admit he was poor at unravelling the mystery of other people, and Madam Kerling was a knotty tangle indeed. She had complained extensively when she'd realised that foreigners—and not just any foreigners, but a large group of exiled sorcerers—were in negotiations with the developer who had, years before, bought up the rest of the street. It was an unfashionable mix of apartments and small business premises which he'd planned to demolish and turn into a summer villa and gardens for the elite of the city…until Madam Kerling's refusal to sell her lodging house stopped him cold.

He'd waited so long for her to die that the fashion for hillside villas had gone the same way as the fashion for mixed-use streets this far from the port and its associated bustle, a fact Madam Kerling had literally stuck her oar—or her cane, to be truly literal—into the negotiations to inform Anika about.

She'd then gone on to detail exactly how little the developer had paid to collect the deeds, and how little maintenance he had invested in the steadily-emptying premises, and which roofs leaked when it rained hard, and where rot had set in, and where mould hastily scrubbed off before the inspection would soon bloom again, and, by the by, she'd heard the developer had fallen on hard times, very much needed to sell, and hadn't had so much as a nibble from a buyer for years even as his tenants abandoned him.

The Taurasi had left Ysthera with six carts filled to the brim with their portable wealth. They'd made it aboard *Steadfast* with only five of those six carts, and only eighty or so of their one hundred and twenty kith. They'd given up the full contents of two carts to pay the captain whose decision to hold firm at the dock—calculated, but still brave beyond measure—had saved their lives.

Madam Kerling's crabby intervention in bringing down the price of Ravenser Odd so that the mortgages were within Taurasi reach had been a stroke of good fortune, a ray of sunshine after weeks and weeks of grey skies.

Mateo had eventually decided that she merely disliked both people and change, and was thus to be treated as a kindred spirit.

The lodging house she'd refused to sell to the Taurasi as strenuously as she'd refused to sell to the developer was narrower and taller than the insula, and had a flat roof. This year-round suntrap was where they had put their woven domed skeps, and planted a garden. They'd negotiated that in exchange for renovating the lodging house, one room at a time. Madam Kerling had snapped, 'Are you suggesting my rooms aren't good enough for you uppity creatures?' and then produced a grand show of begrudging acquiesce, with the stipulation that she make the final decisions on all repairs and refurbishments.

The old woman made a sign of warding as Mateo perforce approached with Jonas at his side, and tugged her shawl tighter about her bony shoulders. The sun was shining and slowly warming the air, but for now it was still cold, and not just for thin Taurasi blood.

'There remains a place for you by the stove in the Come-By-Chance, Madam Kerling,' Mateo told her with a bow.

'I shall not set foot in that den of iniquity,' she told him in her severe, hoarse croak.

'It's a teahouse, Madam Kerling.'

He thought he'd slip by her, but not much did. 'I remind you of the rule about men in the rooms.'

Mateo paused. When Anika had approached Madam Kerling to rent all available rooms in her lodging house, the old woman had been very clear that she only accepted single women, without exception. This left Mateo, with his bad hip, in something of a bind. Taurasi now held a mortgage on the low, broad insula next door, but its six ground-floor apartments, converted from old shops, were too large for a single occupant, even in circumstances where accommodating the entire Kindred wasn't an urgent concern.

Mateo was thus faced with either roosting like an unwanted crow at a feast within one of the Taurasi family groups, or joining the other Taurasi who couldn't readily manage stairs in their congenial communal apartment.

He took the third, most awkward, option and was excruciatingly honest with Madam Kerling.

She had said, 'Young man, I do not care if you have the privates of a woman, you are still a man.'

He'd said, 'I am untouchable to my people. The women of Taurasi have nothing to fear from me, Madam Kerling.'

She'd said, with a snort, 'I don't care about silly foreigner slips. I have innocent local girls under my care in this lodging house.'

Mateo had most definitely *not* said, 'But aren't they all grown women who go down into the city daily to make their meagre living and should be allowed to entertain men if they like, and in fact probably do, except your rules force them do it in the public houses along Aldhelm Row and they have to tolerate it because that's the price of low rent?'

Instead he'd said, 'The women of the empire have nothing to fear from me either, Madam Kerling,' telling the literal truth, since no one had anything to fear from him, but also allowing for a certain interpretation.

Madam Kerling had stared at him in grim silence before saying, 'I see. You are that sort of reprobate. So was my brother. You may have the apartment by mine so I can keep my eye on you.'

And she kept an eye on him so closely that he was now being reminded that he wasn't to take Jonas to his rooms, which was embarrassing on all sorts of levels. He hadn't even realised Madam Kerling applied her rules about male visitors to him.

He said, 'We're going to the roof, Madam Kerling.'

'You cannot fool me, young man, you can still fondle and cosset away on the roof!'

'There will be no fondling, Madam Kerling. No cossetting either.'

Whatever that was. As one of the leaders of the Kindred, his Imperial, both formal Vaer and the local dialect, wasn't bad—he knew "obstreperous", after all—but Madam Kerling still found ways to make him rely on context.

'I was young once too,' she scolded. 'I know the sorts of things you might get up to, you degenerate.'

Mateo risked a glance at Jonas, who gazed upwards, biting back a smile. 'I rather think he has better things to do with his day, Madam Kerling.'

Taking Jonas's elbow, Mateo started to steer him past the harrumphing old woman. She thrust out her cane. 'No male visitors! I do not run that sort of establishment!'

Jonas, adopting a sober expression, efficiently shrugged aside the folds of his cloak and pushed back his left sleeve. 'Madam, I am a respectable physician,' he said, showing her his arm. 'I do not *frequent* that sort of establishment.'

Both Madam Kerling and Mateo stared at the blue-black tattoo of a snake wrapping its way up his forearm. It was a brief glimpse; before Mateo had quite taken it in, Jonas gave a casual flex to make his sleeve slide back down.

Madam Kerling effected a sniff of disdain. 'Most physicians restrain themselves to a laeknir snake about the wrist, what are you trying to prove?'

'That I'm not most physicians, madam.'

'We think much of ourselves, don't we?'

'Someone has to,' Jonas said, with another egregious wink.

To Mateo's outrage, Madam Kerling had to smother a smile. Taking hold of Jonas's arm again, feeling the warmth of his skin through the thin weave of his shirt, he finally managed to tug him past and into the small foyer of the lodging house.

He headed straight up the stairs, not in case Madam Kerling was watching, but, actually, yes, in case she was watching. Jonas was right behind him.

The lodging house had three floors, including the ground floor, which meant two landings, and then the narrow stairs to the roof. Mateo was dismayed to find that his hip and leg began to deeply ache almost immediately. It had been six months since he'd climbed to the roof, where he and the children gathered to soak up the summer warmth. He hadn't noticed how much sorer his hip was incrementally becoming.

He rested on the first landing, casually addressing Jonas to excuse the pause. 'I apologise. One would think I've outgrown interfering older relatives.'

Jonas waved it away. 'I've got at least five years on you, I think—I'm thirty-five—and I'm still bossed about by metaphorical aunts.'

'Nonetheless,' Mateo said stiffly. 'Please forgive Madam Kerling. Insulting you was just a side benefit of flustering me.'

'I didn't notice her insult me,' Jonas said. He touched the fresh plaster, and wandered over to look at the potted plant on the small table under the shuttered window. 'Must've been subtle, was it?'

'Ah, she suggested you'd want to…'

Mateo tangled himself in how to finish that sentence. His own language would have given him some tactful euphemisms to skirt about it, if he'd had to talk about it at all, but he couldn't bring himself to say it in the direct Imperial dialect, offshoot of a language that befitted a famously blunt people as well as nations full of adults suddenly faced with communicating with new overseers. Ystherans didn't say what he would have to say, to explain the insult to Jonas.

Imperials would, though.

'Fuck you? Not an insult, not even close.' While Mateo was still parsing this, Jonas added, 'We don't have to go to the roof. Let's not.'

Mateo realised he was rubbing his hip again. He dropped his hand and started for the next flight of stairs, making himself move without limping. 'That's where the bees are.'

'I believe you when you say they exist. I don't need to actually see them.'

'You actually do if you're going to actually assess the potential to actually sell actual Ystheran honey,' Mateo said flatly, though he wasn't entirely convinced of the necessity himself. Anika had asked him to show the man the hives, so he would show the man the hives.

He refused to slow down, but he made liberal use of the newly installed railing as they went up to the next landing, where he also refused to pause again.

Jonas, however, lingered. 'Fresh plaster here, too,' he said, 'and new shutters, and I like the potted plants everywhere. Did Madam Kerling do this for you?'

Mateo, resenting being forced to rest and *deeply* resenting feeling grateful for it, snapped, 'We did it ourselves. We've done the whole place, room by room. In exchange for the rooftop.'

And also, as they later found out, for peppercorn rent; Madam Kerling charged them even less than she charged the lodgers who couldn't afford anything closer to the city centre.

Some of those women had begged Timon to leave their rooms untouched, holes in the walls, rotting floorboards, broken shutters notwithstanding. They couldn't afford it if their cantankerous landlady raised the rent once fresh plaster and carpentry had been applied. Madam Kerling insisted on it, and she didn't raise the rent.

Madam Kerling, a tangled skein indeed, full of knots, Mateo's elderly Imperial kindred spirit.

'Very nicely done,' Jonas said, in the intractably agreeable way that was rapidly working along Mateo's nerves towards the last one. 'Handy to have practical people good with their hands in your situation.'

They had, in point of fact, practical people who were good with their *magic*, but that was not something an Ystheran refugee could or would ever admit to any Imperial, given the strict prohibition that had been placed upon them when they'd been granted asylum within the empire.

Mateo took Jonas up the last, narrower, flight past a low and stuffy attic space and out into open air. The flat tiled rooftop captured the scarce decent weather Anceral's northern climate saw fit to grant them. Today, with the mist already lifted from the heights and the sun warm overhead, the space was a welcome burst of springtime, the bees gently buzzing about.

The skeps, seven of them, were on the far, eastern, side of the roof where they'd catch the most light and warmth. Over here, by the egress to the stairwell, the Taurasi had set their traditional cushions, and then, out of respect for the lodgers, benches to both store the cushions and cater for people not used to sitting comfortably on tiles.

Jonas made an abortive gesture towards one of the benches and Mateo gave him a scathing look, although his hip was fairly throbbing by now. That last flight of stairs was awkward in the extreme, and not just for him with his damaged hip. The Taurasi had ended up having to hoist the skeps and planters up the side of the lodging house.

They didn't dare risk magic for the task. It was imperceptible to Imperials…unless the Imperial had inherited even a single drop of Ystheran blood, a rare but not impossible ancestry, especially in cosmopolitan Anceral. Their ropes and pulleys might have hidden the levitating effects of the magic, but its subtle glow and quiet hum would have been a giveaway.

The benches were a different matter. Timon had waited until the depths of a foggy night, when the pearlescent glow of magic would diffuse and be indistinguishable from lamplight and no one was around to observe it anyway, and then levitated them straight to the roof, two dark shapes swooping silently upwards in the thick and cloying fog.

Anika had been wild about it the next morning, but by then it was done, and done safely, or at least they'd not had the governor's regulators, the Vigile, show up to execute or exile the entirety of Kindred Taurasi, and probably the few innocent Ystheran individuals who had expatriated themselves to Anceral as well.

'They could have, though,' Anika had fumed. She'd forbidden Timon from the morning ritual for a week, which was a harsh punishment but one which Mateo couldn't in good conscience gainsay. The risk might have been exceedingly low, but the consequences would have been exceedingly dire.

They had all, it had to be said, relaxed more than a little since those early days after their fraught arrival into asylum.

Danae, the twins' mother, was by the skeps. She was wearing a wide-brimmed hat with netting, and an extra-thick undershirt beneath her tunic. Like many experienced beekeepers, she didn't bother with gloves. She exchanged a nod with Mateo, even as she gently rocked one of the skeps, testing its weight, making sure the hive inside had enough stores to make it past the cusp of spring. Satisfied, she moved to the next.

Mateo indicated the skeps, and then turned and waved at the chestnut trees in their planters along the southern edge of the roof. The flower buds were swelling; they would bloom any day now.

'We can't make the bees feed only on the chestnuts,' he said.

They could make the bees feed only on the chestnuts. Danae could dip into Mateo's flow of magic and make an enclosure to keep the foragers within for the duration of the blossom. But she wouldn't, and not only from the risk of overflow or of getting caught out by an Imperial informant. She was fussy about the wellbeing of her girls.

Mateo went on. 'But they prefer the flowers, and they're close. So the honey we'll harvest at the end of the spring flow will be fairly purely made from the nectar of the chestnut. We could claim it as genuine Ystheran honey. If you agree?'

Jonas nodded. 'Where do the bees forage over summer?'

Mateo led the way to the low parapet wall at the northern edge of the rooftop, where they could look out over Ravenser Odd. Opposite was the teahouse, and from here they could see into Anika's bountiful garden beyond it.

He pointed. 'They like Anika's herbals almost as much as the teahouse customers do.'

'Fairly Ystheran, also, then. Not as prized as chestnut honey, but still…'

Mateo made a noncommittal waggle of his hand. 'It's probably not enough. They'd be heading in foraging circles out over the city and mount— hill. We couldn't make a claim on its purity. We brought seeds we haven't used yet, we could sow wildflowers beyond the workshops…'

He trailed off, staring downwards. Anika and two of her helpers were kneeling in the teahouse garden, snipping and plucking leaves, blossoms and seeds for the day's tisanes. The activity was innocuous enough, but it had made Mateo realise he'd positioned an Imperial where he could spy upon the Taurasi moving about their morning routines, any of which might include minor magic.

Five hundred years of applying domesticated magic to one's chores was not a habit broken in a mere three.

He stepped back smartly, saying, 'Let's—'

That was as far as he got before his foot hit a slick patch of hoarfrost on the tiles, protected from fully melting by the cool shadow of the parapet wall.

Mateo's foot slid out from under him, wrenching his bad hip and pitching him helplessly forwards. He slammed into the low parapet and tipped over with a yelp and a flail of arms.

The suddenness of the world going awry. The sick feeling of plummet. The scream of his hip. Mateo was unmoored in the wash of time, plunged back into the day of the exile.

Strong arms locked about him, around his waist and over his chest. Jonas hauled him upright and pulled him close, Mateo's back pressed against his firm chest. For a long moment, Mateo huddled against the solid warmth, seeking only anchor.

Then he caught himself, forcibly regaining his balance, physically and mentally. He shifted his weight, but Jonas didn't let him go, in fact tightened his embrace.

This, Mateo belatedly understood, was because he was trembling all over like a child awoken from a nightmare.

'All right,' Jonas said softly. Though Mateo could now personally attest that the man was indeed much broader than him, and much…*firmer*, he was slightly shorter; his voice thrummed from just below Mateo's ear.

'All right, honey, I've got you.'

Still using one arm to cradle Mateo across his chest, though he casually but significantly adjusted its angle, Jonas shifted the arm about Mateo's waist to get a hand to his sore hip. He gave it a long, firm, slow stroke with his palm, and then another, gradually soothing the agonised protest to a mutter.

Mateo was not sure if the man's stroking touch was genuinely lessening the tight heat centred at his hip or merely distracting him from it. This felt like it was approaching Madam Kerling's fondling prohibition.

He pulled away, and Jonas said, 'Ow,' and swatted at something, and then again. 'Ow! Gods. Why are they suddenly angry?'

'The…gods?'

'The *bees*, Mateo,' Jonas said, deftly managing to sound both endlessly patient and mildly exasperated in the very same breath.

A hum was rising in the air, and it might have been the hives awakening into fury but it was also the sound of Danae's magic in full flight. Her metaphysical receptacle was too small for her to easily aid in defence. It was, however, large enough for her to use her daily allotment of magic to throw bees at Jonas.

Having turned to see two or three red swellings in a line on Jonas's alarmed face and finally recognise what was happening, Mateo shouted, 'Stop that at once!' at her in Ystheran.

'The foreigner is hurting you.' Danae stood in a swirling cloud of bees, unharmed or least unfazed by stings. The only reason that cloud had not descended on Jonas yet was because Mateo was standing too close.

'He's not.' Mateo grabbed the startled Jonas by the elbow and hustled him towards the stairs, saying, 'Danae must have accidentally disturbed one of her queens. We need to be off the roof.'

Jonas hesitated on the threshold of safety, saying, 'Your beekeeper…'

Mateo very much hoped that the end of that sentence involved concern for the abandoned Danae, rather than an accusation of sorcery, and interjected accordingly, 'Will be fine. She knows what she's doing.'

He ignored the alternating throb and stab of his hip as he bounced down the stairs ahead of Jonas, forcing the man to hurry after him. By the time they reached the vestibule again, Mateo had broken out in a sweat from the pain and the rush, and Jonas was not distracted.

'I'd say she knows what she's doing, standing her ground in a swarm for you,' he said, picking up the conversation as if they hadn't just bolted down three flights of stairs. He gingerly touched the stings on his face.

'Your people—'

'You people,' Mateo repeated.

'I really am saying *your* people, I don't know why you can't hear the difference,' Jonas said. 'Your people seem protective of you. Why is that? Your hip? Or…' He spread an inviting hand, raising his eyebrows.

'Blighted Imperials, kinless devils,' Mateo muttered, holding on to just enough of the shreds of his temper to say it in Ystheran.

He stalked out the front door, as much as a man who was fighting very hard not to hobble could stalk, then stopped dead on the stoop as he understood Jonas's mild implication.

Mateo, comparatively tall and narrow, had a more boyish figure than many of his compatriots, but Jonas's forearm had crushed his breasts harder than any binding cloth when he'd caught him. The formal robes and makeup of that morning couldn't have helped the misunderstanding, and the daily working outfit that every Taurasi wore was of no use either. Imperials couldn't or didn't read the significance of how Ystherans dressed their long hair and wrapped their sashes.

'I'm a man,' he said, pivoting on his good hip to confront Jonas, dutifully following him.

Jonas looked politely blank. 'Nice to have common ground?'

'I'm aware I look like a woman to Imperial eyes, but I'm a man,' Mateo managed to elucidate. 'They don't protect me because I'm some delicate flower of feminine fragility.'

'I didn't think you were,' Jonas said. 'I mean…'

He touched his hair, and his midsection, indicating hairstyle and sash to prove that he'd read them in the exact way Mateo had just assumed he wouldn't. And of course he could read them—he'd even read the message of Niki's meticulously neutral styling. Otherwise he'd have labelled them, wearing their hair in a way that, locally, only women wore, Mateo's *daughter*, not his *child*.

Mateo was just beginning to feel embarrassed at his presumption when Jonas said, 'I was actually assuming the overprotectiveness is because you're of high status in the tribe.'

At this, the direction of Mateo's ire flipped like a kite on a tight string. 'They are *not* overprotective and we are *not* a tribe.'

'No?' Jonas slowly shifted his weight, unperturbed by Mateo's sharp tone. 'Aniketa's the equivalent of a tribal chieftain, though, right? The Heart? That makes you the shaman? What am I saying wrong?'

And he *still* didn't sound annoyed, the even-tempered arsehole.

'Those words,' Mateo said frostily, 'were selected deliberately by the empire to make Ystherans appear as foreign as possible. Imperial priests might just as readily be called shamans and your extended families might be called tribes and your leaders chieftains.'

Jonas wisely stayed narrowly focussed on his original question. 'So you're the Taurasi priest?'

'My title can be translated as Soul, as Anika's is usually translated as Heart,' Mateo finally conceded. Their true titles were *desmadonos* and *arestesphor* respectively, but those were too complicated to properly translate, just as *klados* had to be grossly summated to Kindred. 'I am somewhat like the Imperial conception of a temple priest.'

'I have to say, you're pretty cranky for a spiritual leader,' Jonas said.

'You don't have to say it, you just want to,' Mateo retorted with another distinct increase in venom. Jonas had inadvertently hit on his own fears about how poorly he fulfilled his role among the Taurasi.

He became aware in the same moment as Jonas that they had an audience. Mateo looked with chagrin at his landlady and a few of her Imperial tenants who were by her on the stoop. They'd been arrested on their way out to work or back from the bakehouse, and were watching the interplay avidly.

'Is that man bothering you, our Theo?' one of them called, more in tones of incitement than support.

Jonas, for his part, eyed the handful of Ystherans who had paused attentively on their way to or from the teahouse. He folded his hands together and summoned a sunny smile. It was somewhat skewed, thanks to the swelling of the stings across his cheek.

'Mattias,' he said smoothly. 'I'm trying to facilitate a trade deal beneficial to all involved parties. Should we both get back to that, perhaps?'

Mateo, grimacing, slowly rubbed his temple. 'Ah, right. Come with me. Anika will treat those stings.'

And have strong words for Mateo regarding the significant differences between the charming off of the pants and the stirring up of the angry bees and vengeful application of such.

CHAPTER 4

'THIS SHOULD EASE THE IMMEDIATE PAIN,' Anika said, as she bent over a seated Jonas, rubbing one of her cooling salves into his swollen cheek. 'And I'll give you some to take away for when the itching starts.'

She'd already efficiently removed the tiny barbs and handed him a cup of infused willow bark and peppercorns. He was holding the cup in both large hands, patiently submitting to her practical doctoring. He smiled up at her as she worked.

Anika had made it clear to Mateo how important it was to keep Jonas on side, and was now putting down coin in that regard. The salve was cover for the very subtle application of healing magic. Anika, Heart of Kindred Taurasi, might not be their most powerful wielder, but was certainly the most skilful. She would have excoriated any other Taurasi for trying this on an Imperial, but she trusted herself enough to take the risk to be sure Jonas went away happy with them.

Mateo experienced a heart-stopping moment when Jonas turned his face into Anika's hand, as if he'd perceived the shimmer of the magic cupped within her palm and flowing to her fingertips as they stroked away the swelling.

Oh, but no. The man was just responding to the touch of an attractive woman, of course. A respectable woman of the empire—a delicate flower of feminine fragility—wouldn't stroke the cheek of a man on first acquaintance. The girls lodged with Madam Kerling might. And Imperials assumed that foreign women would.

But Jonas said, 'I haven't been fussed over by a little sister in a while.'

He took an obliging sip of the tisane as Anika stepped back. She'd left some of the swelling in place, but he'd be labelling the salve as a miracle cure, which wouldn't be bad for the potential trade deal, all told.

'So, I thought I'd come back tomorrow afternoon to try the spice tea and tour the workshops,' he went on. 'Make a bit of a list to present to the consortium. That would be in the *Imperial* afternoon, Mateo.'

'Our afternoons are the same, it's our *hours*—'

Anika nudged Mateo's ankle and he subsided, not without a scowl at Jonas's amused look. She gave Jonas a smile; Mateo could see the relief in it. He himself was feeling more ambivalent, which could not have been a surprise to anybody.

He said in Ystheran, 'What if he scares the customers?'

Droves of Imperial women arrived at the teahouse every afternoon, making the climb in the back of comfortable awning-covered carts, settling in around Anceran-style tables. The spiced tea ritual always took one hour—one Ystheran hour. Order a second pot and it would take a second hour. The Taurasi had assumed this would effectively dissuade Imperials, but instead it was the perfect excuse for a particular class of woman to meet with friends and linger in a way they were not permitted to do in the taverns in the heart of the city.

Further, the customers felt no need to pay attention to the ritual, except perhaps the first time they attended. This was an affront to good manners, and a blessed relief, because Ystherans didn't want Imperials paying close attention to anything they did. And also because Imperials with large purses, a passing fancy for a cosy domain that only they and their select friends—and all of their wider social circle—knew about, and an hour or two to spare had proven generous in their spending habits.

In short, the Taurasi had accidentally, but profitably, created a warm haven for wealthy Imperial women in their quaint Ystheran shop selling herbal tea and artisanal works. Imperial men came here only rarely and not ever unaccompanied by their womenfolk. Mateo supposed they'd be rather disparaging about it all, as if their private gatherings in their exclusive city spaces were any more elevated.

Mateo, a knotty tangle consisting of tetchiness, anxiety and too much rumination, suspected that the Taurasi were benefiting from an infatuation that would pass before it could become a routine. Jonas, showing up like a well-built, confident, attractive—and that was plenty of adjectives to be going on with—*tomcat* among cooing pigeons might end the infatuation in short order.

He knew he found it disconcerting to have his sanctuary invaded by an Imperial man who smiled like that, and he didn't even have a cultural bias against pirates.

So they might be risking their current major source of income on a dice throw for a proposition which was by no means assured of coming through and which relied on the dictates of what could turn out to be another short-lived fashion for Ystheran culture.

He said, more surely, 'He will scare the customers.'

Anika tilted her head as she considered where on the continuum of ridiculous to possibly valid Mateo's latest worry lay. Once a decorative tail of silken hair would have cascaded gracefully from her topknot when she assumed that thinking pose. She'd not worn it since the day of the exile, joining the older women in the plain topknot far too young. Mateo still missed it.

'I do see your point, my sweet,' she replied at last. 'I'm not sure we can risk saying no to him, though.'

'Imperials,' Mateo muttered. Even the ones who weren't overtly throwing their own weight around still had the full and ponderous weight of the empire behind them.

'When I say afternoon,' Jonas added, once again blithely ignoring the fast, quiet patter of Ystheran, 'I mean more towards sunset. Will you still be open?'

'Conveniently, yes,' Anika said.

Convenient, yes, Mateo thought, eyeing Jonas with narrowed eyes and wondering exactly how good his grasp of the impure Low Ystheran dialect was. Jonas had, after all, been a trader. He'd openly confirmed Low had been on his ship's route. He'd been there often enough to learn the signals of hair and sash, too.

Jonas smiled back at him, and perhaps there was a twinkle in his eye that suggested, *You think I'm following the conversation? Prove it, honey.*

Mateo huffily tugged his sash tighter. He did not have to prove it. In Ystheran, he said, 'Anika, he understands us.'

'No one in this city understands High Ystheran, especially spoken this fast, my sweet.'

This was an indisputable point. 'Fine, you win this round,' he said to Jonas, frustrated to discover he did have to prove it after all.

He did tend towards the unfounded worries like bees aswarm in his head; Anika was right, of course, to answer him with patience, not alarm.

'Oh, good,' Jonas said. 'And what round would that be, Mateo?'

'Don't even pretend.'

Mateo was once again hampered in his dramatic stalking off by his aching hip. Outside, he discovered the Taurasi children playing a chase game about the street as they waited for him. It was a sunny day, and the teahouse was full of Jonas, so he collected his little class and took them to the open field at the far end of the street, where the chickens pecked about the street's communal well, fed from the waters of a spring further up the hillside. The Taurasi had found an abandoned shrine at the spring's head, a low moss-covered stone arch already beginning to crumble. It had been one of Mateo's first tasks to usurp a forgotten god's shrine for the Shattered One so that the ritual waters could be as sacred as they were on Ysthera.

The toddlers, of which the Taurasi had an inordinate number, turned their face up to him like flowers following the sun. They were hypnotised by the aura of the Soul, the subtle glimmer of the goddess's blessing. Mateo shooed them over to the older children, who were less impressed; all Taurasi, all Ystherans, outgrew their open fascination eventually, and stopped staring or falling to their knees. They were all blessed by their goddess, after all. The Souls were merely blessed in a different way.

The children gathered into a loose circle of cross-legged attention about him. Lucius, who had attended the morning ritual, was among them, and looked agonised when Mateo's eye fell upon him. He was right at that awkward age between cleaving to Mateo as the prime Soul, or waiting until Niki assumed the mantle of auxiliary Soul to join their cohort. His shamefaced look suggested he'd chosen Niki.

Mateo gave him a small and hopefully reassuring smile; he'd be more worried if more than a few of the true adults made the same choice, because then his niggling fear that he was failing them in some way would start to seem much less niggling.

He began to count the toddlers, sitting entranced at his feet, and made himself stop, because Nikiti was watching him closely. He did not want Niki to think he was seeking a replacement for his neophyte. He nodded to them.

They closed their eyes, taking a deep breath as they sought within themself the gift of the goddess.

Mateo knelt, ginger with the hip, among the collection of enthralled toddlers. There was very little he could do to help Niki now.

Sabine had used the metaphor of fire, when she'd been teaching her nervy young neophyte how to find and control the flow of magic. The goddess's threefold gift to the Soul was an inferno, and immunity from being scorched by that inferno, and the strength to contain and control the inferno. The Soul's gift to the Kindred in turn was a kitchen hearth, taming the wildfire that could burn them all to ash and turning it into a steady flame, safe and useful.

Mateo's own sense of it was more water than fire. The natural analogy, especially for an islander, might be a wild and stormy ocean, great waves that would crash upon and drown his Kindred if not calmed and contained. Instead, Mateo's gift felt like the tranquil surface of an immense lake, the water still and pale; he'd experienced it as such during the trance in which he'd heard the goddess whisper Her name. His strength was the wall that held back the deep and heavy expanse that would crush the Kindred before they had a chance to drown. He carefully plumbed the vastness, the unrestrained power of divinity. His was the hand on the tap that could draw the thinnest of streams and safely flow it to his people.

But Niki responded more to Sabine's fire metaphor. They also liked to help Danae while she melted her beeswax into sheets and rolled them into candles, absorbed in the soft scent and smooth feel. Therefore, back on Ysthera, in their first lessons, they'd liked to visualise the power within as a flame dancing, lively but kept tame on a wick.

On the day of the exile, Anika's frantic drag on Mateo and Niki's power had almost splintered Mateo's tap, and it had melted Niki's candle to a lumpen stub. Mateo, older, more experienced, had recovered. His neophyte…had not. Niki's flame was guttering, and had been so for three years.

They opened their eyes and shook their head at Mateo, their natural exuberance as dimmed as that metaphorical candle. Mateo put his hand on their shoulder, feeling the tension, the vibration of their fear and shame.

'It's all right,' he said calmly. He was better at reassuring children than he was at reassuring himself; that was mostly because he had the memory of Sabine's wisdom to guide him. He repeated the words she had given him when he had been late to find his way to the ritual himself. 'The worst thing you can do is push too hard. Trust our goddess; Her blessing is upon you.'

'She's asleep,' Niki whispered. 'Does She even know what's happened to us?'

This was the sort of complicated philosophical question that prime Souls liked to sink their teeth into; a solid five hundred years of arguments circled about it. Mateo, on the other hand, had been an auxiliary Soul on the day of the exile and now not only had more insistent worries than tossing over abstract theologies, but no one to discuss such lofty matters with anyway.

He was, until and unless Niki came into their power as auxiliary Soul, the only person in all the world who knew the true name of the Ystheran goddess, their Shattered One. One day, there would be more Souls again—neophytes arose in every generation—but until then, it was one foot after another, walking doggedly away from cataclysm.

'She does,' he said, with far more certainty than he felt. 'She knows, and that's why She hasn't opened Her gift fully to you yet. We have to make it safe for you first, and remake your candle.'

'With wax from which bees, exactly?' Niki demanded, but with the start of their cheeky smile.

'And that's where the metaphor falls apart, you horrible child,' Mateo said. 'We'll get there, Niki.'

He squeezed their shoulder and turned to the older children. In a minor reprisal of that morning's ritual, he slowly trickled magic into their developing receptacles, both he and Niki closely watching their faces. There was no flooding, no testing and expanding their limits. This was about becoming used to the flow of magic, in and out.

To that end, Mateo placed in front of them a torn jacket, layers of woollen batting spilling from the rip. His reward was a heartfelt chorus of groans. Children baulked at chores, even ones they could do with magic.

'No complaining, you awful creatures,' Mateo told them.

The children giggled, but: 'Why can't we ever do anything *fun*?' one of the littlest asked.

'We could do lots of things with our magic, couldn't we?' Mateo said encouragingly. 'Tell me why we don't.'

He received the answer in a ragged, resigned, recitation. 'Our promise to the Shattered One.'

'We promised,' Mateo said. 'Her gift, and our promise. We will never use our magic to do *anything* fun, ever.' They howled at him in mock outrage. 'What? What did I say?'

'We can do fun things,' Lucius said, showing the others a whirl of golden light that he turned into a glowing ball; he tossed it up and caught it. The toddlers, until now rapt on Mateo, watched it avidly, burbling amongst themselves.

'Not in front of Imperials,' Mateo reminded him. 'But, yes, we can play with our magic, of course we can. So what *can't* we do?'

'Fly!'

'Turn invisible!'

'Make other things disappear!'

'Crush our enemies,' intoned the littlest girl.

'All of those things,' Mateo said. 'Especially that last one, because that one is our *choice*, yes? Our choice, and our promise, and our duty.' The children were looking wide-eyed and sombre. He brightened his tone. 'We can…'

'The shield!' they all shouted excitedly.

'Defend ourselves, yes, and—'

'Fix people!'

'Heal others, yes, and—' He pointed at the jacket.

'Chores,' they said, a good less excitedly.

'You'll appreciate it when you're older,' Mateo told them, and nodded to Niki.

Niki knelt among the other children to direct the outflow of the magic. These were their agemates; some would become their auxiliary Coterie. They all had to learn to work their household magic seamlessly together.

The children bent their attention towards the tear in the jacket.

Niki began to murmur directions. This was where they came into their own. Mateo at their age, learning his role among his own cohort, had been a bundle of anxiety and second-guessing—not too much had changed—but Niki had the same smooth confidence he'd envied in Anika back then. Niki's Heart would not be as burdened by their Soul as Mateo's Heart.

He shook away the intrusive thought and pulled a couple of the toddlers, finally beginning to squirm, into his lap. One of them was sticky, and he wrinkled his nose.

'Watch,' he murmured. 'This will be you soon.'

'We clean up the mess,' Niki told the others.

The wool batting edged back into the quilted square of the jacket like a worm inching into soil.

'We sew up the tear.'

This was the trickiest bit; it took concentration. Agonisingly slowly, the ragged edges of the rip joined together and knit back into a whole. They'd done well. There was only the slightest patch of darker blue to show where the damage had been.

'We make sure it's right inside.'

A few of the children laid hands on the jacket, brushing over the repair, patting flat the restored batting with both fingers and magic. They didn't need the physical touch; Mateo should have corrected them, but he let it lie. They'd get there. So would Niki.

'Done!' the older children cried. Niki sat back on their heels and grinned at Mateo.

Mateo released his armful of toddlers and sent all the children off to play with Lucius's ball, and went about the rest of his daily chores, centred on the handful of Taurasi animals, donkey and chickens and cows.

Children, and animals, and only in the teahouse on the very busiest of days—Anika knew him far too well to inflict him on their customers too often.

Then came his solitary turn in the bathhouse, privacy being the one Soul privilege he didn't baulk at. Then the evening meal, baked bread and pots of beans and vegetables, almost the same as back on Ysthera except some spices were more expensive here and so were added with a lighter hand. The city workers brought up grilled meat on skewers from the cookshops at the bottom of the hill to round it out.

And then, at last, he settled carefully on cushions beside Anika, the twins perched on another pile of cushions on the far side of the low table, set with three Kindred cups of wine and one Soul cup of herbal tea.

Darius knelt nearby, silent and watchful, as alert at the end of the day as he was at the start, despite the increasing incursion of silver through his hair, making the shock of white hair around the scar on his scalp less striking. They could not persuade him to give up his guardian duties; nor could they persuade him to partake with them when they indulged in this brief nightly relaxation of their own Coterie duties.

'Are you well, my sweet?' Anika said, the moment the long tail of Taurasi had bid Mateo a respectful good night and departed. She laid her hand over his forehead. 'You've got your bees in the head today, don't you?'

'Sorry,' he said meekly. 'I think the Imperial guest sent me up the mountain.'

The twins had both seen Jonas this morning, but that was all. Anika turned to them now and explained who he was and what he wanted. She added the sad news about *Steadfast*, to pitying exclamations from both twins. Mateo wanted to ask if she had known about the sinking before that morning, but there was little point. If she had known and not told him, the answer was simple: she was protecting her Soul, as all Taurasi were bound to do.

'I will tell you now I think it is a good opportunity and recommend we make the deal,' Anika finished.

'Teo?' Timon asked.

'You *know* I think change is terrible and Imperials are terrible and we should run in the opposite direction,' Mateo said. 'Would you like to hear my list of what-ifs or would you like to get to bed before the sun rises?'

The Coterie sniggered. Andrea said, 'Mateo is right, though, it will bring change to Ravenser Odd.'

'What do you care?' her brother demanded. 'Don't you want to live down in Anceral now?'

He spoke with some scorn; he wouldn't even *visit* the city. Neither would Mateo, but that was more out of respect for his kith's feelings rather than Timon's stubborn lack of curiosity, verging on outright hostility.

'That's Selia, not me,' Andrea said indignantly. 'I don't know that I'd move with her. And I was not ready for her to suddenly bring it up at the meeting.'

She looked apologetically at Anika, who waved it away. 'It's bound to happen eventually. Unless Madam Kerling sells us her lodging house.'

The very idea made them all chortle again. Timon put his arm around his sister. 'Sorry, Dee. I just… Well. You know.'

They did know. Timon had been one of the large minority of Taurasi who'd recognised the irrefutable logic of unbinding the Souls' tame magic to fight off the impending Imperial invasion. Ancient tales of the loss of their homeland and subsequent threefold gift of their broken goddess had not deterred them.

His faction had been outvoted by a narrow margin, *chillingly* narrow in retrospect.

He went on. 'You're so much better at embracing new things than me. I couldn't work with the Imperials like you do.'

'Brother,' Andrea said scoldingly. 'Don't you see that if I spend all day out there, I need an Ystheran sanctuary to come home to? I want change up here as little as you and Teo do. Before we know it, the empire will have woven its threads into every aspect of our lives, and we'll never unpick them.'

'I am also somewhat tired of change,' Anika pointed out. 'But this is where we live now. We do not get to go home.'

She spoke the simple truth calmly, as if Taurasi had not come to her all day, in tears or in confused rage or in bleak staring silence. They would come to her like that for weeks and likely months to come, Mateo supposed.

Anika went on, 'Perhaps it's time to start living like we live here, don't we think?'

Timon bowed his head, accepting his Heart's mild rebuke. Andrea nodded, and that was the vote: the opportunity Jonas had presented to them on a platter would be embraced. Even Darius, reluctantly, added his own nod when Anika sent a subtly questioning look her uncle's way. It would be put to the vote during the next meeting, but Anika's sway, with full Coterie support, would push it through.

Andrea and Timon finished the last sips of their wine. Then they crawled around each end of the table and pounced upon Mateo in a communal embrace that they took care did not jostle his hip.

'No hugging,' he muttered, hugging them back. 'I'm sure I've made this clear.'

Darius excused himself in their wake, heading for his own solitary bed upstairs in the insula. For a solid year after their arrival in Anceral, he'd waited outside on the porch until Mateo retired. These days, he'd unbent enough to trust his Soul to walk across the empty street both without trouble and in time to avoid getting locked out by his unreasonably strict landlady.

Anika slumped against Mateo, fond physical contact containing a fair amount of tired wilt. 'How's your hip, my sweet?'

'Fine.' He didn't want to have to say he'd slipped on the roof she'd sent him up to. He didn't want to admit he could no longer manage stairs that had been manageable last summer.

'If you say fine to every one of my recipe tweaks, I'll never know what's working,' she said severely. 'You seem stiff.'

'And you, Ana?' He quoted her back to herself. '"We suffer, but we need not suffer alone", yes? You had a long day, on the heels of a feisty meeting this morning.'

Anika sighed, partly amused, but partly very much not. 'Oh, it's fine. Sometimes I wish Penelope would just challenge for Heart. She'd be welcome to it.'

'The thought chills my very bones,' he said. 'Please don't let her.'

'I can't stop her,' Anika said, smiling. 'I promise not to suggest it to her, though.' Her smile turned mischievous. 'Though days spent just brewing tisanes and smiling at customers in my cosy little teahouse sound extraordinarily pleasant at the moment. Maybe I should have given up on being Heart altogether and just joined Kindred Leporasi after all.'

When Mateo and Anika were fourteen or so, the fact that as soon as he ascended from neophyte to auxiliary Soul, he would be untouchable to any Taurasi—a strict Ys00theran tradition—had loomed darkly over their mutually infatuated adolescent heads. They'd given solemn consideration to the only acceptable solution—for Anika to relocate to another Kindred, likely her mother's, and request alliance back to the Taurasi auxiliary Soul.

But it was by no means certain that the hoped-for alliance would have been allowed, prior arrangement or no; Mateo had later learned firsthand that even a formal agreement to alliance was not the thing itself.

Anyway, by then it was clear that Anika was a strong candidate for Heart; the opportunity would be lost if she went to another Kindred, where migrants from other kinship groups were always welcome but whose former statuses were very much not.

Anika had made the practical choice for the common good that even now marked her successful tenure as Heart. And so, Mateo's first love had run the gamut from friendship to infatuation to heartbreak to friendship, and Taurasi had the Heart it needed in such trying times.

'You would have been lost with them,' Mateo said now.

'Perhaps if I had been with them, I could have persuaded more of them to vote against blighting the magic,' Anika countered. 'If I recall correctly, many of them did vote no, just not the majority. Then two Kindreds might have made it off Ysthera.'

'And perhaps, if you had not been with Kindred Taurasi, we wouldn't have made it off Ysthera at all. We'd have died on the mountain. Or, perhaps, without your support, we wouldn't have had a majority vote against using wild magic in the first place. Perhaps Timon would have been the auxiliary Heart and his faction would have carried the day, and we all would have drowned last week, if the wild magic hadn't destroyed us first.'

When Anika screwed up her face, Mateo triumphantly added, 'Admit it, I am much better at the what-if game than you.'

'Much better at unrelenting pessimism, anyway,' Anika said, paradoxically sounding a good deal more cheerful.

This sudden cheer, when it had so conspicuously absent before, prompted Mateo to mumble, 'I worry about you.'

'Teo, you worry about everything.' Mateo looked at her anxiously—somewhere in his uncertain future lay the moment when Anika finally ran out of patience with him—and she smiled and nudged him. 'I'm the Heart. This is my role, and I wanted it enough to choose it over you.'

'That's— What? No, I've *never* thought of it like that—'

'I know! I'm sorry, my sweet, I was just making fun, of myself more than you.'

'I'm worried…' Mateo paused to breathe, and Anika let him, patience not exhausted quite yet. 'I'm worried I am not strong enough for you. Not…not compared to Sabine. If she had not been lost, you would not be left with a Soul so susceptible to human foibles.'

Anika wrapped her arms around him. 'As if Sabine was *not?*' she said. 'As if all Souls aren't also just human? One day you'll realise how very strong you are, under all those nerves. You brought us down the mountain, Mattias Taurasi, Soul of my heart.'

'*You* brought us down the mountain, Aniketa the Unconquerable, Heart of my heart.'

She hesitated, pulling away to send a significant look at his hip. 'You know, there's a tradition passed down among healers, that if you refuse to experience grief in your head, you'll experience it in your body.'

Mateo must have looked blank, because she tsked. 'You lost loved ones last week, too, Mateo, just like you lost loved ones on the day of the exile, and all you're thinking about is whether you're being strong enough or not.'

'We *all* lost loved ones,' he said. He felt the familiar ache in his chest, and lifted his hands to press over his heart. 'You did.'

Anika caught his hands, and pressed them to her own heart instead. 'It was not your fault.'

He would accept that when Anika accepted that what had happened to Nikiti wasn't hers, and there was a reason the Heart was not asking the Soul how that day's practice had gone.

He cleared his throat. 'My grief isn't any bigger than anyone else's.'

'It's not… Teo, my sweet, it's not any smaller.'

Neither is yours, he wanted to say. But it was fruitless. He carried a weight from the day of the exile, and now another, from the loss of their home in a second, more catastrophic, devastatingly final way. So did Anika. So did they all.

He did the only thing he could, and put his arms around Anika, and they held each other in that brief moment of respite from their duties. He could only hope it gave her as much comfort as it gave him.

'I better get to bed before Madam Kerling bolts the door and locks me out,' he said finally.

'That woman,' she sighed.

He let her help him up off the cushions in a way he wouldn't have if there'd been witnesses, and limped to the door.

'Sleep well, Teo,' she called after him.

He knew he wouldn't.

CHAPTER 5

THAT NIGHT, MATEO FELL INTO THE dream again. He always knew it was a dream; he could never wake from it. He also knew it wasn't really a dream. It was the true memory of what happened the day the Taurasi left Ysthera.

It is mid-morning on the last spring day Kindred Taurasi will ever experience on their Sunlit Isle.

They've been loading the carts for several days, and at work from dawn this morning. The carts are full now, with people lined up along the sides, and the beds laden high with their most portable valuables, chests and bales containing silks and jewellery, and coins and gems. Everyone has been permitted one personal item of mere sentimental value, as long as it is not furniture.

There has been a long argument between Penelope and the prime Coterie as to whether the pottery wheel handed down through her direct family line for generations counts as furniture and as to whether her status as former Heart—the Heart who led Taurasi during the last invasion attempt, no less—means she is exempt from the rule regardless. She is currently hiding her genteel seething beside the second wagon, which does not hold the pottery wheel.

The weavers did not even make the attempt on behalf of their looms. The jewellers have their tools tucked about their persons. Danae bid farewell to her hives, but she has collected queens and their servants and used her allotment of magic to put them into a sort of stasis, untried. She hopes for the best, as do they all. The older children have been given responsibility for the seeds and seedlings; Niki, though they hadn't yet adopted that name, sits beside those crates, looking uncharacteristically sombre.

It is an orderly retreat. The Taurasi are carefully closing the doors of their cottages behind them. None of them truly believe they will never come back from the exile that is currently their only option.

Sabine, the prime Soul, comes to lean on the cart beside Mateo, where he is already seated by Anika, idly kicking his heels against the side. Except it is not idle, it is anxious. Lean and long-limbed, Mateo is both a natural worrier and a natural runner, and he and Sabine have long since discovered that running up the mountain eases his fretful mind. There had been no time for that this morning and he is suffering accordingly, the bees at work in his head as busy as real bees on a sunny day.

Sabine squeezes his hand. 'Mattias, my dearest boy,' she says soothingly. 'All will be well.'

Mateo nods and makes a concerted effort to stop fidgeting. Anika pushes her shoulder into his, and it helps. Timon, Andrea and Talia, the rest of the auxiliary Coterie, are climbing up on to the cart next to them. Talia, bright-eyed, topknot tail swinging, gives Mateo a fond pat and Anika a fonder kiss.

A voice hails Charion, Heart of Taurasi. Sabine turns, then, and Mateo looks up, too. It is Zanthas, Heart of Kindred Gallasi, coming along one of the narrow paths that wind between the Ystherans' mountainside villages. He has with him a few of his Coterie, but not the Soul. Sabine and Mateo would have sensed the approach of another Soul, each presence forming an unbroken web over the whole island.

Mateo is relieved to see Zanthas's son and heir, Elias, is also absent. Mateo and Elias have not been lovers for many years now, and yet it is still ever awkward to encounter him.

'Come to say goodbye, I suppose,' Sabine says, a touch disapprovingly.

Zanthas was not so neighbourly at Klados, the council assembly, when, one by one, the Hearts announced their respective Kindreds' acceptance of the need to let loose their magic and then Charion rose, Sabine, Mateo and Anika with him, and informed them that Kindred Taurasi was voting no.

Zanthas, in fact, led the bitter recriminations which ended in Charion calmly announcing the departure of Kindred Taurasi in its entirety. The Taurasi had understood that this would be the outcome, when they'd cast their vote against the rest of the klados. They could not, in all good conscience, shelter from the empire under the aegis of the very wild magic they themselves refused to embrace. The decision against freeing it was the decision to leave Ysthera.

It is still galling to watch Zanthas stride past the carts without a second look, calling out a jovial greeting to Charion. Darius and a few of the other guardians move towards them, but Charion waves them off, not without a smile for his severe husband. Zanthas has not brought along his own ceremonial honour guard, after all, nor his Soul, and is dressed in simple clothing. This is not a formal meeting. Therefore, Sabine glides over to stand by the last cart, closer to Charion, but refrains from joining her Heart.

The two leaders exchange shallow bows, but then Zanthas grasps Charion's hand. He's a hearty older man, of Penelope's generation, hair gone to silver, but still strong across the shoulders. Charion looks startled as his hand engulfs his own. It's almost an Imperial-style clasp, and there's nothing any Ystheran values about the empire right now, not even those currently emigrating into its embrace.

'Come now, old friend, let us not stand on such ceremony. You know why I have come.'

Charion smiles apologetically. Their Heart is a gentle man, much taxed by the strife between the Taurasi and the other Kindreds. 'There is no point going over this again. We have not, and will not, change our minds, Zanthas.'

Zanthas glances about with raised eyebrows, acknowledging the packed carts for the first time. 'Not even now, when reality must surely be sinking in? This does not have to happen.'

'No.' Charion looks thoughtful. 'No, it doesn't.'

After a pause, Zanthas says, 'I see. You are persisting in this notion that it is everyone else who is wrong. Look.'

He puts a jovial arm around Charion, and Darius, keeping a respectful distance with the other guardians, stiffens. But no Ystheran is a threat to another Ystheran, and Darius does not need to be jealous of Zanthas.

Charion, still wearing his rueful smile, allows himself to be turned so Zanthas can gesticulate over the vista. The sky is bright blue. Taurasi will never see its like again.

Far below, at the bottom of the steep zigzag main road down the mountain, a compact trading ship with striped sails awaits them at the long Low wharf. Out to sea, small white-capped waves ripple in the wide bay near the shore, fading to the dark blue of the deeper water westwards. Imperial ships patrol out there, the bold black raven-and-wheel emblem on their sails too indistinct to make out at this distance.

Zanthas points towards those ships. 'They are blockading us for the crime of resisting their invasion.'

Charion, in his turn, gestures to Low, to *Steadfast* moored at the deep-water end of the long dock. 'They are not doing such a wonderful job at the blockade. We thank the Shattered One and Her sacred Remnants for piratical-minded traders, do we not?'

'This is not a joke,' Zanthas says severely, though Mateo knows Charion was not joking. 'They already revile us for our magic. When they come back—and they will come back—they will no longer be trying to conquer us. They will be trying to eradicate us.'

Beside Mateo, Anika stirs, touching the inner pocket of her light jacket. As auxiliary Heart, and moreover someone who has taken the trouble to learn to read, Charion has awarded her the honour of carrying the documents from the Imperial authorities in Ingelrii, the southern port where Taurasi has been given leave, with strict conditions, to disembark.

The Taurasi are settling within the Vaeringan territories under a *deeply* ironic political asylum.

Despite himself, Charion has been drawn into the same old argument that Ystherans have engaged in since the empire first tried to invade in his youth. It was the argument he and Sabine won with the Taurasi, but lost with the rest of the Kindreds.

'We held them off with our magic before, and can do so again. We do not need to resort to breaking our promise.'

'The empire will swallow you all, Charion,' Zanthas says. 'Stay. Defend Ysthera with us.'

'Gladly,' Charion says. 'If we use only our domesticated magic.'

Zanthas laughs mockingly, though it is he who forgot the new vocabulary. '*Fight* with us, then.'

'We made the sacred promise of peace to our goddess. To turn away from that is to surrender to the empire before it even attempts to send its marines ashore.'

'We can afford the luxury of peace no longer, old friend.'

'We had this lesson five hundred years ago, Zan. Our Most Holy, broken. Meredonia, destroyed. Five Kindreds, lost. How many Kindreds will we lose when we again fall to the temptation of wild magic, and thus scorn the gift granted to our ancestors when they made landfall safely on Ysthera?'

'Bedtime tales leave you trembling,' Zanthas says pityingly. 'Wild magic did not cause the Shattering. Wild magic did not force us from the shores of Meredonia. Wild magic did not destroy five Kindreds. And the Souls did not guide the seven surviving Kindreds to Ysthera.'

Charion glances over to Sabine, who is frowning. It is difficult to hear the traditional stories so readily scorned. Mateo wonders if it is a necessary step on this path, to first denigrate the Souls, whose domesticated magic is so much *less* than wild magic, from which their discipline, their promise, their faith, shields their people.

The other Kindreds fear imperial invasion far more than they fear untrammelled magic, but it seems to Mateo that both ways from this agonising crossroads lead far, far, from Ysthera. The other Taurasi speak hopefully of coming home one day. Mateo thinks their home is already forever lost.

But then Mateo is a morbid creature sometimes. He looks about, at Anika, at Timon and Andrea and Talia, at the children whispering in the next cart over, their parents smiling at them. Sabine is right. All will be well.

Zanthas then says, 'Our goddess is dead,' and this is shocking heresy, worthy of the blight that is the goddess turning Her face from him. 'You belittle Her final gift by forcing your Soul to keep it chained.'

'No.' Sabine, raising her voice from by the last cart, sounds too sharp, and she takes a moment before she resumes her usual serene tones. 'She merely sleeps, or we would not have magic at all. Her gift *is* the chains. It is you who tarnish it by trying to take them off. We made Her a promise.'

'And She promised *us* Her protection, and where is She now, when the empire musters against us? *Dead.*'

More Taurasi than just Mateo flinch as Zanthas again makes that blighted accusation.

Charion, sighing, makes a soothing gesture, patting the air between Sabine and Zanthas. 'Please, let us not rehash the same arguments. We accept the decision you have made. We do not share it. We are going.'

Again, he looks at the quietly watching Taurasi. Lucian, Anika's father, is strapping down the contents of the last cart. The last few children have ended their game of chase and are climbing up to sit with their siblings and parents and grandparents. There are even some few Ystherans previously of other Kindreds, who came quietly to join Taurasi after the vote, defying the cultural expectation that kith cleave to their Kindred's rulings.

All is ready.

The Heart of Taurasi receives the resolute nods of his people. 'We go.'

'That is the final choice, then,' Zanthas says. He sounds almost sad. He exchanges looks with his silent Coterie, and calls out to the carts. 'We would like to invite those of the Taurasi who were outvoted to join Kindred Gallasi, if you do not wish to be punished for a folly that is not your own.'

Mateo peeks at Timon, one of the more vocal of that faction. The other man pulls a face and gives a nonchalant shake of his head. No one else moves.

'Punished,' Anika repeats. She sounds puzzled.

'He means by exile,' Talia says. Her mother was Gallasi, allied into Taurasi. One of Talia's uncles is standing with Zanthas. He hasn't looked at his niece, or at her father on the front cart, amid the prime Coterie.

'Oh, Taurasi,' Zanthas says softly, so softly Mateo has to strain to hear him. 'To not merely refuse to protect Ysthera against the Imperials, but to actually join them? Traitors.'

'No. Our ship awaits us at the dock, Zanthas.' Charion nods, politely but in firm dismissal, and starts to turn away.

Before he can, Zanthas takes his hand again. 'Charion,' he says, and his eyes are suddenly inhumanly cold. 'You brought this down on yourself.'

And he scorches magic through Charion and drops his smouldering corpse to the ground.

There is a beat in which no one reacts, a single beat that lasts all of eternity.

Then comes chaos like a tidal wave.

Darius bellows—it is the last sound he will make, and it is a wordless howl of grief and rage—and charges, sword yanked from its sheath. The other guardians are with him, iron blades drawn for the defence of the Taurasi on the carts. Some of those are huddled, weeping, covering their children. Some few let out shrieks as what they witnessed sunk in, but are now silent in shock. Others leap off the carts and run forwards with neither thought nor weapon readily to hand.

The Coterie shake off their own shock and throw up a shield, which saves the guardians' lives when the wild magic Zanthas and his own Coterie fling at them bounces harmlessly off it. The Gallasi are themselves shielded, and the blades of Darius and the other guardians cannot break through.

'Taurasi, we go,' Lucian calls, loud and firm. His voice cuts through the panic, a lighthouse in the storm, and the Taurasi turn to it. 'Darius, protect the carts.'

Darius turns on his brother a look of utter loathing. Mateo has no doubt he intended to follow Charion into death, taking as much of the

Gallasi Coterie with him as he could. But he obeys. He leads the guardians onto the carts, shoving stray Taurasi before them.

Lucian turns Anika back too, where she has run to him, not a daughter seeking comfort from her father, but the auxiliary Heart, instinctively taking up the mantle, trying to patch the gaping hole rent in the prime Coterie when their own Heart fell.

But her father shakes his head to her, as he shook it to his brother. He seizes her arm and runs with the others to the rearmost cart, but he pushes her over towards Mateo. 'Stay with your Coterie, Ana,' he says. 'Get the carts to the dock. We'll shield.'

Sabine leaps up beside him on the last cart, spry in the urgency of the moment and already aglow. She is flooding her Coterie with magic, and they are thickening the shield, spreading it over all six carts. She looks calm enough, even with tracks of silent tears on her face, but a Soul in desperate circumstances can easily overrun a novice Heart, stop her heart, destroy the Taurasi's last chance of escape. Lucian is right to send Anika back to the auxiliary Coterie.

Anika clambers back up to Mateo, pushes him off the side and into the middle of their cart, and sets all the carts jolting into motion. She is sobbing.

And then she is not. She will never cry in front of the Taurasi again.

She commands the Coterie with cool calm: Talia to add her strength and direction to the shield the prime Coterie has spread over the carts. Timon and Andrea to steer and keep the Taurasi from being flung off.

Because Anika hasn't merely set the carts rolling down the steep switchback. She is still pushing at them, speeding them up. She is dragging heavily on Mateo's magic.

All Mateo does is kneel amid the crates and trunks and send out magic towards his Coterie. Darius is crouching beside him, sword still drawn. The rest of the guardians are spread about the other carts. Mateo is not panicked, not yet. The Taurasi Coteries have never trained against attack by other Ystherans, that would be unthinkable—this is *unthinkable*—but they have trained against invasion by the empire. They are safe under their shield.

There are shapes overhead, indistinct though the strong honeyed glow of the shield. Some of the shapes are dark and human—the Gallasi Coterie have become *phalaros*, the blighted, what the empire would label sorcerers, and are flying after the Taurasi to batter at their shield. Other shapes are long, sinuous, pale smudges.

Talia whispers, '*Skiaskylos.*' Shadow-dogs, an ancient story from the fall of Meredonia.

They plunge and claw and bite at the shield.

The shield trembles.

They reach the first switchback, and Anika slows to turn the carts around the sharp bend. 'Everybody hold on,' she shouts.

Back on the straight, steep descent of the next leg, Anika's watching the prime Coterie on the last cart, her gaze tracking back and forth as she assesses the strain of reinforcing the shield against the assault. She's turning to reassign Timon or Andrea to help them when it happens.

A child falls from the second cart, a tumbling movement in the corner of Mateo's eye. And Kalinda, of the prime Coterie, shifts her attention to catch him and push him back to safety. She shifts her attention for just the barest of moments, a half-breath taken to save a child.

The shield falls.

The Gallasi surround the rearmost cart and pour boundless magic upon the prime Coterie and the other Taurasi riding with them. Without their Heart to hold them steady, the Coterie has dissolved into individuals fighting for their lives, flinging their domesticated magic up to block fatal strikes. Sabine kneels in their centre, looking up, her face as serene as ever, lit to near-incandescence with the magic she is blazing outwards to her Coterie and to any other Taurasi reaching for it.

Anika swings the carts around the next switchback, barely slowing this time. Taurasi cry out and pitch alarmingly, but everyone holds on, fingers and magic clinging tight to the wooden sides.

The other shapes have come clear, hunting hounds made of mist, and yet solid enough.

That much is apparent when one stoops down and rips Sabine from the cart.

The Taurasi scream. Mateo doesn't. He chokes. He can't make a sound. He can't breathe.

He crawls across the cart, towards the prime Coterie's cart. He does not know what he is thinking. He's not thinking. The Coterie needs a Soul. He doesn't remember that he is experienced enough now that he doesn't need to touch a Taurasi to gift them his magic. It doesn't occur to him that it is too dangerous to try to jump to their cart when they are rattling along at this speed.

The other danger does not occur to him either, until Anika puts a firm hand on his shoulder. 'No.'

Lucian and the other Coterie members have started to scrabble along their own cart towards Mateo, a panicked instinct as they desperately hold off the much stronger wild magic with only whatever of Sabine's magic is left within their depleting receptacles.

Anika stands tall, swaying only slightly with the rattling of the cart, and holds her hand up, stopping them. She looks her own father in the eye, and shakes her head.

Just as a novice Heart teamed with a strong but panicking Soul might die of it, a desperate prime Coterie could drain an inexperienced Soul to the very quick in mere moments, taking unwitting advantage of his naïve, terrified generosity with the goddess's gift.

Lucian matches his daughter's stance, tall and straight in the centre of the sixth cart. He nods to her, and turns to issue orders to the Coterie.

Suddenly, the sixth cart is slowing, veering, heading back up the mountain. The Coterie gush forth the last dregs of Sabine's magic, drawing off the blindly questing shadow-dogs, the Gallasi vainly trying to call them back towards the main target, which…

Well. It's Mateo now.

The remaining train of carts speeds away, and Mateo and Anika kneel side by side, watching uselessly as, one by one, the Taurasi prime Coterie exhaust their magic and fall, murdered by the Gallasi or their shadow-dogs. Her father is last, crouching protectively over the civilian Taurasi to the very last breath he takes.

Anika says nothing. She does not look away.

The shadow-dogs fall upon the last of the Taurasi in the sixth cart in unrestrained slaughter. It's a relief when the cart, bodies strewn in its wake, tips and rolls down the side of the mountain, spewing a colourful rain as trunks of silks and jewels split open on the rocks.

The rest of the cart train is approaching the next switchback. It will send them back in the direction of the shadow-dogs and their masters where they swirl above the wreckage of the rolled cart and its horrid jetsam. They are massing like a storm about to break upon their heads.

'I need everything you have,' Anika says, not taking her eyes from the chaotic mass in the sky overhead.

'It's yours,' Mateo says.

'Taurasi,' she cries, magically amplifying her voice. 'You must hold yourselves to the carts. We cannot help you if you fall. Hold yourself and your children.'

Tersely, she directs Talia to bring the shield back up, and Timon and

Andrea to leap, with a mix of magic and agility, to the first cart, to wipe obstacles from their path in between adding their strength to the shield.

'Hold on,' she shouts one more time.

Then she turns the carts, and plunges Kindred Taurasi straight down the mountainside.

It is not a descent, but a plummet, its sole intent to outrun the shadow-dogs, for the erstwhile auxiliary Coterie cannot hold a shield their obliterated prime Coterie could not. They are falling, but it is a controlled fall, Anika's face set in fierce determination as she holds five carts and near one hundred people steady and sends them past switchback after switchback in favour of the direct route.

They are halfway down when the Gallasi catch them and once again assault the shield. Timon and Andrea are doing their best to help Talia, but the speed of the descent does not leave them much time to do anything other than shove boulders aside and alter the inexorable trajectory of the cart train just enough to dodge full-grown trees.

Darius has pushed Mateo to lie in a narrow space among the strapped-down boxes on the cartbed, kneeling over him, his weight heavy. Mateo wishes he was not lying on his back, looking up at the shield, counting the shadows beyond it, measuring every little shiver it gives. He should close his eyes. He won't.

He is flooding out magic now, pushing it not just to the Coterie but to all the Taurasi, silently pleading with them to just hold on, to just hold the shield, to just hold the course.

But people are not holding on. People are tumbling off the sides of the carts, fingers torn lose from handholds and straps. Mateo, desperate, pushes out even more magic, because he does not understand what is happening until it happens to Talia. She's been on top of the crates in his cart this whole time, the main pillar of the defensive shield.

Strong, merry Talia, Anika's love and her ever-steady comfort, firm and unyielding in holding the shield.

She gasps. Her face goes ashen. Her bright eyes dull, appallingly fast. She falls. Her body hits the crates, rolls, slides, and vanishes off the side.

Mateo flooded her with so much magic so fast that he stopped her heart.

Anika looks back up the mountain at Talia's body, a discarded doll in the dust rising in billows behind them.

The shield has fallen with Talia, and in that instant, the shadow-dogs stoop upon the Taurasi. They cannot find Mateo, not at first, because all five carts are drenched in magic. The guardians strike at them, but their blades do nothing, and they are torn from the carts until only Darius is left. There is nothing but screaming and thrashing and useless panic, rippling up and down the carts.

As impossible as it seems, the carts move even faster, their wheels, splintered and cracked from the rough decent, nearly all off the ground now. Anika is near-literally flying the carts down the mountain.

They're almost to the flat when a shadow-dog finds Mateo wedged in his narrow shelter. It knocks Darius aside with a slash of claws and bites clumsily into Mateo. It only just grazes his hip with its front teeth, but it instantly sinks them deep and jerks him up off the cart.

Darius, bleeding from a gash in his head, lunges and seizes him around the shoulders to pull him back down. Anika, never faltering in her control of the carts, grabs on too, and they both grapple with their full weight to hold Mateo.

Mateo screams in agony. He is being torn in two.

The shadow-dog twists in the air, knocking Anika loose. The supernatural creature is, as its mythic name implies, vaguely hound-shaped, but its tail is spiked. It sweeps the brutal spike towards Darius, who is being dragged up off the cart after Mateo and still will not let him go.

A glint of something brassy scythes overhead, the tearing sound of its passage almost drowned out by the frantic hum of Taurasi magic. It rips through the solid mass of the shadow-dog just before it stabs Darius, shredding it into misty wisps and dropping Mateo and Darius back to the bed of the cart.

Later, Mateo will be told that their brassy salvation was the giant harpoon, the ballista, of *Steadfast*. The ship has fired upwards upon the Gallasi, to far better effect than the guardians' blades. The ballista tore low above the line of carts, dissipating three shadow-dogs before shredding Mateo's assailant above the final cart.

Now, however, he barely registers anything except that the pain in his hip is excruciating but that the thing that had its teeth in him is gone and he is safe in Darius's arms.

His guardian is silently weeping, the tears cutting a clean path down his bloodied face, as he cradles the Soul of Taurasi.

The carts hit the village road hard, the leading edge of the front cart shattering and showering the Taurasi still clinging there with wickedly jagged splinters. Timon's face is cut open, and Andrea is lucky not to lose an eye. They still wear the scars.

The carts scream along the road towards the dock, not losing an iota of speed on the last shallow decline through the outbuildings of Low. Low is deserted; the foreign merchants have already been expelled.

'Anika,' Timon shouts, bleeding freely, unable to spare a hand to clap to his wounds. 'Anika, slow down. *Steadfast* is holding. She's holding!'

Anika does not slow down. Later, much later, she will tell Mateo that her mind in this moment is nothing but a clenched fist beating *get them out get them out get them out* against the inside of her skull in time with the slam of her heart against her ribs. She does not even hear Timon.

Mateo is letting her pull magic out of him hand-over-hand. His head throbs and he feels wetness on his face, and touches it. His fingers are painted red. His nose is gushing blood to match the leak from the messy holes in his hip.

Ystherans do not pray to their goddess. She was shattered into twelve shards, and now sleeps, deaf to praise or petition alike. Even Her name is lost to all but the Souls.

But now, looking at his wet fingers and feeling the blood drip down over his mouth and chin, feeling the hot wet stabbing in his hip, feeling the tidal ebb of hope, Mateo silently makes a single, heartfelt plea.

Please.

He receives no answer, of course, except that, perhaps, in his extremity, something stirs within him. He opens bloodied hands and somehow is able to gift even more magic to Anika. It could be a blessing from his goddess. It could simply be wishful thinking and the last drop from a dry well.

Overhead, the soaring Gallasi swirl up their wild magic and fling it towards the ship. Perhaps this is retribution for the incursion against the shadow-dogs, or perhaps it is a pre-emptive strike on the Taurasi's escape route, or perhaps it is both.

No one on the ship would be able to see it coming. They can likely see the shadow-dogs, to have shot something at them, but wild magic itself would be as invisible as domesticated magic to non-Ystherans. It is, after all, only a difference of degree.

Anika raises both hands, still sucking magic from Mateo. He's bleeding from his ears now, too, and his eyes feel like they might burst, but he will not fail his Heart by denying her his gift. She snatches the Taurasi's personal shields from their control, eliciting more screams, and throws the whole mess upwards.

It is blunt force born of despair and it bats the assault aside just before it hits the ship to sink Taurasi's last hope. She spreads her upflung fingers wide, and the last few shadow-dogs about to pounce shred into tatters and whip away in the wind.

They clatter onto the dock, five carts of Taurasi, trembling, sobbing, bruised and bleeding and bitten, weak with shock and the tantalising promise of escape so close.

Even now, Anika does not stop.

She pulls on not only Mateo but also—in her well-hidden terror, to her later everlasting shame—little Niki, who is gamely offering up their own developing power without sensible restraint. She simply picks up the entire contents of the carts, Taurasi, crates, trunks and all, and dumps them on the deck of *Steadfast*, setting the ship to violently rocking.

With Mateo crumpling bonelessly to the deck and Niki crying out in fright and pain, Anika seizes the last of their freely-offered magic to shove the yawing ship away from the dock, leaving the old wooden planks and struts cracking and collapsing in its wake.

She wrenches *Steadfast* out of the harbour and halfway across the bay in a single, soundless swoop of power unmatched in Ystheran history.

Aniketa the Unconquerable has saved Kindred Taurasi.

She's almost killed both Soul and neophyte doing it.

CHAPTER 6

MATEO SLEPT LATE AND WOKE IN a much better mood. Part of that was the inaccurate ending of the nightmare, a warm, steady voice saying, 'All right, honey, I've got you,' in his ear as he collapsed, bleeding from every orifice, aboard *Steadfast*.

In reality, of course, that had not happened, and Mateo knew that to his core. Not in five hundred years would the Taurasi have allowed any outsider near their bleeding and unconscious Soul, not even one claiming to be a physician. Bereft of magic, they'd have used knives and nails and teeth to keep strangers at bay.

In reality, he'd awoken more than two full weeks later, already in Anceral, after a sea journey that could not be described as horrific only because its onset had taken that honour for itself.

The sailors, still reeling from Anika's magical shove, were left scrabbling to get underway before the Imperial ships of the blockade closed in. Then a storm—unseasonal and unlucky but still just a storm, Anika said—assailed them. Mateo and the children and the injured had sheltered berths, but everyone else huddled under awnings behind the water barrels, helpless to do anything but watch as the crew passed ropes under the hull to keep the ship lashed together and then, wrapped in oilskins, tied each other to any sturdy brace to weather it.

By the time they were becalmed on the far side, they'd taken such damage, and were so far off-course, that Captain Velasco had turned *Steadfast* to limp for her homeport instead of taking her passengers south to Ingelrii. This must have been the part of the journey Niki and the other children had enjoyed under Jonas's care.

They should have reembarked on a new ship immediately, but with Mateo still unconscious, the Kindred slipping ever further into shock and despair, and their funds finite, Anika made the decision to hold. In the back of her mind must have been the bleak knowledge that the other Kindreds knew Taurasi had intended to make for balmy southern Ingelrii. Between the expulsion of the last Low merchants, the reinforced blockade, and the destroyed pier, Ysthera had no way to learn the refugees had gone north to Anceral instead. That ignorance bespoke a safety they'd never had to consider before.

She'd had to face the Anceran governor and plead for yet more mercy from a long-standing enemy that hated and feared her people. The Ystheran defiance of the first invasion—their shield rising shimmering around the entire island, the whole klados working in shifts to hold it for weeks—introduced the undefeated Vaer to real magic. The repelled marines had saved face by claiming it had not been a magic wall at all, but human heads on spikes in an unbroken line along the narrow white beaches, powerful sorcerous curses known as nithing poles, a lie still infecting Imperial opinion more than a generation later.

Regardless, the failed invasion ended the eastern expansion, toppled an emperor, ruined the battle wizards whose magic was now revealed to be either inferior or utter fakery, made the people question their gods, and in general shook Imperial foundations all the way to the very heartland.

The Ingelriin governor had been convinced, over months of negotiation, that Taurasi refugees come crawling, hobbled and penitent, into the benevolent empire under the massing threat of a second invasion was a coup, a victory of the smuggest sort. More of the contents of the carts had gone in bribes to persuade Anceral's governor of the same logic. Anika won permission to stay.

Meanwhile, the Taurasi, decimated but still numerous, had been forced to separate, away from their Heart and Soul. They'd had to spread out across the city and crowd into whatever quarters they could scrounge, a dire situation that could not have been making them any less miserable.

And Mateo had slept through it all.

The moment he'd opened his eyes in a grubby little inn on the outskirts, Aniketa the Unconquerable, waiting at his bedside, had prostrated herself to the bare floor beside the narrow bed. She'd called him by his archaic title and begged his forgiveness for almost killing him, for snuffing Niki's nascent gift. He'd begged hers, for actually killing Talia, for *sleeping* while the Taurasi had suffered. There had been much mutual self-recrimination.

Normally, the memory of that treacherous day and the miserable weeks that followed would have left Mateo in the same sort of mood as yesterday. But between the unexpectedly decent night's sleep and un-expectedly comforting ending of the familiar nightmare, he'd recovered enough composure to realise he'd been terribly cranky and rude yesterday, and was going to have to make amends.

Penelope was, of course, not cranky and rude this morning about the ritual being late, but was politely vocal about it to everyone else as they came in on Mateo's tail. She was also very polite and understanding about the plan, now successfully voted on, to sell, among other things, the spiced tea to Jonas's consortium.

'Without the ritual, dear?' she asked Anika. 'That's a touch…heretical, wouldn't you say?'

'I mean, it's not a *particularly* sacred ritual,' Anika said, though caut-iously. 'We've all been guilty of occasionally drinking it without first…'

She trailed off, because Penelope had drawn herself up. '*I* most certainly have never done such a blighted thing,' she said, with sweet emphasis, glancing about her faction, mostly the Taurasi of her own gen-eration, but with a hearty sprinkling of young Taurasi as well, and receiving nods of sanctimonious agreement.

Anika came fairly close to scoffing in disbelief, if Mateo was any judge of it. 'Well. We will modify the recipe so it doesn't taste of…blight. Expect a visit to the pottery workshop late this afternoon, Penelope.' She raised her voice to address the full gathering. 'We must all work together to make this trade deal happen, Kindred.'

'Indeed,' Penelope said, in the supportive voice that made Anika wince even before she went on, 'After all, we lost so much wealth our first weeks here, didn't we, dear?'

'Just…everybody be nice to Jonas Nebrija,' Anika said with a sigh.

The day was busy; it was market day, when a small group of Taurasi headed down the hill with long lists in their heads, the food and spices they couldn't grow themselves and the materials they needed for the workshops and Timon's renovations. Once they returned, everything had to be distributed or stored; the workshops and Timon's little band would set to work revitalised, and the cooks would set to baking fish, which they always had fresh on market day.

It was also the day the Taurasi lit the fires under the big copper vats in the shed behind the bathhouse and boiled hot water as if they were truly subjecting themselves to the rigmarole of laundry. It both hid their use of magic to complete the heavy chore, and let them help out their Imperial neighbours, who would bring their soiled linens to wash and drape over the copious lavender bushes behind the shed, without overt curiosity as to where the Taurasi linens might be drying.

Mateo was currying the donkey in the paddock at the far end of Ravenser Odd when Jonas finally arrived late that afternoon. The little ass had taken the Taurasi down to the marketplace and back up again laden, and she always deserved extra fussing over afterwards.

They hadn't had beasts of burden on Ysthera; magic pulled the carts and did the heavy lifting. That would be just a bit blatant in Anceral, given the prohibition the empire laid on Ystherans. Mateo had thus discovered how pleasant it was to care for a large, calm animal, how grounding it could feel.

He laid his forehead against the donkey's long face, feeling the hair prickling his skin, breathing the animal scent. She ignored him.

In the other field, the chickens were pecking busily about the fenced-off vegetable beds by the well. Chickens were soothing too, but they'd had those on the island. Their milk cows, kept for cheesemaking, idly licked the blossoms of the single apple tree in the back field. Cows were idiots, and not soothing at all, though it was probably more heresy for a Taurasi to wish for goats. Mateo delegated the milking without mercy. He hoped Jonas had no bright ideas for Ystheran cheese; he didn't want more cows.

'Heilsa, Mattias, good afternoon,' the man himself said from behind him, and he started, making the donkey flick her ears.

Darius had escorted the Imperial in. He nodded now to Mateo, and backed off a scant five paces to assume his usual attentive pose, keeping a narrow gaze on Jonas.

Jonas turned from watching him to address Mateo. 'Bodyguard or boy friend?'

'That is Anika's uncle,' Mateo said, appalled. 'Which is to say, practically *my* uncle.'

'Bodyguard, then?' He waved a hand to encompass the quiet street. 'Against what?'

'You,' Mateo said, 'obviously.'

Jonas snorted with amusement, and Mateo looked at the sky in frustrated self-reproach.

'I apologise,' he informed the scudding clouds before sending Darius a speaking look. Darius ignored him as studiously as the donkey did. Mateo put his hands on his hips. 'Darius, go ask Anika to start the spice tea ritual for Jonas.'

Darius, deprived of the opportunity to stand about looking menacing, stomped off on this errand. Mateo dipped his head to Jonas. 'There. Just me here now, and the other ass.'

The other man gave him a friendly grin, his only acknowledgement of the lame apology. 'What's her name?' he asked, scratching the donkey between the eyes.

She nuzzled at his hand, the traitor.

'She doesn't have one.' Jonas looked, so far as Mateo could tell, mildly aghast. 'I do apologise, truly. I am aware you are being very helpful to Taurasi.'

'Don't take that sentiment too far,' Jonas said. 'I'm here to help my mother's friend, really. And the trading consortium.'

'Oh, when it comes to the negotiations, Aniketa the Unconquerable will...' He dared try out a local phrase. '...nail your arse to the wall.'

Jonas voiced a small and satisfied noise that made Mateo twitch. He had the horrible sense he'd just used the Imperial slang incorrectly and given Jonas a very wrong impression about Anika. He opened his mouth to refute himself and was stymied by the sheer embarrassment of having to explain and the distinct possibility he was wrong on any number of points. Even he could tell that Anika liked Jonas.

'You with me, honey?' Jonas prompted, not quite as ignorant of Mateo's inner turmoil as he'd hoped. 'Pottery workshop? Before it, you know, closes.'

'Yes, all right, I apologised,' Mateo said crossly. He gave the donkey—name her? Like a pet?—a last pat and took a chuckling Jonas back down Ravenser Odd towards the pottery workshop.

'Your hip sore today?' Jonas asked him as they walked, which was irritating—Mateo had thought he was doing a decent job of hiding it. 'I think you wrenched it pretty badly on the roof yesterday.'

'It is not substantially worse than usual,' Mateo said, falling back on the traditionally honest but elliptical Ystheran communication style rather than the bluntness that Imperial forced on its speakers.

'You're telling me it hurts all the time,' Jonas cheerfully translated. 'I can help with that, you know. Despite your scepticism, I am actually a physician.' He patted his left forearm, where the laeknir snake hid under his sleeve.

'Anika helps me.'

'Anika's not giving you anything strong for the pain.'

Mateo shook his head. Anika *couldn't* give him anything strong for the pain; it'd sully the magic. On bad days, he'd take a small dose of whatever she saw fit to mix up for him straight after the morning ritual, but that was all.

Jonas didn't take the hint. 'Does she not know about poppy milk or—'

Mateo glared at him. 'There is nothing Aniketa does not know about herblore.'

Jonas held up his hands. 'Understood, Mateo, I did not intend to impugn your girl friend. I just wondered if she was fully aware of the breadth of the pharmacopoeia she can access now she's within the empire's bounds. She can do better than willow bark and holly leaves.'

'Assume she does,' Mateo said sternly. 'And she's not my girl friend. Well, she is. But not in the way you seemed determined to presume.'

The other man, smiling, made a tip of fingers to forehead that Mateo, after a moment, recognised as some sort of salute. He huffed and led the way into the workshop, back stiff. He could feel Jonas's amusement radiating off him as he followed.

He'd been a bit too flummoxed to remember to warn Jonas or even steel himself before Penelope spotted him and dropped to her knees with a fluidity that belied her years. Mateo was more than half her age, and could only wish for her ease of movement.

'Your Soul is here, dears,' she informed the other Taurasi expectantly in Ystheran. Mateo supposed he could only be grateful she'd refrained from using the overdramatic archaic title.

Her assistants and apprentices hovered in dismayed stasis, caught between Penelope's velvet-clad and yet iron hand on the reins of tradition, and Mateo's well-known dislike of the old-fashioned status displays. They had to live with him, and work for her; they were in a bind.

'Just do it, then,' Mateo snapped at them.

They dropped to their knees in painful-sounding clacking unison, dipped their foreheads low, got back up again and returned to their tasks. Penelope and Mateo both sighed heavily, the one because the brief genuflection had not been nearly ritualistic enough, the other because it had happened at all.

'That's a thing,' Jonas said. 'Did you just order them all to get on their knees? Because that's, ah…'

'No! Well. Yes, if you want to be literal about it.'

'Imperials usually do,' Jonas said. He strolled forwards, holding his hand out to Penelope, who looked down her nose at it and bowed instead. 'Good evening, madam.'

Penelope, as former Heart, was one of the few Taurasi who did not go down to the city yet still had a decent grasp of Imperial, as much as she disdained it and anything to do with the empire that had tried to take her homeland twice in her lifetime.

'We do not respond to that title, dear,' she informed Jonas, her accent thick. 'You may address me as Penelope. Kith Penelope, should you wish to be exceptionally polite.'

'Hmm, and do I wish to be exceptionally polite, do you think?' Jonas asked with what Mateo was coming to realise must be a near-unshake-able equanimity.

Penelope stared at him, quite arrested in her passive-aggressive ploy. Eventually, she said, 'It might be wise.'

Jonas smiled the sort of smile that men like him rolled out for grand-mothers and great-aunts. 'Kith Penelope, would you do me the honour of showing me around your workshop?'

Mateo wasn't sure whether to be impressed or annoyed that this blatant bit of flattery worked. He didn't have to do anything further to finagle Penelope's cooperation, and merely trailed uselessly along behind the pair as Penelope showed off the wares and Jonas took notes on a thin codex-style tablet.

But when he paused by the pottery wheels and asked, 'How fast do you think you can increase production to meet increased demand?', her demeanour cooled noticeably.

'We are an artisan workshop, dear,' she told him, 'not some sort of Imperial factory.'

'Understood,' Jonas said mildly. 'It's just, the pottery is going to be one of the most popular products. It's beautiful, you see.'

'Yes, I'm aware.' Penelope looked about the ceramics she designed and personally oversaw the creation thereof. 'However, some of us care more for preserving our artistry than base commerce.'

'And some of us have to feed the artists, Penelope,' Mateo said, on Anika's behalf.

She made a harrumphing noise which was not too far off the sound Mateo had made outside in response to Jonas's teasing salute.

One of the younger workers, mostly tasked with preparing clay, and therefore subject to frequent lectures on its inferiority, spoke up.

'Penelope, there's space at the other end of the workshops. We could add a few more wheels, maybe.'

This, unfortunately, piqued Jonas's interest, and so Mateo took him through the rabbit warren that was the communal artisan workspace.

Before the Taurasi had bought the street, there had been, between the little wooden bakehouse and the street's decaying bathhouse, a long row of derelict shopfronts and tiny workshops that once made things like shoes, floral bouquets, elixirs, and the like.

When it came to renovating Ravenser Odd, the Taurasi priorities had been first to restore and expand the bakehouse into the much larger tea-house—not because they had expected it to be such a solid source of income but because a teahouse was a more circumspect place for the whole community to gather for the ritual than a dedicated space that Imperials could only interpret as a temple to a secret god—and then building a new stone bakehouse and kilns next to the old bathhouse and the small laundry shed with its huge copper vats. All those structures needed ready sources of heat or hot water or both, and so were logically grouped together.

Then it had been renovating the bathhouse and the living quarters, the Taurasi-owned insula and Madam Kerling's lodging house. Even subtly resorting to magic, the small renovation team on its string-thin budget was still finishing up the last touches across all these projects.

Therefore, aside from some structural reinforcement, the only improvements to the workshops had been to knock holes in the common walls, either for easier access between premises, or for better natural light.

It was a cold, dusty, rundown, jumbled space, and Mateo was frowning as he ushered Jonas through. He should have anticipated Jonas would want to see it, and it was not a good advertisement for Taurasi's capacity for fulfilling its side of the potential trade deal.

Near Danae's small workstation for processing wax into candles and herbal balm bases for Anika, currently vacant, Helena was bent over one of her angled tables, completing close work on an intricate bracelet, her helpers beside her, the glow and hum of magic apparent.

Ystheran jewellery was unsurpassed in all the known world, for it was the only jewellery in which skill was entwined with magic to craft literally inhuman works of art.

Mateo cleared his throat. 'That's our jeweller,' he said, loud, 'and over there are the looms.'

The weavers, set up in a series of half-walled bays, were using magic too, infusing into their handlooms and the cloth itself.

All the magic cut off abruptly, and the Taurasi artisans straightened from their work and tried very hard not to look guilty.

'Are you going to tell them to get on their knees?' Jonas whispered.

'I am not inclined to do that, no,' Mateo said.

'But I love it,' Jonas said. 'So stern. Go on, please?'

'Stop making fun of our customs. Blighted bloody Imperials.'

He was irritable enough to not even bother to switch to Ystheran for that last peeved mutter, but Jonas only laughed. 'Just teasing you, Mateo.'

He gave the Taurasi a friendly wave as he followed Mateo through a knocked-out wall to the far end of the workshop premises.

Here, Mateo paused to offer a meek 'Sorry,' as he remembered yet again that Jonas was not only the facilitator of a lucrative trade deal that his Kindred desperately needed, but also that, as *Steadfast* crew, they quite literally owed him their lives.

'What are you sorry for, honey?' Jonas said, glancing at him in what seemed genuine confusion.

'Being me, I suppose,' Mateo said.

He got a smile and a shrug. 'A bit of vinegar makes the meal.'

Mateo blinked at him in incomprehension until Jonas started having to fight another smile. 'You are *strange*,' he said at last.

Instead of perfectly justifiably quibbling over which of the two of them was stranger, Jonas unleashed one of his ridiculously loud roars of laughter. One of Helena's helpers peeked through the doorway in alarm, before ducking out of sight before Mateo could scowl and shoo her away.

Wiping at his eyes, the Imperial subsided. 'Oh, honey, you're—'

'Hilarious, I know.'

'I've always been a bit of an odd fish,' Jonas said. 'My mother was always telling me I was too— Hah. You won't believe me.'

'What?'

'Too gentle for a life at sea.' He paused, studying Mateo's face. 'There, I knew you wouldn't believe me.' He was still smiling, but there was the slightest of edges to it. 'Meanwhile, my father tells me I'm too formid-able-looking to be an entirely easy prospect for our patients.'

This struck Mateo as both a fair assessment, and yet also as unfair as Jonas must feel it to be. 'I'm sorry.'

'No business of mine what people think of me, honey,' Jonas said with another of his casual shrugs. 'That's on them.'

It felt pointed, but then Mateo had not exactly been trying to hide what he thought of Jonas's incursion onto his street. The man's equanimity about it was purely down to not at all caring, it seemed, and that was actually quite a sensible place to sit.

Mateo offered a small and wisely silent bow and turned away to wave a hand around the dim, empty space before them, once a small warehouse bookending the run of premises. 'We haven't needed this space yet.'

Once more, Jonas showed more grace than Mateo might have been capable of, genially taking the change of subject. 'You are going to need this space, very soon. You're going to have to upgrade this whole…' He looked about, and back the way they had come, where dust was floating in the beams of slanting light piercing through the broken shutters. 'Shall we call it your artisan precinct? That has a nice ring to it.'

'It does,' Mateo said, highly relieved to find something to be agreeable about. And then ruined it by saying, 'We don't have money, though. For upgrades. We've used up the last of our reserves just getting this far.'

They could, he thought sourly, perhaps finally sell off the last sets of the ceremonial robes and jewelled status markers.

'I'll talk to Anika about loans,' Jonas said, unperturbed.

Rather than go back past the illicitly magic-wielding artisans and Penelope, Mateo unlatched the door of the warehouse to take Jonas along the street. The peeling, cracking door had swollen from the incessant light rain and mist in the years since the warehouse had last been used, and he had to shove at it to get it to move half an inch. Jonas came close and helped, his body warm and solid beside Mateo as he gave the obstinate door a thump with shoulder and hip. The door wedged open in a shower of grit and cobwebs that Jonas shielded them both from with one arm. He flashed his smile to acknowledge their minor shared victory.

Jonas had nice eyes, actually, a pale hazel uncommon in the region, set off by dark, thick lashes.

'You're tall for an Ystheran, aren't you?' he said cheerfully, head indeed tilted upwards so he could meet Mateo's eyes in return.

'Maybe you're just short for an Imperial,' Mateo said, crossing his arms.

Jonas tossed another grin over his shoulder as he stepped onto the street. 'Everyone's short for an Imperial, except the heartland Imperials, right?'

Down the gentle slope of Ravenser Odd, the Anceran clientele was emptying out of the teahouse, light chatter rising on the cooling air. Anika stood on the porch, exchanging last pleasantries with her departing customers, many of them carrying packages and full baskets. The merchant consortium had had its idea proved in principle: Ystheran artisanal products were walking off the honeycomb shelves lining the back wall.

She saw Mateo and Jonas, and waved. 'Come down for the spice tea now,' Mateo said.

An older Anceran woman, one of their regular patrons, grasped Anika's hands in hers, earnestly saying, 'It's so good to have the Come-By-Chance open again. Please allow me to express our dismay, our distress, when we heard the fate of your beloved Sunlit Isle.'

Mateo pulled a face. He imagined a great many Imperials actually thought the Ystherans had received their rightful comeuppance for practising what the empire called sorcery, and experienced not a whit of distress on behalf of the doomed inhabitants when the island had cracked and sunk.

'To think, no one knew the mountain was actually a volcano,' she went on.

'Indeed,' Anika said. 'Five hundred years and we never suspected such.'

The woman took out a wrapped item from the basket slung over her arm. She bowed, an almost-endearing attempt at Ystheran courtesy, and even proffered the gift by laying it ritualistically on both flat palms as per Ystheran tradition.

'A small token to convey our condolences.'

'Thank you, Freydis,' Anika murmured, serenely accepting the gift and returning the bow.

Freydis took her final leave with a last few coos of sympathy and Mateo ushered Jonas forwards. The teahouse was now empty of Imperials, with a few younger Taurasi sweeping and washing up; two worked together to close up the big front shutters as the meagre warmth of the day began to leach away into evening. All these tasks were normally helped along with magic, but they'd been warned about Jonas and were working the mundane way.

Anika paused at Mateo's table to investigate the gift with him. It was a finely crafted rosewood box with brass fastenings; upon opening the box, they discovered a set of the Ystheran tile-matching game, Lithos. They'd introduced their Imperial clientele to Lithos to help fill the time the spice tea ritual took, and it had proven almost as popular as the tea.

Ystherans made the tiles from grey pebbles, smoothing and shaping them using magic. The patterns, inlaid with nacre and lapis lazuli, were abstractions—gentle hints of ears and horns, feathers and scales, fronds and leaves, spirals and curves—of the whole klados, including the five lost Kindreds, as well as the flora and fauna of the Sunlit Isle.

This set, however, was crafted from walrus ivory from the heartland, and the symbols inscribed in silver and gold on the surfaces had been transformed from the organic Ystheran style to an angular echo of Vaer runic writing. Both Mateo and Anika stared, taken aback.

'I can't tell if this is quite thoughtful, or in extremely poor taste,' Anika said eventually, in Ystheran.

'Both?' Mateo hazarded, watching Jonas for any reaction that showed he'd understood.

It was a blighted travesty, to his mind, and he knew Timon would agree, but he didn't want to say that in front of someone he truly did think must have some grasp of their language.

Anika smiled and raised her hand towards the kitchen, where one of her helpers was hovering with a tray. Jonas received his pot of spice tea, but Anika set out ginger tea, sweetened with honey, for Mateo.

'We're trying this for your hip,' she told him.

She turned to Jonas, and began to rattle off the spices, some powdered, some steeped whole, and their tasting notes. They were quickly engrossed in not just the flavours, but the pharmaceutics of it, the herbalist and the physician bonding over their mutual interest.

Mateo sipped his tea, clicking the creamy ivory tiles of the Imperial Lithos set through the fingers of his other hand. They were, he had to admit, lovely to touch, the smoothness of the polished ivory contrasting with the slight irregularity of the etchings.

He began an idle game, drawing tiles at random to make a pleasing design. No Taurasi would play a real game with him, in case they accidentally vanquished their Soul. Not even the Coterie, who had to deliberately suppress the general cultural awe in which Souls were held to serve their specific Soul, could bring themselves to play him properly. It didn't matter; the solitaire game was meditative, and he let himself relax, focus becoming hazy.

The ginger tea, spicy under the honey, suited his tastes. Its clear amber glow was very much the same as the clear amber glow of his magic.

He was then reluctantly amused to note that both ginger honey tea and Ystheran magic were the same colour as Jonas's eyes.

Anika had whisked off to the kitchen to fetch something pertinent to the botanical conversation. Jonas leaned across the table. 'Tell me what I did to win that smile from you, honey, and I promise I'll do it again.'

'Just existed, really,' Mateo said absently. Jonas raised his brows and Mateo's attention snapped from admiring the lambent shade of gold. 'I just meant you have pretty eyes. Well, that's not any better.'

He set his cup down and began to hastily tidy the tiles away, avoiding the gaze of the other man.

But Jonas merely laughed. 'You have rather lovely eyes yourself, Mateo.'

Anika returned, carrying a few jars of ground spices, just in time to overhear. 'Teo, is he flirting with you?' she asked in both Ystheran and tones of unalloyed delight.

'No!' Mateo said. 'I mean… No. No. He's just friendly. And shush, Anika, he understands Ystheran, I swear he does.' When Anika shook her head with a fond smile, he said, 'Why does no one ever listen to me?'

'Because, my sweet, you are a catastrophiser.'

'That's because I had a catastrophe happen to me!'

'We all had a catastrophe happen to us,' Anika said, 'but you were a first-rate worrier even before then, you know you were.'

Mateo could not deny this. Anika kissed the top of his head affectionately before setting the jars in front of Jonas, unsealing them in a puff of warm spicy fragrance.

As she and Jonas sank back into their conversation, Mateo sighed, just a little. It was plain to him that Jonas could not have been flirting with him, because he was far more interested in Anika.

Which was fine. Just…fine.

CHAPTER 7

JONAS BEGAN TO VISIT RAVENSER ODD regularly, though never at regular intervals. He'd appear in the midmorning, well after the ritual was complete, or late afternoon, while the teahouse customers were safely ensconced, to see how the renovation of the workshops—the artisan precinct—was coming along, or pass judgement on less sacred versions of the spice tea recipe, or collect samples of the pottery, weavings and jewellery likely to have the widest appeal.

He remained friendly, curious and cheerful, projecting a phenomenal amount of goodwill in the face of Taurasi attitudes ranging from cautious to suspicious to outright hostile. Eventually, most of the street decided that even if Imperials in general could not be trusted, this Imperial in particular was acceptable.

It helped, to an excessive degree, that he'd been crew on *Steadfast*. Ystherans were already inclined to trust traders of the bootlegger bent, running the blockade to keep the Sunlit Isle on the trading routes. Those seafarers with their bright striped sails were a nation unto themselves, barely Imperial at all except for their homeports. But that Jonas had been one of the crew under Captain Velasco that day… Any simmering opposition to his presence on the street melted away once that was widely known, and Anika made sure it *was* widely known.

Even Timon pronounced him likeable, eventually, after he and Jonas returned dusty from the workshops one afternoon. Timon had taken Jonas's desire to cast his eye over the renovations doubtfully but with relatively good grace, given he and his team now had three solid years of experience in tackling such projects and all Jonas had were a few old trading contacts from a past life. However, the Imperial, with his passing knowledge of how freightage worked, had given some advice, just in time, about the arrangement of the doors for ease of lading onto carts, and thus won Timon over.

'Do you think he'll get suspicious about how fast the renovations are coming along?' he'd asked Mateo while Jonas was off rinsing his hands, grimy from fossicking about the workshops.

'I don't think he's the suspicious type,' Mateo said. 'Curious, yes. Suspicious, no.'

The ever-helpful Jonas also let Anika know that the consortium would be prepared to make loans towards expanding Taurasi capacity for artisanal production, but also warned her that it would be detrimental for the contract negotiations. She drew the funds against the mortgages on the insula and teahouse and workshops instead.

'Is that risky?' Mateo asked.

'Everything's risky, my sweet,' she'd said.

'You're reassuring today, Ana.'

Change continued apace. The Taurasi narrowly voted in favour of sending their children to the local Imperial schoolroom, Anika casting the deciding vote, which she had greatly hoped to not have to do. After a rousing argument between Nikiti and the Heart and Soul, in which Anika could not bring herself to exert her full authority against the child she had harmed so badly, the Taurasi's precious neophyte had been allowed to go along with the other children, their cohort from whom they should not be isolated.

Anika was likely feeling her risks quite heavily right now.

Mulling over that, and myriad other worries, because that was how his mind worked and it would not shut up about it, Mateo went along Ravenser Odd one cool afternoon, rugged up in his quilted jacket. He dodged around a few puddles, left by a morning squall, common in spring.

The older children had started school shortly after the vote, Taurasi adults taking turns to escort them to and fro from their mornings at the local temple. It meant the nascent ritual with Nikiti took place in the afternoons now, in the privacy of Helena's apartment since the stairs to the roof had become problematic. Mateo's time with the children had become even more important, in respect of keeping them properly Ystheran.

Mateo had just finished with that—the children had been full of excited chatter about the new games they were playing and the marks they were learning to read and make in wax, and had used their daily portion of magic to draw those esoteric runic symbols in the air, but at least they still listened to him with rapt attention and had not yet come home talking of other gods and demanding other rituals—and had come down to pat the donkey.

Perdita? he mused as he rubbed her nose. *Claudine? Fionna?*

In the field next to him, Lucius, who had switched from trying to grow a moustache to having a patchy try at stubble, was on herding duties for the toddlers, full of phrenic energy after the session with the Soul.

Mateo had been feeding Lucius extra magic since that morning. He chose a Taurasi or two every day to practice their control of the flow, and wrangling the toddlers was definitely a worthy application. It also gave Mateo the chance to assess kith for those empty Coterie slots. It wouldn't be Lucius; he was definitely meant for Niki's cohort.

The young ones had been feeding the chickens, but the grain bucket was already discarded. Lucius was using the flowing magic to both corral and entertain the little monsters by juggling glowing amber balls and rolling them around the field. The cows watched with the dully placid curiosity typical of their kind. The little ones were enthralled, chasing and jumping, squealing with delight.

Mateo took the opportunity to count them. There was the same number as usual.

Then Lucius snapped off the magic and put his hands behind his back, blushing horribly. His charges, deprived of their entertainment, started wailing. Mateo assumed one of Madam Kerling's lodgers was home early and heading for the bakehouse to collect bread or a bowl of the ever-simmering bean and vegetable soup-cum-stew that the Taurasi kept replenished and warm over the same low coals that baked the bread.

When he turned, however, he saw that Jonas was striding along Ravenser Odd, escorted as ever by a glowering Darius. He'd gradually been discarding the blatant trappings of the sea trader—the jet earrings, the calf-length breeches, the heavy weatherproof cloak, the plaited wristbands—and today was in a simple linen shirt, dyed palest blue, and long trousers, warm enough for a local in the spring daytime. He'd kept his knife and necklace.

'What's your deal, friend?' Jonas asked Darius as he waved to Mateo. As usual, he made the question as congenial as could be. 'Surely you know by now I'm not here to do harm? Afternoon, Mateo. Hale and hearty?'

'Maybe he's just wondering why you're here yet again,' Mateo snapped in the teeth of this polite greeting, flustered by the close call, not the first one they'd had with their ubiquitous Imperial visitor. Jonas raised his eyebrows, smiling, and Mateo winced. 'Sorry. But didn't you say you're working with your father now? How do you have time for this?'

Holy Remnants, Imperial was a blunt language.

'You're right, I should've taken on more of his clients by now,' Jonas said. 'He's given me leeway to do my civic duty.'

Ancerans had a whole raft of familial, religious and civic responsibilities; it was one of the points of commonality with Ystherans. 'Does brokering a minor trade deal count as civic duty?'

'I'm acting for the good of my city, so, yes. What's with these kids?' He leaned over the fence, eyeing off the collection of tearful tots. 'My little chicklings, heilsa. Am I so frightening? Your Uncle Darius thinks I am.'

Darius scowled dreadfully at this, which merely made Jonas's smile widen. He was probably thinking about little elves again.

Mateo decided to pre-empt bloodshed. 'Darius, help Lucius take the children inside.'

Darius transferred his glare to Mateo but joined Lucius in corralling the children through the little gate out of the field. He marched off after them like a menacing mother duck following its ducklings.

'You've got a healthy number of youngsters there,' Jonas said, watching them go with something very close to affection.

'Yes. Well,' Mateo said. 'Turns out there's a predictable reaction to coming terrifyingly close to a horrible death, and a predictable result nine months later.'

Especially when both magic and herbs were temporarily unavailable; it was the same reason Timon and Andrea, and other Taurasi, wore their scars. The *Steadfast* crew—Jonas, perhaps—had been able to set fractures and tend open wounds, but they couldn't work the miracle of Anika's magic healing.

He forcibly returned himself to the conversation. 'Hence, a truly trying number of toddlers.'

Jonas gave an agreeable nod. 'Personal experience?' Mateo stared at him, head on one side. 'Is one of the little ones yours, Mateo?'

'Ah, no. No. I am untouchable.' It was Jonas's turn to look blank. Mateo reluctantly elaborated. 'I am considered untouchable by my people. I hold myself apart.'

'Oh, the priest thing,' Jonas said. 'You're *for* the community, so you can't be *of* the community.'

This was a good enough summary for an Imperial, so Mateo shrugged a vague agreement. He realised he was being self-absorbed. Jonas was proving adept at asking questions in a gently curious way, and somehow Mateo had yet to learn a thing about him except he'd been a trader and was now a physician.

But he was only just opening his mouth to ask after Jonas's potential children and person to make or raise them with when Jonas said, 'So you've never…'

Mateo's eyes widened at the rather graphic gesture with which Jonas finished his sentence. He was appalled to have been asked; a cultural bias towards answering questions honestly and therefore being circumspect about asking questions in the first place had crashed headfirst into the Imperial tendency towards bluntness in all things.

'I am untouchable to Taurasi,' he said stiffly. 'Not other Ystherans.'

He should have anticipated the next question, he supposed. 'And foreigners? Or do your people—'

'You people.'

'Stop that—*your* people not allow you to be sullied by the touch of'—his tone became teasing—'filthy foreign dogs?'

'We're the foreign dogs,' Mateo said automatically, before giving it some genuine thought. 'I…' He looked down the street at the teahouse. 'I think they'd cope. As long as it wasn't an actual Imperial marine.'

It'd be hypocritical if they complained, really, even if he did have special status among them. The Taurasi were a small population; not all their toddlers had two Ystheran parents, and that would only become more common.

He played with the gate latch, flipping it back and forth. 'The question has not arisen.'

'What, never?' When Mateo glanced around, surprised, Jonas smiled at him. 'Three years in the bosom of the empire, Mateo—'

'*Bosom?*'

'—you've never once considered a local dalliance? Three years is a long time to be celibate.'

It had been…a good deal longer than three years, actually.

'I don't know that I'm all that interested.' To Jonas's polite look, he felt obliged to add, 'My last…affair…did not go so well. He wanted to treat me like a woman.'

Jonas cocked his head. 'I don't see Ystherans treating each other too differently,' he commented. 'Not compared to some territories within the empire, anyway. Is it different when you're courting?'

'We don't have courtships—'

'Oh my gods, are you *kidding* me?' Jonas crowed in delight. 'You have rituals for *everything else*, you have one for drinking *tea*, and not for weddings?'

'*Yes*, for weddings,' Mateo said crossly. 'But we don't have courtships, our elders arrange alliances with an eye to the bloodlines. They're the equivalent of your marriages, except they end after a pre-agreed time.'

'Right, no courtships,' Jonas said. 'But you didn't call it an alliance, you said affair. So you do have more casual arrangements?'

'We do. Though this man was meant to be an alliance,' Mateo said. 'It…didn't work out.'

'Because he treated you poorly.'

'No, not poorly as such, just…like a woman.' Mateo sighed. There were a dozen euphemistic ways he could say it, if he had to say it at all, but an Imperial was going to have to be beaten over the head with it. 'He always wanted to *take* me like a woman.' He saw the understanding dawn. 'And I'm not a woman, and it turns out I don't especially enjoy being had like a woman, *as pleasant as other people find it*, but he was how I discovered that.'

'He sounds like a dick,' Jonas said in his usual cheerful way, with a decided gleaming undercurrent in his voice.

'It wasn't so bad, mostly. I mean…it was tolerable.' When Jonas made a noise, he corrected, 'Fine. It was fine. Absolutely, um…fine.'

And it had been. Elias had never hurt him, or forced him. It had been consensual, just…not all that satisfying. And there'd been an incident on Elias's birthday that still made Mateo wince whenever he remembered it, embarrassing enough that he deeply regretted blurting it out to Anika back then, in the teeth of the strong taboo surrounding openly discussing sex.

When Gallasi had publicly and without explanation ended the agreement to alliance shortly afterwards, he'd been hurt and humiliated—and very quietly relieved. He'd even murmured a thanks to the Shattered One, and Ystherans did not typically disturb Her sleep with prayer.

'Adequate?' Jonas asked.

'Decent enough.'

'You know how to devastate a man, don't you? Tolerable? Fine? Decent enough? Stab him right in the heart, why don't you? Though this particular man sounds like he deserves the lowest rating on'—Jonas waved his hand up and down—'your idiosyncratic scale.'

'We were both quite young,' Mateo said, wondering how he'd managed to get into this conversation and how to end it. Bluntly, he supposed. 'Look, Ystherans don't talk about sex like this. *Ever.*'

'And that's exactly why you end up having shitty sex, honey,' Jonas said with a grin. 'Could I just point out—'

'This is going to be awful, isn't it?'

'—that it would've cost him nothing to let you get on top and fuck him if that was the shape of your desire, and before you make the riposte you seem to believe is obvious, when you go at it enthusiastically enough, the configuration of the cock or cocks involved doesn't come into it at all.'

Mateo put his hands over his ears. 'Holy Remnants, please stop. *We don't talk about this.*' Jonas chuckled to himself until Mateo lowered his hands and blurted, 'How did you know I wanted to be the one doing the…'

'The fucking?' Jonas said helpfully. 'Say it, go on. Go on, let me hear it.'

'…the fucking?' Mateo managed, though only in a strangled whisper.

Jonas let out one of his loud cracks of laughter. 'So easy to corrupt!'

Mateo must have made an *extremely* indignant face at that, because the impossible man practically cackled. He poked Mateo, gently, without a trace of malice. 'Because, my friend, you're stern and controlling, and that often goes hand-in-hand with wanting to be charge in bed, that's how.'

Mateo stared at him for so long that Jonas evidently felt obliged to give him another nudge. 'You with me there, Mateo?'

He shook himself. 'I'm not… I'm mostly just anxious, and grouchy about it.'

Jonas shrugged like it made no difference. 'I'm not actually here to discuss recreational sex—'

'Neither am I!'

'—I wanted to show you this.' From a pocket, Jonas took an intricate length of silver set with red stones. 'Came across this ruby bracelet for sale in the central market. Ystheran, or no?'

The chickens had gone to roost; Mateo closed the hatch on the henhouse before taking the bracelet from Jonas. Absently, he walked off, holding it up to the waning light.

'It's not Taurasi, but there are other Ystherans in the city, they might have sold one of their heirlooms.'

'Mateo? Should I follow, or…'

Mateo belatedly explained, 'I'm showing it to Helena, our jeweller. Yes, follow.'

He led the way to the artisan precinct, blushing because Jonas had started sniggering the moment Mateo had directed him—in a stern and controlling way, apparently—to follow. He trotted along beside Mateo with a great show of meek obedience.

Helena was still at her workstation in the artisan precinct. She gave a startled bob when Mateo interrupted her, an aborted genuflection, before saying in Ystheran, 'Why are you looking so disconcerted, Mattias, is he bothering you? Should I call Darius?'

'No,' Mateo said, in Imperial for courtesy's sake. 'Look at this. Genuine? Oh, stop it!' That last was directed at Jonas, who had buried his face in his hands to smother his smile. 'I am *not* stern and controlling.'

'You sure aren't, honey,' Jonas said generously.

Helena, frowning between them, took the bracelet. She only needed a single glance. 'Not genuine. You can see tool marks. It's a copy of an old Caprinasi style—a good one, actually.'

Jonas, holding a polite expression of mild interest, said, 'Oh, yes, that's right. Ystheran jewellery is famous for showing no sign of earthly make. Can I see how you manage it?'

Mateo and Helena exchanged a look. They managed it, of course, with magic; Ystheran jewellery showed no sign of earthly make because Ystheran artisans barely touched the pieces with their delicate tools, and magically smoothed out any marks they did happen to leave. Their compatriots without magic in the city did not even try to replicate true Ystheran jewellery, turning their talents to other, less delicate, metal-work.

The nice thing about having a reputation for being obstreperous was that Mateo could be just as obstreperous as he liked.

'No,' he said, and took Jonas's elbow and marched him out of the workshop with a brisk nod of thanks to Helena.

'Proprietary information, is it?' Jonas said, laughing. 'All right, I'm not insisting, you can let me go.'

His left sleeve had ridden up, and Mateo again glimpsed that physician's snake tattoo, just the tail entwined around the man's strong wrist before the rest of it disappeared up his arm. He stopped, arrested.

Ystherans did not mark their bodies in any way, natural scars excepted; even their earrings, such important status markers back on Ysthera, were clipped on, on the lobe or, profusely, over the shell of the auricle. They found the ink Imperial sailors sported to be both strange and fascinating, like writing—or perhaps, like the Imperials found the idea of Ystheran magic.

'We'll have to clamp down on faux products or they'll flood the market—I suggest you develop a hallmark, do you know what that is? Ah, are you with me there? Oh, the tattoo.' Jonas pulled back his sleeve in an instant. 'Have a proper look, then.'

The snake twined realistically up his arm, curving strokes of ink evoking the muscular strength of the coils, an intricate pattern of light and dark diamonds representing scales. It ended at his elbow with a flicker of tongue. It was sleekly attractive and oddly compelling; Mateo had to link his hands together so he wouldn't trace a finger along that well-formed arm and touch the tender skin in the crook of the elbow where the tongue flicked…where a tongue could flick.

Jonas seemed, for once, insensible to Mateo's struggle. 'It's taboo for Ystherans, is that right? Do you find it repulsive?'

Was that what the man was reading in Mateo's expression? He shook his head, and did touch then, very lightly, the last twitch of tail on Jonas's wrist, to prove he didn't find anything about Jonas anything close to repulsive.

'It means chaos, in Imperial mythology?'

'Both protection and destruction,' Jonas said, obligingly rotating his wrist under Mateo's fingertips. 'I, however, am of trader heritage, and the snake reflects our philosophy. Shedding useless regrets and other relics of the past, being wise and measured in all things in the present, anticipating but not fearing the future. That's my mother's side. On my father's side, it's a straight-up call on the Anceran goddess of healing, called Eirina under the empire but once known locally as Angitia, snake-witch.'

Since Mateo's touching was rapidly edging into the realm of caressing, he pulled his hand back. Jonas gave him a bright smile, edging towards wicked. 'I've got *Steadfast*'s wayfinder sigil inked on my pectoral, want to see that?'

He slapped his left breast with the corresponding hand and was already lifting his shirt with the other, exposing a thick stomach, a trail of hair between navel and waistband, a slight paunch padding the heavy muscles of a man who had not been a stranger to physical labour.

'No!' Mateo said, demonstratively covering his eyes to hide the sudden strange liquid flip low in his own stomach at the unexpected sight of smooth brown skin, the unexpected impulse to run his palm over it without even the excuse of touching a tattoo.

Though, if he let Jonas take off his shirt, he'd have the excuse of the wayfinder sigil to touch his chest…

'Stop that!' he said, more to himself than Jonas, who was just being friendly and didn't deserve to be subjected to such blatant fetishism.

'I suppose you don't want to see what I've got tattooed on my arse, then?' Jonas said, grinning. 'Hint, ever seen the helm of awe?'

'Yes,' Mateo said, since the only thing more popular to inscribe on public walls in seaside Anceral than that quintessential protection sigil was penises. And then, in alarm, 'I meant I've seen it before, not that I want to see it on your, on your, on *you!*'

Jonas had ostentatiously set his hands to the ties of his trousers. Now, with another bark of laughter, he let his hands fall back to his sides. 'Just teasing you, honey.'

'I'm not very good at being teased,' Mateo mumbled, blushing again, because he should have realised that not even an Imperial, not even an extremely easy-going and apparently shameless one, would actually be so blunt and forthright as to drop their trousers in a public street. Not on a day that wasn't a festival day, anyway.

'You don't have to be,' Jonas said. 'I'll keep amusing myself, and you go ahead and ignore me.'

Mateo, shaking his head at himself, turned towards the teahouse. Darius, having obeyed Mateo in so far as escorting the children down to be fed, was standing cross-armed on the porch, watching Jonas with narrow eyes.

'But, really.' For a vertiginous moment Mateo wondered if the man was going to invite him to a private viewing of his arse. 'What is Uncle Darius's deal?'

Unable to tell if he was disappointed or relieved, Mateo said, 'He's the last surviving Taurasi guardian. The others were killed on the day of the exile. He's…'

'Lonely,' Jonas supplied when Mateo sought and failed to find words. He was suddenly, if not sombre, then solemn. 'Guilty. Seeking redemption for a perceived failure that wasn't even a failure and wasn't even his fault if it was, but try telling him that.'

'Yes,' Mateo said, deeply surprised. 'All of that.'

'I know what it is to owe the dead a duty,' Jonas said, 'and I know it can be hard to let those feelings go. Better for him if he can, though.' He touched his left forearm in another absent-minded call on the laeknir snake. 'Better for him to remember that his lost friends would be deeply grateful to know he survived.'

'As are we.' Mateo paused then, wondering if Darius understood that. 'He never talks?'

'We thought he was injured at first,' Mateo said, touching his hair where the telltale white tuft lay on Darius. 'But we suspect it's a vow of silence until he feels he's redeemed himself.'

'Right. Difficult task. Not to ask the obvious question—'

'Except you're about to.'

'—but why would Ystherans need armed guardians at all? You had magic, back on the island. Magic enough to hold back the might of the Vaer Empire.'

'Ystherans are pacifists,' Mateo said, using the word the empire used for a way of life that grew out of a sacred vow to a broken goddess. 'Well, Taurasi are. Oh. That means Ystherans are, now.'

It was strange, to know Taurasi was the last Kindred, and yet discover that fact over and over by tripping on a turn of phrase or running headfirst into an outdated adage. The other day, Helena had burnt herself on a bakehouse oven and exclaimed, 'Seven surviving Remnants!', and then had to hide her face until she could control her tears because there was only one surviving Remnant now.

He felt a touch on his shoulder. Jonas had put a hand there. 'You with me, Mateo?' he asked, his smile gentle, in stark contrast to the easy teasing of a moment before.

Mateo concentrated, grasping the thread of his thought with both hands. 'And pacifists sometimes need assistance maintaining their idealism. Hence armed guardians. They are permitted to fight, if doing so will bring fighting to an end. It had devolved into a ceremonial honour guard position.'

Again, he faltered, because the Taurasi guardians had more than done their duty during that frenetic plummet down the mountainside. Again, he felt Jonas's soothing touch, grounding him, pulling him away from the memory of Darius's altogether more forceful approach, kneeling atop him to keep him safe and sheltered while the shadow-dogs dived upon them, a painful pressure on his chest that had never since quite gone away.

Addled by a mere hand on his shoulder, he said, 'Would you like to stay to dinner, Jonas?'

Jonas brightened. 'Delighted.'

'It's just samosas—grilled octopus and chopped vegetables wrapped in thin pastry, quite spicy, you might not like them. You probably won't.'

'Sounds lovely. Sounds very much like the pasties you can buy fresh cooked from the cookshops. I'll take you to one sometime.'

'I can't leave the street,' Mateo said flatly, ruining the conviviality. 'Sorry. I mean, thank you, that would be lovely, but…'

Jonas, meanwhile, was looking most uncharacteristically grim. He took Mateo's arm and drew him under the portico of one of the old shop-fronts, away from the various Taurasi about their last chores. Mateo saw Darius stiffen and start towards them, and waved him back.

'Mattias, are you a prisoner?' Jonas demanded, leaning in close to his ear, his hand firm around his upper arm as if he planned to drag him to freedom right then. 'You can tell me the truth, is Darius a guard, not a guardian? I'll help you get out.'

'No! No, I mean, I *can* leave the street, I just…don't.'

Pricklingly aware of how close Jonas was standing, how intense his eyes suddenly were, Mateo directed his gaze upwards, at the amber radiance of the eternal light outside the teahouse. It was Mateo's own magic that made it glow, though Timon had installed a lamp-and-mirror arrangement for it, so that it was lit up even for those with no Ystheran blood.

This trick was to avoid the tiniest chance of an Imperial with distant Ystheran ancestry commenting on the eternal light, and their imperceptive friends responding, 'What beautiful golden light?' which would be an unutterably stupid way to get thrown out of the empire for breaking the prohibition against magic.

Jonas followed his gaze. 'The light?' he asked. 'Is this something to do with being the Taurasi priest?'

'The Soul,' Mateo said. 'If I die…'

'All right.' Jonas stepped back, tension gone as if it had never existed. 'People do go about their business on the city streets and manage to not die most days.'

'I'm the last Soul in all the world. They're protective.'

'Overprotective.'

'Entire way of life dependent on my continued existence,' Mateo countered. At least until Nikiti ascended to full command of the gift of the goddess.

Jonas raised his eyebrows, silently inviting him to elaborate, which was when Mateo realised how far the man's easy friendliness had walked him along the path to giving too much away. 'Oh, this is… No, not talking about it, Jonas.'

'And I thought we were friends, Mateo,' Jonas said, with, as usual, a cheerful grin and no offence whatsoever.

And that was a problem. That was dangerous. Somewhere in the last few weeks of his incessant visits, Jonas had indeed collected Mateo's friendship, though who could tell why the affable man wanted it.

'I don't know why you're so cagey,' Jonas added.

'Worship of foreign gods is prohibited,' Mateo said, feeling numb. He started to walk towards the teahouse, urgently wanting to hand Jonas over to Anika, who would not have let herself walk into this dangerous position.

'But not in private,' Jonas said. 'The empire knows very well how to hold a community together and keep them placid. Same as speaking your own language, forbidden in public, fine in private. And your people—'

'You people.'

'You *know* I said *your* people, are fine speaking Ystheran in front of me. So why so worried about even talking about your religion?'

Because it wasn't a religion in the way Imperials thought of religion. It was magic. Jonas could be as friendly as he liked, but Ystheran magic, even the small domesticated magic of the Taurasi, revolted and terrified the empire in equal measure.

Mateo found he did not want Jonas to be revolted and terrified by him. He also, equally, did not want Jonas running to the authorities and getting Taurasi exiled for a second time, if not worse.

'Sacred,' he said. 'Dinner?'

CHAPTER 8

ANIKA WAS INORDINATELY PLEASED BY JONAS staying for the evening meal. Mateo supposed this was what an Anceran courtship looked like, visiting frequently, bringing gifts—Jonas had brought her a packet containing a variety of leaves and roots from different herbs hard to find locally—and being generally pleasant company.

He was pleasant enough company, in fact, and familiar enough now, that the Taurasi were relaxed about hosting him during their Imperial-free evening, even if it meant they couldn't use their usual minor magic to prepare the meal, pack away the high tables their customers preferred, and set out the Ystheran tables and cushions.

Even Penelope took a moment to exchange a few polite words with him, saving her little dig solely for Anika. 'I suppose you know what you're doing, dear.'

Anika contained a sigh. Mateo bristled. 'I invited him, Penelope.'

'I know, dear.' She looked at Anika again. 'I really do hope you know what you're doing, Aniketa.'

Jonas joined the Coterie around their table in the back corner, perfectly comfortable on the cushions beside Mateo. Andrea delivered him a serve of wine. Imperials took their wine from communal dishes, but he knew enough of Ystheran customs to look suitably honoured at the presentation of a guest cup, marked by the Taurasi horns.

Mateo was interested to see if he'd still pour the traditional libation to the gods on their shiny wooden floor, but even there, Jonas adapted and merely tugged on the leather thong about his neck, pulling a medallion free from under his shirt so he could rub a few drops of wine over its bronze surface.

He tucked it away, murmuring a few words under his breath, and looked about. 'Why don't you sit at your table for dinner?' he asked Mateo forthrightly. 'I hope it's not because I'm here.'

Mateo followed his gaze towards the table by the little ceramic stove in the other corner. He knew he sounded vague as he said, 'No, I just don't.'

He had no explanation for the habit, except that he preferred cushions, just like his compatriots did, and his hip had used to only properly ache in the morning. Once it and the teahouse warmed up, he hadn't needed the sop of the bench, especially not when it left him sitting above everyone else in an uncomfortably symbolic way. He hadn't paid attention to how sore he was in the evenings now, too.

He realised he was absently playing with his Soul cup again. It wouldn't be quite so awful to knock it off the low table and onto cushions, compared to off the high table and onto the bare hardwood, but he still pushed it away to a safe distance. He peeked to see if his fidgeting had garnered Penelope's disapproving attention. It had. He folded his hands in his lap, a scolded child.

Jonas had observed the interplay, and was grinning. 'Is it really so bad if it breaks?'

The Coterie made pretend-shocked sounds. 'Anathema,' Anika said, smiling mockingly. 'Blight.'

'It's over a hundred years old,' Mateo said. A succession of previous Taurasi Souls had managed to not break this one, though one had chipped it and repaired it with gold. 'It's made from clay from the Sunlit Isle. We can't get clay as pure as that here.'

'Bet you could,' Jonas said, without turning a hair; he received slightly more genuine shocked noises. 'The Vaer Empire stretches thin across half a world, my overdramatic friends. There'll be clay of the purity you need somewhere, and a trade route to get it here.'

Mateo frowned. 'I'd rather not be the one to test that notion.'

'It's just a cup, though. A hundred years old, very pretty butterflies, last relic of a lost civilisation, sure. But just, after all that, a cup.' After a pause in which the Taurasi's silence made their argument for them, he said, 'Then why dare use it at all? Keep it safe on a shelf.'

'Just because it's fragile doesn't mean it shouldn't be allowed to fulfil its proper function before it breaks,' Anika said.

Mateo's hands clenched in his lap, matching the sudden clench in his gut. He didn't dare look up to meet anyone's gazes. Anika hadn't meant her comment, a teasing sally aimed at deflecting Jonas, to fall like crushing rock upon his shoulders, of course.

It wasn't something she'd ever say to him—*you are too weak to be our Soul and I fear you will break before Nikiti ascends*—but it was one of his most enduring what-ifs. On his darkest nights, it was something he thought all the Taurasi believed.

He felt Jonas shift his weight, arm brushing his. But whatever their visitor had been about to say was interrupted by the arrival of Niki and a few other children to the table.

'What's the name of your sword?' Niki asked Jonas.

'Heilsa to you, too, Nikiti,' he said indulgently.

'Heilsa! Does your sword have a name?'

'Are you asking,' Jonas said, highly amused, 'if I *named* my *sword*?'

'Don't Imperials name their swords?' Niki demanded.

They'd apparently been delegated to be the one asking the rude questions, because the other children were peering around them with big-eyed curiosity.

But while Anika tried to shoo them all off, Jonas merely chuckled and said, 'Blooddrinker? Ironbiter?'

The children gasped in delight.

Jonas called over to Darius. 'Uncle, I'm about to draw my blade, don't murder me.'

He slowly, keeping half his attention on the glaring guardian, drew out his short knife from its plain leather scabbard and showed it to the children, keeping it just above the surface of the table. 'This,' he said, 'is not a sword. It's an old type of knife called a seax, which has come down to me from my paternal grandfather, who came to Anceral from the west, from Chalcadea. Since you ask, let's name it Brightknot.'

'That's not very bloodthirsty.'

Jonas smiled. 'It's very useful for disembowelling a raider in close quarters.' He twisted his wrist indicatively. The children made appreciative noises.

'Oh, I think—' Anika started.

'Or slipping up behind someone and slitting their throats in a fog.'

'—you can run along now, children!' Anika finished, and then, when they'd raced away full of delighted whispers to receive a scolding from Helena, put her hands on her hips. 'Jonas!'

'Too gentle for a life at sea?' Mateo said.

'I used this thing for cutting rope and gutting fish,' Jonas said, chuckling. '*Steadfast* was too fast and our captain was too clever to get boarded by raiders.'

'Do you have children?' Andrea asked disapprovingly; Mateo was pleased to discover he wasn't the only one who'd been lulled by Jonas's perennial friendly curiosity into forgetting to ask questions in return.

'I have nieces,' Jonas said. 'They like thinking their uncle's a bit dangerous.'

'All children aren't the same. You're lucky you didn't terrify ours.'

But here, Jonas, dropping his smile, took a long slow look about the quiet people clustered on their cushions across the teahouse floor. 'I rather think it takes more than a blunt old knife to scare Taurasi children these days.'

The Coterie stilled. Following Jonas's lingering look, Mateo understood what the man was seeing, what it had taken Mateo months to *stop* seeing—the gaps that ran through the Kindred like the scars left by an avalanche, healing over with new growth but still visible to a knowing eye.

They'd brought out most of Penelope's generation, the elders of Kindred Taurasi. But the loss of the sixth cart, the entirety of the prime Coterie and all but one guardian… There was a bottleneck there. Darius, Danae and Helena were three of the few left in that cohort. And Mateo had been responsible for losing a swath of his own agemates—those Taurasi with enough experience to try to use his panicked flood of magic on the day of the exile, but not enough experience to survive the attempt.

'Half of them are orphans, aren't they?' Jonas continued relentlessly. 'So are half of you, at *least*. I've met your mother'—he nodded to the twins—'and, by the gods, I am certainly familiar with Uncle Darius. But…'

'Yes, I lost my father that day,' Anika said simply. 'I lost my mother—and the twins lost their father—when Ysthera sank…if not sometime in the three years prior.'

Anika's mother was Kindred Leporasi. She'd returned to Leporasi when the formal alliance with Lucian had come to its negotiated conclusion, and, despite pleas from both father and daughter, stayed there after the vote, as their traditions insisted she should.

The same sort of narrative had played out for the twins' father, of Kindred Serpasi. Formal inter-Kindred alliances were, by design, impermanent; relationships weren't, but none of that had mattered, when faced with banishment. The Coterie, and all Taurasi, had grieved the family left behind in the weeks immediately following the day of the exile. That they had been literally lost only when the island had sunk was almost—almost—irrelevant.

'Gods, that must have been a hard day.' Jonas was still relaxed, his body language open and sympathetic. 'You too, Mateo?'

'I lost my foster-mother,' he said, striving for the same calm as Anika. 'My own parents…died when I was very young.'

'Like Niki,' Jonas said with a nod.

Anika and the twins tensed. They'd been as unaware as Mateo, it seemed, that Jonas had had time and opportunity to innocently chat with their neophyte during his various visits to the street.

'So, yes, we're mostly orphans here now,' Anika said, once again deploying light charm as a diversion. 'Sad little waifs that we are. Or is it elves?'

Jonas smiled obligingly, but he also reached out and took one of Mateo's clenched hands. He gently slid his fingers under the curl of Mateo's, and unfolded the fist into a flat palm, which he laid his own palm over.

'I didn't mean to put you back there,' he said. 'It was terrifying just to watch those carts plummeting down the mountain, let alone what it must have been like to be in the middle of it.'

'Yes,' Mateo said, looking at the strong hand pressing down on his with some confusion.

'Yes,' Anika echoed. 'I don't think we were ever in a state to properly thank your captain for waiting for us that day. It took great courage.'

'Let's not get too sentimental,' Jonas said. 'The lady of *Steadfast* exacted her price, didn't she? We were generously compensated for our courage.'

He was watching Anika closely as he said this, as if expecting to catch a flash of resentment—Taurasi had paid well over the agreed rate for safe passage to the mainland, after the dramatic embarkation. Penelope had even had the gall to murmur about extortion, though not for some months after they'd settled safely into Ravenser Odd.

Anika merely shrugged. 'Your consortium be warned,' she said. 'I'm a better negotiator than I might have appeared back then.'

'I doubt it not,' he said, bowing slightly. He gave Mateo's hand a squeeze and let go to drain his cup. Mateo clasped his hands together to replace the missing warmth. 'The sorcery that day, though…'

'Never left the island,' Anika said quickly.

'*Sank* with the island,' Timon said.

'You sure?' Jonas asked casually. 'Don't like to think of that sort of thing floating about my city.'

'Absolutely. More wine?' Anika leaned over to add another dash to Jonas's cup. 'And I'll get your tea, my sweet.'

'I can get it,' Mateo said, shifting on his hip.

'I'm getting it,' Timon said, standing. 'Stay there, Teo.'

He brought the brewpot over, and Andrea helped Helena and Selia bring the plates over. The conversation was congenial, not touching on weighty matters like the loss of generations and islands. Eventually, Jonas stood to take his leave, rolling his shoulders and stretching his back after the unaccustomed evening on the floor.

'Thank you, Taurasi,' he said, smiling down at Mateo and at the Coterie, and around at the room of quietly-conversing Ystherans. 'Lovely evening.'

'Do come again to dinner with us again, and bring your nieces,' Anika said. 'And your…'

She hesitated. Thanks mostly to magic, Ystheran marriage alliances didn't necessarily lead to children, and so the elders paid more attention to strengthening ties and developing strategic blocs among the whole klados than they did to enforcing particular pairings, except where bloodlines were too important. Imperial marriages, on the other hand, were only between husband and wife, but there were just as many pairing types in their less formal arrangements—their dalliances, to use Jonas's own word.

'…favourite person?' she finished weakly.

Given how well she and Jonas had been getting along, Mateo thought crossly, it was a touch late to be trying to determine if he had someone tucked away by his home hearth. It might not even be relevant if he did or not, depending on the shape of the arrangement.

Hands on hips, Jonas said, 'Oh, I'm a man content with my own company for the most part.'

Mateo felt a flash of disappointment, on Anika's behalf. But Andrea, who'd been her usual quiet and contained self for much of the evening, laughed.

When Jonas smiled at her questioningly, she said, 'I've noticed down in the city that the ones content with their own company are the ones who never do seem to have any trouble getting other company at the merest click of their fingers.' She snapped her fingers demonstratively.

Jonas's smile broadened. 'Ah, well. Let me finish my business on the street first, and then we'll see who might deign to click their fingers at me.'

With one last grin around the table and a rather meaningful glance Anika's way that Mateo accidentally intercepted, he strolled out.

'Remnants, he truly is an odd fish,' Mateo muttered, mostly to cover the strange roil in his stomach at that last look from Jonas.

'I mean, against all inclination, I like the man,' Timon said. 'But are we really allowing this, Anika?'

'Don't deny our friend a chance for some pleasure for once, brother,' Andrea said. She and Anika were smiling at each other.

Point taken. Odd fish or not, Jonas was attractive and agreeable and would be a respite of sorts for Anika. Mateo had no call to feel so ambivalent about it.

CHAPTER 9

ONE OF THE MANY LOCAL OBSERVANCE days fell a few days later, and Mateo was on the steps of the lodging house, waiting for the children to return from school, still trying to feel appropriately glad for Anika. Jonas was a decent man, kind, good-humoured and attentive. Anika had been alone and quietly grieving for too long. She deserved him.

Mateo wished he didn't feel so strange about it, though part of that was just generalised unease, plaguing him since he woke up. He had days like that sometimes. More often, since Ysthera had vanished beneath the waves.

Rubbing his hip, he glanced up at the sky, sun-bright, the day warm enough that he had finally left his jacket on the hook in his apartment, though he hadn't yet forsaken the undershirt. The entire city would grind to a halt when the sun reached its peak, the whole afternoon meant for devotion to the god or goddess who was being honoured today. In truth, after due observance at the relevant temple, the more secularly-inclined Ancerans turned their holy day into a holiday. The teahouse would heave with custom this afternoon, and the Taurasi would eat roasted meats tonight, brought back by the city workers from the generous temple offerings.

At the moment, however, Ravenser Odd was startlingly quiet. Andrea and Selia, and the other city workers, weren't home yet, though the children were overdue; Helena had departed some time ago to escort them home early from the nearby temple schoolroom. The artisans had been thrown out of their precinct for the day while Timon's crew moved equipment about, and had seized the opportunity to disappear up the hillside for a picnic by the sanctified spring, taking the toddlers and elders with them. Anika and her helpers were hard at work preparing the spice sachets and tisane blends for their busy afternoon, and the accompanying snacks. The Ystheran traditional *globi*, little golden dumplings filled with ricotta and honey, were popular.

Mateo was the only Taurasi left idle on the street. That was probably why the general sense of impending doom was getting the better of him. Mateo did best when he was kept busy so that his thoughts could not buzz uselessly about like a hive of bees thwarted by cold rain. Once he would have run the mountain trails, outracing the circling thoughts, but that wasn't an option anymore.

Madam Kerling stomped out of the lodging house, cane in one hand, basket of yarn in the other, the nailbinder sticking out of one ball and gleaming brassily in the bright sunshine. 'What are you standing about for? I cannot abide idleness in young men.'

'I'm due to teach the children, Madam Kerling,' Mateo said. 'They seem late home, given temple duties today.'

He thought he'd managed to hide his unnecessary fretfulness about this, but Madam Kerling paused. 'It does no good to chase wolves around your own head,' she said severely, though also, strangely, comfortingly.

Her girls were due home soon, too, after their temple observances. She sat on the steps and took out her yarn work, a dark mass that resembled a shroud.

Oh, I am very morbid today, Mateo thought.

'Stop hovering and find yourself something to do,' Madam Kerling snapped.

'I'll go help in the teahouse.' He could at least chop herbs until Nikiti and the others arrived.

Madam Kerling harrumphed. 'It is a sacred day. Your teahouse should not even be open this afternoon.'

Mateo said, 'If the customers thought it was sacrilege, they wouldn't come, would they?'

Not to mention, if they closed on holy days, they would be closed a good deal; Imperials had a ridiculous number of deities, all of whom were greedy for the acknowledgement of festivals and temple rites. The whole empire counted out its year with feast days.

'That is no excuse, you contrary boy.'

The warm brightness of the spring day flickered and dimmed as a shadow passed over the sun.

Madam Kerling muttered a querulous curse, hunching over the close stitches. 'Stand out of my light, my eyes are not what they were.'

Dread hollowed Mateo's core. Not wanting to, every part of him rebelling at the need to, he looked up.

There was white mist in the air, and the mist was rapidly coalescing into fog, and the fog was rapidly turning solid, and the solidity was rapidly taking shape, and that shape was death.

Shadow-dogs were upon them.

He saw, then, the strong amber glow of Ystheran magic, rising up the steep road towards Ravenser Odd. It was Helena, face a rictus of fierce concentration, using her daily allotment of magic to hold a shield over the heads of the children as they all ran up the hill, wasting no energy at all on screaming.

In fact, with Niki at their head, they merely looked resolutely intent on reaching safety. Jonas had been right—it took quite a lot to scare Taurasi children, these days.

The shadow-dogs, three, no, four, were swooping overhead, diving at the shield to break it.

It was sickeningly familiar, and for a moment Mateo's world swung about him, tipping and darkening.

'Get inside, Madam Kerling,' he said softly.

He heard her stand up. She whispered, 'Oskoreia.'

Mateo did not know the word—he supposed it to be the rough equivalent of *skiaskylos*—but it was apparent she could see the creatures in the sky. That was right. He had not been conscious to hear it firsthand, but Anika had told him that *Steadfast*'s crew perceived the mist-form of the shadow-dogs that day. They'd have had to, to have fired their big harpoon.

'Get inside,' he repeated.

Heedless of his aching hip, he ran down the steps. He was shining bright, already flooding magic towards Helena, who had no hope of holding up that shield for much longer without help, and all along the street. It would bring out the Taurasi to see what had their Soul in a panic, but more, it would be as good as a whistle to the shadow-dogs.

Those things weren't hunting the children per se. They were scenting Nikiti, and Nikiti's nascent power.

'I'm here,' he shouted. 'Come to me.'

It was unnecessary. The shadow-dogs were already turning, tasting his magic. The sinuous creatures elongated and twisted about each other as they sought the source of the rich magic, and then they were arrowing at him, roiling fast like steam from a kettle spout.

This had not been his brightest idea ever.

He spun around to run; running straight across to the teahouse meant racing the shadow-dogs in a dead sprint he couldn't possibly have won even before his hip was damaged, natural runner or no. But Timon was at work in the artisan precinct, and Mateo thought he could get himself over there in time.

He collided with Madam Kerling, who had not, after all, gone inside. He knocked her flat and tripped over her. He landed on his hip but registered the spike of agony only as the barest afterthought amid the clamour of his panic. He heard her gasp as he struggled to his knees next to her.

The shadow-dogs dived at them, silent, huge white teeth bared. He had a moment, a single moment, to consider abandoning an old lady for the sake of Taurasi, before he hunched over to shield her.

'Get off, fool!' She struck him across the ear and knocked him away.

He took it for terrified flailing before she stabbed up with her nail-binder and pierced a shadow-dog right in the centre of its icy eye.

Madam Kerling let go with a cry of pained fury as her tight fist collided with its eye socket, but she shoved the gleaming needle further in before she did, and it plunged in all the way to the decorative knob on the end.

The shadow-dog dropped like a stone to the packed clay of Ravenser Odd.

Madam Kerling tucked her hand to her chest, but, undeterred, she shook her other fist at the sky. The remaining shadow-dogs circled together, twining about like eels in a barrel. They formed a banked mass, a stormfront.

The Taurasi shield shimmered into a thick sheet between the crouching Mateo and spittingly furious Madam Kerling and the menace overhead.

Mateo tore his gaze away. Anika and her helpers were at the teahouse door; Timon's renovation team, but not Timon, by the newly-installed lading door to the artisan workshops. All had their focus intent on the shield. A rustling hum along the hillside trail at the far end of Ravenser Odd indicated the rest of Taurasi was running back from the picnic in haste, magic blooming.

Darius, no doubt absolutely despising having had to choose who to protect, was already with Helena and the children, hurrying them along into the teahouse behind Anika's blockade. He had his sword drawn, for all the good the guardians' blades had done on the day on the exile.

At which thought, Mateo's attention came back to Madam Kerling and the dead shadow-dog, indisputably slain by, of all things, a nailbinding needle. She was looking between its solid ghost-white body sprawled before her and its misty littermates overhead.

'Scared for a taste of the same, are you?' she shouted at them, shaking her fist, radiating defiance.

She couldn't see the shield the Taurasi were holding up, of course. 'Ah, we should go inside, Madam Kerling,' Mateo said. His voice was wobbly.

He tried to take her sleeve to pull her across to the others, now clumping together into a single defensive mass, faces grim or terrified or determinedly fierce or a mix of all those emotions and more. Beyond them, he saw the Anceran lodgers arriving home, staring and pointing at the shadow-dogs.

He could hear their murmurs. 'Wild hunt,' they were saying, or 'Wish hounds.' Some said, 'Oskoreia,' like Madam Kerling had.

They didn't sound frightened. They were seeing some heartland story come to life, an enthralling battle between their friendly little elves and some other legendary creatures. They didn't know the Taurasi shield was protecting them from something that was not in any way a fairy tale.

Anika strode out from the midst of the Taurasi holding up that defensive wall. She was in a flood of magic, the normally gentle glow a blaze, the soft hum a roar. He felt the draw on him, an insistent pull like a hook in his belly. He allowed it.

Raising her hands, she swept clawed fingers through the air, and a shadow-dog shredded.

The local girls cried out, thrilled. Then, behind the residents, came Jonas, holding the hands of two dark-haired girls. He was looking at the shadow-dogs too.

He said, 'We're all seeing this, right?'

Anika dropped her hands, face stricken. She'd committed a cardinal sin, performing such dramatic magic—not wild, of course, but dramatic-ally showy all the same—so openly. Even if a witness happened to have the telltale drop of Ystheran blood, the shield was a mere golden glow, harmless, perhaps even beautiful if one could shake off the Imperial indoctrination. On the other hand, ripping apart her enemies, even deadly supernatural ones, with her bare hands was not a fantastic demonstration of the innocence of Ystheran magic and the firmness of Ystheran pacifism.

She'd been lucky, though. Everyone had been so busy staring at the display overhead that they hadn't seen what caused the disintegration. Or, at least, no one was pointing and screaming accusations of sorcery.

The remaining pair of shadow-dogs seemed to dislike an audience as much as the Taurasi did. They whirled upwards and away, fading into mist that puffed away.

For a long moment, the shield stayed solidly in place. Then Anika, serene again, raised her hand and the Taurasi let it shimmer into nothing, an unsettling echo of the way the shadow-dogs had faded out. Mateo immediately cut off the flow.

Darius marched across to him, grabbed his wrist, and began to drag him away from the dead shadow-dog and into the shelter of the teahouse surrounded by his kith.

'Hey, hold up, uncle,' Jonas said as Mateo winced, his already-abused hip protesting the sharp tug. 'You're hurting him.'

Anika hurried over. She settled Darius with a hand to his arm. He reluctantly let go of Mateo's wrist but stood at his shoulder, glaring at Jonas, whose young companions hid behind him, and at Madam Kerling and her lodgers, who were standing fascinatedly about the felled shadow-dog while their landlady declaimed her role in bringing it down.

Anika looked up at Mateo with worry in her dark eyes, whole body leaning towards him in a silent question. He gave her a quick nod of reassurance. Alarmed, yes. Harmed, no.

'This is the same thing as attacked you when you left Ysthera,' Jonas said, absently patting the girls clinging to his sides.

'This is not a good time, Jonas,' Anika said.

Jonas missed a beat in the comforting patting. 'Do you think they're coming back?'

'They're gone,' she said, in a tone of voice that decreed it would be so. 'But you need to leave.'

Mateo, unable to match her diplomacy at the best of times and currently completely incapable of even approaching it, blurted, 'We don't want foreigners in Ravenser Odd right now.'

'We're the foreigners,' Anika said. 'But, yes. You should go. I'm sorry, Jonas, but please. Go.'

'Understood,' Jonas said, because of course he did. He held his hands fisted together, knuckles snugged to knuckles. 'We turn inwards when we're frightened. I just need to check that Madam Kerling is not injured. And you, Mateo.'

Now the panic was subsiding and Mateo's heartrate was slowing towards normal, he had the wherewithal to acknowledge that Jonas was not wearing his usual long-sleeved shirt and trousers. Rather, he was dressed in a more traditional outfit of tunic, sky-blue, tied at the waist rather than belted, and falling only to mid-thigh. The snake tattoo was striking, writhing almost like a living thing as his forearm flexed with his movements.

The other bicep—the formal tunic left him bare all the way to the shoulders—sported a tattoo of the raven-haunted Imperial tree, surrounded by runes. Just below it lay tangled lines of white scar tissue. He had on the local sandals, too, the straps winding up his strong calves. It must be to do with the holy day.

It was an *excessive* amount of smooth brown skin. The man *definitely* availed himself of the depilation services of the barbers.

'And I have my nieces here, and they're quite frightened themselves, actually.'

Anika looked at the two little girls peeking around Jonas. They were in holy-day outfits, too, bright ankle-length tunics. One was staring raptly at Mateo, until the other, taller, one leaned around Jonas to give her a rebuking tap.

He could see Anika pulling herself together, making calculations, balancing and triaging the competing needs assailing her: her threatened Soul set against her frightened people set against anxious children on both sides set against Imperial witnesses set against physical evidence lying on the street set against the terror of knowing shadow-dogs had somehow found them.

He watched her pack that last one away; she had no time to indulge it on her own behalf when every single other figure in her calculations needed dealing with of one sort or another.

She nodded, once, briskly. 'What are your nieces' names?'

'This is Asta and Hilda,' Jonas said. 'My sister's children. I thought they'd like an outing to the teahouse.' He made a face, grimly amused at his own timing.

'Heilsa, Asta and Hilda,' Anika said, bending slightly towards Jonas's nieces. 'The big white dogs were scary, weren't they?' The girls looked uncertain. 'They're gone now. Would you like to come meet some new friends while your uncle makes sure everyone's all right?'

She was apparently betting that the novelty of new playmates would calm both the Taurasi children and these two. She held out her hands to them. The girls stared at the hands with wide eyes. Even Jonas was wearing a slight frown.

If they had happened to *not* be looking up when Anika had disinteg-rated the shadow-dog, if they had seen her do it… Well, it wouldn't be the misty white dogs who seemed scary.

After a moment, her smile and confident calm, and mostly an encour-aging nudge from the uncle who must be able to recognise that the teahouse was the safest place in the city right now, persuaded the girls to let go of Jonas and take a hand each. She led them over the street, where the other Taurasi were already following her example, calming them-selves so they could calm the children.

Over her shoulder, she said in Ystheran, 'Teo, get Jonas and Madam Kerling out of the way so Timon and Darius can deal with this thing's body.' She checked, and then looked about. 'Where is Timon?'

Timon was running up from the mouth of Ravenser Odd, looking flushed. The palaver would have been visible skywards all the way to the bottom of the hill and beyond.

'Where were you?' Anika said, not quite accusingly.

'I needed to fetch extra fittings before everything closed for the day,' Timon said, not quite defensively. He waggled the wrapped package he was holding.

Anika shook her head, still on the edge of reproof. 'What a time to finally decide to go down into the city.'

'I couldn't keep making my helpers do something I wouldn't do myself,' he muttered. 'I have to start living like we live here, right?'

How safe they'd all felt, for two-thirds of the Coterie to leave the street without a care, for Mateo to be so lax in appointing the fourth and fifth members without thinking of what the lack would mean if threat came a-hunting.

They'd left Ysthera and assumed wild magic could not find them. Ysthera was *gone*, and wild magic had found them.

Mateo shivered. No. No, there was a simple explanation for this, and Anika would tell him what it was as soon as they got the Imperial residents out the way and Jonas off the street. The only source of any magic was Souls, and Mateo was the only Soul left in all the world. There was some other explanation for this.

Jonas had gently separated Madam Kerling from her enthralled girls, and was persuading her inside her lodging house in unruffled tones, pre-sumably the voice he used at his father's clinic. He sounded simultaneously competently authoritative and immensely reassuring, and Madam Kerling followed him readily, her lodgers flocking in her wake.

Mateo took a few steps after them, watching as Timon and Darius bent over the dead shadow-dog. Darius pulled the nailbinder from its eye, sword at the ready. Timon hovered beside him, magic coiled but not yet deployed. Far from leaping back into life once the needle was out of its eye, the creature faded away into nothing, truly dead. Timon gave a satisfied nod.

Mateo, still horribly unsettled, joined Jonas in the lodging house foyer. He'd seated Madam Kerling on the hard bench where male visitors waited for the girls to come down for chaperoned visits. Most of the lodgers vanished up the stairs to gather and gossip, but some lingered to fuss over their irascible landlady. Under Jonas's instruction, one trotted over to the teahouse to fetch a restorative tisane.

A few welcomed the chance to fuss over Mateo too, cooing, 'Are you all right, our Theo?' He nodded mutely to this and to Jonas's quick glance his way.

Jonas squatted next to Madam Kerling in a flex of bare thighs that Mateo had to make himself look away from. He raised his arm to flash the snake tattoo, but only perfunctorily; it was on full display already.

'Where does it hurt, Madam Kerling?'

'This addlepate pushed me over and then squashed me,' she said grumpily, waving a trembling hand at the awkwardly hovering Mateo. 'I'll ache for days. He's lucky I didn't break something! And I want my nailbinder back, you reprobate.'

'I wasn't *trying* to shove a little old lady over,' Mateo said, just as grumpily.

'Who are you calling any of those things, you foreign noddy?'

Jonas swept a quick smile up at Mateo. 'That's what the tisane is for. You send Mateo to fetch you a pot of Aniketa's special herbal blend whenever you like.'

Mollified in direct proportion to Mateo's sigh, Madam Kerling added, 'Otherwise, my hand might just hurt some.'

She held out the hand she'd used to stab the shadow-dog. It was red and blistered where the side of her fist had jammed into its eye socket; the shadow-dogs might look like mist to Imperial eyes, but they were solid enough in their effects. Jonas hummed with carefully modulated interest, while Mateo, with no bedside manner whatsoever, openly winced.

Jonas sent another helpful lodger over to the teahouse, this time for one of Anika's medicinal salves, and dispatched Mateo to source some clean strips of cloth.

By the time he came back, he was limping badly, and Madam Kerling was well and truly soothed with a cup of herbal tea and salve all over her hand.

'I suppose you think you're charming, young man,' she was saying in haughty riposte to some smiling sally from Jonas.

'So I've been told on *many* an occasion, madam,' he said cheerfully, with one of his winks.

Her frosty façade almost cracked with a return smile, to Mateo's great indignation. He handed Jonas the clean cloths he'd asked for.

Jonas wrapped the salved hand. 'Now you should go rest,' he ordered. 'I want to see you taking better care of yourself.'

She almost tittered. Once one of her girls had led her into her apartment to lie down and the others had disappeared upstairs, Jonas turned to Mateo. 'Your hip?'

Was aching. 'Is fine.'

'Is not. Let me take a look.'

'There's really not much to be done for it, Jonas.'

'I respectfully disagree.'

Mateo huffed. He stood conspicuously still, arms folded, sore hip angled towards Jonas as the very slightest of concessions.

Jonas sucked air over his teeth to make a cross-culturally distinctive *I-know-you'll-hate-this* sound. 'I need to literally *look* at your hip. Both hips preferably.'

Both considered Mateo's clothes, the four layers of the usual Ystheran day-to-day outfit—undershirt, wrap-tunic, sash, loose trousers—covering his hips. He would have to get a good way to undressed to let Jonas look.

'I really am a physician,' Jonas said. 'I know I haven't been my most professional self around you, but I won't be looking at you in any sort of lascivious way. It won't even cross my mind.'

'Of course it won't.' Mateo ran his thumb repetitively over the edge of his sash, trying not to let himself become too anxious at the thought of undressing for Jonas. 'I mean, why would it?'

Jonas shook his head, smiling ruefully. 'Right. Why would it, indeed?'

Mateo was abruptly grateful that every Imperial dialect encouraged bluntness. 'You're confusing me.'

'I realise that. Can I look at your hip, or no?'

He had probably, slowly, reluctantly, been getting around to asking for advice about his hip from Jonas anyway, given they appeared to be friends now. But he was still tense and upset. He didn't currently feel like he had the fortitude for it.

But Anika had told him to occupy Jonas while she exploited the presence of his nieces to help calm the Taurasi, and while Timon and Darius got rid of any last scraps of evidence of sorcery. They could do nothing about the story that would rip around the city, but they could at least leave nothing incriminating if—when?—the Vigile came sniffing.

'Come to my rooms,' he said at last, forcibly making his hands stop fidgeting with the sash.

Down the hallway past Madam Kerling's apartment, Mateo's small quarters consisted of an antechamber, minimally furnished with a pile of sitting cushions, a low table with a row of combs and brushes and other Ystheran paraphernalia, and a second chamber holding a sleeping platform and clothes trunk. A small plumbed washroom with hot water, installed by the Taurasi, was further down the hall, nominally shared with Madam Kerling, though she had declined to make use of the polite offer on the grounds that it was foreign and indulgent. Mateo didn't tend to linger here, spending most of his time outside or in the teahouse.

He stood in the centre of the antechamber and undid his sash. This let the tunic fall open, making it obvious it was really just a soft half-robe with short but draping sleeves. As Jonas politely but expectantly waited, he took it off, and then his long-sleeved undershirt. He'd been expecting to help in the teahouse this afternoon, so his breasts were firmly bound, which provided enough modesty that he didn't feel too strongly the need to cross his arms defensively over his chest. He didn't normally feel uncomfortable about his body, but it seemed different with Jonas, through no fault of the man himself.

Sighing, Mateo undid the laces of his trousers, and tugged them down over the top of his hips.

'That's good, that's enough,' Jonas said.

He knelt in front of Mateo and set his hands gently on Mateo's hips in a weighing, testing sort of way. His fingers brushed the top hem of Mateo's undergarments. He removed his hands, and sat back on his heels.

Mateo assumed Jonas had noticed the scarring on his hip. Imperials could see the dog-like shapes in the mist, and they could see the indisputably solid body of the dead one, and it should be no surprise they could see the evidence of one's teeth imprinted on his body. The holes it'd left had been real enough.

But that wasn't what had caught Jonas's eye, after all. 'You wear silk underthings.'

'They're comfortable.'

They'd sold off almost all their silks, the gorgeously extravagant ceremonial robes, brightly dyed and painted, but the money for the undergarments would have been minimal—they would have been taken for rags—so Anika had indulged him, as she so often did.

Jonas took a deep breath. 'Do you ever think,' he said, 'that the gods enjoy punishing us for hubris and sending us these little trials to test us?'

Mateo's heart gave a skip. He found he'd put his own hands to his hips, touching the skin where Jonas's fingers had rested. He folded his arms instead. 'Strange time to start a philosophical discourse.'

'Is it, though?' Jonas said musingly.

Clearing his throat, Mateo said, 'I think most gods are just trying to get through their day like everyone else.'

'Just like us, hey?' The other man gifted him a wry grin.

'The little gods, anyway. The…minor ones.'

'Demigods, you mean? Imperials call them volsungs.' Without waiting for an answer, Jonas shifted his weight, returning to business. Or not. He reached to tap Mateo firmly on the sternum, just above the fold of his arms. 'Unsolicited advice?'

'No, thank you.'

'I don't think you know how unsolicited advice works, Mateo.'

'I don't think *you* know how it works, Jonas.'

Jonas, smiling, tapped the tight cloth over Mateo's chest again. Strangely, it made Mateo relax. He didn't think an Imperial, even the impervious Jonas, would so casually rap his knuckles between the breasts of someone he even slightly considered a woman.

He said, 'The theatres in the city. Corsets for highlighting assets, corsets for minimising assets—bandeaux, they're called. Have someone look into it for you. Much more convenient than the wrapping.'

'Oh. All right.' Mateo tilted his head back, stared at the ceiling. He let his arms drop. 'Sorry. Again.'

'You've had a nasty shock,' Jonas said. 'I'm flattered you're tolerating me at all.'

Mateo glanced guiltily down at him. He was tolerating this only because Anika had told him to get Jonas out of the way. That was not the act of a friend.

Jonas, meanwhile, had folded the tops of the silken drawers down and put his hands back on Mateo's bare hips. His breath was warm over Mateo's stomach as he made that tiny satisfied sound at what he'd discovered.

I wonder if he makes that noise when he—

Shutting his eyes, Mateo mercilessly cut the thought's throat. He understood what was happening. He'd spoken of it to Jonas not so long before, when he'd been explaining their bounty of toddlers. He'd had a brush with death, and his body was reacting. That was all.

He opened his eyes to find Jonas gazing up at him. 'Have you consulted with a physician about this before?'

Mateo cleared his throat again. 'Anika called some in, when we first arrived, but that was more because I was…weak in general.'

'From your seasickness,' said Jonas, smiling wickedly as if refraining from making a sarcastically disbelieving gesture only by the merest whisper of willpower.

Mateo scowled at him. 'They mainly looked at my urine and recommended I drink other animals' urine. I…didn't.'

'You're lucky there wasn't dung involved.'

'That was when Anika decided to stop wasting our limited funds on Imperial medical training.'

'My father—and me, now—treats those without the means for endless expensive cures. So he's a great proponent of simplicity: keep wounds clean, eat as well as you can, and move. Anika's on top of the first two. What you need to do here is the third.'

Mateo was sceptical. 'It hurts when I move.'

'Ah!' said Jonas, greatly pleased. 'The thing about this kind of injury is your body wants to protect you by contracting the surrounding muscles, but that just ends up making it all worse. So, here, everything across your lower back and down your leg has tightened up, and it'll be up in your opposite shoulder, too, right? So it all feels worse than it has to. You need to stretch. Can I show you?'

At Mateo's nod, Jonas rose and came around behind him. He circled his right arm all the way around Mateo's waist to rest the hand on Mateo's stiff left hip. 'All right. Step this leg forwards. Nice big step, I've got you. Good.'

His solid body—half-naked—was close up against Mateo, supporting him. His left hand came to Mateo's left thigh. Mateo stared down at the coils of the snake tattoo around his forearm, eyeing off that flicker of tongue in the crook of Jonas's elbow.

'Bend your knee. That's it. Not too far, for now. You hold that for a few breaths, then do the other side too. You'll eventually get to kneeling on the back leg. Breathe into it, Mateo.'

Mateo went very still in Jonas's arms, trying to remember what breathing was, feeling the heat where their two bodies touched almost as a throbbing. He was silent and compliant as Jonas slowly brought him back up to standing square and changed his grip, one hand on Mateo's hipbone, the other on his other thigh, slowly spreading his fingers to gently but inexorably ease Mateo's hips open, his own hip set into Mateo's lower back as the pivot.

All the while, he kept up a cheerful commentary. 'Now, you don't want actual pain here, but you do have to let a good, slow stretch take you past the point of discomfit until it starts to feel good, right? As it loosens, you can take it deeper.'

Mateo wobbled, and Jonas firmed his grip, not even shifting his feet to catch Mateo's extra weight against him. His voice sounded husky in Mateo's ear as he said, 'I think I better put you against the wall.'

'I think you better, yes,' Mateo said, which was not what he had meant to say, but which was apparently all he could say.

Jonas, still behind him with big hands on his hips, gave him a friendly nudge with one thigh, and shuffled him towards the wall. 'More pliant already, hmm?'

Mateo, meanwhile, was quietly panicking. This couldn't be what it felt like, surely. If an Imperial wanted sex, they didn't tease about it, did they, and dance about sprinkling euphemisms. If they were interested, they asked. Jonas hadn't asked; therefore, he wasn't interested.

He'd also assumed he himself was not interested, but his body was very much contradicting him, insistently so.

All right, he had apparently, confusingly, consented to a rough fuck against the wall. He didn't know how to renege without incurring, at best, the other man's injured pride and, at worst, his anger. He wasn't even sure he wanted to renege, entirely, because even though he knew he wouldn't much enjoy it, his body was demanding that he have a try anyway.

Fine, the sex itself would be over with quickly enough, and then if he was lucky he might get some kissing, which was the one part of this enterprise he was likely to appreciate.

He was more likely to get that beforehand, he remembered. He mumbled, 'Is kissing permitted?'

Jonas, for his own meanwhile, had positioned Mateo's good hip against the wall and was saying, 'Counterintuitive, I know, but actually you want the support on this side so you can bend into the stretch a bit further without overbalancing.' He paused. 'Sorry, I didn't catch that?'

'Is—' Mateo stopped himself. 'Is this what we're using the wall for?'

'So you can do these exercises alone. You'll probably want to do them first thing in the morning and last thing at night. Gradually increase the number of repetitions. You'll find it helps immensely, *if* you're disciplined about it. Good? And I'll give Anika our recipe for mandrake salve for you to massage in, too.'

It was very odd to feel so relieved and so utterly disappointed at the exact same time. 'I see. Do you and your father treat a lot of patients with sore joints, then?'

'I mainly learnt this trick with my mother. She was getting quite arthritic in her last few years. Salt air's supposed to be good for that, but she found a regimen of stretching and salve more helpful. Kept her seaworthy, anyway.'

'Oh, you were thinking about your mother.'

Mortified, Mateo quickly turned away to dress. The man was his *friend,* temporarily acting as his *physician*, and just trying to do that job. Mateo should have realised he'd not in any way be propositioning him; Jonas had even said as much.

Jonas muttered, 'It's a sight better than what I could have been thinking about.' He raised his eyebrows. 'Why, what were *you* thinking ab—'

Madam Kerling hammered on the common wall between her apartment and Mateo's antechamber. 'Just because you've had a fright does not give you leave to have a strange man in your bedroom, Mattias Taurasi!'

'I guess she's feeling better,' Jonas said with his usual grin. 'I should check on my girls.'

CHAPTER 10

I N THE TEAHOUSE, JONAS'S NIECES, BAREFOOT and giggling, had introduced the Taurasi children to the concept of an imaginary tea party. Darius was somehow sitting, cross-legged and straight-backed, in the circle of young ones, ominously sipping pretend tea from a pottery cup decorated with sunflowers. He shot daggers at Jonas when he and Mateo paused at the doorway.

'Asta's pretty persuasive,' Jonas said, smiling back at him with deep pleasure. 'She's the elder of the pair. Hilda's the younger. Obviously.'

Jonas was, obviously, politely reminding Mateo of their names. 'You're looking after them today for your sister?'

'For my father. They're his wards now.'

Mateo knew what that meant; all the Taurasi knew what it meant, since the day of the exile. Both parents were dead—Jonas's sister was dead. 'Oh, I'm sorry.'

Jonas absently made the tap and sweep of the fingers he'd made when talking of his lost crewmates and said, as he had then, 'Long time past. It's Eirina's day today. My father has duties at the sanctum all day, so I've got the girls.'

'But you're a physician, too,' Mateo said.

He started to reach out to touch the snake, its tongue so complacently flicking over the smooth skin. He clenched his hand, dropped it back to his side.

'I paid my respects already, with the girls, but I'm a devotee of Njorda.' Jonas tugged on the thong about his neck to show Mateo the bronze medallion he'd glimpsed the other night, a large coin with a distinctive low-beamed trading ship embossed on its face. 'Goddess of safe conduct through the storm, you could say. Sailors usually follow Her, and I spent the first half of my life asea with my mother. Deities don't tend to like it when you, ah, change chariots mid-race.'

'Doesn't that annoy your father?' Mateo asked, trying to imagine this careful balancing of parental desires, a thing alien to his very existence.

'He already inveigled me away from my mother's vocation to his,' Jonas said. 'He knew better than to push his luck.'

'Oh, but then why were you on *Steadfast* on the day of the exile?'

'I was still crew then.'

Slowly, Mateo spelled out, 'You only became a physician after *Steadfast*—' He stopped, suddenly so cold that the golden glow of the lights in the teahouse seemed to dim momentarily.

Jonas turned to look at him. 'Ah. Mateo, don't get too fretful about this.'

'She was a family trading ship, wasn't she?' Mateo said, voice flat. 'You lost more than some hired-on crew when she foundered. You lost your mother and your sister.'

'And aunt, their husbands, and a couple of cousins, and a few crewmates I was especially fond of,' Jonas said, rubbing the scar on his right bicep. 'Somewhat lost the passion for the sea trade after that, and my father offered an apprenticeship.' He tsked at Mateo's expression and said again, 'Long time past, Mateo.'

It was a mere three years past.

Ships went down all the time, foundering in storms or blown off-course and running into reefs in uncharted waters. Traders knew the risks; it was the exact reason that kinship crews were a dying tradition.

Mateo looked at the two orphaned girls, sitting happily in a circle which contained many other orphans, and wished very hard to not have to know that the mutual orphans had wild magic in common as well.

He didn't want to know, he didn't want to hear. It was an utterly selfish impulse. He had to ask. 'How did she sink?'

Please, please, please, I do not want to know that we brought it down on your family.

'Storm,' Jonas said. 'Gods are fickle fuckers, sometimes.' Notwithstanding, he kissed the medallion and slipped it down the neck of his sky-blue tunic with a murmured, 'No offence, Njorda, you old sea witch.'

Not Ystheran magic, just a storm. The guilt did not exactly ebb away—a storm might have an unnatural source—but it did recede enough to gather momentum for a surge in a different direction.

'I don't understand.' He set his hands to his stomach, running his thumbs along the top of his sash. 'Jonas, I don't understand how you can be so… I've been whining about my whole world sinking to the bottom of the sea, and yours did too, and you haven't said a word.'

'My whole world did not sink, not even close.' Jonas opened his palms towards where his nieces sat, shooting them his beautiful smile. 'I've lost much, yes, I'll carry them in my heart forever, yes, but I've plenty left right here in front of me. I don't have to let their loss be so heavy a weight that it holds me down. That's no way to live.'

'But *how* do you…'

'Practice,' Jonas said. 'Look at it this way. The Ystherans have, or had, the ability to murder each other at a distance, so therefore you're pacifists.'

Mateo opened his mouth; it wasn't quite why they obstinately cleaved to their peaceful ways. But on the other hand, Jonas's assumption made pragmatic sense, Imperials' favourite kind of sense. He stayed quiet.

Jonas smiled like he'd caught the suppressed impulse to correct him. 'Meanwhile, we're a sea-trading family, so therefore we know every time the ship leaves port that it might be the last voyage. We keep half an eye on the winds and half an eye on death.' He examined Mateo's face uncomfortably closely. 'Not to be morbid about it. I lost half my family, but while I had them, we didn't waste a single moment not loving one another to the best of our abilities, and that's a great comfort.'

Mateo looked about the teahouse, cosy and inviting and full of just a handful of the people he loved: the children, engrossed in their game; Anika, chopping herbs in the kitchen while she nodded sympathetically along to something one of her helpers was confiding in her; Timon joining in on rolling out the high tables; Penelope staring narrow-eyed at the copper mechanism of the water-clock like she was counting out the drips to calibrate it, which she likely was.

'That does sound like a comfort,' he admitted, before blurting, 'Aren't you angry? Don't you…' He bit his lip. 'Blame someone?'

'I was raised to see anger and regret as pointless, temporary, emotions,' Jonas said. 'And when it comes to blaming myself or blaming other people, I've had years and years of practice of…' He set his forefinger on the head of the snake at his elbow and ran it all the way down his forearm, tracing the sinuous curve. '…letting it go.' He reached the tail and flicked his fingertips across his palm, illustratively releasing a burden into the ether. 'Because holding on to bitterness or regret about a past I cannot change does no one any good, least of all me.'

Drinking in the quiet, peaceful industry of his people about their daily routine, as soothing to them all as one of Anika's tisanes, Mateo said, 'I'd be scared of losing the other half of my family.'

'I can't control what happens in the future. I act to head off foreseeable dangers, of course, but otherwise, there's no point losing sleep over it.' Jonas shrugged. 'I can count on one hand the things worth losing sleep over.'

Mateo couldn't help a marvelling laugh. 'I lose sleep over everything.'

'I could have made a guess at that, sure. I know you're carrying your own weight, just like the rest of the Taurasi.' Jonas hesitated, considering him speculatively. 'I'm going to overstep my bounds.'

'If you know you're overstepping them, are they really bounds?'

'What a typically refreshing way of looking at it. When you do the stretching, try something for me, all right? Don't think about the past, don't think about the future, just think about…the stretch. Just be there, with the stretch.'

He was sounding, in a way that was both disturbing and comforting, like Sabine, until he said, 'It might help with the drifting off, you see. *Not*'—he'd sped up, watching Mateo's face in that strangely intent way—'that I'd say a word if you were drifting off into a pleasant reverie. But you're not. You're going someplace dark. Somewhere you should try not to linger, if you can help it.'

'I don't need your advice.' Mateo was speaking stiffly, all the more so because Jonas had recognised his instinctive offence and tried to head it off.

'Understood,' Jonas said easily. 'Apologies.'

Mateo narrowed his eyes. The man's ready capitulation was beyond irritating. Jonas bit back one of his *honey-you-are-hilarious* smiles. Just then, Anika emerged from behind her counter, heading towards the door to the herb garden.

Jonas called across to her, 'Anika, a word?' The Taurasi froze for a moment before they resumed their work. 'Sorry. I forget your people don't raise their voices.'

He wouldn't think that if he'd ever attended a morning meeting. 'You people.'

'You know what I said.' He smiled at Anika, who had obligingly trotted over. 'I didn't mean to summon you. I didn't want to step inside with my sandals on, but they're a right scrote to unlace for a quick visit.'

Both Anika and Mateo looked down at Jonas's sandals. Under the thin straps of leather crisscrossing to just below his knees, Mateo saw another of the tattoos, high up on the side of his left calf. This one, as far as he could make out, was not an Imperial symbol but rather, some sort of seashell, a spiral shape decorated with intricate patterning. He checked Jonas's other leg: bare of ink. His right thigh bore more of the same welted scarring as on his right arm, and his left thigh was unmarked, and Mateo really needed to stop staring at the man's legs.

'I want a word about those wish hounds earlier,' Jonas said. 'You said sorcery never made it off the island, but that attack suggests otherwise. Is sorcery loose in my city?'

It was very blunt, for all that Jonas seemed relaxed. Just moments ago, he'd said, *I act to head off foreseeable dangers, of course* and that, *of course,* was what he was doing.

'No,' Anika said promptly. 'Like Timon said, it all sank with Ysthera. We think it was a…like an aftershock of an earthquake, arriving belatedly, not to be repeated.'

This explanation sounded plausible; as to its truth, Mateo had as little idea as Anika did. He had been the Taurasi auxiliary Soul on the day of the exile. There was much he had not learned. He'd definitely learned nothing of wild magic, except the injunction against using it. That he had no idea how to go about setting his magic free in such a blighted way was a natural offshoot of the injunction. He didn't even know if Sabine would have one day taught him more on the taboo subject.

But, yes, if an entire island full of so-called sorcerers had suddenly faced destruction, a last gush of wild and desperate magic might have burst out. It might have taken the form of shadow-dogs, and swept with the winds towards the only Soul left in existence. It felt possible, edging towards likely.

And Jonas's true concern was to be sure sorcery wasn't endangering Anceral and his remaining family. There, Mateo was on solid ground. He was the only source of magic in all the world. Therefore, Anika could aver with stone-cold certainty that sorcery was not loose in the city, and Mateo could give a firm nod of agreement, and neither of them was contravening the Ystheran cultural bias towards honesty.

Jonas looked between the two of them, and his gaze flicked briefly over Anika's shoulder, towards his nieces. Then he gave a nod of his own. 'I'd say your customers will be arriving soon. Be warned, they'll have heard the story of the wild hunt by now. So you're either going to be very quiet, or very, *very* busy.'

Turning from them, he clapped his hands, once again startling the Taurasi. 'Girls. I know Uncle Darius is your favourite uncle now, but it's time to go.'

Under the coverage of the universal complaint from the tea party circle, Anika murmured, 'Ask him to an evening meal soon.'

'Will you come to dinner another time?' Mateo said obediently.

He assumed the invitation was another prong in the Heart's soothing strategy. For his own part, he was oddly grateful to Jonas in a myriad of ways: for not holding a grudge, rationally or not, about the fate of his family ship; for demonstrating that it was possible to recover, even thrive, after a dreadful tragedy; for not pushing about the sorcery he had witnessed, both today and on the day of the exile; for being as patient as the Taurasi with Mateo's irritable outbursts…or conversely, for recognising when he had truly gone too far and Mateo's irritable outburst was justified—Mateo couldn't tell which of them had been in the right on that last occasion.

'Love to, Mateo.' His nieces presented themselves and he took their hands. 'Why are you so sticky?'

'Ah?'

'Honey cake,' the smaller one, Hilda, announced. She had her uncle's wide smile and cheerful manner, plus the extra weapon of dimples.

'Uncle Jiji, they gave us *so much* cake!' Asta added. She looked the more serious of the two, but not right then.

'Oh, good!' Jonas said with hearty sarcasm. 'Thank you, Taurasi.'

'You're welcome, Uncle Jiji,' Anika said, and Jonas returned her smile with an appreciative grin.

Andrea came up onto the porch just as he finished helping the girls into their sandals. The brewery had closed for the holy afternoon. She exchanged nods with him, and gave the girls a polite wave. She watched them march off along Ravenser Odd before turning to Anika and Mateo.

'Heard there was a kerfuffle,' she said, which turned out to be an understatement. She was the harbinger of an influx of their Anceran customers, who had also heard there was a kerfuffle.

The teahouse was very, *very* busy.

CHAPTER 11

Jonas didn't visit for over a week, counted in Anceral from market day to market day, longer than the Ystheran sennight. It was an unusually long hiatus between visits, though Anika did not seem concerned, and waxen message tablets, and even some paper or papyrus scrolls, made their way to the teahouse unabated, as well as the promised mandrake salve recipe.

Since Timon apparently left Ravenser Odd now, Mateo sent him down to the theatre district for a few bandeaux; he didn't like to send Coterie off the street so soon after their unpleasant surprise, but he also didn't like to ask anyone else to run such an intimate errand for him. Timon returned successful in his quest and incessantly humming some rhythmic tune from one of the theatre plays.

Jonas had been right, a bandeau was more comfortable and more convenient. Mateo found himself using them almost every day, duties in the teahouse or no. He also, grimly but with dedication, obeyed the man's instructions and carried out the stretching and massage regime twice daily, trying very hard to keep his mind right there, on the edge-of-pain stretch and the subtle relief of the release.

His thoughts insisted on turning, not to his usual myriad worries, some more justified than others, but to Jonas. He'd been absent long enough for Mateo to wonder if the shadow-dogs had scared the man off once he'd put some thought into it, or if he'd finally got sick of Mateo's self-absorption…which was apparently strong enough to make him assume he could be worse than shadow-dogs.

But then, following a few miserable days of rain, light but incessant, their Imperial friend strode, congenial as ever, into Ravenser Odd to take Mateo up on his meal invitation. He was, thank the Shattered One and all

Her lost Remnants, back in his trousers and long-sleeved shirt, and a short cloak in the local style as a nod to the cool evening. He brought a gift of honey-coated almonds and juicy dried apricots from the garden of his family's villa.

This time he lingered afterwards, as the Taurasi, except for Timon, out late on some errand, settled into their evening society, with singing and strumming—Ystherans were always ready for a melancholy tune—and taletelling and gameplay.

Jonas played several games of Lithos with Penelope and her closest cronies, and was trounced without mercy. He was still laughing at the totality of his defeat in the last round when Timon arrived back. The Taurasi made shift for bed then, and the Coterie were left alone for their last indulgence of the night.

Their guest joined them at their low table, and without a whit of self-consciousness, rearranged Mateo's cushions, and prodded at him to rearrange him as well, until Mateo's hip was sitting comfortably, and he himself was sitting alarmingly close to Jonas. Anika and the twins sat across the table, watching this process with varying degrees of knowing interest.

Timon still looked chilled from being outside in the misty Anceran evening, and was also avoiding specifying where he'd been. He was in a good mood, though. 'And what do we think this is about, Teo?'

'I think,' Mateo said, 'that he's seen how much you all fuss over me and he's joining in.' He switched to impatient Imperial. 'It's fine. I'm *fine*, Jonas.'

Timon smirked at him. 'I see you're choosing to take it with as much graciousness as you usually show us.'

'Do people ever get demoted from the Coterie, Anika?' Mateo asked, and the others chortled. Even Darius, kneeling watchfully a little way away, smothered a brief smile.

'Everything all right?' Jonas asked, as usual ignoring their rude use of a foreign language in front of a guest. 'I mean about the wish dogs? No more problems?'

'As I said, not to be repeated,' Anika said smoothly.

Over the last ten days, she'd presented the story she'd told him to the teahouse patrons, who had flocked agog and apparently ready for their own theatre performance directly out of legend. They'd seemed almost disappointed when Anika had insisted it was an aberration, never to recur.

Anika was right, of course. The Taurasi had taken longer to believe it, but as the days had passed with no further incursion, they'd begun to relax again. After all, where could wild magic possibly be coming from? Anika's explanation seemed less like a story to appease the Imperials and more like a solid theory.

Jonas nodded without overt curiosity. He took out a scroll from the bag he'd brought the other treats in, and made an Ystheran-esque bow as he presented it to Anika. 'This dinner serves somewhat as an impromptu celebration. The trade deal is finalised.'

Anika accepted the scroll with both hands, inclining her own head. She smiled at the others. Mateo tried to smile back. He should have been happy, but his first reaction had been dismay that Jonas had no reason to visit anymore, which was exceedingly selfish of him.

'I wanted to surprise you,' Anika told them. 'I'll tell everyone tomorrow morning. I think we got a good deal?' She tilted her head queryingly to Jonas.

'Now that the contract is safely signed and lodged, I may confirm that you negotiated yourself extremely favourable terms,' Jonas agreed. He smiled. 'And the favour I owed to my mother's friend is discharged. I'm now free to do as I like.'

'Oh, you're free to do as you like,' Anika parroted.

They exchanged a significant look, which Mateo took as part of their quiet courtship. Oh. Of course. Jonas had plenty of reason to still visit, and Mateo was still being selfish to be just as dismayed by that realisation.

He was surprised, and horrified, when they both then looked to him, as if for permission. But, leaving aside the appalling notion that one or both had noticed his inappropriate and hopefully temporary crush on his Imperial friend, here was a chance to not be selfish.

'You should do as you like,' he said. 'Definitely.'

'Well, then.' Anika smiled over at Jonas, and lounged back into the cushions with unusual self-satisfaction.

'It calls for a proper celebration, what do you think, Ana?' Andrea asked.

'Yes, go on.'

Andrea fetched a bottle from behind the kitchen, and five tiny cups of delicately wrought metal, and Timon brought over ginger and honey tea for Mateo from the pot kept at a simmer at the back of the stove. He'd already had his evening dose of twice-daily tea.

The bottle, stoppered with wax, held a syrupy liquid the same luminescent amber as the ginger tea, and Ystheran magic, and Jonas's eyes. But it was nowhere near as innocuous. Andrea sliced it open and poured a dash for everyone except Mateo.

Jonas touched a drop of the liquor to his medallion before taking a sip. His eyes slipped closed in ruminative pleasure. 'My gods, you people—'

'You people,' the Taurasi chorused.

'You better believe I said "you people" this time,' Jonas proclaimed, as indignant as Mateo had ever heard him. 'You've been fobbing me off with pottery and weaving and you've had bottles of this behind the counter the whole time? You should have been building a distillery, Taurasi.'

'We can't make it,' Anika said. 'Apricot liquor was the specialty of Kindred Caprinasi. This is the last bottle.'

The Taurasi looked at each other. It was the last ever bottle. They'd tripped over the loss of Ysthera again.

'There's the real tragedy right there,' Jonas said cheerily.

'Excuse me, it is too soon to be making jokes about the destruction of our people,' Andrea said, though she did, in fact, sound amused, if reluctantly. Jonas had that effect.

'Who's joking? This is why you should write things down.'

Mateo huffed. 'Sorry we failed to anticipate the cataclysmic destruction of six-sevenths of our *klados.*'

He did not manage the same lightness of rebuke that Andrea had. Timon tipped his glass, willing to be indulgent towards their guest. 'Don't mind Mateo, being grouchy at you is how he shows he cares about you.'

'He must care about me *a lot*,' Jonas said, to the amusement of the others. Mateo felt his face heat. 'But, seriously. This is…' He held up his cup in deep admiration. 'This is bottled summer filtered through liquid silver.'

'My, that's lyrical for an Imperial,' Andrea said.

Jonas snorted. 'You all realise I'm just an Imperial subject, right? Heartland Imperials are the big, blond ones with the long swords and the formal language. I'm an empire mongrel. My Chalcadean grandfather was garrisoned here after Anceral was conquered. Not,' he added with a small smile, 'that she took much conquering. They're a seafaring people, we're a seafaring people; they had their false battle wizards, we had, ah, knowledge of true wizards'—his smile became cheeky as he saluted the Ystherans with a tip of his cup—'and we did warn them to not think of Ysthera as an eastwards stepping stone, by the way; they had a plethora of gods, we only had two more than them; they dangled a worldwide trade network at us… Oh, we slid right on into their embrace, especially once they decided they liked our villas more than their halls.'

Some of those old wooden halls still lay under oak and over spring, quietly decaying on the western outskirts of Anceral, by a burial mound said to hold the narrow ship and treasure horde of an ancestral king. If he'd been local, he'd have been called a chieftain. The whole area was desolate, said to be haunted.

'Other peoples have not had quite the same consensual experience in their grapple with the Imperials,' Timon said, though not too harshly. He was still mellow from his mysterious outing and the liquor, and didn't look like he planned to start being too belligerent about an argument that was close to his heart.

Jonas made a thoughtful noise. 'Yes, the Imperials have committed atrocities in their bid for empire. Two hundred years ago was a different world. It'll be different again in two hundred more years. I can't even imagine what two thousand years will bring. Would they slaughter us locals wholesale if we pushed back too much against the governor and the tithing? Possibly, but they'd really rather not, so they try not to give us too much reason to push back. We're at equilibrium, and it's not a terrible place to be.'

'You're saying we and them,' Mateo said, 'but you're quite…'

Almost absently, he spread his palm over the rough weave of cloth covering Jonas's bicep, where the Imperial ash was inked. He looked up to see his Coterie staring at him.

He snatched his hand back, and excused himself with perhaps too much haste. 'I saw the tree rune when he was half-naked.'

Jonas laughed. 'When I was wearing a traditional outfit as dictated by my religion?'

'That too,' Mateo muttered. 'If you wear the tree-of-life symbol, and the other ones—'

'What other ones?' Andrea asked.

'Oh, I have to be a bit more than half-naked for you to see *those* ones, madam. Kith.'

The Coterie returned to staring at Mateo with renewed interest.

'I haven't *seen* them, he's told me about them! And they are very Imperial.'

'Most of them, sure,' Jonas said readily. 'The wayfinder for my mother's ship, and the helm of awe because you won't find a sailor who doesn't ink that protection somewhere on their body.'

Where is it, Timon mouthed at Mateo, because Jonas had delivered that last snippet with half-lidded eyes and a smile that outright encouraged the question. Mateo scowled and took a sulky mouthful of ginger tea, once again greatly amusing the arseholes who were meant to be his friends.

'This one isn't runic.' Jonas bent his knee. Turning his ankle, he slid his trouser leg up, revealing his muscular calf and the seashell inked there. 'A nod to my father's side. The Chalcadean symbol of eternal life.'

Mateo looked; Anika looked; Andrea, who didn't like men that way, looked; and even Timon, who didn't like *anyone* that way, looked. Jonas took another sip, smiling around at them, basking in the silent appreciation of his shapely form.

'The ash tree,' Mateo insisted, more sharply than he'd meant to. The effort of wrenching his gaze away from the long muscles of the man's well-formed calf had disconcerted him. 'That can't be anything other than a full endorsement of the empire.'

'My father's grandfather was a child-slave in Chalcadea, with no path to freedom,' Jonas said. 'He could hardly decry the invasion that liberated him. He lived a life he would not have had, his freeborn son had the opportunity to travel the empire with the garrisons, and *his* son, my father, gets to use his intellect and compassion as a physician instead of labouring as a slave in a salt mine. So, yes, honey, I proudly wear the tree.'

'It's like he sets me up to seem as rude and unreasonable as possible,' Mateo said to the other Taurasi, though he was still fairly convinced Jonas could follow the Ystheran.

Andrea smiled at him. 'Does he set you up, *honey*, or do you set yourself up?'

'Oh no, Anika, now we have to demote Andrea as well.' While his Coterie were laughing, Mateo turned to Jonas, smiling to himself as he drained his cup. 'Sorry.'

'What for, Mateo?'

'You know, being me.'

'Who is in your ear telling you you're not delightful just as you are, because it's not your friends here, is it?'

Mateo, disconcerted yet again, blurted, 'They have to tolerate me, I'm their Soul.'

This earned an immediate outcry from Anika and the others. In the fuss, Timon refilled Jonas's cup to brimming, and the others' cups too, though Darius, ever on duty and nursing his first cup with sips the size of raindrops, waved the bottle away.

Jonas took a generous sip and picked up the thread of the meandering discussion. 'Of course, my father's people faced the same choice you Ystherans did when the Vaer came knocking.' He abruptly tossed back his cup in a single swallow. 'Except they didn't decide to, you know, trade their chance at eternal reward for sorcery to hold off the invasion.'

'They might have,' Mateo said, instantly irritable again, 'if they'd had any magic at all to give them the option.'

'A very strange tack for you to take, honey, given the Taurasi famously chose to exile themselves from Ysthera rather than take that option.'

Mateo glanced at him and away. Jonas was correct. Mateo was being bloody-minded in arguing for the use of sorcery, which the Taurasi had been, perforce, loudly public about repudiating when they'd arrived in Anceral.

He'd been with Sabine and the majority of the Taurasi when they'd voted to keep their small and domesticated household magic rather than grasp for the raw, deep, dangerous wild magic needed to not merely hold off the mighty empire once again agitating at their doorstep, but to permanently repel it. He'd been standing beside Sabine and Charion when the six other Hearts had justly spat at them for Kindred Taurasi's betrayal.

Ysthera, for five hundred years, had been at peace because all Kindreds agreed to follow identical strictures. The Taurasi, riven between breaking that concord or breaking their holy promise, cleaved to the latter as the higher claim. They hadn't chosen to exile themselves. They'd had no choice but exile.

Timon shifted, finally sitting up. 'To stand and die fighting,' he said, 'or bow to the empire and watch our way of life die by a thousand cuts.' He added, with distaste, 'Stylus cuts,' because Ystherans, after all, cherished their oral storytelling tradition and saw no use in the endless bureaucracy of Imperial recordkeeping.

Anika casually tapped the floor beside her cushion with her knuckles. Timon straightened further. 'The second choice, of course! We are endlessly grateful that the empire extended refuge to the Taurasi.'

'You don't need to tell me that,' Jonas said, laughing. 'You think Chalcadeans aren't still telling their children bedtime stories in the old language, following old recipes and old customs, doing their best to preserve a way of life from a hundred or more years ago? Empires fade, my friends, empires fade.'

'On that cheerful note…' Anika murmured.

She looked across at Mateo, who understood she wanted him to change the subject. Jonas could pretend indifference to treasonous talk as he liked; he wasn't heartland Imperial, but he was still Imperial, assimilated into the empire and grateful for it. He couldn't think of anything to say.

Timon leapt in the wrong direction. 'They don't, though.' At Jonas's raised eyebrows, he went on recklessly. 'They don't just fade away. They overextend, and are harried at their edges, and collapse. And if your Chalcadeans are going to sit back and let other people do the harrying, they'll be Imperial subjects for another hundred years and more. Holy Remnants, as if they could preserve their culture with *lullabies.*'

Mateo held his breath but Jonas merely smiled, making a seesawing gesture with his free hand. 'So they rise up and fight, and by some miracle they win, and the Imperial garrisons fall back to protect the heartland, and then what happens? The Chalcadeans might fall to fighting among themselves, right up until the next invaders sweep on in—bearing in mind the Vaer united to prevent an invasion in the first place, from this very region, in fact. Or Chalcadea might return to the old ways after all, and that's not necessarily for the best either—remember, they had slavery. *Everywhere* had slavery, until the first empress said no.'

The Taurasi bowed their heads, acknowledging the point, which Jonas should not have had to make again. Slavery was anathema, only slightly less an appalling blight than the idea of using the gift of their goddess to hurt another person. If the Vaeringan Empire, perhaps destined to fade like other empires before it, could be remembered for one good thing, it would the outlawing of slavery across its dominion.

'You do have to allow that, in some ways, the empire has brought benefits,' Jonas added, looking between Mateo and Timon as if he knew very well they would allow no such thing.

Timon predictably scoffed. 'Tell me what they've done for us that they didn't first take away from us. Stop glaring at me, Anika, he likes it.'

'I do,' Jonas said. 'I'm not the argumentative sort—'

'Neither am I!' Mateo protested, since Jonas had flickered a glance his way.

'I didn't say you were, honey.'

'There was a look.'

'There was no look.' Jonas lifted his hands, smiling. 'I insist, I'm not argumentative—'

'Definitely a look that time,' Timon murmured helpfully, and Andrea elbowed him.

'—but I do enjoy a robust exchange of opinion. And look, sure, for just about any technological advantage I could name, Ysthera had magic in its place, so I'd feel hard done by in that regard, too. But Ysthera was increasingly insular in a modern world. No literacy, limited trade, no embassies... Do you know what happens when you're the only people with magic in all the world, Taurasi? Everyone decides you're elves who may or may not actually exist.'

'Fine with us,' Mateo said, 'if it'd meant the empire's marines forgot we existed as well.' Timon nodded, but Anika and Andrea didn't.

'All right.' Jonas touched the contract scroll, still on the table. 'Peace, my friends. We're arguing over the fates of homelands none of us will see again. We can't go back. So we move forwards in the world we have. That means letting the past inform us, but not rule us.'

'You must see our hurts are very much closer than yours,' Mateo said, before his brain could remind his tongue of the loss of *Steadfast*.

'I concede your past is more recent than mine,' Jonas said easily. 'Still can't be changed.'

'Our future can be,' Timon said.

'Our future lies together in Anceral, where our benevolent conquerors rule us with the lightest of hands.'

'If you have to specify benevolence,' Andrea muttered, '...are they?'

Jonas smiled. 'Make the best of it, my little elves, you might have washed up in a worse refuge.'

Timon set down his cup with a sharp click, brow furrowed, thoroughly roused. His Ystheran accent had thickened, its melodic swoops made ugly by the anger of his words. 'The empire indisputably harmed us, and I'm not going to wave it away with a "get over it, it could've been worse". We lost the whole island, and that's pretty fucking *worse*, Jonas.'

Anika murmured Timon's name, low, as she took up the bottle and tipped another dollop into Jonas's cup. Even Mateo winced. He could not bring himself to *entirely* blame the abstract empire for the fate of the Ystherans who had turned to blighted magic against their goddess's interdiction.

Their Imperial guest, however, remained perennially unoffended. 'You're right, Timon. They have done great harm, for questionable good.' He paused. 'Do you think the emperor lies awake at night, worried about you being right? Does it make you feel better, to be right?'

Timon face flushed, opened his mouth, then shut it abruptly. Mateo was willing to wager his Heart or his sister had just kicked him.

'I would never tell any of you to just get over it,' Jonas added with a warm earnestness. 'I'm suggesting moving on in your own time, and in a way that lets you heal and help others heal, and with thought to future safety and freedom. And future joy, too. Don't forget that.'

Something about those last words, or Anika's increasingly vehement frown, shifted Timon from his stubborn sullenness. Expression almost guilty, he gave a stiffly conciliatory, 'Peace.' He raised his cup. 'I do understand you intend well, my friend.'

Jonas lifted his own cup in silent accord, and they all shared a slightly awkward toast.

'I don't see why we shouldn't try to distil this,' Andrea said suddenly, holding up the bottle and then topping Jonas off again. 'I've been working at the brewery down the hill long enough to have a go at it.'

'Distilling's like brewing,' Jonas agreed, possibly relieved to let the topic turn—although relief was likely another of those pointless emotions he so readily dismissed.

Or perhaps he was already tipsy. They were only a quarter of the way down the bottle, but he'd been receiving frequent refills and it was strong stuff.

'I bet you could, Dee.' Timon also seemed willing to be turned to safer ground, with body and accent softening as he settled back into good humour. 'It's just apricots.'

'Mostly,' Andrea said judiciously.

Anika looked briefly saddened. 'And it's not like we're stealing the recipe off Kindred Caprinasi.'

Timon said, 'Though we've only got the little patch of land between the bathhouse and the back fields left and I was thinking of building a cottage for our Soul there.'

He shot a glance at Anika and received an approving nod, but Mateo said in surprise, 'I don't need that.'

'We really just need a simple still set up under shelter,' Andrea said. 'You could put a shed behind the apple tree, and we could plant an apricot orchard there too. We could…get around the lack of sunshine at that end of the street.' She meant with magic.

Timon nodded; it seemed both twins were intent on ignoring Mateo's continued demurrals until Timon turned to him to say, 'You can't live under Madam Kerling's gimlet eye forever.'

'Not to be morbid…' When no one helped him finish the thought, Mateo was forced to spell it out. 'As much as she might seem it, she's hardly immortal. Her heir, whoever it is, will either be more reasonable, or be willing to sell.'

Timon pulled an odd face. 'How many more years are you willing to abide by her rules, Teo?'

'They don't bother me.'

'Might they not *start* bothering you?' Anika asked him gently.

He shook his head in bemusement, while the Coterie exchanged a cryptic round of looks.

They and Jonas then turned to careful sips of the liquor while they tried to parse out the flavours. Anika was, of course, quite practiced at this with her tisanes, but the others indulged in a great deal of florid pronouncement—'Hazelnuts! Overtones of hazelnuts!' 'There's no hazelnuts, you dolt.'—while all four became fully, wonderfully, intoxicated.

Peace, indeed. Mateo had cause to exchange several amused glances with the silently watchful, yet increasingly relaxed, Darius.

At last, Andrea confiscated the bottle, with the last third thickly sloshing, to save for taste tests against her distillation attempts. Jonas scooped the dregs of his tiny cup with a supple hook of his little finger, and licked out the very last drop with his tongue.

Dexterous. That was the word Mateo was suddenly struggling to recall in any language at his disposal.

'All right.' Jonas set the cup down and stretched. 'This has been exceptionally pleasant, my lovely little elves, but I should start for home.'

'You shouldn't walk home in your condition,' Anika said lazily. She flopped back against the cushions between the twins. 'I'll make you up a pallet, you can sleep by the stove.'

'No, no, I'm fine,' Jonas wobbled to his feet. 'By and large. And I can hardly ask the equivalent of a king to make me a bed.'

'We don't stand on ceremony here,' said Andrea.

'Not these days, anyway,' added Timon. 'Otherwise we'd all be on our knees every time Mateo walked in.'

Mateo hushed the drunken fool, but Jonas looked at them with half-lidded eyes. 'You *should* all get on your knees when Mateo walks in,' he opined with drunken gravity. 'He's a shining glory, this one.'

He swayed over, quite dangerously, kissed Mateo on the very top of his head, and, muttering some Imperial slang under his breath, staggered past Darius in the direction of the back door out to the privy.

Mateo turned from staring after Jonas in confusion to discover three unblinking gazes fixed on him with the intensity of the slightly sozzled.

'What?'

Timon said, 'I think we have to tell him.'

'He likes you, Teo,' said Anika.

'He does not.'

'He's flirting with you constantly,' said Timon.

'What? He's not flirting with me.'

'He doesn't call anyone else honey, honey.'

'Yes, he does!' Mateo paused. 'Doesn't he?'

'Or a shining glory, for that matter, honey,' Andrea said.

'He called me stern and controlling.' This was, from the reaction, not quite the convincing negatory evidence Mateo had thought it would be. 'And he's interested in Anika.'

All three howled with laughter for an unconscionable length of time.

'Definitely isn't,' Anika said. 'He's interested in my herblore. No, it's all you, *honey*.'

'Shush, he's coming back.' He wasn't, quite, but Mateo wanted the conversation to end forthwith.

'We're speaking Ystheran,' Andrea said.

'He was a trader, he understands Ystheran.'

They all scoffed. Anika waited until Jonas really did come back and was in earshot before asking, still in Ystheran, 'Mateo, is Jonas flirting with you?'

'No,' Mateo said crossly. 'I already told you. And stop it, by every single lost and holy Remnant, he understands us.'

'Absolutely not flirting?' Anika said, ignoring his scowl in favour of closely watching Jonas, who was smiling at them all with the indiscriminate sociability of the most affable of drunks.

'Absolutely not. He's just friendly. That's…that's just how his face looks.'

'He cannot understand us, my sweet, because if he could, he would whack you across the back of the head for being obtuse.'

'No, that's what *you* would do.' Mateo rose. 'Sorry, Jonas, we're being *very* rude.' The others just laughed to his glare. 'I'll walk you to the road.'

'Sure, honey,' Jonas said. 'I'd like that.'

Darius stood too, but Mateo waved him back down; it was a small miracle, or a sign of how far along the amiable Imperial had come in the trust of the Taurasi, that his guardian obeyed.

Outside, the air was cold and misty, and Mateo was shivering by the time he'd slipped into his sandals, even ensconced in his quilted jacket off the hook by the teahouse door. Jonas, back in his cloak, put a comfortable arm around his shoulders, somehow managing to tuck him into his solid warmth despite being slightly shorter. They walked together to the mouth of Ravenser Odd under the amber glow of the eternal light, diffusing in gold fragments in the mist.

'Thanks for the lovely evening, Mateo,' Jonas murmured.

'Are you sure you're all right to walk all the way home?' Mateo asked him. 'It'll be very dark, beyond the eternal light.'

The city streets were generally set with large white stones, known as tiger's eyes, to catch the moonlight and help people find their way, but they would be no use in the mist, which would only become thicker as Jonas descended from Ravenser Odd. Mateo realised he didn't even know what quarter of the city Jonas lived in. The man had become a familiar presence so quickly, and deflected their curiosity so well with his own, that Mateo had forgotten he never did get around to asking those polite small-talk questions.

'I'll pick up a link-lamp at the bottom of the hill. Unless you're offering me a bed?'

'We don't have beds, we have sleeping platforms with mattresses and bedding.'

Jonas sniggered. 'Offering me a bedding?'

'Um.' Mateo, still tucked against him—just for the warmth—gave him a careful look. 'Anika offered you a bed.'

They were face-to-face, and felt even closer as Jonas said, 'Yes, but are *you* offering me a bed, honey?'

'If...you...want...one?' Mateo said, entirely unsure if he was currently engaged in flirtation or not.

The teasing of his Coterie had got into his head; Jonas, he reminded himself, was sweetly inebriated on top of being congenitally good-natured, and it must be very annoying to have friendliness mistaken for more, especially by the likes of Mateo, who was so far on the other end of the scale from congenitally good-natured that he'd fallen off it.

'Hmm. If we're talking about what I want...' Jonas brushed Mateo's hair with the back of one hand, knuckles skimming over the end-of-day loosened strands. His amber eyes had caught the diffused radiance from the eternal light; they were almost aglow. 'I'd rather talk about what *you* want.'

Transfixed, Mateo got out, 'What…do…*I*…want?' with agonising slowness.

Jonas smiled, then, and shook himself, breaking his intent focus. He moved so that he was still keeping Mateo warm, but wasn't quite so close. 'Let me know when you know. Hey, does it bother you when the lodging girls call you Theo?'

Mateo wondered if Timon had slipped some of the liquor into his ginger tea, since he was having so much trouble keeping up. He shook his head.

'I thought that sort of nickname was for close family. Or, you know, close friends. If you find it presumptuous, I could talk to them for you?'

'They're pronouncing it wrong, so it's fine. It's Teo.' Mateo said it the proper way, *Tay-o*.

'Teo,' Jonas repeated softly, rolling the intimate name over his tongue so it was honey-slow in the middle. 'Nice.'

A flutter rolled in response, deep in Mateo's stomach. 'Jonas, you can call—'

Something moved below them in the mist, and he recoiled, a sharp flick of panic shooting through him in concert with the pang of his hip.

'It's people,' Jonas said, holding on to him. 'Just people. Not wish hounds.'

People. A small crowd of them, coming up quietly from the city through the mist at this time of night. The only reason Mateo didn't rapidly retreat to the teahouse was because Jonas still had an arm around him. His free hand, however, was on the hilt of his knife, his seax, for all he'd claimed he'd only used it on rope and fish, and he somehow shifted his stance to seem much bigger.

Physician? part of Mateo asked dubiously. *Trader?*

He suddenly remembered how piratical Jonas had seemed, that first day he'd walked into the teahouse, how close to menacing Mateo had found him, only a few weeks before.

'Should I call for Darius?' Jonas asked in his ear.

They were Ystherans, Mateo realised, as the shadowy figures emerged from the mist, eight or nine of them, distinctively petite and fine-boned, round-faced, black-haired, dark-eyed. His first thought was that the handful of solitary Ystherans in the city had briefly banded together to either lay a petition to the Taurasi or outright attack them to drive them away. The tale of the shadow-dog would have frightened them beyond reason. It should have occurred to Mateo to visit them, or send someone to visit them.

And then he stiffened as their faces came clear. At that, Jonas turned and shouted, 'Uncle!'

The leader stopped short when he saw Mateo, and went to his knees, and laid his forehead to his hands, outstretched before him upon the ground, a full obeisance followed instantly by the others.

'Shard of the Divine,' he said in High Ystheran, speaking Mateo's archaic title reverently into the hard clay of Ravenser Odd.

Mateo found his tongue. '*Elias?*'

CHAPTER 12

IT TOOK SOME TIME TO BE rid of Jonas, since Mateo had announced Elias's name with far more consternation than joy, promptly overriding Jonas's usual facility for presciently taking his leave. It took Darius, materialising at Mateo's elbow, and then Anika's reassurances, before he finally accepted that this was perfectly normal Taurasi business, or at least none of his, and headed off down the hill, far more sober than he had been.

'Do you think he realised they're not local Ystherans?' Mateo asked Anika as together they led the small group—the Gallasi auxiliary Coterie, it looked like, and a few others, though none of the ones who had attacked on the day of the exile—into the teahouse.

Anika made a noncommittal sound. She didn't want it known around the city that more refugees had arrived in the wake of the destruction of Ysthera, and so, without outright lying, had implied to their easy-going Imperial friend that this was just a late visit—from local Ystherans—for some ritual they were being coy about.

Jonas was not the suspicious type, but he certainly hadn't looked happy as he'd left. And if they'd arrived en masse by ship, there would be no holding back the news. Though, on that note, Mateo could not sense the presence of another Soul within the usual bounds that they could sense one another, roughly twice the distance between Ystheran villages.

He frowned. Supporting a whole second Kindred would tax him, if their own Soul was not functional.

'Where are the rest of you?' Anika asked Elias. She'd also be thinking about rumours scattering like rats from the docks.

'This is all of us,' Elias said. He sounded exhausted.

The Taurasi looked at each other in silent shock. It had never crossed their minds that if the Gallasi Coterie could get clear of the destruction of the island, they wouldn't bring the whole Kindred out. It had never crossed their minds that if only a few Gallasi could escape, they would do so, abandoning their people, their children, their *Soul*.

Elias looked hurt, and a little angry, at their confused silence. 'We had no choice. You don't know… You *can't* know what it was like.'

If he had been Taurasi, Anika would have put a soothing hand on his shoulder, but as it was, he was Gallasi, *phalaros* from a lost island, and so she merely raised her hand in a quelling gesture.

'What do your people need most?' she asked. 'Food, sleep, healing?'

They needed everything, it turned out, and Andrea roused more of the Taurasi so they could all set to work, putting together a quick meal, setting up extra sleeping spaces in the insula, bringing bowls of warm water for washing, addressing the physical wounds and travails of their escape from the sinking island and their long journey here.

By then, Anika had barely pried any more information from Elias, except to learn they'd made landfall somewhere south and come overland, off the roads, north to cold Anceral. That was a relief; there'd be no gossipy sailors spreading tales, at least.

The Gallasi were falling asleep over their bowls. The Taurasi helped them to bed.

The newcomers slept all the next day, through the morning meeting, which buzzed with questions, and through the morning ritual, and through the daily routine and the midday meal and the afternoon teahouse Imperial crowd, which Anika monitored extra closely. The fuss about the wish hounds had just about died away, and there were no rumours about sorcerous refugees.

The teahouse was full for the evening meal when the Gallasi haltingly made their way over from the insula, after a long visit to the baths, reported on breathlessly by the excited Taurasi children. His people arrayed behind him, Elias knelt before the Taurasi Coterie, making a low formal bow.

'First things first,' Anika said. 'Are you well? What more do you need?'

'Your shelter and your care has been ample.' Elias was looking better; all the Gallasi looked rested, and more alert, washed and in clean clothes, colour returning to their wan cheeks. 'We need only the dawn ritual, which we humbly beg leave to attend tomorrow.'

'Morning ritual, and naturally,' Anika said; she and Mateo had already anticipated and mutually decided to grant the request. 'Were the shadow-dogs yours?'

Elias blinked. 'Shadow-dogs?' he repeated slowly, voice thickening.

The Gallasi exchanged uneasy glances behind him. They'd been longingly eyeing off the bowls of soup and plates of sliced fruit lined up on the kitchen counter, and had clearly been taken unawares by the abrupt question and Anika's brutally brisk attitude, honed by years within the Imperial embrace. The Coterie had discussed this approach, too.

'We were attacked, a week or so ago,' Anika went on mercilessly. 'You, yes?'

'Yes,' said Elias. He had no choice; a lie would have been too apparent, thanks to Anika's blunt ambush. 'I suppose it must have been. They followed us from Ysthera, but then they disappeared. We thought… But they must have sensed the Soul as we approached Anceral, and rushed on ahead. We didn't think…' He turned to Mateo. 'I'm so sorry.'

Anika stood poised for a moment of thought that must have felt agonising to the refugees. Then she nodded towards the food. The Gallasi collected their bowls in something just short of a stampede. They knelt on cushions in a cluster near the rear of the teahouse to eat, but Elias, with the air of a man bravely resigned to his fate, knelt with the Coterie around their usual table.

They let him eat in peace, but afterwards, when normally the Taurasi with storytelling or musical talents would entertain their people, Anika instead lifted her hand and opened it towards him, an invitation which was by no means optional. Elias bowed, still stiffly formal, and began to speak into a fraught silence.

He was hesitant at first. 'Do you want to know just about the sinking of Ysthera, or should I start from the day you ran away?'

'We're aware of what happened on the day your father and his Coterie tried to murder us as we peacefully emigrated,' Anika said, eyes cold, cutting off a discontented murmur from the Taurasi. 'Feel free to begin your story after that point.'

'Goodness, three years of living in the empire has made you direct,' Elias said. 'I will be so, as well. I know you and I have not always gotten along'—he cast a meaningful sort of look towards Mateo, who frowned in confusion—'but I think you should try, given our circumstances.'

'Oh, yes? And I think you are presuming far too much if you think Taurasi intends to open its arms to you without hesitation.'

'We're Ystherans,' Elias said, sounding genuinely stunned. 'We're refugees, just like you were. We've travelled weeks to reach you.' When Anika did not appear moved, he added, 'We *renounce* unbound magic, of course we do. Succumbing to the blight of the temptation to use it was the biggest mistake we ever made.'

There came a distinct lessening of tension among the Taurasi, including the twins sitting silent and stern beside Anika. Darius, kneeling by the Coterie as always, did not relax. Neither did Anika.

'We would agree with that,' she said. 'Continue, then.'

'After…that day, all the Souls eventually opened themselves to wild magic, and fed it to us. It was— Well. I can't deny it felt good.' He spread his hands with a disarming smile. 'No. It felt *amazing*. We were gods.'

The Taurasi gasped, and some cried out in protest.

'It went wrong!' Elias called. 'I'm just telling you what it was like at first. We all felt so very powerful. We were immensely, arrogantly, pleased with ourselves, and positively thrilled to see the empire's blockade grow ever thicker. We couldn't wait till their fleet tried to land their marines on our shores. We even sent out attacks on some of the ships.'

Mateo remembered Jonas, speaking of the loss of *Steadfast* with casual calm. *Gods are fickle fuckers, sometimes.* 'Just Imperial warships?'

'Of course. But it was at a distance, unsatisfying. We wanted to *fight*. Yes. Yes.' He nodded around the teahouse and the shocked Taurasi. 'Such power begs to be used; you can't imagine the sheer *pressure* to use it. It was the wait that destroyed us. All that power, all that waiting, months and months of it. Some of us started jostling for position. Which kith made the best Heart, which Heart would lead all the Kindreds, that sort of thing. There were…duels.'

Elias was lost in his story now, gaze abstracted, unaffected by the continued quiet reactions of the Taurasi hearing heresy after heresy, quintessential blight. 'Some of the Coteries were destroyed, and the kith of those Kindreds fought over who would take their place. Then we didn't even need Coteries anymore, because we all had our hands in an endless well of power and no one was weaker than any other. And once we'd tasted it, we wanted more and more. Some of the Souls began to die. Others began to crack. Some began to declare we'd done wrong, and we forced—' His voice failed. 'We forced them. Then Sabine—'

Mateo inhaled sharply, and he wasn't the only one.

The communal gasp was enough to jolt Elias from the grim tale. He looked around, wide-eyed. 'Did you not know Sabine survived falling off your cart?

'We did not,' Andrea said, when even Anika couldn't answer.

'She tried to resist, but in the end, she was with the other Souls, giving us her magic.'

Mateo pushed to his feet. He was still staring at Elias, stricken to his core. The pain was almost physical. Sabine hadn't fallen, like Elias said. She'd been snatched from the cart, taken by a shadow-dog. They had presumed her dead. They had left her. They had left her behind, and she'd turned to wild magic.

He blindly stumbled away, seeking no particular place except solitude, and Anika intercepted him, wrapping her arms around him. Her low, calm voice was in his ear. 'We didn't know. We couldn't have known.'

'I should have known. I should have felt her. I should have—'

He remembered, then, his formless plea for more magic, on the day of the exile, and the stir he thought he'd felt in response. He'd wondered if it could have been his sleeping goddess, responding to his desperate need. But now he knew Sabine hadn't been killed outright, that feeling was far more likely to have been—had almost certainly been—

He rocked in distress, and felt Anika's arms tighten, and more arms coming around them: Timon and Andrea. His Coterie held him as he fought his way to calm; this was a shameful display in front of his grieving people who needed him to be as strong as Anika.

'Send everyone out,' Anika whispered to Timon.

'No!' Mateo wriggled free. He wiped his eyes. 'I'm fine. I'm fine. Sorry. Elias, you may continue.'

'Are you sure?' Elias asked solicitously. 'If it's too much for you, sweetling…'

'To know we left our Soul pains us all,' Anika said. 'As losing your own Soul on the day Ysthera sank must have hurt you.'

It was a subtle but unkind rebuke, and the Taurasi, already appalled, turned startled eyes on their Heart. She raised a hand in an apology aimed more at her people than at Elias, who had meekly bowed his head as if under a lash. Mateo straightened his shoulders and knelt back on the cushions, watched by the entire teahouse. His Coterie surrounded him.

All humble compliance, Elias went on, 'You can infer that we lost the island just how our ancestors lost our original homeland, to the endless, incessant infighting of powerful people in too small of a space. The Gallasi were lucky. We got to a boat in time. We got away.'

'The Gallasi?' Timon's question was fair. If they had lost most of the

Kindred to an Imperial retaliation on the mainland, the Taurasi needed to know what might be coming in their wake.

'*We* got away,' Elias repeated, pointing at the cluster of newcomers at the back of the teahouse. Into the silence that greeted that, he said, 'We saw it all from the water. The mountain cracked open like the wrath of the Shattered One fell upon it in a single blow. It split the island in two. The sea boiled and steamed. The— The—'

He abruptly dropped his head into his hands. The Taurasi made sounds of sympathy and concern. Some moved towards the Gallasi, kneeling with them, touching their shoulders. Anika refrained from rolling her eyes but she did send a frustrated look towards Mateo, who shrugged in helpless agreement. Elias, a man of charm and quick intelligence, had always been artful.

Elias lifted his chin to continue, radiating stoic courage for his audience. 'We used the last of our magic to escape the eddies and rough waters of the sinking, and made landfall as soon as we could. Then we made for Ingelrii on foot, engaging in beggary and petty theft to sustain us.'

'Ah,' Anika said.

'Yes. The expulsion of the foreigners and the redoubled blockade cut us off from all news. We had no idea you'd changed plans. We'd reached the Ingelrii outskirts before we heard you'd come to Anceral instead. You can't know… You will never know how grateful we are to have arrived at last.'

Elias fell then, onto his face, in full prostration. 'Shard of the Divine, you will never know the depths of our regret. Our goddess gave us Souls to keep Her magic tame and we learnt that truth to the bitter blighted dregs. We beg leave to join Kindred Taurasi as penitents, our promise to the Shattered One renewed.'

The Coterie had also expected this. Anika once again surprised their kith by pausing for far too long, flint in her dark eyes, before finally saying, 'Of course.'

She rose and addressed the Taurasi. 'I know this has been shocking. To know that Sabine—' She cut it off. 'But it lightens some of the weight to know we can provide refuge for other survivors. I ask that you retire from the teahouse now. But please, spend time with each other tonight if you need it, and find me tomorrow after the morning ritual if you want to talk.'

The night bells in the city below were tolling as the Taurasi made their way out, taking the other Gallasi with them. Mateo counted the peals. It was three bells since sunset in Anceran time. The water-clock, when he checked, said it was just past the twentieth hour of an Ystheran day. It was an early night for the Kindred.

The others went into the kitchen, making up a brewpot of ginger honey tea for Mateo, opening a jar of wine, slicing figs.

Alone together for a moment, Elias smiled at Mateo. 'Morning ritual? What happened to dawn?'

'Holy Remnants, we'd all be miserable if we tried to force Teo out of bed too early,' Timon called over as he splashed wine into four cups.

Elias, leaning comfortably back on one elbow, slowly raised his eyebrows at Mateo, mouth turning up at the corners. Mateo flinched. Elias hadn't actually been so unsubtle as to call him selfish, but that was the message he received from the familiar look.

Anika knelt beside him to put his pot on the table. 'Trying a spoon of turmeric in with the ginger, tell me if you like it.' Her gaze lingered on his face, and then she turned on Elias. 'Did you say something to Mateo?'

'Are kith not allowed to talk directly to the Soul in this Kindred?' Elias asked innocently.

Anika said, 'You're not doing this again, Elias.'

'Doing what?'

'He didn't say anything,' Mateo said. Elias *hadn't* said anything. It was Mateo's sensitivities making him overreact. 'Anika, I'm fine.'

'Did anyone else make it off?' Andrea asked Elias, setting the plate of figs in front of him, giving Anika a puzzled frown as she did so. 'Did you see other boats?'

'No. It was too sudden. Too chaotic. We were lucky.'

Timon set the tray of drinks down and took the cushion next to Andrea, who'd settled beside Elias. 'Lucky you had magic left to help you escape?'

'Well. Yes, I suppose. I know you don't want to hear it, but wild magic is not in itself blighted, no matter what the elders used to say. It's just...overwhelming. It was our actions that tainted it, nothing inherently evil within itself. When we— When my father began to force the Souls—' He made a display of choking, shame suffusing him. 'I'll never forgive myself for going along with it.'

Mateo turned his cup slowly, looking at the butterflies. 'Did Sabine die thinking we'd abandoned her?'

Elias rushed to reassure him. 'No, no, not at all. She was very strong. You must all miss her very much. You'll never see her like again.'

Mateo nodded, but Anika put her hand lightly on his back. 'We have her like right now,' she said, that touch of cool rebuke back in her tone.

'Yes, of course. Though…' He trailed delicately off.

Anika shifted her hand to Mateo's knee, a firm squeeze there disallowing him from walking into the trap. Timon, unaware it had been set, said, 'What?'

'Only three in the Coterie? Shouldn't it be at least five by now, for a Soul of any great calibre?'

Mateo looked down, fighting shame. Anika's hand was still on his knee, grip tightening. He put his own hand over hers, his turn to silently warn her about Elias's games.

But Timon just snorted, and Andrea gave one of her unexpected laughs. 'Oh, no,' she said. 'You've got it very wrong. We don't work quite how we did back on Ysthera. The whole Kindred is his Coterie. You'll see, when we make the shield at tomorrow's morning ritual.'

Mateo raised his gaze, astonished; he hadn't known that was how the Kindred thought of the communal shield. The twins offered him smiles and bows, and he felt his shoulders release. Elias would find it difficult to slither his way in here, he thought.

'I see.' Shifting slightly, Elias looked at them all, earnest. 'You know, the Taurasi are the true lucky ones. You said holding off the empire with wild magic could only lead to disaster, and you were proven right.'

Andrea raised her cup in silent salute. The other raised theirs, and Mateo raised his cup of ginger tea.

'To lost Ysthera,' Andrea toasted, and they echoed her.

Elias did too, but once he had taken a sip, he said, looking mostly at Timon, 'Though we cannot hold the unbound magic responsible for all of it. Domesticated magic would not have been enough to hold off the marine garrisons forever. Ysthera would have been lost anyway, to the endless empire instead of the endless waves. Even knowing what happened, some would say we were right to try to fight. All would have been lost anyway.'

Timon fidgeted and was silent. Anika said, 'And we'd have kept our promise to the Shattered One.'

Andrea leaned her shoulder into her brother's. 'And we'd still have our Sunlit Isle.'

'And a diminished way of life,' Elias said, 'under the thumb of the Imperials.'

He was an expert at speaking without words, and so his glance around the teahouse made the silent corollary plain. It was outrageous. The teahouse was their sanctuary. Andrea needed somewhere to come home to, Timon somewhere to structure his days, Anika somewhere to centre herself, Mateo somewhere to breathe. It was their sanctuary, and Elias sullied it with one sly look about, but none of them could challenge him on it because he hadn't actually said anything—and because at least one of them agreed with him.

'If they hadn't put all of us to the sword out of fear of our magic, and handed Ysthera over to colonists,' Timon couldn't help but say, and then quickly shook his head when Andrea leaned harder against him.

'You have no fear of similar here?' Elias asked. 'If they find out that Souls are the source of our magic…' He tsked. 'They'd have slaughtered every Soul on Ysthera.'

He smiled sympathetically at Mateo as if he hadn't just pointed out the death sentence that hung over him and Nikiti should Taurasi let its most secret of secrets slip.

It was brutal, but indisputable. It was also indisputable that Souls manifested in every generation. If the magic-fearing empire discovered the truth and committed efficient murder, it would destroy many of the Taurasi's traditions, perhaps enough to sunder much of what made them Ystheran, but it wouldn't eradicate magic.

'We have no fear of that here,' Anika said. 'We are Anceran citizens and protected by their laws just like any other citizen.'

'We might,' Andrea said, 'have washed up in a worse refuge.' She nodded to the others, knowing they'd pick up on the quote.

'Such trust,' Elias murmured. 'While they pick away at our language and our traditions and our practices and tempt our children with notions of easy wealth until they grow up to beg for crumbs from their overlords and forget all about their lost people.'

'You're saying nothing new, Elias,' Anika said tiredly.

Again Timon shifted uncomfortably; he was either disliking how much he agreed with Elias, or how much Elias sounded like him in his most bitter moments. He finished his cup with one gulp and stood.

'Appointment down the hill,' he muttered to their surprised looks.

For a man who had until recently never gone into the city, he was vanishing down there on a regular basis ever since sourcing Mateo's bandeaux. If he had been anyone else, Mateo would have suspected he'd met a performer at the theatre. He certainly seemed as embarrassed and secretive as someone heading to an illicit liaison.

On the heels of his departure, Andrea made her farewell bow, drawing Darius in her wake. Elias, however, lingered, looking between Anika and Mateo while they sipped the last of their cups, quietly confused by his presence; tradition dictated he should have left with the others.

'Do you need reminding where your quarters are?' Anika enquired eventually.

'I wish to address the Soul alone.'

'And why is that?'

Elias arched his eyebrows. 'May the kith not approach their Soul for private succour in this Kindred?'

They could; they were supposed to. They went to Anika instead, by community-wide but unspoken agreement. Mateo slipped his hand into Anika's and gripped tight, silently indicating his strong desire to not be left alone with Elias.

He hadn't lied when he had told Jonas that Elias hadn't treated him poorly. But it had been some ten years since their relationship, and with age and distance he recognised that he had dutifully fallen into it because of the opportunity for Taurasi to form a prestigious alliance with Gallasi. He hadn't had anything more than a mild attachment to Elias, driven mostly by feeling flattered he'd caught the Gallasi heir's eye, and—of course—worried in case Elias lost his reciprocal regard before the alliance was in place.

Which he had. Their relationship had died in the same moments as the formal agreement to alliance, not least because, just before Zanthas, Heart of Gallasi, had renounced the agreement, Elias had finagled Mateo into an outbuilding behind the Klados hall and taken him with oddly gleeful haste. In retrospect, it reeked of full knowledge of his father's intentions.

And there had been that little incident a few weeks before, that still made Mateo squirm in remembered shame.

Maybe he *had* lied when he'd said Elias hadn't treated him poorly, but only to himself.

'If he wishes it,' Anika said, 'but perhaps not so soon after you have given us such bad news so callously.'

Elias offered a thin smile. 'You have changed in your years under Imperial rule.'

Anika visibly bit back a response, no doubt along the lines of it not taking years in Anceral but a single day back on Ysthera to have changed her.

Her silence let Elias continue unchallenged. 'You used to at least try to be subtle in your dislike of me.' He turned to Mateo. 'That's why she used her influence with her father and Charion to break our agreed alliance.'

Mateo started. 'Gallasi broke it.'

'My father had an eye for politics.' Mateo's face must not have hidden his disgust at that ellipsis; Elias grimaced. 'Yes, well. He broke it because he knew Taurasi was about to, and he'd rather you were humiliated than us.'

'That's a convenient story.'

'And yet your Heart is being suspiciously quiet right now.'

Not wanting to give Elias the satisfaction—he was worse than Penelope for sowing dissension—Mateo reluctantly turned to Anika, who did indeed look apologetic, to the point of outright guilt.

She said, 'Feel free to fetch yourself more wine, Elias.'

When he'd gone, smiling, behind the counter, taking the tray of empty cups with him, Anika shifted closer to Mateo.

'It was after what you told me,' she said quietly. 'About what he did to you on his birthday.'

Mateo wrapped his arms around himself. 'You told your father— You told Charion and *Sabine*?'

'I had to, they wouldn't have broken the agreement unless they truly understood *why*—'

'No,' he said and shuffled back from her, ignoring the twinge in his hip at the unaccustomed motion.

His head was buzzing. He had told Anika about that horrible, embarrassing incident in *confidence*. He had been willing to oblige his Heart to make a coup of an alliance, smallest Kindred to largest. He'd been humiliated when Gallasi broke it, alleviated by quiet relief.

To discover that Anika had moved to protect him—and hadn't told him, like she *always* didn't tell him—and he'd felt *relief*, when all the prime Coterie must have known the whole story and looked at him with such *pity*. Layers and layers of disgrace and shame were falling upon him like successive winter snows, deeper and deeper: how Elias had treated him, how Gallasi had treated him, and Taurasi because of him, how *Anika* had coddled him, how the prime Coterie must have thought of him.

He lifted his head. 'I did not need your intervention then,' he said coldly, 'and I don't need it now. You may go, Aniketa.'

'Teo—'

'Go. A kith has requested a private consultation with the Soul, and I am granting it. You are dismissed.'

Arms folded, gaze down, he heard her soft exhalation. She rose. 'We'll talk tomorrow.'

'As I see fit.'

She paused, then bid both him and Elias a good night in her usual composed tones. He heard her footsteps go evenly up the stairs, and the door to her apartment overhead open and close.

Elias knelt on Anika's cushion, still warm from her body heat. He put his cup down, and Mateo's soul cup, full near to the brim with dark wine.

'Sorry for that,' Elias said, wearing his sincerest manner. 'Let's have a drink together, sweetling, it'll help you feel better.'

Mateo stared at the wine. Its surface looked oily. 'I don't drink wine, Elias.'

Elias covered his mouth. 'I'd forgotten.' His breathing rang heavy, then he bent over, folding into himself. 'Holy Remnants, I'd forgotten the Souls don't spoil the magic,' he moaned into his hands.

'I suppose the blighted didn't have to worry about that.'

Elias shook his head, still breathing hoarsely, and Mateo repented his caustic response. This grief looked raw, real. He put his hand to Elias's shoulder, and Elias instantly shifted into his arms.

Untouchable, Mateo started to say, since Elias's face nuzzling into his cheek and hands coming possessively about his waist suggested the Soul's sobriety wasn't the only tradition he needed reminding of.

Elias kissed him.

CHAPTER 13

Mateo had once enjoyed Elias's kisses, even if the rest of the business left him cold; it was how he'd usually ended up naked under the man, after all, reservations melted away under the expert application of his mouth.

And he'd been craving something like this—warm mouth, gentle caresses, intimate touch—in a way that had been almost entirely absent in the three years of the Taurasi exile. It was just unfortunate for Jonas he'd been the unwitting recipient of the craving.

Better, he supposed, to slake it somewhere slightly more appropriate.

And so, for an interval that had nothing of time or weight to it, Mateo softened into Elias's touch, the familiar taste and scent of the other man, making an obligingly appreciative sound against his lips as he deepened the kiss. Elias's fingers brushed over his skull, and then sank into his hair, pulling out pins and loosening it from its bun to spread in a glossy fan over his shoulders. He ran firm hands over Mateo's chest—the kiss hitched as he discovered Mateo had bound his breasts today—and then began to work at the knot of his sash.

Which was when Mateo remembered that letting Elias kiss him meant letting him have him. And he remembered that he hadn't, on balance, overly enjoyed being had by Elias.

Mateo started to pull back; Elias protested and tugged him closer again, fingers insistent in unravelling the sash. The movement jerked at Mateo, pinging the sore hip. He winced and pushed Elias away, rising and stepping stiffly away with one hand upraised in denial, the other pressed against his hip.

It had been quite well-behaved lately, between the stretching and the mandrake salve, and the renewed ache made him irrationally angry.

'What's the matter?' Elias asked.

Mateo pushed down on his hipbone, counterbalancing the pain like Jonas had demonstrated for him. 'Just—hip's hurting.'

'Come on, then,' Elias said, with a hint of impatience. 'Come lie down with me here on the cushions, then.' He held out his hand for Mateo.

'I don't want to.'

Mateo had meant to pause, to make it look like he was at least regretful about turning his erstwhile lover down, but it came out as a blurt, immediate and heartfelt. He absolutely did not want to lie down on those cushions with Elias.

Elias's eyes narrowed. 'Why not? You're not untouchable till I've officially joined the Taurasi tomorrow morning. This is our last chance. Come on.' He patted the cushion, more a command than an enticement.

Mateo did not point out that this logic felt very much like following the letter of the law rather than the spirit. It explained Elias's impatience. He said, firmer, 'Elias, I don't want to.'

Elias tsked. 'You used to be so biddable,' he said. 'Oh, don't get pissy, sweetling, you could be grateful for the attention. It's not like you have options here. Unless you're stooping to consort with the locals.' He laughed.

Like an open-handed gift from Anceral's plethora of gods, the teahouse door opened, and Jonas came in, politely barefoot, cloak a touch damp from the evening mist he must have walked up through, carrying a cheesecloth parcel in one hand and a bag looped over the wrist of the other.

'Evening, Taurasi,' Jonas called cheerfully over his shoulder, though he addressed the greeting and his glowing smile entirely to Mateo, so intent on him, and juggling his items while he shut the door, that he hadn't yet glanced around or noticed the deep quiet. 'Sorry to barge in, you know how I feel about lit lamps and unlatched doors. I brought up some of those pasties I told you about and some… Oh.'

He'd set the parcel and bag on Mateo's table by the ceramic stove and turned with his fingers on the clasp of his cloak, finally taking in the emptiness of the teahouse, Mateo standing at its centre, Elias in the far corner at the Coterie's low table.

Mateo momentarily saw the scene from his perspective, Mateo with loose hair, reddened lips, half-unravelled sash, Elias, straightening from his lounge upon the cushions and looking deeply annoyed at the interruption.

Jonas took half a step backwards, an unfamiliar expression on his face that Mateo, after a moment, decided must be chagrin. '*Really* sorry to barge in.'

Mateo saw salvation politely retreating out the door, and lunged after him, ignoring another pang from the tightening hip.

'Jonas, good evening,' he said, seizing his hand in the Imperial style. He manoeuvred close enough to say in his ear, 'Will you play along, my friend?'

'I'll play any game you like, Mateo,' Jonas murmured in a warm brush of air over his cheek.

This was the sort of friendly, imperturbable response he'd grown to expect from Jonas, and there was something about his suddenly husky tone and heavy-lidded eyes that encouraged Mateo further. He'd been about to kiss Jonas's cheek to give himself the excuse that a simple refusal did not provide, but he abruptly decided that kissing his mouth would be more convincing.

He half-expected Jonas to draw back, or make a surprised sound, or have some other reaction that would give the ploy away. Instead, when Mateo's lips touched his, Jonas sighed, making his small, satisfied noise. He slid one hand to Mateo's hip—his sore hip, supporting it—and the other around the nape of Mateo's neck under the inky fall of his hair, kissing him back with a slow and yet—and this was clever of him, actu-ally—comfortable intensity.

It was not the awkwardly tentative or desperately passionate kiss of new lovers. It was the sort of kiss exchanged between people who had done it plenty of times before and were looking forwards to doing it quite a few more times to come.

So. Very much more convincing, then.

Mateo broke off first, and looked at Jonas blankly.

'And I'll play *this* game all night.' Jonas peeked over Mateo's shoulder even as he began to play with his hair, running its silky length between his fingers. 'You want him jealous?'

'I want him to think he'd have to go through you to get to me,' Mateo explained. They were still speaking quietly, and in the local dialect as well; he didn't think Elias would catch it.

Elias said, then, his voice sharp and brittle like shale, 'Mattias, who, by the seven surviving Remnants, is this Imperial?'

One surviving Remnant now, thought Mateo, and felt again the nausea that had come upon him, upon all the Taurasi, when they had heard the news about Ysthera, and then again tonight, when Elias had so abruptly told them about Sabine.

Jonas's arm tightened about his waist, and he realised he had sagged against the other man. He rested his head against the warm strength of Jonas's shoulder before gathering himself and offering a small, nervous smile.

Just the game we're playing, he reminded himself, as Jonas smiled back, slow, amber eyes alight. *Just friendly.*

Jonas favoured Elias with another look from the corner of his eyes; it must, Mateo realised, be greatly annoying the other Ystheran. 'And is it a fight you want him to *win*, honey?'

'Gods, no,' Mateo said, resorting to the mild Imperial blasphemy for emphasis.

Again, Jonas made his small noise of satisfaction. His arm still slung casually around Mateo's waist, he shifted them both from their close conversation to casually include Elias in a way that made it blatant that the other man was intruding. It was a masterful deployment of body language.

'Teo,' he said, which was, truly, an inspired touch, as was the affectionate tuck of a lock of Mateo's loose hair behind his ear. Jonas was *really good* at this. 'Who's your little friend?'

Elias stood up, hands on hips, face one tight glower. It didn't help him; Jonas might have been a smidgeon shorter than Mateo, but Mateo was the tallest among his own people. Elias was the shortest—the littlest— of the three of them.

'This is Elias—' Mateo had been about to give Elias's Kindred, and stuttered in confusion.

Anika wanted to keep their arrival secret, so he couldn't name Gallasi nor could he, for the life of him, come up with the names of any compatriots in the city. But he couldn't call Elias Taurasi; Jonas knew the Taurasi, by sight if not by name, and would wonder where this one had been for the last seven weeks—not to mention why Mateo wasn't untouchable to him.

Besides, something in Mateo rebelled at it. Elias *wasn't* Taurasi, not yet. He finished awkwardly. 'He's one of the visitors who arrived last night.'

'Nice,' Jonas said, playing the ignorant Imperial to the hilt. 'I brought up dinner. It *might* feed three…' He gave a shrug and a doubtful wince of his whole face that strongly implied that it would definitely not feed three.

Here, Elias's ingrained Ystheran conditioning towards social courtesies finally appeared. 'Oh, no, I should not intrude,' he said in stiff and formal Imperial, accent heavy.

Jonas said, 'If you're sure,' while somehow making it obvious he was actually saying, *Yeah, you shouldn't.*

Elias bowed and made his farewell in the circumspect Ystheran manner, and Jonas made his own farewell in the bluff Imperial manner, and Mateo stayed nestled in the comforting strength of his arm and let him, because, *really*, the playacting in this game was *masterful*.

As Elias opened the door to depart, Jonas winked at Mateo. Acting very much as if he had been waiting for privacy, and had, in his eagerness to get his hands on his lover, simply mistimed his move so that Elias hadn't quite left yet, he pulled Mateo into a close embrace.

He murmured, 'Mmm, Teo,' against the skin under Mateo's ear, stubble tickling.

Earlier, he'd used this most intimate of diminutives casually, as if he'd been invited to use it a considerable while before. This time, however, he managed to pronounce it like he was moaning it in bed, breathy and needy and wanting.

Mateo felt his face blush scarlet, and Elias slammed the teahouse door much harder than he had to.

'Hah,' Jonas said, now laughing. He rested his forehead on Mateo's shoulder, still with arms wrapped around him. 'How'd I do, honey?'

'Good,' Mateo said, staring wide-eyed over Jonas's shoulder. He slowly put his hands on Jonas's sides, feeling his solid bulk. 'Good. Ah, this is— That was…good. Thank you, Jonas.'

'Any time, Mateo, truly *any* time.' Jonas still wasn't letting him go. 'Who was that? Not going to cause you trouble tomorrow?'

Mateo realised Jonas wasn't moving away because he couldn't; Mateo was unconscionably clinging to him. He found himself wanting to shift even closer, lean on that warm, muscular body. But for all his Coterie's teasing when they'd been flown on apricot liquor, Jonas really was just a kind and amiable man who considered Mateo a friend. If he'd had any flirtatious thoughts towards him, he'd surely, *surely*, be showing signs of jealousy over Elias.

He forced himself to let go, resignedly saying, 'Only in so far as word will very rapidly spread that I'm letting an Imperial have me.'

Jonas did step back then, giving him a quizzical look. 'It's not trouble, as such,' Mateo reassured him.

'Let them think you fucked me,' Jonas said. 'Judgemental people seem to judge that way round a bit less.'

Mateo discovered they were still standing too close. He went over to the stove, poking in a few twigs from the woodstore to coax flames back from the embers. This task complete, he had no excuse not to say, 'That's not… It wouldn't be…'

'We are going to finish a sentence sometime tonight, aren't we, honey?'

'I don't have the physical arrangement,' Mateo said, a touch crossly, as Jonas no doubt hoped to make him, to encourage the blurt. 'You know that.'

'Sure. I'm not sure where it's relevant right now?'

'No one's going to think I fucked you?' Mateo spelled out, almost revelling in the indelicacy of Imperial bluntness. 'I can't fuck people?'

Jonas snorted. 'This is that dick of a former lover voicing his opinions again, isn't it? I'd like to punch him in the face.'

'If it's any consolation, you did just metaphorically punch him in the face,' Mateo said, jerking a thumb at the recently slammed door.

He hid a wince; he was going to give away the arrival of Ystherans fleeing the sinking. He hoped Jonas would assume he'd been talking about a fellow Anceran Ystheran when he'd talked of his past lover, rather than making the connection that Elias must have escaped from Ysthera.

'That was him?' Jonas turned and looked at the door like he was considering chasing after Elias. 'If I'd known, I'd have rubbed it in a bit more. I want to go stand under his shutters and moan your name. Oh, Teo, honey, take me right here against the wall.'

This last was in that husky, needy voice and Mateo may have had to bite down on a whimper. He raised a stern finger. 'Be that as it may—'

'But you'd been kissing him,' Jonas said, sounding startled now. 'You were going to sleep with him if I hadn't walked in. And you know he's a dick and you *know* the sex would have been bad.'

'I was trying to extricate myself!'

Jonas got the intently serious expression he occasionally wore. 'Was he forcing you?'

'Not forcing,' Mateo said. 'Just…pressuring.'

Slowly, Jonas said, 'Honey, do you think that's much better?'

'Not…now you point it out, no,' Mateo said. 'He just… He just always needed a good reason for why not. That's what that whole game was about. You were helpful. And surprisingly good at it.'

This compliment did not prove the distraction he'd hoped it would. 'I may have to go give him a literal punch in the face now. Don't give me that bewildered look. You know what a good enough reason for why not is?'

'Not an Imperial who'll punch you in the face, then?'

'No, Mateo.' Jonas began to undo the package he had put on the table earlier. He was moving with some frustration, and the thin wrapping tore, releasing a spicy, savoury scent into the air. '*No* is a good enough reason for why not. Hey, care to fuck?'

'Um...'

Jonas continued the conversation with himself. 'No, I don't want it. All right, then, let's not. That's how it should go. Anyway, hungry? I do have wine, too.'

'You...did actually come up here to eat with me?' Mateo asked, feeling even more bewildered.

Jonas looked up at him, eyes crinkled. 'Yeah, honey. It's a snack, really. I know you'll have already eaten with your family. But I thought I'd bring up those pasties I talked about, since you can't go to them. I actually did bring plenty—I thought Anika and the others would still be about as well, but I suppose they're having an early night?'

Ignoring the question, Mateo lowered himself onto the bench, hand pressed to his hip again. He was touched, absurdly so, to think that Jonas had been going about his life down in the city and had spared a thought for the grouchy, awkward Ystheran of his acquaintance, enough to pack a picnic and bring it up here on an evening which surely held better prospects for a man like him.

But when Jonas returned from the kitchen with plates and cups, he blurted, 'I can't drink the wine, though. Oh, by the Remnants! I meant, thank you, Jonas, this was truly a lovely thought.'

'It's grape wine,' Jonas said. He was smiling down at the pasties as he divided them up onto the plates. 'The Sunlit Isle had grape wine, didn't it?'

'It's not the taste or... It's because I'm a Soul,' Mateo explained. 'The Soul. It—' It sullied the magic, the same way poppy infusions would, but, of course, there was no saying that to an Imperial. 'It interferes with my duties.'

'Which are? Just teasing you, Mateo, I'm not really asking, I know you don't want to answer.'

'Thank you,' Mateo said, humbled yet again by the easy acceptance.

'You're welcome. I should have realised you don't drink when not even the apricot liquor tempted you.'

He glanced over Mateo's shoulder, however, at the Soul cup on the other table, full enough, and low enough, that he must be able to see the dark liquid inside glinting in the lamplight. He filled his own guest cup without comment.

'That—' Mateo started, and then discovered he couldn't explain it.

An Ystheran had forgotten Souls did not drink alcohol? That made sense if they'd spent three years with no concern for the sanctity of the magic they were receiving. But it would make no sense to Jonas, who had only ever seen the Taurasi falling over themselves in obeisance to their Soul, extremely unlikely to forget a single one of his preferences.

Jonas made his libation to Njorda and took his own sip. '*Are* we finishing sentences tonight, do we think?'

'Yes!' Mateo snapped, and winced again. 'Sorry.' He rubbed fretfully at his hip.

'Your hip hurting again, honey?' Jonas opened the bag he'd set on the table, and showed Mateo a cloth pillow of sorts, small and flexible. 'This is packed with tourmaline beads. It can mould around your hip, and—'

He rose, tipped the pasties off his plate onto Mateo's, and carried it and the pillow to the ceramic stove. He set the plate atop the stove and the little pillow on the plate; the glazed plate would transfer the heat without the cloth scorching.

'—the beads will warm through and hold the heat for hours.' He glanced over slyly. 'Ystheran hours, even.'

Mateo shut his eyes, though he was basking in the teasing. 'You must think I'm awful.'

Jonas sat beside him to share his plate. He picked up a pasty, considering it with great gravity before saying, 'Teo, I think you're lovely.'

Craning to peer into Jonas's cup, Mateo said, 'Then you were either already drunk when you got here, or that is an especially potent bottle.'

He was rewarded by Jonas's shout of laughter and a friendly nudge of his shoulder. Mateo picked at a pasty. It was delicious, still warm, spicy shreds of chicken and peas wrapped in a flaky pastry. But he had no appetite, and his thoughts kept wandering, to the news about Sabine, to his quarrel with Anika, to his altercation with Elias.

'No good?' Jonas asked, when he'd eaten two to Mateo's almost-half. 'Not Ystheran enough?'

'I really am awful,' Mateo said to the table.

Jonas leaned his shoulder against his. 'I'm teasing, honey, I promise. Is that thing with…who was it, Elias? Is that still bothering you?'

'Partly. And he…brought some bad news with him, that we weren't at all expecting.'

'All right,' Jonas said. 'So we don't have to keep talking around it, that's more bad news from the fall of Ysthera, right?' When Mateo bit his lip in consternation, he added, 'They were far too raggedy the other night to be local, and we'd know if another city had exiled a group of your compatriots.'

Mateo had no choice, then, but to nod. Jonas looked satisfied, which made Mateo realise he hadn't known at all, not for sure. He sat up straighter, indignant to have confirmed the sneaky guess.

Jonas grinned, giving him another bump, shoulder-to-shoulder, before leaning against him companionably. 'Sorcerers?'

Such a simple Imperial word, encompassing all that the empire feared in one swoop. There was no true translation of *phalaros*: the blighted, who swallowed unbound magic and tainted it and let it taint them in turn; the heretical, who turned their backs to their goddess and broke their promise to Her; the pitiful, who lost Her blessing and pretended not to care.

Mateo said merely, 'They've renounced that.'

'And that's good enough for you?'

'They can't do sorcery here,' Mateo said firmly, and shook his head when it looked like Jonas wanted to ask more.

Jonas shrugged. 'Can you tell me about the bad news, then?'

'I could,' Mateo said doubtfully. 'If you wanted? I mean… We all thought my foster-mother died on the day of the exile, and now we know she survived until the island sank. And it shouldn't matter *when* she died, but it does, because it means…'

Jonas slid an arm around him. 'It means you think you left her.'

'We *did* leave her.'

'You'd have died if you'd slowed down for an instant on that mountain, honey, let alone tried to go back for someone. You'd *all* have died. Would your foster-mother have wanted that?'

'She was our Soul,' Mateo said. 'We should have gone back for her. I should have.'

'Ah,' Jonas said. 'And what, precisely, gives you the idea a single one of your people would have allowed their precious Soul to sacrifice himself for another?'

'She was the better Soul, and the better person.'

'Then she definitely wouldn't have wanted you to make the sacrifice for her.'

Mateo, even in the depths of his cloud, had to snort at that logic. Jonas tightened his hold, tucking him in closer, offering silent ballast. 'I'm surprised Anika left you alone with Elias after that news.'

'Um,' Mateo said. 'I had a fight with Anika, too.'

Jonas managed to both wince and smile. 'Haven't we had an eventful evening.'

Again Mateo couldn't help but make an inarticulate noise of something close to amusement. 'Or, at least, I peremptorily dismissed her, very rudely, before we could really have a fight. The stupid thing is I'm happy she did what she did, I just didn't like that she didn't tell me about it at the time. Which was *ten years ago*, Jonas, so please do tell me I overreacted.'

Jonas didn't. He made a soft sound, that could be interpreted as sympathy or as an invitation to keep talking. Mateo, to his own surprise, kept talking.

'This was back when Anika hadn't perfected the contraceptive tea, so I still had bleeds sometimes. And I didn't like sex when I had my bleeds, because it hurt, and Elias didn't like sex when I had my bleeds, because it was messy, but it was his birthday, you see, and I wanted to do something nice for him.' He added, bleakly, 'Sometimes it does occur to me to do nice things for other people.'

'Never thought it didn't, honey, go on.'

'So I… We were… together… and I was… cuddling with him… and he asked, don't you have your bleed, and I said, yes, but we can do other things, and he said…' Mateo slumped. 'He said, if I can't put my cock in you, I don't want to do other things. Well. He didn't literally say that, you'd be hard-pressed to say anything that direct about sex in Ystheran, but that was the gist. And then he pushed me off him and… left. As if, if he couldn't have proper sex with me, I wasn't worth touching, or talking to, or spending any time with at all.'

Jonas was silent. Mateo glanced at his face. He was staring straight ahead, unblinking, lips pressed together.

Hesitantly, Mateo continued, 'So, obviously that was all very embarrassing and… lowering, and I was hurt enough to tell Anika about it, and she got Charion, our Heart at the time, to break the agreement to alliance. And I found out tonight, and was… less than understanding about it.'

'Right,' Jonas said after another agonising pause during which Mateo valiantly resisted the urge to keep blurting more out. 'Here's how I see it. Since Ystherans don't talk about sex, you must have either been *very* hurt to go to Anika, or very much hoping she'd act exactly as she did—'

'Probably both,' Mateo suggested, 'but not consciously.'

'And so, on the one hand, Anika was right—'

'I know. She's always right.'

'No one's always right,' Jonas said. 'But in this case, she was, and I don't know why she didn't outright *murder* that utter *dick*—'

'Pacifism? We're pacifists?'

'—but, on the other hand, she should have talked to you about it, especially because she must have had to tell your elders what had happened—'

'Yes!'

'—which I think you would have hated.'

'Yes,' Mateo said, turning his face into Jonas's shoulder out of sheer gratitude that the man understood why he was being so unreasonable.

'And tomorrow morning she's going to apologise for being too angry and determined to rescue you to remember to consult you back then, and you're going to apologise for snapping at her and sending her away instead of talking it through with her tonight, and everything will be fine. No need for thinking it's a catastrophe, honey. It's, at most, a spat.'

Mateo breathed out. The what-ifs had been lining up: what if Anika stayed angry at him, what if she had finally had enough of him, what if, what if, what if, and Jonas had neatly flicked away the queue. 'Yes.'

'And I know I don't have to tell you that his behaviour that day reflects poorly on the character of only one person, and it's not Mattias Taurasi.'

'Yes.' He made himself sit up, surrendering the warmth of the man's shoulder.

Jonas half-lifted his hand towards his face, and then let it drop. 'You can lose your shit with me, you know.'

'I can do *what* now?'

'Freak out,' Jonas cheerily translated, which wasn't any clearer. 'I'm not going to judge you for it, honey. You're safe.'

'Imperials!' Mateo said. 'You butcher your own language worse than anyone else's.'

Jonas snorted. 'Cry on my shoulder, then, if you really find the slang so incomprehensible.'

'Oh,' Mateo said. 'No. I don't. Because Anika doesn't, and the twins don't, and… Well, everyone's lost just as much as me, so why should I cry when they don't?'

'I have to say…' Jonas paused, lips curled, but Mateo stubbornly refused the bait. 'You're all so busy being brave for each other and trying to take each other's weights that you're forgetting to put your own down, and you must know you've all ended up carrying much heavier weights than you have to because of it. It's like your hip. The instinct is to tighten up around the pain, but you have to move through it.'

Mateo shifted away in instinctive defensive recoil; Jonas let him loose and his hip promptly reminded him he'd strained it tonight. Reading that second flinch as readily as the first, Jonas slid off the bench and retrieved the tourmaline pillow from the top of the stove.

It was warmed through, when Jonas tucked it over his hip, and the heat melted into his skin, almost as good as leaning against Jonas when he sat back down on Mateo's other side.

'How's the stretching going?' he asked, completely willing to change the subject in the face of Mateo's discomfort.

'It's… Sorry, my hip really has been better lately, I'm just tense. I used to… What you said, with the stretching, about staying with the stretch? I used to run up the mountain. It helped keep me not drifting. And it helped me when I was in moods like this. But I can't run anymore. The stretching… helps. Exactly as you said it would.'

Jonas glowed. 'Good.'

'Sorry I snapped at you about it,' Mateo added in a mutter he hoped didn't come across as sullen as it sounded to him.

'That's all right. It truly doesn't bother me, honey.'

'Oh yes, because what other people think of you is pointless.'

'Not to them, I'm sure,' Jonas said, grin blooming. 'But no concern of mine.'

'Isn't that a touch… distancing?'

He earned the *honey-you-are-hilarious* look. 'Ah, do I *seem* distant to you, Teo?'

To which Mateo could only shake his head. 'But you did say you're happy with your own company?'

'Sure. Everyone can be, perhaps even should be, happy with their own company.' Jonas once again read Mateo's thoughts. 'It doesn't mean I don't enjoy other people's company. And I think, considering that story, given it's a bit on your mind tonight, I should tell you—I very much enjoy your company.'

'Of course you do, I'm hilarious,' Mateo said. Then, quieter, 'Thank you, Jonas.'

'You are very welcome, Mateo. Is there anything else I can help you with tonight?'

'I think,' Mateo said, 'I would like distraction, please. If you can.'

Something like the opposite of a shudder went all the way through Jonas, a ripple of utter stillness. 'What kind of distraction?'

'*Your* company would suffice, if that is acceptable.'

Jonas shifted his weight. 'That's simple enough, then, food and wine and safe shelter and fair companionship. What else could there be to want?'

'You make everything so easy.'

Mateo couldn't help a note of wonder, and Jonas got that glow again—he very well might not care a single whit for other people's poor opinions of him, or perhaps even their good opinions, but he was not entirely immune to a dash of praise every now and again.

He pulled the plate closer indicatively, and they settled to snacking again; the pasties had cooled, but were still tasty. In between occasional bites, and sips of his wine, Jonas told stories about his nieces, and then stories of the torment he and his sister had put his parents through as children, and then, as the jar of wine grew steadily lighter, increasingly ribald ones involving crewmates. Mateo might have felt the tipping towards guilt and sadness over his losses, except Jonas was very good about keeping his anecdotes light and amusing, never skirting close to the wreck of *Steadfast*.

They cleaned up when they were done, Mateo taking the leftovers out to sort into the compost bin and chicken scrap bucket—thanks to magic, they did not have a pest problem in the teahouse or anywhere in Ravenser Odd, but there was no need to make keeping it that way more difficult than it had to be—and Jonas collected the plates, and the cups off the Coterie table, to wash up. He left his own cup, only half-empty, beside the also half-empty wine jar, and popped the tourmaline pillow back on a plate on the stove, its fire long since gone to embers but its ceramic surface still warm.

Mateo latched the back door behind him, and paused to watch Jonas gingerly cleaning the Soul cup, the gilt emerald butterflies catching the low light as he wiped the cloth around the inside. He hadn't seemed drunk, perhaps merely even freer with his generous laugh, but he was taking great, slightly squinting, pains to not break the just-a-cup. Mateo could have told him to leave it for Anika's helpers in the morning, but he just watched, feeling fondness unfurling ever more in his chest.

Turning from setting the cup safely back into its alcove, Jonas smiled at him. 'Can I make you up a brewpot, Mateo? No? I'll finish my cup, then, and get going.'

They settled back on the bench into a companionable silence, slightly turned towards each other. Jonas looked Mateo over curiously, and touched his own hair as he said, 'I don't think I've ever seen an Ystheran with their hair down before.'

'Oh!' Mateo said, feeling his face heat again. He was so comfortable with Jonas, he'd forgotten his hair was loose, something he'd only normally countenance when alone with his Coterie, or for specific public rites, mostly funereal. 'That's… You wouldn't have, no. Unless you'd… It's a little like being naked, actually.'

He combed a few locks back out of his face, fretful now he'd announced that minor exaggeration. He coiled it into a bundle at his nape, but Elias had scattered the pins when he'd loosened it.

'I'll find them,' Jonas said, when Mateo began to rise.

'Then, in the cushions.'

A noncommittal noise from Jonas. He fossicked around by the low table in the other corner and returned with a silvery handful. He sat on the bench beside Mateo, and pinned his hair for him, hands moving gentle and sure over his scalp and neck.

'A man of many talents,' Mateo said.

Despite himself, despite the drift of his thoughts towards how those gentle hands might move elsewhere over his skin, despite his opposite conviction that Jonas was friendly and helpful and nothing more, he could hear that his tone had cooled to cautious, he could feel himself tensing.

He'd kissed Jonas at the start of their pleasant evening together. Jonas had… liked it. Surely the man expected more now, especially after being so nice for several hours on end. He could talk of taking a no all he liked; he wouldn't be expecting a no.

'Nieces,' Jonas said easily. 'Well. People in my life who are particular about how their hair is dressed.'

'I'm not particular about it.' He felt Jonas's puff of laughter on his nape. 'We just have our ways.'

'I know, honey.'

Jonas ran his thumbs firmly along the line of tension along his neck and shoulders. Mateo, instead of relaxing into the indisputably agreeable touch, tensed further. Jonas paused, gave him a casual tap on the shoulder to indicate he was finished, and moved—not just sliding along the bench they'd shared all evening, but getting up and going all the way to the other side of the table.

After a moment—here was that mingled relief and disappointment again—Mateo said, 'Thank you. I think…'

As he trailed off, he caught Jonas starting to smile; Mateo was about to be asked about finishing sentences again. He glared and blurted, 'I think most men would have wanted something from me in return for that favour.'

'Pasties and a hairdo?' Jonas said, with an unusually sardonic sort of look. He drained the last of his wine and set his cup down with a decisive click.

'A lovely evening. And…letting me kiss them.'

'*Letting* you…' Jonas knocked his knuckles on the table, almost over-turning his empty cup. 'That dick really does deserve a punch, doesn't he?'

'Why? I mean, why this time?'

'He soured you on sex completely and he made you think it was your fault.'

Mateo examined this gem from all angles before saying, 'I've had good sex, Jonas.'

Jonas coughed something that sounded like, 'Anika.'

Mateo bristled. 'That's none of your business!' Jonas dipped his head in an apology gracious enough that Mateo reluctantly brought himself to say, 'I've had perfectly lovely sex, just…not with men.'

'So you're saying he's ruined you for other men and not in the good way.'

'What's…the good way?'

'I hate him,' Jonas announced with an almost Ystheran flourish of melodrama. 'I hate him so much.' To Mateo's stare, he said, 'Someone like you, and all he could think to do was fuck you?'

'But, be fair,' Mateo managed, 'what else could he have done, given our respective, um…'

Jonas spluttered. 'Oh my gods, is that a fucking question? Plenty of things. A million things that don't involve doing what one party doesn't want to do.'

'Is this what Imperials talk about socially?'

'Depends on the context,' Jonas said, with a glimmer of wickedness in his eyes which suggested to Mateo exactly what the context might be. 'Among friends, sure.'

Mateo stared. 'You…do that with friends?'

'I don't do it with *enemies*, honey.'

A chain of faulty logic was making itself abruptly, stridently, apparent. Mateo's friends were Taurasi. He and his friends were untouchable to each other. Jonas was also his friend. They were therefore also untouchable to each other.

Except Jonas wasn't Taurasi. He was a self-proclaimed empire mongrel, and it seemed he did not put his friends in the untouchable basket.

On the heels of this loud and looming understanding came a quiet, and thoroughly *disquieting*, possibility.

Jonas still had that alarmingly roguish gleam in his eye. 'Come on, Mateo. Don't you want to ask what a few of those million things might be?'

'No,' Mateo said, wishing very hard to put his hands over his ears like a child confronted with unpleasant truths. He felt very hot.

The Imperial chuckled. 'It's just friction and motion in various combinations, no need to get exercised.'

Self-respect, vague but insistent, forced Mateo to at least act like he could cope with this conversation; that was no doubt Jonas's intention, and it was manipulative, which was easy to overlook because he was so friendly about it. Mateo resisted this blatant, friendly manipulation for the space of precisely three heartbeats before giving in.

'What things, then?'

Jonas's eyes lit up; he just about rubbed his hands together in anticipation, if only metaphorically with his gleeful expression. 'To start with the screaming obvious, my stern and controlling friend who wants to be in charge in bed,' he said, '*you* could have fucked *him*.'

Mateo choked. 'To end with the equally screaming obvious, with *what?*'

'You implied you've been with women. Same general concept, different technique. Depending on the shape of your mutual desires, use your fingers, your tongue—'

'My…'

'—or, as they say, if you can't grow your own cock, a store-bought phallus is fine.'

'What? *What. No one* says that. I could live for *millennia* and not hear anyone say that.'

Jonas went on blissfully, 'Leather, marble, ivory, wood—very well polished—vegetable, if you must. Obsidian's a popular luxury choice. Jade, imported.' He looked through the wall in the direction of the pottery workshop. 'Ceramic.'

'Holy Remnants,' said Mateo and then just sat and stared into space, quite done with acting anywhere near like he was coping with this conversation.

'Are you with me, or did I snap something in your brain there?'

Rallying, Mateo said, 'Just imagining the look on Penelope's face were I to ask her to make me a massive clay phallus.'

Jonas was laughing now, warm eyes crinkled. 'Massive? Ease a fellow in, won't you? Or, ah, ease it into a fellow.' He went off into helpless chortles that set Mateo off, too. 'Oh, honey! If I'd known you had such a low sense of humour, I'd have managed to make you laugh long before this.'

'No, you'd've horrified me,' Mateo said, wiping at his eyes. 'I think I am horrified, really. How do you know all this?'

'Because life's a smorgasbord,' Jonas said with a wink, 'of which I have partaken generously.'

'No, but, really, Jonas…'

'Really, Jonas?' the man himself encouraged when Mateo couldn't go on.

'*Are* there men out there who would let someone like me do that to them?'

'Mateo, honey,' Jonas said, shaking his head with warm exasperation. 'How obvious do I have to make it that there's a man right here who would beg you to do that for him? Don't you *dare*.'

That last was because Mateo, disbelieving his own deduction despite the glaring evidence to the contrary, had started to look around to find the hypothetical man.

'Really fucking obvious, I see. Me, right? *I* want you to fuck me.' Mateo stared at him helplessly. 'Ah. I think I might have given you too much to mull over too suddenly. I blame the wine.' Jonas shuffled himself off his bench. 'I'll leave you to it. Send me a message once you've thought about it, yes? Either way, and no trouble if it's no. Have a good night, my friend.'

At the looming loss, Mateo jerked into action; heedless of the warning twinge as he shifted forwards, he hooked his hand around Jonas's wrist. He held there for a moment, catching his breath at his own audacity, before standing and shuffling close enough that Jonas had to look up at him.

Mateo brushed his mouth over Jonas's, and heard him sigh. 'I think I've thought enough for one evening.' He shut his eyes. '*Make* it a good night for me, Jonas?'

'Thank *fuck,* I was beginning to think you'd never get down to it,' Jonas breathed. Mateo's eyes snapped open in time to catch his huge smile. 'You better fucking *believe* I'll make it a good night for you, honey.'

CHAPTER 14

MATEO CLOSED UP THE TEAHOUSE, WHICH took longer than it had to because Jonas was snugged right in behind him, kissing the curve of his neck. He'd assumed the man would be insistent, hands roving everywhere now he had his permission, but all he did was curl his strong hands around Mateo's sides, lightly running them up and down his ribs.

'Gods,' he murmured. 'I was putting your hair up for you, and all I wanted to do was bite…right…here.' He grazed his teeth on the bare skin where Mateo's neck met his shoulder, leaving tingles in his wake.

'Oh,' Mateo said, pressing back. He could feel a hard bulge, slotting against his arse. Jonas made an appreciative noise. 'Oh, you bite?'

'I do anything you ask me to do, honey.' He smoothed a thumb over Mateo's skin, soothing the nibble. 'And nothing you don't.'

'But what if I ask to do something *you* don't want to do?'

'Not to give offence, but given how long it took you to even notice me flirting with you, I doubt you could be that inventive.' He laughed, tightening his hold. 'You are trying *so hard* to think of something really perverted now, aren't you?'

'I am and I *can't*.' It was difficult to be too cross about it. The rest of Jonas's words infiltrated. 'Does that mean you *have* been flirting with me this whole time?'

'Oh my gods, Mateo, friendly *and* flirting, they're not mutually exclusive.'

Jonas's cheerful sally tugged at Mateo, making him pause and frown. Jonas chose that moment to turn him about and pin him to the door he was yet to manage to latch behind them. Mateo could feel all his taut strength, and the muscular length of his solid thigh pressing between his legs, offering delicious friction.

'You're having second thoughts,' Jonas said against his mouth. He tasted of wine.

'No second thoughts,' Mateo said, but uncertainly.

'That's because you've already blown past second thoughts all the way to fifth thoughts, right? Not on my account, honey.'

'Yes, but—' Mateo said, and Jonas laughed again. '*But*, how drunk are you, exactly?'

'Not,' Jonas said firmly, and kissed him.

Mateo revelled in the light scrape of his artful prickle of stubble, very different to Elias's smooth and domineering kisses. They'd been kissing in the teahouse, too, for a timeless span; he'd been the one to press Jonas into taking him to his apartment, because he was moments away from letting the man fuck him on the communal cushions and even unsure why he hadn't done it already.

'You've had a horrible evening, and you told me a horrible story, and I can't have you thinking I'm pushing you for sex when I can make it just as good for you if you want to keep it right here,' Jonas had said.

'I've actually had a perfectly lovely evening since then,' Mateo had pointed out. 'And I would like… I would *very much* like…'

And Jonas hadn't made him finish the sentence.

And now they were on the porch, kissing in the glow of the eternal light *and* the porch lamps, and Mateo was practically rutting on the man, chasing the friction of the thick thigh pressed firm to his core, and he didn't care who saw, though, actually, he did, so he broke off and turned to properly latch the wretched door.

His hands were shaking; he couldn't flip the latch. Jonas helpfully extinguished the lamps and returned, not bothering with his shoes, though he'd had the wherewithal to collect both his cloak and the tourmaline pillow before they'd come outside.

Jonas stroked one trembling hand. 'Honey, you nervous? You don't need to be. Nothing you don't want, ever.'

'I think,' Mateo said, inspecting the tremor with an almost detached fascination, 'I think I'm mostly very, very aroused.'

Jonas made a sound in his throat. He simultaneously pushed his whole body against Mateo and reached around him. 'And I'm just going to latch that door for you so we can get off this porch as soon as fucking possible.'

Mateo tugged Jonas onwards towards the privacy of his apartment, also failing to find his shoes. They stumbled across Ravenser Odd in the cool drizzle of the evening, into the lodging house vestibule, and then,

Jonas near-giggling behind his hand and Mateo urgently shushing him, tiptoed past Madam Kerling's door.

They were at Mateo's door at last. They knocked against it a few times while he once again failed to manage a very simple latch thanks to Jonas's mouth on him.

'Quieten down, you reprobate,' Madam Kerling shouted from her apartment, knocking back; that was her cane, which she used to bash on the common wall when his existence was annoying her.

Jonas broke off to laugh, head buried in the crook of Mateo's neck where he'd been kissing and nibbling. 'She's going to hear some louder noises than that tonight.'

'Oh no,' Mateo said in horror.

He tugged Jonas inside, across the antechamber, and straight into the sleeping chamber, which, thank all the Remnants, was on the other side of the apartment from the common wall. It was cosy, lit luxuriously gold—one of the young Taurasi had been in on their nightly chore of lighting a lamp and warming the sheets, since Madam Kerling had disallowed even a small stove out of fear of fire.

Jonas dumped his cloak and the heated pillow on the side table by the ewer of fresh well water and turned to Mateo.

'Right.' Managing to look serious, he smoothed his hands over Mateo's shoulders, a firm, slow touch. 'Right. What do you want, honey?'

'Oh,' Mateo said, flatfooted. 'I thought… I was hoping for sex?'

Jonas started laughing again, hands heavy on Mateo's shoulders. He rested his forehead in the crook of Mateo's neck again. Mateo allowed himself a grimace, secure the man couldn't see him. He was messing this up, obviously, but it wasn't kind to outright laugh at him.

'I'm not laughing at you, Mateo, honey,' Jonas murmured, once again proving that mindreading was not an unknown skill among Imperials. 'I'm just happy.'

'Happy?' Mateo repeated, somewhat dazed at the idea he could make Jonas happy.

'Ecstatic, even.' Jonas brushed a thumb over Mateo's cheek, gaze soft. 'And since I'm also hoping for sex, I think between the two of us, we might manage it. I meant what sort of sex would you like?'

Sensing that a diffident *The usual sort?* would set him off yet again, Mateo prevaricated with an 'Undress me?' while he tried to work out the answer that would best please.

'Can I loosen your hair?'

Mateo nodded, and Jonas slid the pins free, setting them one by one on the table by his cloak. He ran his fingers through the jet length of it, coiling the silky weight into his hands and letting it loose again.

'Gods, you're a lovely man, truly.' His fingers began to work at the hastily re-tightened knot of Mateo's sash. 'I'm surprised there's not a five-hour ritual for this.'

Mateo had gone still under the touch. He was thinking of Elias, fumbling at the sash; how close he'd come, to submitting to something he didn't want just because it was familiar. Thank the holiest of Remnants for Jonas. But what if this was just his gratitude towards Jonas, and Jonas's tipsiness, overwhelming the good sense of two people who had a perfectly decent friendship in place, and this ruined it?

'Oh, there is,' he said absently while his thoughts tangled in the ever-eager what-ifs. 'A two-hour ritual.'

'Good thing we're getting started now, then.' Jonas paused in unwrapping the sash. 'You with me, honey? You saying some sort of rite in your head right now, or are you fretting, or a bit of both?'

Mateo dragged his attention back. 'It's a wedding ritual,' he said. 'No, it's for taking off wedding clothes. They're…elaborate.'

'Must be, for two hours.' Jonas hadn't resumed unwrapping. He had the end of the sash in both hands. He was watching Mateo, eyes bright in the low lamplight of the shuttered room.

He's waiting for me to tell him to stop, Mateo realised, and the surge of panic he felt at the very thought of Jonas politely going away was enough to overcome his unfounded surfeit of worries. He took one step back and felt his legs hit the edge of the broad, low sleeping platform; with an accompanying tug on Jonas's shirt, he was flat on his back on the thinly stuffed mattress and Jonas was kneeling over him, smile beatific. Mateo shoved at the shirt's hem, silently indicating that Jonas was to immediately make himself naked.

Eyes still intent on him, Jonas asked, 'Know what you want yet?'

He wished the man would stop asking and get on with it.

'Teo,' Jonas said gently. 'I think you like kissing?'

'Yes,' Mateo said, glad to discover mutual solid ground. 'I very much like kissing.'

'Then let's do that.'

Jonas lay beside him. He murmured something reverential under his breath, and his mouth found Mateo's. He had a hand cupped on Mateo's face and the other on his shoulder, and his mouth was slow and insistent and Mateo made an urgent noise and rolled on top of him, pushing him onto his back, heedless of anything but the taste he was chasing.

'Oh, there it is,' Jonas said, voice muffled as Mateo pulled the shirt off over his head. 'Stern and controlling. Don't. Some people like stern and controlling. To be clear, I like it. I like it a lot. And you are very good at kissing.'

'*I'm* good at kissing?' Mateo repeated, astonished.

'Did you think it was the other person? No, honey, all you.'

Mateo, musing on that, began to explore Jonas's bared torso, the light fur there, the well-developed muscles of his chest and shoulders, a few scars that must have come with shipwork, smaller than the messy ones on his bicep and thigh, the softness of his belly over the broad working muscles of the abdomen, and the promised wayfinder sigil inked over his left breast, just above a dark nipple. It was an eight-pointed and knotted star, encircled by staved runes, themselves surrounded by a narrow border marked by smaller symbols, probably the name of the ship. Jonas's offering coin, on its leather cord, lay on his chest by the sigil.

Mateo traced the blue-black lines and Jonas lay back, eyes slitted like a purring cat's under the light touch of his fingers. Jonas tilted his chin to offer up his mouth, but not just that: he put his hands over his head, palms splayed open and inviting, beautifully muscled arms flexing. Mateo considered this, fingers spread flat on Jonas's chest, not sure if he was interpreting the pose correctly.

'Teo, take my wrists and hold me down,' Jonas said, in his blithely patient way. 'And kiss me like you're fucking my mouth with your tongue.'

'Holy Remnants,' Mateo blurted, and obeyed.

For a few moments he was conscious of their mouths moving against each other, and then he sank drowning into the sensations, Jonas's taste and scent, the light rasp of his stubble, his firm, broad body under Mateo's own lankier length, his mouth opening to take Mateo's tongue exactly as prophesied, his soft sounds of abandoned pleasure.

Mateo knew a rapidly rising need like a tidal wave, becoming more and more insistent until at last he broke away to gasp, 'Are you making me ask you twice to get my clothes off, or…?'

Jonas, smiling, pushed Mateo to sit upright on top of him. Mateo straddled his hips, rocking tentatively against his hard cock. Sucking in a breath that sounded approving, Jonas gripped Mateo's bad hip with a murmured, 'All right there?'

At Mateo's nod, he finished unwinding the loosened sash, and pushed open Mateo's cross-wrapped tunic with a gentle caress of his thumbs. He slipped it off, and Mateo helped him with the undershirt.

When he saw the laced bandeau, he said, with a genuine pleasure that saved it from being smug or condescending, 'Oh, you *can* take advice.'

'I don't think I'd be here with you if I couldn't take your advice,' Mateo pointed out.

'And let's thank our respective goddesses for that.' Jonas ran his hands over Mateo's sides where the bandeau sat smooth. 'Off or on?'

'Whatever you like.'

'Teo, honey,' Jonas said, a delicious touch of authority stealing into his tone. 'Off or on?'

'Off,' Mateo decided, on the grounds that Jonas apparently had broad tastes and therefore probably liked breasts well enough.

Jonas unlaced the bandeau, and, avoiding the nipples, ran his hands around and under Mateo's small breasts in a soothing cupping gesture, in the same way he might have lightly rubbed any body part recently freed from constriction.

But then he asked, 'Can I touch?'

Mateo was entirely indifferent to attention paid to his breasts; he almost said, 'Whatever you like,' again.

But he was not as entirely oblivious as anyone would be well within their rights to assume. He said, 'Yes,' because he knew that was what Jonas wanted to hear.

Jonas ran his thumbs over Mateo's nipples. Mateo was clinically interested to see that they stiffened under the touch. Jonas's voice was husky as he asked, 'Can I kiss you here, too?'

Again, Mateo assented. He leant down, arching his body against Jonas so the other man did not have to lift himself too far to lick and suck at first one nipple, then the other.

After a moment of that, though, Jonas let his head fall back with a thoughtful hum. He looked up at Mateo. 'See, you said yes to me kissing your breasts in the same way you said yes to me kissing your mouth, but you plainly enjoy it on the mouth and you are plainly not enjoying it on the nipples.'

'I don't hate it,' Mateo said.

'Do we recall,' Jonas said, tracing a finger along Mateo's throat and down along his sternum, 'a conversation in which I indicated that if I was rated "decent enough" after a fuck, I would be devastated? You may not realise that "didn't hate it" comes a couple of notches lower on the rating scale, honey.'

Feeling hot, Mateo mumbled, 'I just thought… Well, it's *you*. I thought I would probably enjoy it more with you.'

'That's sweet. But you don't.'

'But I don't *hate* it,' he said earnestly.

Jonas laughed, pressing his face between Mateo's breasts so that Mateo felt his breath huffing soft against his hot skin. 'Acceptable, is it? I'll slot that into the scale. Above "tolerable" and below "adequate", perhaps.'

'I'm making a hash of this. I'll understand if you want to stop.' *Please, please, don't want to stop.*

'How about we don't shy at the first hurdle and make a deal instead?' Jonas said. 'Tonight, we only do what you know you like. We can experiment another time, hmm? Stop making that face, of *course* I'll want in your bed—your sleeping platform—another time.'

'Will you?'

'Three times, but that's a hard limit.'

'All right,' Mateo managed to say around his disappointment, before catching the glint in Jonas's eye and swatting his shoulder. 'Oh, stop, I'm too…*me*…to know when you're teasing.'

'I know, it is a source of true hilarity.' Jonas did sober then, catching Mateo's face in his hands. '*Is* it all right that your hair is down?'

'Yes,' Mateo insisted.

'And that the bandeau is off?'

'Yes.'

'All right.' Jonas kissed Mateo lightly, a testing, tasting brush of lips. Carefully, he rolled Mateo on to his back, and lay on his side beside him with his head propped on one hand, smiling down at him.

'What are we doing?' Mateo ventured after a moment.

'Whatever you ask me to do, honey,' Jonas said. 'Whatever you know you like, and ask for.' Mateo was silent. 'Come on, honey, ask.'

'Your fingers?' Mateo said, after steeling himself for yet more of this utterly exhausting plain talking. 'Not inside me, but, ah, *on* me? I'm confident you know what I mean.'

'I can do that.'

Jonas unlaced Mateo's loose trousers, cradling his hips as he lifted them to tug the garment free. His hands caressed the silk of Mateo's underclothes, a firm slide over the smooth fabric that set Mateo biting his lip and clutching at his shoulders. He spared a scant moment amid the overwhelm of sensation to realise that Jonas still wasn't noticing the scarring on his hip.

'I cannot tell you how good it feels to touch you, honey,' Jonas murmured. His fingers eased under the silk, and stroked.

Mateo's hands on Jonas's shoulders turned to claws on the instant. 'Feels good to *be* touched,' he managed to say, each word gasped between noises which were embarrassingly like whimpers.

Eventually, Jonas eased the scrap of silk down and off, and returned to lie fully atop Mateo, as if he could feel Mateo's slight apprehension about being fully naked and wanted to offer his body as shield. He himself still had his trousers on, and Mateo could feel every inch of his cock pressing hard through the cloth. It felt large and thick and quite adamant about it, and Mateo's apprehension became less slight.

Jonas adjusted his weight, setting his strong, supple forearms on either side of Mateo's head and giving Mateo an indulgently affectionate look. 'Tell me what you *actually* want now?'

Mateo was silent, breathing jagged as he fought off dismay. He'd been responding wrongly. Had he not been enthusiastic enough? He hadn't been lying; the steady friction of Jonas's fingers moving under the silk had been wonderful.

'Stay with me, Teo.' Jonas brushed a kiss over Mateo's forehead. 'I know you liked that just then. But I'm guessing there's something else you'd like even more.' He eased back to lie beside him again and waited patiently, watching his own fingers tracing patterns on Mateo's stomach and hips and along his thighs. 'Go on, honey, I want to hear you say it. I want to hear you ask me for it.'

Again, Mateo was lost in silence, this time from the sheer agony of flaring desire struggling against the unfamiliar idea of demanding something, anything, from a bedding partner. But he knew what he'd once liked from other lovers, tentative alliance prospects, and what he hadn't had from Elias in any enjoyable fashion, and what he intuitively grasped Jonas would be fairly fucking spectacular at, given the man was practically begging him to demand it.

'I…would like…your…mouth…' he eventually informed the ceiling.

'You bet your pert little arse you would,' Jonas agreed with a grin, and slid down.

He did not zero in on Mateo's sex, but spent a good deal of time kissing his way over his stomach and thighs, following the loose swirling patterns his fingertips had laid down while he'd waited for Mateo to gather his fortitude, careful with the soft, enticing rasp of his stubbled cheeks over Mateo's tender skin.

Only when Mateo's heavy breathing had turned into desperate little moans did Jonas finally touch his tongue to the urgent throb between his legs. Mateo jerked hard and sobbed, clutching his fingers into the sheets in lieu of raking them over Jonas's scalp.

'You go ahead and grab my head, honey,' Jonas murmured, and, later, 'Relax, Teo, it doesn't matter how long it takes. You don't know how good you taste.'

Mateo's unalloyed pleasure had indeed begun to be abased by the notion that a man with a cock and two good hips would have been done by now and surely, *surely*, Jonas had not signed on to this enterprise with the expectation of spending half of it on his metaphorical knees. He glanced down at Jonas helplessly, his fingers caught in the man's short curls.

'Mindreader,' Jonas concurred. He had one big hand spread across Mateo's thigh, holding him open to his tongue, and the other around Mateo's bad hip, supporting it, not letting Mateo accidentally wrench it as he arched into Jonas's tongue without volition. 'Let yourself go, honey, I've got you.'

He lowered his head again, and Mateo fell back against the pillows and finally let go of every last worry, firmly closing the door on what-if. The pleasure jolted through him, the gentle suck and lick of Jonas's mouth drawing little quakes and shudders that demanded response. Trusting that firm, safe hand on his hip, he began to thrust against Jonas's mouth. Jonas moaned encouragingly, the vibrations thrumming through Mateo and halfway down his thighs like the spread of a river delta in flood.

He found himself muttering, 'Oh please, oh please, oh please,' incoherently, halfway between plea and prayer, as he felt the crest begin to crash over him.

He tightened his hold on his lover's head as he drove his hips upwards, restrained only by Jonas's supportive hold. Pulses so sudden and intense they were almost painful lanced through him like blinding forks of lightning in a night storm. He cried out, loudly, and pressed the side of one hand into his mouth to muffle himself, while his other hand pushed down at Jonas's head, holding him in place to wring the last few glinting flashes of pleasure from his core.

'Holy Remnants, sorry,' he groaned, when he had his breath back and realised he'd been essentially trying to smother the man between his legs.

'Why?' Jonas crawled up the mattress and flopped next to Mateo, wiping his glistening lips. 'That was glorious. I knew you knew what you wanted. Next time you'll sit on my face and you'll fucking love it.'

Mateo whimpered, all he could manage by way of fervent agreement. Once he'd gathered himself, he asked, 'Would you like to fuck me now?' He had his arm flung over his eyes, which made it easier to find the words.

He felt Jonas roll closer, putting a hand on his stomach. 'Didn't we decide we're only doing what you know you like tonight? And you know you don't like that.'

'I think I would like it from you,' Mateo said stoutly.

'I think you are very sweet,' Jonas said, 'and I think what you mean is you would like to do it *for* me, but I don't need it, honey.'

Jonas was lying close enough that Mateo could feel the man's rigid length pressed against his thigh. 'Um,' he said, shifting his leg to give the ironclad evidence a nudge.

'Oh, I could use a little help, sure, but I don't need to fuck a man who thinks he has to offer a hole to keep me happy.'

Mateo dropped the shield of his arm, protesting, 'It's not like that.'

'It's a bit like that,' Jonas said. 'You're not a martyr and I'm not willing to take your sacrifice, Teo.'

Mateo peeked at Jonas anxiously. He didn't look or sound angry, but Mateo could feel his own tension winding up, coursing into his shoulders, down his body. His last lover, annoyed at him for fucking incorrectly. Jonas, annoyed at him for…not-fucking incorrectly, he supposed. He couldn't get this *right*.

'Stop,' Jonas said softly. 'I've had a lovely time so far. I'm hoping to continue having a lovely time. I don't need your cunny or your arse for that, all right?'

Mateo's mind was still turning it over, but his body responded to Jonas's gentle but very sure tone, and his tension ebbed away. He gave a helpless nod.

'All right. So let's get my trousers off.' Even as he was saying it, Jonas was unlacing and shimmying out of his trousers and drawers with enviable athleticism. 'How would you like me, honey?' he asked, with a complacent spreading of his muscular thighs, and why not, because they were beautifully decorated with more ink and his cock was magnificent now Mateo did not have to contemplate fitting it inside him.

And at least he knew what he was meant to do from here. He shifted to kneel over Jonas, lowered his head to let his silky hair trail down Jonas's chest, traced his fingers along the newly-discovered inked lines high on his inner thighs—runic writing he couldn't hope to read but could readily guess was a minor prayer for stamina—and swirled his tongue around the tip of his cock, tasting the astringent flavour there as he dispassionately planned his technique. He had practice; Elias had liked receiving this, much more than he'd ever liked giving it—and, frankly, Mateo had been far better at giving it than Elias ever had been—but Elias had also not been as big as Jonas.

Jonas's hands on his shoulders stilled him. 'I'll spend instantly if you do that, and I don't want this to end so soon.' He gave a light tug on a lock of Mateo's hair. 'Why don't you come on up here and tell me what you want to do to me.'

He drew Mateo to straddle his hips again, but here Mateo baulked. 'Why don't you ask for something? You made *me* ask.'

'Yes, but you're fussy and I'm not.' Jonas flexed his stomach muscles to lean up and kiss him, robbing the words of any insult Mateo might have wanted to excavate from them. 'Not to say I'm not fussy about the company I keep. I'm just not fussy about what we might mutually decide to do together.'

'And we are going to mutually decide to…' Mateo prompted hopefully.

'Want me to hand it to you on a platter?' Jonas asked, smiling, not adding, *Like everyone's always done for you your whole life*. 'All right, honey. I've got a suggestion for you. I'm wondering if you'd like to hold me down with a hand on my throat—'

'Holy Remnants.' It came out as a reverent whisper.

'—and jerk me off until I beg for mercy. But, Teo, honey? Don't you dare give it.'

'*Holy Remnants.*'

'Yeah, you'd like that,' he said complacently.

Mateo *did* like that. He licked his palm, making it slow because Jonas seemed to enjoy the sight, and wrapped his hand around Jonas's swollen, leaking cock, the other hand pressing lightly over his collarbones. He endeavoured for strict obedience to moans for harder and faster, until Jonas opened his eyes and began to accompany every plea with a tiny shake of his head and an absolutely piratical smile.

From this, Mateo understood he was to torment the man by refusing to do what he was asking for and pleasing himself instead. He shifted his grip around the silk-sheathed rigid length and took complete and merciless control. He followed only the hint that Jonas didn't want it to end soon, and brought him to the edge of that unwanted ending over and over again. By the time he issued the final stern permission, Mateo had rendered Jonas thoroughly helpless and undone, and truly begging.

Jonas did not, it turned out, make his small, satisfied noise when he spent, though Mateo might have preferred it on behalf of his landlady, if the noise he did make as he bucked and spasmed under him hadn't been so joyous and gratifying.

In fact, Mateo liked it all so much that his lover was obliged to see to him again—'you lucky fucker,' he muttered as Mateo writhed under his fingers, 'you could take this all night, couldn't you, and meanwhile my flesh is willing but weak'—and then he collapsed in a languid haze of sated pleasure with his head on Jonas's chest and his arms wrapped around him, heedless of the mess.

After a time, Jonas eased away. Mateo, mostly asleep, nonetheless sighed to feel his warmth retreat. Jonas layered the blankets over him, and Mateo heard him quietly moving as he went about some necessary administrative work. He dampened a cloth and cleaned himself up, and brought it over to wipe Mateo's belly and thighs. Then he moved the blankets just enough to mould the pillow of heated tourmaline beads over Mateo's bad hip. The heat was already sinking deep into the low ache of Mateo's hip, loosening the clench there, much as Jonas had loosened a few achy clenches tonight, all over.

Jonas pulled the blankets back over Mateo, sat on the bed and touched his shoulder. 'All right, honey,' he murmured. 'Am I staying the night, or going?'

'You have to go?' Mateo sleepily repeated.

'I should—I have an early appointment before attending my father's clinic—but I don't have to. But I also don't want trouble for you in the morning.'

Mateo caught his hand and tugged. Jonas slid back under the blankets and curled around him in a satisfyingly cuddly fashion. The last thing he remembered was a soft kiss to his temple.

CHAPTER 15

THE DONKEY AND THE ROOSTER CONDUCTED their usual competition at sunrise to wake the street. Mateo normally stirred at the cacophony, pulled a pillow over his head in defiance of any sliver of a notion of the traditional dawn ritual, and went straight back to sleep. He was often a restless sleeper until this very hour.

This morning, however, the other body in the bed rolled over and jostled him before falling back into slumber, leaving Mateo wide awake and astonished at both himself and the world. Letting the tourmaline pillow slide off his surprisingly limber hip, he pushed himself up against the wall at the head of the sleeping platform, and looked down at this most peculiar of creatures, his new lover.

Jonas lay sprawled on his stomach, the bedding slipped down so that his broad, muscled back and thick arse and thighs were laid out like a banquet. Mateo smoothed the palm of his hand over the expanse of tattooed brown skin, feeling ridges and hollows, scars and patches of coarser hair, leaning over him so he could trace all the way down his back along lines of ink the colour of an old bruise.

Jonas indeed wore the helm of awe on his lower back but it was too large to be confined to just his arse, as expansive a canvas as it was. Like the wayfinder sigil, it was circular, eight angular staves arranged like spokes from its centre, a ring of more indecipherable runes enclosing them, and then another ring about it all, the long scaly body of a snake-thin dragon, its head looping around to fiercely grip its own tail between its teeth.

He paused with his hand curved about the arc of dragon on one solid butt cheek like he was weighing the density of a melon, feeling a rush of desire like liquid heat, already pooling low in his belly.

'Bet you're thinking about fucking this quality piece of arse,' Jonas said without opening his eyes. Mateo started and jerked his hand away, sitting abruptly upright. 'Ah, I believe I've been clear as to my feelings on the matter. Go ahead and check out the merchandise, honey.'

'Someone was lucky to get to ink this on you,' Mateo told him, stroking the dragon's head.

Jonas chuckled indulgently. 'Gods know, sailing between trading ports is tedious when the winds are right and the chores are done. A willing friend or two makes the hours race along.'

Mateo ran his hand over the sigil, thinking about that. Someone—two someones?—bent over the willing Jonas, touching him just here. Maybe here. Probably here.

He traced the runic lines he'd noticed the night before, delving high between Jonas's thighs. 'I'm surprised you're not covered in tattoos, then.'

Jonas spread his legs, inviting Mateo to explore further, and murmured, 'Lying still for ink was a long way down the list of my favourite pastimes shipside.'

Reluctantly lifting his hands away, Mateo had to clear his throat before he could say, 'Thank you for last night.'

Jonas finally opened his eyes, without lifting his head. 'That sounds like the start of a brush-off. Is it?'

'No. No, it's not.' Mateo squirmed as Jonas peeked up at him. 'How were you so good at giving instructions while still making me feel like the one in control?'

'Because you *are* the one in control, Teo. You'll always be the one in control, hear me?' He rolled over and gave his teasing smile. 'Here, anyway. It's not given to humans to control *everything*, as much as you might like it otherwise.'

Mateo could feel his response coiling through him, humming under his skin. 'Was it… Did I…?' *Please you*, he couldn't quite make himself ask.

Jonas's smile became knowing. 'I believe you're the one with the rating scale. Dare I ask if you'll add a level above "adequate" now?'

'I think I have to extend the scale all the way up to "outstanding",' Mateo said honestly. 'And an extra point for the distraction technique. It worked.'

Jonas grinned and tugged him down for a kiss. His stubble was heavier this morning, scratchier. He'd have to see a barber practically daily, the vain creature. 'I better get going. Sun's well and truly rising.'

'Will you come back tonight? No! Not tonight. Some…time.'

'I'll come back tonight,' Jonas said, looking puzzled. His expression cleared. 'Oh, are you overthinking this, honey?'

'I mean, did you have to ask?' Mateo said. 'You *know* I am. But I'm not expecting nightly attendance. I'm not trying to… I mean, it's just friction and motion, I know. I don't have expectations.'

'Right.' It had to be the first time Mateo had ever heard Jonas sound unsure. 'I said that, didn't I? Right. Yes. That's a no to overthinking and a yes to tonight.'

'And. Where might one acquire. Certain previously discussed items. For…'

'Phalluses for fucking?' Jonas said helpfully, and laughed as Mateo blushed. 'One might ask one's good friend to fetch an assortment for one, should one be so bold as to give an indication of one's preferred girth and length.'

'By all the lost Remnants,' Mateo moaned into his hands, which had flown up of their own accord to cover his burning face. 'Jonas, are you sure? It must be very hard to think of me as a man right now, let alone a man who…delivers the fucking rather than receives it.'

His hair was loose and wild from all the writhing and stroking and caressing last night; his breasts were unbound and, though small, felt heavy on his chest. He was still wet between his legs. Naked of clothes and all adornment, the cultural markers Ystherans understood even if Imperials missed them, there was nothing masculine about his body at all.

'Honey, I think of you as Mateo, my Teo,' Jonas said. 'I'd want to be with Mateo whether he was man or woman or both or neither at different times. But you're a man and I don't need you to strap on a massive cock to know it. I *would* like you to strap it on so you can do me like you want to do me.'

'I probably don't need it to be massive, as such,' Mateo mumbled, still addressing the palms of his hands.

All this disconcerting plain talk had its upside. He wanted Jonas; he wanted him splayed under him, moaning with all his intoxicatingly unfettered pleasure; he wanted to have him, urgently.

He emerged from shelter and said, in a rush of determined directness, 'Can I suck you off?'

'Do you mean now or while you're fucking me? Because that's an agreeable bonus about a detachable phallus, if you hadn't thought that far ahead.'

He had *not* thought that far ahead. '…Now?'

'I'd love that, I really would.' Jonas shot a pointed look towards the shuttered window, where morning light was streaming through the wooden slats. 'I'm late, though. Tonight?'

Mateo nodded. Jonas pushed himself up and kissed him messily, laughing as Mateo tried to press his advantage and climb on top of him. 'I really am late,' he said, sliding away between kisses. 'I'm probably missing something important right this very moment.'

'More important than getting your…' But as daringly as he'd waded into the sentence, he couldn't bring himself to end it.

'Yeah, it's not overly flattering, is it?' Jonas stood by the platform, unselfconsciously naked and hard, smiling down with arms boldly akimbo. 'Tell you what, finish the sentence and I'll crawl back into bed.'

Mateo shut his eyes and blurted, 'Cock sucked.'

He opened his eyes to the reward of a truly stunning grin from Jonas. 'Oh, well done, you.' He clambered back up onto the mattress with flattering alacrity. 'Lucky this is going to be embarrassingly quick.'

'Is it?'

'Honey, I've been fantasising about you far too much for this to end in any other way but pretty much the instant you put your mouth on me.'

'You've been fantasising about me?' Mateo repeated in blank surprise.

'No, I've not at all been finding it more and more impossible to think about anything other than you,' Jonas informed him, straight-faced.

'You're very good—'

'I know I am.' He smirked, flexing back on to one elbow.

Mateo huffed. '—at hiding what you're thinking, then.'

'I can be, if I have to be.'

'But why wouldn't you just say something? You're Imperial, you people just say something.'

'You people, is it?' Jonas no longer seemed in any sort of hurry, slowly wrapping a handful of Mateo's dishevelled hair about his fist without exerting any pressure. 'Partly, I was amusing myself, seeing how long it would take you to notice.'

'Years, probably,' Mateo said, gloomy at the very thought.

'Months, maybe,' Jonas said, sounding not nearly gloomy enough.

'You must have thought I was very stupid.'

'No, I figured if you're only thinking along the lines of your traditional alliances and such, you're going to have trouble recognising Anceran flirtation. I knew you'd get there in the end—I was enjoying the anticipation.'

Mateo tugged his hair free. 'Presumptuous!'

'Honey, you kept looking at my laeknir snake like you wanted to throttle it for daring to put its tongue on me—believe me, I was enjoying the anticipation.'

He laughed when Mateo covered his face again—he'd been both oblivious and obvious, a blighted combination—and tugged his hands down.

'And I did feel obliged to finish up my business here first.' Jonas frowned as he said this, looking at the shutters again, the ever-increasing light sending fingers through the slats.

'Well,' Mateo said, shifting to kneel between Jonas's legs without more than a thought to the open display of his own naked body; Jonas's naked body was too eye-catchingly beautiful for that. 'Then it's to the good that we finally got that contract signed.'

Jonas abruptly wriggled away and rose. 'You know what, I really am late, Mateo, and I really do need to get it sorted.' He moved quickly about the room, collecting his far-flung clothes. 'I'll have to get my boots from the teahouse. Do you want me to tell Anika I was too drunk to make my way home and you made me up a pallet?'

Mateo shook his head at the change in mood, and at the very idea Jonas's overnight stay could be kept secret or waved away. Madame Kerling would know, the moment Jonas stepped out the door, and the whole street would know as soon as he stepped off the stoop, if Elias hadn't risen early to spread the news personally.

He sat back, hands quiescent in his lap, quietness falling over him, the buzz of the what-ifs somewhere below it like a hive blanketed under snow. He wasn't truly worried—he didn't think the Taurasi would mind, not if it was Jonas—but it didn't matter. Jonas's precipitous departure had begun to shift him from his sated, languid mood.

Jonas, finishing his rapid reclothing, glanced at him, and then paused and turned all the way to face him. '*Very* sorry to rush off, honey. It's not you. I'll make it up to you tonight, that's a promise.'

Mateo felt his smile return, quite outside his control.

Jonas, still keeping the warmth of his attention centred on Mateo, tidied his hair through the expedient of running his hand through the short curls a few times. Mateo was mildly jealous, since his own fine hair would take some effort to tame into smoothness after the travails of the night. He brought over one of Mateo's light silk robes, the silver one with green butterflies aflutter over the wide sleeves, and leaned over to gift him a last kiss, more fond than enticing.

'I love to leave a man smiling,' he murmured. 'See you soon, honey.'

After he'd gone—cheerfully, and loudly, greeting Madame Kerling to an inaudible response, the sequel to which Mateo would be subject to later and at length—Mateo shrugged into the short robe and lazily contemplated getting up and ready for his own day. Jonas may have been late for his appointment, but Mateo was still early for the morning ritual.

He yawned and lay back down, idly touching his thighs where Jonas had lavished attention.

He was still in bed when the raid started.

CHAPTER 16

THE VIGILE GUARDS WHO ARRESTED MATEO did not touch him more than they had to, in transporting him to a small plain building within the governor's complex. Only after they'd manacled his wrists to a shackle set in a heavy oak table and backed away slowly did he understand that this was not due to respect but to fear.

Hip already aching, stomach roiling, he examined the room where he'd been deposited. It was light and airy, and showed a few signs—patterns of dust and fading—that suggested it'd held more furniture before they'd turned it into what he supposed was meant to be an interrogation chamber. Two more chairs were on the other side of the table from his own chair.

The smell of fresh wood shavings where the shackle had been screwed into the tabletop was still strong. He supposed normal prisoners were thrown straight into the dungeon.

He was sick with the memory of being marched out of the lodging house and into the cool morning air of Ravenser Odd.

Vigiles pouring into every building, barking incomprehensible orders.

Thuds and smashes coming from the teahouse.

Madam Kerling strident and swearing on the lodging house stoop.

The looks on the children's faces as they were herded from the insula out into the chilly morning and separated from their adults.

Anika, suddenly tiny as she was surrounded by armed men, holding her hand up to Darius to prevent him drawing his sword, but staring after Mateo like she wanted to give the guardian an entirely different signal.

Gallasi shouting, until Elias quieted them, a look on his face that read almost as gratified.

Taurasi forced to their knees in the middle of the street in a rather spectacular error of judgement, except Mateo hadn't replenished anyone's magic in the morning ritual yet.

He'd felt tendrils as many of them begged for magic—and he'd also felt the suppressed yet palpable rage of a people sundered forever from their beloved island home and helplessly watching the start of another round of calamity. He'd looked to Anika and they had slowly, despairingly, shaken their heads in refusal, each helping the other hold the pacifist line against the most extreme provocation.

The last thing he'd seen, as he was pushed into the back of the cart, was his kith, kneeling with their hands on their heads, eyes as blank with shock and fear and anger as they had been in the first days of their arrival in Anceral.

Overhead, the eternal light winked out, both magic and lamp flame, because Penelope could not help but add extra drama to any situation.

And yet, it still wasn't the most awful moment of his life.

It was the only thing keeping him from panic. Though… They'd left him to stew, and he was talented at that. His thoughts circled agitatedly and he tried to centre himself with his most reliable truths: he'd survived trials by bigger fires than this one, and Anika would be coming for him.

What if she doesn't? his thoughts buzzed at him. *If she was coming, she'd be here already.*

The last thing he'd said to her had been a demand to stop interfering, so what if she decided to let him live with the consequences of that command. What if the Taurasi had decided to let him go, like they now knew he'd let Sabine go? He knew it was ridiculous, *but what if it wasn't?*

At last, the door opened to allow an older Imperial woman to stride in. Mateo instinctively classified her as high-ranking Vigile due to the number of garnet studs in her bronze epaulettes. He met her eye with an equanimity that was by now entirely false.

She was blue-eyed, large all over, broad across the shoulders and hips, with a military stiffness to her bearing and rigorously tamed and braided hair which was that peculiar shade of yellow that seemed strawberry blonde until closer inspection showed there was no red in it at all. She looked every inch the warriors her ancestors had been, those fierce and free raiders who had haunted the tides until the exigencies of collecting taxes and tithes across their wide dominion had tamed them into civilisation.

In short, Heartland Imperial by birth and breeding.

'My name is Henrike Helgasdottir,' she announced crisply.

Excessively heartland Imperial, really.

She took one of the chairs opposite and dumped a handful of papyrus scrolls on the table. Already untied, they unrolled in all directions. She stopped one with the flat of her palm. 'I am Commander of the Vigile. You are Mattias, Soul of the tribe Taurasi?'

'You only call us a tribe so you can raid us without conscience,' he said.

'Mouthy, aren't you?' she said. 'Given your current predicament.'

Mateo looked at his manacled hands. 'I've had worse days.'

'Day's not over, son,' she said, which matched the thread of his thoughts closely enough to shift him another notch towards panic. She consulted a papyrus and looked at him questioningly. 'We do have you recorded as…'

Pretty butterfly-decorated silk robe, loose raven-black tresses, unbound breasts, refined of feature, high of cheekbone, slight of body, short by her standards, and probably still looking ravished from the night before. It was a fair question, he supposed, if any question could be counted fair under these circumstances.

He said, bracing himself, 'I am a man.'

'Oh, yes. Some of our temples do that. Quite a few tribes within the empire do it, too.' She smiled to Mateo's scowl. 'Does the—' She looked at her records again. '—Soul have to be a man? Strange, we had you people pegged as loosely matriarchal.'

When they had first arrived in Anceral, Anika had casually, almost as a joke, told the Taurasi what to do if they happened to get arrested by the Vigile or some other power in the web of Imperial and Anceran authorities, on suspicion of using magic or anything else more mundane: mouth firmly shut until she could get to them.

Having belatedly remembered this instruction, Mateo merely stared at her.

'Don't you want to know why you've been brought in, Mattias? No? Would you not like the chance to save every Ystheran in the city from exile? Or worse, of course.'

Mateo did not get the impression this was an idle threat. His thoughts, already whirling, turned to the swarm of bees. He lowered his forehead to his chained hands. Sometimes he wished he could pray.

Then he sat up straight and met her eye again. 'The Taurasi are here under formal political asylum. The rights of the citizen apply to us as to any other within Anceral.'

The woman, Henrike, smiled broadly. 'You are making the claim that you have not violated the strictures set upon you under the terms of your asylum?'

That sounded like a leading question if ever he'd heard one. *Shut up*, he told himself. *Wait for Anika. She* will *come*. 'We have not violated any stricture.' She watched him knowingly, and the silence was weighted. 'Is this to do with the shadow-dogs that flew over the city last week?'

Oh, Remnants *blight* him and his nervous blurting.

'It wasn't,' she said. 'But since you bring it up…'

'We had nothing to do with that.'

'They appeared over your enclave.'

'Our *public street*, and not by any doing of ours.'

'Where did they come from, then?'

'I could not say.'

'Cannot or will not?'

He certainly would not say they had been a harbinger of survivors from Ysthera. He gave over Anika's teahouse theory. 'A last burst of sorcery from the Sunlit Isle as it sank.'

'And it took weeks to arrive?' Henrike asked sceptically.

'How would we know how far and fast sorcery can travel?'

'Why did it come here?'

Because they followed Elias, and then they arrowed in on me. 'I don't know.'

'No attempt was made to report it to the authorities.'

'The authorities obviously knew about it already,' Mateo snapped.

'What about the other instances of sorcery?'

If she thought the rapid back-and-forth would make him give something away, she would have to be disappointed, because he had nothing to give. 'What other instances?'

'Seven weeks ago, and last night.'

Mateo shook his head. 'We know nothing of that.'

She stared at him, blue eyes piercing. She could only be seeing puzzlement shading towards alarm.

'You had visitors arrive, night before last.' He almost, but not quite, suppressed his jerk of surprise and Henrike gave him her shrewd smile again. 'Assume we know a lot more than you think we do, Mattias.'

'How d—' He bit his tongue. He said, 'They were not in Anceral seven weeks ago, they were not in Anceral last week, and they were wholly within Ravenser Odd last night. They're naught to do with any sorcery in the city, same as the Taurasi.'

She sighed heavily. 'I'm asking you to cooperate, son. I have it on good authority that you are the only Taurasi who does not use magic.'

Mateo finally began to suspect the obvious. They had an informant on the street, someone who thought they had seen magic. One of Madam Kerling's girls, perhaps. Or could it be Madam Kerling herself? That didn't seem right, not after her grimly pragmatic reaction to the shadow-dogs. Magic did not scare her, not even the blighted sort the Imperials called sorcery.

'None of us use it,' he said stubbornly.

'He said you'd be awkward.' While Mattias was still frowning—one of the hauliers who delivered Timon's building material or their bulk orders of grain, some of whom dumped the goods at the mouth of the street rather than set foot within its sorcery-tainted confines?—she rocked her chair back and tapped the door behind her.

'You better come in,' she said.

There was a pause about the length of someone taking a deep breath, and then the door opened.

Jonas walked in.

CHAPTER 17

MATEO HAD TIME TO FEEL HORRIFIED that Jonas had been caught up in the raid, before his tightly controlled expression, so unlike his usual open affability, gave away the truth.

It struck Mateo so hard that he let out a choked laugh because that was all he could do.

'I believe you know Jonas Nebrija.'

He shut his eyes. The swarm of thoughts in his head had gone still, as abruptly as if Danae had quelled an angry hive by magic.

He heard Jonas quietly say, 'Your men could have let him dress, Heiko.'

'My men were terrified of sorcery if they lingered too long,' she said. 'I had to pay them a danger percentage on their wages as it was.'

'All right. But the shackles aren't necessary.'

'Take them off, if you think so,' Henrike replied carelessly.

Mateo felt the gentle touch of the man who had made love to him the night before. He could still smell Jonas's scent all over his skin. Jonas, standing close, solid and warm, held his wrists and unlocked the manacles. Mateo sat back, rubbing where the heavy iron had begun to chafe. He did not open his eyes, and kept his head bowed.

He could feel anger and misery trying to rise, and he fought the welter of emotion away. There were plenty of answers he might have liked to demand from Jonas his friend and lover. There was only one answer he needed from Jonas the informant—how much had he seen?

The Taurasi's domestic magic was so entwined into their way of life that they did not go through a day without using it. And they had grown to trust Jonas, part of the crew who had saved their lives, whose presence on the street had been benign enough that it was too easy to forget he was a local Imperial.

What had he seen, that had made him go to the authorities? And when had he seen it? Before—*before*? It must have been; the raid had come too close on the heels of his departure for it to be after.

Timon had asked, 'Do you think he'll get suspicious about how fast the renovations are coming along?' and Mateo had said, 'I don't think he's the suspicious type.'

It was too much. He laughed again, a ripple of dumbfounded sound. Then he said, strained, 'I have nothing more to say.'

'That is not a wise choice, son,' Henrike said.

Mateo still hadn't opened his eyes; he couldn't. Large hands settled on his shoulders and he knew Jonas's familiar touch even before the man said, 'Really in your best interests to talk to the boss, Mateo.'

The boss. Mateo shrugged convulsively. 'Don't touch me.'

Jonas leaned close, his breath warm against Mateo's skin, speaking very softly in his ear so Heiko couldn't hear. 'That's not what you said last night, honey.'

Mateo did open his eyes then, his gaze involuntarily flicking to Jonas's face as he sucked in a sharp breath. Thick between them was his vulnerability, his pleading gasps of *oh please, oh please, oh please* as his climax engulfed him. He hadn't thought Jonas capable of such cruelty.

He realised, then, that he hadn't yet truly comprehended the betrayal. He could have no idea what Jonas was capable of, because Jonas was an *agent*, not the friend or the lover he'd pretended to be, and not even a simple informant.

He paused to try to make that sink in, and, as it did, their tactic came clear. They were trying to provoke him. Jonas looked relaxed, but Mateo could sense the tension in his focus. Henrike, the boss, was in same state of alert readiness, her hand resting casually by her waist, not quite on her hilt, but not very far away either.

Provoking someone you suspected of sorcery into deploying said sorcery within a very small room seemed a somewhat pyrrhic strategy. But it told him, very clearly, that Jonas—the agent—had fucked up. He didn't know nearly as much about the Taurasi as he thought he did, if he and his boss truly thought Mateo could wield magic against them.

But then: 'See, no magic, Heiko,' Jonas said, straightening and dropping the lightly mocking tone. 'If he was going to lash out with it, he would have done it then. He doesn't ever use it. He shines, but he doesn't glow.'

He shines, but he doesn't glow. Jonas had to be one of the rare Imperials with Ystheran heritage who could see the manifestation of magic and a

Soul's subtle aura. His mother's family were long-time sea traders; just as Mateo had suspected Jonas could understand Ystheran—and he surely, surely could—he should have suspected this, too.

He had been very stupid.

Henrike was peering at Mateo through a strange object, a small, smooth stone with a hole hollowed through its middle. 'I'll have to take your word for it,' she said as she lowered the stone. 'I can't see anything through this, but it's hard to prove a negative.'

She turned back to Mateo. 'You are here because you are the only Taurasi we can trust.'

'I'm here because you raided lawful citizens of Anceral,' Mateo said, keeping his gaze down.

'Mateo,' Jonas said, and his customary pleasant and paradoxical mix of patience and exasperation made Mateo bite his tongue. 'I have seen every single Taurasi except you use magic. I hate to say it, but not a one of them is a lawful citizen.'

Mateo had nothing to do now but dig in and deny all until Anika got here, and she would come, she *would*. He fretfully gathered his hair, twisting it with one hand into a low knot. Even if he hadn't been only half-dressed, the loose tresses would have made him feel naked.

Jonas spread a handful of hairpins, bronze, not the intricate Ystheran silver. They must have been his nieces'.

Mateo didn't touch them. He let his hair cascade over his shoulders again.

Henrike tsked. 'I don't blame you for resisting. Loyalty is also greatly prized in the heartland.'

'Oh, is it?' Mateo said, stubbornly addressing the sarcasm to the table, glaring at the pins.

She glanced at her scrolls. 'Your Heart, Aniketa Taurasi.'

He kept his head down and refused to respond, though his heart skipped.

'When we had the first episode of sorcery, we, of course, asked Taurasi for assistance. Aniketa refused, repeatedly. Understand that that makes you all look extremely guilty. And thus we have Jonas knocking on your door with an irresistible trade deal.'

Jonas gently squeezed his shoulders. 'Someone in Ravenser Odd is using sorcery, Mateo. We need your help to find out who it is.'

'This is ridiculous,' Mateo burst out. 'No Taurasi is using sorcery. It is not possible.'

Sitting up at the anguished sincerity in his tone, Henrike lanced him with icy eyes. 'And why not?'

Because I'm their only source of magic, was not a politic answer. It was the one thing that under no circumstances could the empire discover. It was the one thing they had managed to keep secret from the spy, and it chilled him to think that if Jonas had walked into the teahouse that first morning even a single Anceran rushlight earlier, he would have seen it all.

He deflected, with merciless disregard for his own compatriots. 'What about the other Ystherans in the city?'

'We raided them too, to see what shakes loose. But we've been watching them. Like you, they don't use magic.'

The Ystherans in Anceral didn't use magic because they had voluntarily ceded the blessing of a Soul. He didn't use magic like the sun didn't use sunlight.

And the Imperials did not know that. Jonas had fooled him, but Kindred Taurasi had fooled Jonas. There was comfort, of a sort, to be had in that. *Teo, my sweet*, he heard Sabine murmur in her serene way, *all will be well*.

Except Sabine had been spectacularly wrong about that. He pressed his hands to his bare knees—the robe was uncomfortably short—to stop himself from jiggling. It was Anika's voice who calmed him, Aniketa the Unconquerable, telling him to bide his time, be silent, and wait for her. He was her Soul, and she would come, and all he had to do was shut his mouth and wait.

Once again, his resolve was instantly shattered when Henrike casually said, 'Aniketa is our chief suspect, of course.'

'*What?*' he exclaimed in a throttled-back shout. 'That is— That is a filthy accusation. You are out of your blighted Imperial minds.'

'She does, after all, spend her days brewing up what some might call potions, just like a drya from the old tales.'

'They're tisanes! For a *teahouse*!'

'I see we hit a nerve.' She picked up the strange hollow stone and peered at him again through it.

Mateo recoiled from that and, unable to help it, turned to the spy.

'Jonas, please,' he said, hating himself for the pleading note creeping into his voice. 'Please, you know Anika. You know she would never use sorcery.'

Jonas squatted and rested his hands on Mateo's hands where he'd clamped them to the chair, willing himself calm to very little effect.

'Mateo, we *can't* know that. I know she's responsible for the Taurasi. And I know she's smart, and determined, and—'

He cut off as a tumult of shouts and thuds rose from outside, rising in volume and urgency as it neared. All three of them looked at the door, Mateo with some trepidation. Anika did not use sorcery, but that didn't mean she wouldn't come in wielding her own magic to the absolute top of its bent, never deadly except to the Taurasi's chances of remaining sheltered within the empire.

'And I know she'd shred the entire world for you,' Jonas said, rising and stepping back in the same motion and turning to face the door.

'We don't use magic,' Mateo shouted as the door flew open, in a desperate attempt to smother Anika's outrage into a simmer.

But it was Darius who stormed in, sword drawn and face like thunder, eyes flashing like lightning.

His face might have thunderous with rage but it was livid with bruising. He'd been beaten.

Mateo said, 'No,' and stood up, reaching for his guardian.

'He resisted during the raid,' Jonas said woodenly and for the first time seemed shamefaced when Mateo turned a savage look on him.

Darius stayed Mateo with an upraised hand, and stood to attention as Anika stalked in behind her martial escort, dressed in the formal robes and cosmetics of the Heart. They hadn't used overt magic to reach Mateo after all, just a bared blade, exotic prestige, and uncompromising effrontery. In fact, now Mateo had enough air to think about it, Anika might not have any magic left, given he'd been hauled away before the ritual.

Flustered Vigiles hovered behind Anika. Henrike, looking amused, waved them off.

Anika's expression was set hard with the same grim determination that had seen Taurasi plummet down the side of the sacred mountain and onto *Steadfast*. The moment she saw Mateo, however, it broke and she wore instead the despair he had awoken to after his weeks-long coma.

The despair she had worn when she had prostrated herself and, in guilt and sorrow, called him by his archaic title. He had to head that off, urgently.

He went to his knees in her stead and said, 'I apologise for my disarray, my Heart, they would not let me dress.'

Which was as close as he could get to saying, *They do not know what I am. Do not give us away.*

Anika got the hint, or at least his obeisance snapped her into the game they had to play with the authorities. She pulled him up and into her arms for a very long hug. He felt the gentle tug of her call on his magic, and he just as gently refused it, shaking his head minutely where he rested his forehead against the top of her head. She held him at arm's length and examined him.

'I am unharmed, Ana,' he said softly.

She cast a look over his shoulder, at Jonas. She was coldly disgusted, but not surprised. But then, Jonas had known about Darius's condition—he must have been at the raid. Anika would have had her moment of betrayed realisation then. All the Taurasi would have, a second shock in the wake of their Soul being taken from them.

'Very much unharmed,' Mateo added in the teeth of that look.

Jonas, equanimous as ever, moved the spare chair around from Henrike's side of the table to Mateo's and gestured for Anika to sit. He himself stood by Henrike, a match, unconscious or not, to the silent and glowering guardian by Anika's side.

Anika brushed off her bright silk robe with an imperious flick of her hands and sat like a queen. She stared at Henrike.

'Aniketa Taurasi, I presume,' Henrike said. 'I'm Henrike Helgasdottir, Vigile Commander. I'm the one who wrote you all those messages requesting your assistance.'

'I know who you are,' Anika said. 'As you see, I am done with being left waiting. I am sure the governor expects my embassy to be treated with as much respect as any other.'

Mateo was sure she'd have already been pleading her case before the governor, if Taurasi had had enough spare wealth to put together a suitably impressive bribe. Henrike gave her a look that suggested she knew it.

'Let's be clear,' the Imperial commander said. 'We are currently holding your priest—'

'Not our priest.'

'Jonas tells me he's a priest.'

'*Like* a priest, I said,' Mateo said.

'It's hardly our problem if your agent provocateur does not readily comprehend analogy,' Anika said, even as she tapped Mateo's leg; *be silent*, that warning reminded him.

Henrike smiled. 'We are holding Mattias Taurasi, your Soul. Do you want him back, Aniketa?'

'Under what grounds are you holding him?'

'Under the grounds that I bloody well feel like it and you forfeited any right to complain when you and your people violated the terms of your asylum.'

'Imperials,' Anika said scathingly. 'We're all equal under the law until you decide we're not.'

'Indeed,' Henrike said. 'And we're all following that law until you decide to use magic.'

Anika snapped, 'We do not use magic.'

In her head, in the heads of all the Taurasi, it wasn't a lie; she meant they didn't use what the empire labelled sorcery, which was what it was actually worried about, whether it knew it or not.

'Grandmother was half-Ystheran,' Jonas said, tapping a thumb to his chest. 'Seen it. Literally.'

Anika eyed him. She was, Mateo knew, running through his exact calculus, triangulating what Jonas might have seen and what they could still brazen out with denials.

'I do not wish to play charades,' Henrike said then, low and deadly. 'I need no more than the word of a man from a respectable family to condemn you all before the magistrates of the city and, make no mistake, Aniketa, we are not talking exile, but execution.'

Jonas opened his mouth, and then closed it tight. Anika did not blink but Mateo felt tension thrum through her at the threat. Again, she reached for his magic in an instinctive shiver; again, he denied her and this time she nodded in understanding. Jonas might have seen the Taurasi wield magic, but he had not seen it flowing to them from Mateo. As subtle as Anika was, it was too big of a risk in this confined room.

Regally, she said, 'State what you require.'

'You already know, do you not? We requested—politely—your assistance, and you refused. I was just explaining to Mattias that your, shall we say, lack of civic duty narrowed our options in terms of considering suspects.'

'You still want me to investigate your supposed case of sorcery?' Anika said scornfully. 'You are jumping at shadows. No sorcery escaped the destruction of Ysthera.'

'You saw for your own self wish hounds swooping on your street not very long ago, Aniketa,' Henrike said. 'I would think that would make you admit sorcery is on the loose.'

Anika's mouth thinned and she shook her head. It had been a singular and explicable occurrence; it had targeted only the Taurasi Soul; it had been vanquished. Like Mateo, she was by no means inclined to admit anything of the sort.

Jonas said, abruptly, 'My mother and much of my distaff family were sunk by white mist out of a clear sky in a southern port, Anika.'

Mateo heaved a breath, and Anika went very still and alert.

'Multiple witnesses averred that *Steadfast* was sent down by an unnatural storm while at anchor surrounded by other ships, none of which were touched. Now look me in the eye and tell me you didn't suspect precisely that when you heard *Steadfast* was lost.'

'We didn't even know she was lost until a few weeks ago,' Mateo protested.

Jonas snorted. 'I've been dying to ask you, Mateo. Do your people— *don't*—deliberately keep you this naïve or is it the unintended fruit of overprotecting you?'

Mateo glanced at Anika. She was maintaining rigid dignity but he saw the guilt stirring under it as Jonas levelled a hard look her way. 'Very well. Yes, I did know about *Steadfast*. She went down mere weeks after she saved us. I didn't know *how* she was lost. I assumed coincidence lest I fall victim to paranoia.' This last was more to Mateo than Jonas.

Jonas shrugged. 'We took your money to do a risky job. It was a fair exchange. Many a trading ship takes a contract and then is lost to more natural storms en route.' Now he straightened, standing square and solid, face unwontedly stern, the determined matter-of-factness erased. 'However,' he said, sounding out each syllable like the blows of a sword. 'However, seven weeks ago, sorcery came to Anceral and my lost mother's oldest friend'—he nodded to Henrike—'told me Taurasi *wouldn't help.*'

The silence was pained after he snapped those last two words, a ringing accusation.

He repeated, softer, 'The Taurasi refused to help.'

Anika stared straight ahead, avoiding all of their gazes. 'I see how that might make you angry.'

'Anger is a pointless emotion,' Jonas said, 'and I did waste some little time in pointlessness, yes. But I don't choose to act out of anger. I choose to act because action is needed. If typhoid struck my city, I would act to mitigate it. Sorcery's struck my city—I act to mitigate it.'

She sighed. 'I thought it was a trap,' she said, voice slow and tired. 'I knew it could not possibly be sorcery, and I thought that either the authorities'—her turn for a nod towards Henrike—'were overreacting to some unusual but perfectly mundane event in the wake of the news about Ysthera, or the authorities were baiting a trap in the wake of the news about Ysthera, and it seemed to me likely the latter. And so I chose to ignore it.'

Mateo felt her squeeze his hand before she added, 'I see now that was one of a series of mistakes I have made recently.'

'One for which you do not wish Taurasi to pay,' Henrike said. She sounded insufferably self-satisfied and Mateo felt a sudden flash of anger, brief but intense. 'This is what will happen if you wish to maintain your tenuous grip on all you hold dear. You will do as you should have done weeks ago, and accompany Jonas to investigate not one but now *two* murders which, despite your protests, were plainly committed by sorcery.'

Anika and Mateo exchanged a look; the murders were indubitably *not* committed by sorcery.

'Jonas,' Henrike said, a hint of irritation peeking through her commanding tone, 'take them back to Ravenser Odd.'

'We do not need his escort,' Anika said. 'We have our own.' Darius stood even further to attention, no doubt a strain on bruised ribs.

'Take them back. Work logistics with Aniketa. Report to me as soon as you find something.'

'So, this will be a frosty ride home,' Jonas remarked in the face of three Ystherans staring at him with various degrees of dismay and dislike, and gestured them out.

CHAPTER 18

T HEY WERE USHERED OUT BY THE Vigile, or at least two nervous young guards trailed along behind them until they exited the front gate of the governor's administrative compound.

Outside the tall walls, the market cart waited, the donkey mournfully patient. Anika must have had enough magic to aid the little ass in pulling the cart here with two adults. There would be four of them, going back up the hill. He hoped Anika had enough magic left to help pull, because he would not risk giving her any in front of Jonas.

Mateo was limping after so long on the hard chair in a cold room. Jonas automatically put out his hand to help him manoeuvre onto the cart, and for just the merest instant Mateo shifted his weight to accept the help. Then he remembered, and jerked away, which only had the effect of wrenching the hip anyway. Darius, glaring at Jonas, assisted him instead before climbing onto the driving bench.

'Another question I've been dying to ask,' Jonas said as he settled opposite Anika and Mateo.

'While you were spying on us?' Anika asked with silky politeness.

'No moral high ground to be had there, Anika,' he said mildly. 'If you're going to go about using magic anyway, why haven't you magically healed Mateo?'

Because magic doesn't work on me like that, was once again the honest but not the sensible answer. 'It's not the right type of injury,' Mateo said instead.

Jonas looked sceptical. 'Because it was done to you by a wish hound?'

'Something like that.'

Jonas then nodded to Darius, a silent question regarding his current state. Mateo couldn't admit that the Taurasi were most likely saving whatever dribble of magic they had left until he performed the ritual. There was another, truer, answer anyway.

'He will have refused healing. He... He's been looking for an honourable way to die for three years. This will have merely hung an extra reason about his neck. I am sure he will barely notice the additional burden.'

Darius glanced around, just a flash of a look before he turned back to the reins, shoulders hunching. Mateo put a hand on his back, shamed. It had not been right, to use his guardian like that, to get at Jonas.

It had worked, though. Jonas shook his head, looking over Mateo's head, lips pressed together.

Mateo was beginning to realise that he was not, in fact, staying calm and quiet because it was one of his few viable strategies in this situation, but because he was numb. The flash of rage he had felt towards Henrike was the first indication that his true reaction was breaking through.

He began to shiver in the cold breeze. He had been trapped for a long time. It was afternoon, and if it had managed to once be a warm spring day, that had been eaten up by clouds blowing in from over the ocean. Anika pulled a robe from under the seat and wrapped it around him.

He let himself sag against her shoulder, ensconced in the heavier, warmer robe she had so thoughtfully brought for him, even as he saw her glance at his bare feet in consternation that she'd forgotten sandals. He didn't care. She had come for him. She'd been meant to, Henrike had expected her to, *he* had expected her to when he'd been able to squash the what-ifs, and yet he shuddered in the relief of being there beside her in the cart, heading towards home.

Squeezing his arm, Anika let him go too soon to set a bowl of almonds and dried fruit on his lap; he hadn't eaten at all today, but could only stir the mix. His mouth and throat were too dry to face even this light snack, his stomach too sickly. He put the bowl aside.

The glow and hum of magic rose about Anika, lightening the cart, bolstering the donkey's efforts. Jonas merely watched. He did not look repulsed or afraid, just interested, in a way he'd must have been hiding for weeks.

'We don't use our small magic to spite the empire,' Anika said, either in response to his interest, or to divert the conversation further from why Mateo couldn't be healed. 'It's just...built into our way of life. It's like breathing to us. If breathing was outlawed tomorrow, could you stop?'

'Breathing is mandatory. You cannot claim your magic is. Other Ystheran expatriates manage without.'

'They're not Kindreds. To unpick it from a whole Kindred would take years.'

'You've *had* years, Anika. If Teo could do it, why couldn't the rest of you? Why'—turning now to address Mateo directly—'if you have such a strong objection to breaking the empire's rules, didn't you tell your people to stop doing it?' He paused. 'What is it that's making you both frown at me like I'm saying something really stupid?'

At least Anika now had her warning about just how good their Imperial spy was at reading them.

'Just wondering why you think you've got any right whatsoever to use my intimate sobriquet,' Mateo told him.

Anika murmured, 'Teo, don't. We can't antagonise him, we have to keep him on side.'

'I don't know why you're speaking Ystheran,' Mateo snapped, the bluntness of Imperial perfectly matching the sudden, alarming burst of fury, lightning flashing out of a dull grey sky. 'He *understands* it, as I warned you several times but you wouldn't listen. You constantly over-protect me and when I actually needed you to, *you wouldn't fucking listen.*'

His Heart sat back. She tilted her head as if looking at her hands, clenched in her lap, but her eyes were closed.

Mateo shuddered. 'Sorry. No, I'm sorry, Aniketa. I also warned you we would run out of money, and the children would start speaking Imperial all the time once they went to school, and a million other things, and none of those things happened, so of course it was logical not to listen. Sorry. It's not your fault.'

'It *is* my fault.' Anika very carefully touched the corners of each eye with one finger. It was difficult to have damp eyes in the full ritual makeup without smearing it disgracefully. 'It's my job to protect you, and I failed. Holy Remnants, what have I done to us?'

Mateo wrapped an arm around her, an awkward hug side by side on the bench. It was her turn to lay her head on his shoulder. He said, not bothering to speak softly, 'It's not your fault, it's his.'

Jonas said, 'I would very much like to be on your side, if I can be.'

Anika must have felt the tension spike up Mateo's spine; she sat up quickly, ignoring the sheer nerve of the words in favour of the invitation they implied. 'You've seen our magic. You've spent weeks seeing it. You know what we do is harmless.'

Jonas had been leaning forwards, but now reclined, resting his elbows casually against the cart's siderails. 'How do I put this politely?'

'Why would you even bother trying?'

Ignoring the pure acid of Mateo's tone, Jonas lifted his shoulders in silent concurrence. 'I was on the ship the day the wish hounds attacked the Taurasi. And I was on the ship when the Taurasi picked it up and threw it a mile or more across the bay. And half my family was aboard when it sank in mere moments under the mist. And I saw you, Anika, shred a wish hound threatening Ravenser Odd, and so did my nieces. So am I not particularly reassured by any claim, from any Ystheran, that your magic is *harmless*.'

Mateo, driven to agitation, twisted his hair into a knot at the base of his neck, and then loosened it and twisted it the other way. 'It's like fire,' he said, falling back on Sabine's favourite metaphor for the gift contained within the Souls. 'Just because it could burn your house down doesn't mean you extinguish every lantern forever.'

'Someone badly scarred by fire might do exactly that. And someone ordered not to light lanterns by the people extending refuge should consider doing that, shouldn't they?'

Anika shifted herself and took Mateo's hands down and away, before gathering his hair into her own hands. She began to comb her fingers through it, neatening it in preparation for pinning.

Mateo covered his eyes. She could have just handed him pins—she'd either cached extra in her voluminous sleeves or was taking them from her own elaborate braids—but she was doing it for him because it was one way of offering comfort, currently undeserved.

And Jonas had intuited the exact same thing, the night before, and the memory of it closed Mateo's throat and made his chest ache like he'd been kicked by their gentle donkey.

'It is the threefold gift of a fallen goddess,' Anika said, and pressed down hard against Mateo's shoulders when he twitched. There were two threefold gifts, one to the Souls and one to all Ystherans; Anika, of course, was not speaking of the former. 'We were sundered from our original homeland, Meredonia, five hundred years ago. Our goddess gifted us Ysthera, and She gifted us magic, and She gifted us Her protection, and in exchange for Her three eternal gifts, we made a promise to never use our magic to hurt a fellow human.'

'Like the promise you made to the governor not to use magic at all?'

Mateo felt the warm air from Anika's sigh over his neck. 'The sacred vow to our goddess is a good deal more important to us than concessions forced from us under duress.'

'And yet Ystherans can break that holy vow, plainly.'

'Not if we are to remain worthy of Her gift. To be unworthy is to be blighted.'

'I am going to wager,' Jonas said, 'that the contingent who turned to sorcery argued that the bargain was sundered, the promise made moot, after the empire tried to invade the first time. And when it blockaded you for years and started to muster the marines for the second attempt, your goddess's protection must have been looking more than a little tenuous.'

Anika's hands, twisting Mateo's hair into the low bun, paused. 'Exactly so.'

'I would say the mystery sorcerer thinks the promise is even more void now that you've lost the whole island. All they've got left is the magic, so why are you so convinced they wouldn't use it in precisely the way we're telling you they've used it?'

Because they can't. 'Because we would know if they did,' Mateo said.

'I must respectfully disagree, given that they did and you *didn't* know.' He held up a hand. 'Look, I don't like this. You can't imagine how little I like this. But it's for the best if it was the only way to get you to help. You could very well be protecting the culprit without knowing, because you're refusing to even look.'

'It's not one of us,' Mateo said, tugging the second robe tighter around himself.

'I know it's hard to imagine someone you love and trust betraying you—'

'I don't have to imagine it,' Mateo snapped. After a beat in which Jonas looked at him with open surprise and Anika almost jabbed him with a pin, he added, 'I meant because of what happened on the day of the exile, actually. Don't get the idea our little dalliance signified much at all.'

'Moving along,' Jonas said smoothly, and that hurt like a stab in the stomach. 'Two murders, now. The second one—a compatriot of yours, note—might have been prevented if Taurasi had helped Heiko with the first one.'

Anika sighed again, and Mateo could hear the frustration in it. It would be so easy to say, *It can't be sorcery because sorcery, just like our tame magic, can come only from Souls, and I am the only Soul left in the world and even I, in all my obliviousness, would have noticed that.*

Honest, but not sensible.

'When was this second murder?' Anika asked, sliding a last pin into Mateo's hair and sitting away again. Mateo took her hand in silent gratitude.

'Last night. It's what precipitated the raid.' He hesitated. 'I didn't know about it. I was meant to meet Heiko this morning about where to look next, and I missed the message about the change of plans because I was…not at home.' He was careful not to look at Mateo, but Mateo felt his face grow hot anyway. 'I saw her people coming up the hill and turned around to go with them. I was horrified when I realised what was happening, actually.'

'Yes,' Anika said, very dryly. 'So were we.'

Jonas offered a thin smile with no amusement in it at all. 'I wanted…' He shrugged. 'I wanted to head off the worst of it.'

'Then where were you when they were putting Mateo in the cart?'

'And making Anika kneel and *beating our uncle*,' Mateo added, naming his own worst offences.

'The teahouse.'

Mateo recalled the sounds of smashing emanating from the teahouse as he was led to the cart under the appalled eyes of his people. He winced. The guards in there must have quickly rebounded from fear into bravado once it was clear the famously pacifistic little elves were going to hold that line.

And thus the fate of the Kindred cups was clear. Jonas had not done a fantastic job there, as effective as he'd been in his role as spy.

Jonas went on, 'I didn't know they were going to target Mateo. He was the only one of the lot of you I'd identified as completely innocent of using magic.'

Mateo fought very hard to not exchange a look with Anika, and felt, from her stillness, her doing the same. He was reminded that Jonas had not actually been as effective a spy as he might have been.

Jonas nodded ruefully to their silence. 'It didn't occur to me that Heiko would decide that meant you were the only one we could trust.'

Anika cleared her throat. 'The most useful bait,' she corrected. 'And so. Now what?'

Jonas looked for a moment like he wanted to argue, before taking the change of subject as graciously as he always had. He and Anika began to discuss the investigation she'd been coerced into, as superficially congenial as true colleagues. Mateo fell helplessly into his buzzing thoughts.

When they reached the base of the final steep climb to Ravenser Odd, where the sign announcing a temporary teahouse closure had been erected, Darius stopped the wagon.

'Meet me here tomorrow morning, then,' Anika said to Jonas, and jumped down with Darius.

Together, they two and their last gasp of magic began to help the donkey pull the cart slowly up the slope that Mateo, with his hip, had no hope of walking up.

Jonas, too, got down, but he walked along right behind the cart. He'd been told to take them home, Mateo supposed, and the man followed instructions.

He could make the walk in silence, then.

Except… 'Why?' Mateo found himself asking. 'You had my friendship. That was enough for all of us to relax our guard around you. Why couldn't you leave it at that? Why did you have to make it more? Were you collecting an Ystheran for your smorgasbord? Or a…' He waved a hand at his body. '…whatever you Imperials would classify me as.'

'Teo—'

'My name is *Mattias*.'

'—I'm aware I deserve the insult. But—you don't, honey.'

Mateo set his teeth at the gentle rejoinder. 'Or was it just so you could have the satisfaction of beating Elias on my rating scale?'

He saw he'd finally landed a blow; the triumph was bitter on his tongue. Jonas twisted to look away, making a small noise under his breath. After a silent frowning moment, he smoothed his expression and turned back.

'Do you want to hear that I couldn't resist you?' he said. 'I'd made my report to Heiko, you know. I'd told her Taurasi was using magic but I could see no sign of any sorcery—until the wish hounds, which…they attacked you, Mateo. I reported that they couldn't be of Taurasi, because they attacked the Soul, and no Taurasi would deliberately cause that. I said it was time to look elsewhere. Maybe even look for a different explanation.'

'Exactly!'

'And then there was another murder,' Jonas finished, brows raised pointedly. He paused. 'But I really didn't know Heiko would use my testimony about the harmless magic to coerce Anika.'

'You're saying you only betrayed us accidentally, so that makes it forgivable that you were spying on us the whole time?'

'Now that I hear it aloud…' Jonas leaned against the wagon, shoring it upwards with his bodyweight on the agonisingly slow climb. 'Look, I'm trying to say that I owed duty to my mother and her closest friend, and I owed duty to my city. The duty remains unresolved, but it was discharged in respect to the Taurasi, they were in all likelihood innocent of sorcery, you yourself were *entirely* blameless, and I was free to pursue you.' He pulled a face. 'Encourage you to pursue me. Because, *yes*, Mateo, I could not resist you. You *shine*.'

He'd said that before, an oblique clue that he could literally see Mateo's status as Soul—Remnants, he'd even given himself away when he'd been flown on the apricot liquor and fondly called Mateo a shining glory—but this time the significance struck Mateo.

'Oh,' he said. 'Oh, doesn't that put the cherry atop the pile of shit.'

'I'm not trying to excuse myself,' Jonas said quickly. 'I'm trying to tell you that… I don't know. That you shouldn't feel like I fooled you, in that one regard. I wasn't ordered to honeypot you. It, ah, arose naturally.'

'No,' Mateo said. 'It's…'

But he couldn't explain, not without revealing far too many hints about the Soul's true nature.

The youngest Ystheran children were fascinated by Souls. But by the time they grew up, they'd become inured. Ystheran adults treated Souls almost as any other respected elder. Unless they were without a Soul for a time, after travel or illness or anything that took them away from the ritual blessing.

And then they, too, were enraptured by Souls, at least for a time.

Jonas had enough Ystheran blood to see magic and the Soul's aura. His interest was in what he called the shine, not in Mateo. It was almost worse than being betrayed, to discover that, far from tricking Mateo into bed for nefarious purposes, Jonas himself had been tricked by an ancient legacy that was not actually Mateo at all.

It shouldn't hurt. It should be as a splint to a broken limb to discover they were both as foolish as each other. It should be satisfying, in the same way that realising Jonas had failed to uncover the full truth about how Ystheran magic worked had been satisfying. There should be no room for a lurch of his heart amid the dull ache of the more salient betrayal.

He felt Jonas's warm hand on his bared leg, looked up to see his warm smile. 'You with me, honey?'

Mateo blinked. The cart had come to a stop at the mouth of Ravenser Odd while he'd been adrift. 'No, Jonas,' he said tiredly. 'Obviously not.'

He clambered awkwardly from the cart, ignoring both Jonas's chagrined look and his proffered hand. The packed clay of his street felt warm on his bare soles.

Darius hurried on ahead to the teahouse, and Lucius came to unhitch the donkey. He stared at Jonas with wide, hurt eyes. He'd got rid of his nascent stubble. He didn't call the donkey by the name he and Mateo had picked for her after Jonas's mild censure. She'd been Fionna since then, but no more. Lucius led her away to give her a rubdown and her treat, both heads drooping despondently.

By all rights, Jonas should have had some hesitation about strolling into Ravenser Odd, but he walked beside Mateo like he hadn't sold Taurasi down the mountain.

As they approached the teahouse, Anika said, 'We're home. You don't need to come further. You're not welcome here, Jonas.'

'And is this a public street, Anika?' Jonas asked mildly. He added, when she tipped her head back to look at the sky in silent frustration, 'I just need to make sure…'

He came to a stop in both action and word on the teahouse porch, when he glimpsed, through the open shutters, the bulk of the Taurasi standing in serried ranks within the teahouse's wooden walls. He might have been as blasé as it was possible to be after exposure as a spy, but this unnerving sight had stymied him at last.

Mateo huffed an annoyed breath in the doorway. 'I'm fine,' he half-shouted, but was too late.

The Taurasi dropped to their knees with a rustle like autumn leaves and made obeisance. The only one who didn't was Niki, who was slowly sweeping up colourful fragments of glazed clay from the floor. Only a few Kindred cups were still in their alcoves.

Mateo felt his shoulders slump at the sight of the empty niches, but he made himself stand straight and stepped fully inside the teahouse so his people could see him properly. 'I'm fine. I am unharmed and safely returned by Aniketa.'

He hastily added that last, loudly, when he saw Penelope bearing down on them, looking quite severe in the direction of the Kindred's current Heart, who had turned to remove her shoes.

Penelope took both his hands. 'Shard of the Divine, we have failed you.'

She bowed to kiss his fingers in a highly old-fashioned gesture, while he bit his tongue and internally pledged undying fealty to any Imperial god who would make it so Jonas had been briefly deaf.

Naturally, no such intervention was forthcoming. Out of the corner of his eye, he saw Jonas give a small shake of his head. His lips moved as he silently rehearsed the syllables of the ancient title Penelope had been entirely foolish to use in front of him. It was, Mateo remembered, the second time their spy had heard it in recent days. He widened his eyes at Penelope in rebuke.

Her softly lined face flushed. She knew she'd made a mistake in her desire to highlight Anika's failure to protect him.

Just outside, the steady glow of the eternal light flickered into life. Jonas, blessedly distracted, looked back from the porch to frown up at it.

'He's safely home now,' Anika told him, following Mateo inside. 'You can go and I will be at your beck and call tomorrow.'

Elias had come up beside Penelope. 'You,' he said to Jonas, lingering on the porch. 'We don't want to see your face again.'

No doubt it greatly pained Anika to then have to say, 'It's a public street, Elias, we have no grounds to bar him.'

The Taurasi murmured, an undercurrent of ugliness in the susurration. Once again, their anger was at the surface, the suppressed rage of the dispossessed, poised to fall upon Jonas, Imperial spy and tangible symbol of the very empire whose actions had lost them their home once already.

Mateo grimaced, cursing Elias for forcing Anika to defend the man.

'I am going,' Jonas said to Anika, utterly unperturbed by the soft but fierce disapprobation of the Taurasi and the open hostility with which Penelope, Elias, and now the twins, who had come to Anika's side, were all regarding him. 'I just wanted to be sure of Mateo's reception. I needn't have worried, plainly.'

'You…thought Taurasi would be angry with *me*?'

Jonas dipped his head. 'Can happen.'

'How often have you *done* this?'

'First and only time. Heiko warned me, that's all. Your hip is going to start aching from sitting cold in that chair half the day. Don't refuse to use the tourmaline pillow just to spite me, all right?'

Mateo seized the chance to be petty and stared stonily past him in blank refusal to acknowledge the advice.

Jonas raised his hands. 'It's your hip that'll hurt, not mine, it's not the most logical revenge.'

'We're not the most logical people, are we?' Timon interjected, standing very close by Mateo. 'Otherwise, there'd be a fairly logical thing that would be happening to you right now.'

'Understood. I'm going. I want to give Mateo something first.' Jonas took from the pocket sewn into the lining of his cloak a small bundle of cloth, which, upon unwrapping, proved to hold Mateo's Soul cup. 'I saved this during the raid.'

Mateo took it from its swaddling, turning it to stare at the delicate gilt-edged rim, the bright butterflies, the ox horns on the bottom. It was beautiful, and fragile, and well over one hundred years old. It could not be replaced, not with clay that wasn't from lost Ysthera. Jonas had saved it as the other Kindred cups were shattered.

He'd saved it as Mateo was arrested and Darius was beaten and Anika and the Taurasi were forced to their knees.

A spike of rage like a dagger impaled him. 'All of us or none of us, you *fuck*,' he shouted, and hurled the cup to the ground.

It exploded into tiny sharp fragments, detonating over the floor and the bare feet of the Taurasi standing closest, and across the threshold to the porch where Jonas stood.

He didn't know he was going to do it, until he had done it.

The sound of the shattering was still ringing in his ears when Niki launched at him and began to hit at him with great thrashes of arms and body.

'It wasn't yours to break,' Niki wailed. 'It wasn't yours.'

Jonas lurched inside to wrap arms around Niki, and the teahouse lit with the remains of the magic the Taurasi had left over from the day before. It coalesced into the shield, which then began to descend towards Jonas.

A shield could be raised, but it could also be used to push away, or to batter. Anika held up her hands, but an Imperial agent had hurt their Soul and was now touching their neophyte. Ystherans were pacifistic, but they could only be pushed so far. Taurasi had found its line at last.

'Let go,' Mateo hissed, 'let go, let go.'

'They're hitting you.'

'*Let them.*'

Jonas only loosened his already-gentle grip, watching the Ystherans deploy their magic with the same blandly inquisitive expression as when he'd confronted Anika about the shadow-dogs.

He was looking, Mateo realised, for sorcery.

He tugged hard at Jonas's wrist, and Jonas, as obliging as ever, released his hold. Freed, Niki stumbled against Mateo, but this time merely burrowed in for a hug.

'You're right, Niki, it wasn't mine to break,' he said into their hair. They were shivering, little shocks running through them from head to toe. 'I'm sorry, I'm so sorry.'

He caught Jonas's eye. 'Get out,' he said, half-command, half-warning. 'Right now.'

'An impressive communal effort, my kith,' Anika called. 'Well done. Release.'

She'd layered the whip of her authority under her usual calm tones, and the shield, which truly had to be the very last of the magic they had left until Mateo gathered himself for the ritual, lowered.

Jonas looked at the trembling child in Mateo's arms, looked at the shards all over the floor, looked at Mateo, and beyond him at Anika and the seething Taurasi, and at Elias. He made a sound under his breath which was positioned somewhere opposite his usual small, satisfied noise. With a sheepish nod to Mateo that still managed to be gracious, he turned to leave the teahouse.

'That reminds me,' Elias said into the silence. Jonas paused to presumptuously level a hard look his way.

Elias briefly went to the other Gallasi, and brought back his own wrapped object, held safe by one of them until now. In a mimicry of Jonas, likely intentional, he opened the wrapping to reveal another Soul cup, its blue and red butterflies as bright in the lamplight as the green butterflies on the Taurasi cup had been.

'We saved it,' he said. 'I'd like you to have it.'

He held it out to Mateo.

Mateo stared at it. Elias was smirking past him at Jonas, but he could sense the Taurasi's attention fixated on him, intent. Anika was watching, lips pursed. Timon was watching, arms folded. Andrea was watching, posture identical to her twin's. Danae and Selia and Helena were watching. Penelope was watching.

Nikiti was watching.

Only Darius and Jonas were looking away, at Elias, holding out the cup. Mateo was under no illusions what accepting it would mean.

He took it.

'Good,' Elias said. 'You grant me great honour in allowing me to perform this favour for my Soul.'

Yes. There it was, in all its subtle Ystheran glory. He owed Elias now. Mateo turned the Soul cup over and over. He met Elias's eyes. He smiled.

He didn't look around as Jonas left.

CHAPTER 19

MATEO TOOK A SHUDDERING BREATH AS he set the new Soul cup down in the kitchen workspace. He felt wrecked, filthy and reeking of sex and sweaty fear, and cold and sore all over. He wanted nothing more now than to be away from the anxious eyes of his people, nursing his hurts alone.

He had to first stand by Anika's side while she broke the news that the trade deal they had sunk their last resources into was a fiction concocted by a spy, that they were being coerced into investigating a murder the Imperials were looking to pin on an Ystheran, and that the best outcome they could hope for was to stave off execution in favour of exile.

'Go to the bathhouse, my sweet,' Anika murmured.

'Don't you need me?' He hadn't meant to make it such a hopeful question.

'To be blunt, I'd rather not have you here illustrating the very depths of the pit I have dug us down into.'

'To be an Imperial level of blunt,' Andrea added, 'she'd rather not have you here looking pathetic and miserable.'

'Pathetic and miserable,' her brother repeated. 'You've been spending too much time down in the city, Dee.'

Andrea punched his arm. 'Insult me to my face, why don't you?'

Mateo pulled his outer robe tighter. She wasn't wrong.

Darius escorted him to the bathhouse. He'd had a tendency to hover since the day of the exile, but he hadn't trailed Mateo quite so closely, especially not in daylight, since their first months in Anceral.

'Do you want to come in?' Mateo asked him. He had to be sore as well.

Darius shook his head and held back at the threshold, making it plain he intended to stand guard.

'Uncle of my heart, it's all right.' Mateo took his hands. His knuckles were grazed, reddened, swollen. He'd gone down fighting. 'You can rest. I'm safe.'

The guardian shook his head again, jaw gritted.

'Please,' Mateo said. 'I want to just soak for a long time, and I won't do that if I know you're standing out here in the cold.' Darius scowled. 'If you can't bring yourself to rest, go back to Anika and stand by her.'

He waited while Darius weighed his choices, and then his guardian gave him a firm nod and marched off back to the teahouse. Mateo shut the door and breathed in the steam. In the dry antechamber near the door, he hung up the two robes he'd been wrapped in, and let down Anika's makeshift pinning. He recognised the simple jewelled pins—she'd taken them from her own hair.

Moving through to the main area with a towel from the clean stack by the door, he rinsed himself thoroughly, scooping bowlfuls of warm water from the large basin and sluicing himself repeatedly until his hair was soaked and heavy and the grime of his horrid day was washed away.

Then he sank gratefully into the hot communal pool, filled from copper pipes that led in from the terracotta piping outside, those fed in turn by the spring he'd blessed to make sacred.

Back on Ysthera, the bathhouse for each Kindred village had been built over geothermal springs bubbling up out of the mountain, sometimes naturally, sometimes with engineering or magical assistance. The water here was kept at temperature through a combination of engineering *and* magic. The local girls from Madam Kerling's lodging house complained that this little bathhouse wasn't like the numerous Anceral public baths; no cold bath, no scented oils, and, not least, no separate areas for men and women. The Taurasi instituted women-only times and solved one of those problems, though the Imperial girls did need reminding at first to wash themselves before entering the pool. They found it paradoxical but obliged because that was more convenient than going down the hill.

He had been soaking for— He didn't know how long he'd been soaking, because he'd fallen asleep. Now his hip felt better but his neck was cricked from resting heavily on the tiled edge of the pool and he was a little dizzy from the heat. His fingers were pale and wrinkled and he felt waterlogged just looking at them.

It had become dim in the bathhouse, towards evening, the sun sinking behind the tall hill already. Probably half the street was queued up outside, waiting for their Soul to vacate the bathhouse. He'd been selfish again, to so readily abandon Anika, to monopolise the communal bathhouse.

To mourn his personal betrayal, when all of Taurasi had been endangered by Jonas.

He carefully rose from the pool. While he was drying off, he heard the door open. 'Yes, sorry,' he said. 'I'm coming out now.'

'No hurry at all, Teo.' It was Elias. He was carrying a tray, holding Mateo's brewpot, cups, and a stack of folded clothes.

He glanced about, dubious, eyes lingering on the exposed piping. The bathhouse was one of the first renovations tackled by Timon and his team, since running water had not yet been a feature of the decrepit lodging house and insula on the other side of the street. And it had been their first experience working with copper, which was never imported after a legendarily terrible experience with a crooked copper merchant. The piping here and in the teahouse kitchen had given the renovation team endless trouble, which was apparent in the way the pipes often twisted into corkscrews at the barest touch of magic. Timon's team had had to learn the same delicacy as Anika applied to healing.

Given the restraints of time and resources and skill, the team had kept it simple. It was, in its way, striking, pristine white tiles, oaken wooden benches, and gleaming copper pipes, the strange twists a feature. But back on Ysthera the bathhouses had been inlaid with lapis lazuli and nacre motifs unique to each Kindred, and a dozen more luxe touches. Simple became stark, with that in mind, and Elias's mouth turned down as he evaluated the work.

He said, lifting the tray, 'Anika sent me over with your evening tea.'

Mateo wrapped his towel self-consciously around himself. His body hardly ever bothered him anymore; the cues of hairstyle and sash-fold were the only things Ystherans heeded. He'd bind his breasts if he had to be in the teahouse among the Imperials, because their main cues for the feminine were long hair, short height and general daintiness; relatively tall and lean, he wasn't even the Taurasi man most frequently mistaken for a woman under that classification system. Once corrected, however, the locals had to be given due credit for acceptance, even if it was sometimes tainted with patronisation, like Henrike.

But Elias had a way of making Mateo uncomfortable and unable to articulate why. Or at least he did have, when they'd been lovers. Now he kept his eyes politely downcast. Mateo could not have pinpointed why, exactly, the conspicuous respect made him feel judged—but he did edge closer to understanding when he remembered the casual way Jonas had tapped him between the breasts when he'd examined his hip.

He wished for a clean robe to wrap up in, and then realised that was what the clothes on the tray were for. Thoughtful of Anika, of course, and it would have been exceeding thoughtless of her to delegate this job to Elias. It was more likely Elias had commandeered the job from someone else.

Unless. Unless Anika was finally annoyed with Mateo, for his accusation in the cart and for his paucity of spirit and self-absorption when the Taurasi needed him, when Anika needed him. She hadn't seemed annoyed, but Anika was good at hiding her emotions behind her political smile.

Or perhaps she was just so busy in the aftermath of confessing her mistakes—his mistakes, their mistakes, but she would shoulder all of it—that she just had, after all, thoughtlessly let Elias bring the tray.

In the teeth of Mateo's long silence, Elias shifted. 'Timon was meant to bring it over, but I wanted to talk to you so I collected it first.' When Mateo just stared at him blankly, he added, 'You still drift off like that, do you? I thought you'd outgrow that habit.'

'If anything, I do it even more often since your father—'

But Mateo made himself stop there, just as Anika had bitten back her own retort last night. Yes, he felt antipathetic towards Elias, but it was no good excoriating the man for what the prime Coterie of his Kindred had chosen to do. There was no way forwards from that. He and his band had survived their own cataclysm and learnt firsthand the dangers of unbound and blighted magic. They were to be pitied, not blamed.

When Elias, head bowed, set the tray down on one of the slatted benches lining the wall, Mateo took the clothes and turned away, slipping into the bandeau and then the familiar daily outfit before letting the towel drop. He firmly fastened his sash, gold-embroidered emerald, and tied back his hair, twisting it into a loose loop at the nape of his neck in lieu of making the bun. He picked up the tray; he'd drink his tea with his Coterie, and eat something for the first time that day—he was surprised Anika hadn't added a plate of something light to the tray.

'Come on, Teo, don't rush off,' Elias said, putting a hand on the tray to push it back down. 'I was hoping you'd have tea…would let me sit and have tea with you, here where it's nice and warm.'

Mateo said, 'No, I'm not going to do that right now.'

Elias's eyes flickered; Mateo supposed he'd had to resist rolling them and sighing, like he always had when they'd been lovers.

Jonas wouldn't have rolled his eyes. Jonas would have smiled, endlessly, fondly patient.

And Jonas was a spy playing a part to keep Mateo lulled and compliant. Of course he'd smiled when Mateo had been abrupt with him. *Some people like stern and controlling.* Hah.

Perhaps the aura of the Soul had drawn Jonas into bed with Mateo, but his role as spy would have had him playing his part there, too. He could hardly have broken character in the last act, duty discharged or no.

Jonas, provocatively splaying his hands over his head and glowing with pleasure when Mateo gripped his wrists and held him down. Playing his part, staying in character, the consummate professional.

Elias, ignoring Mateo's glare—which, to be fair, most Taurasi also ignored, or how would they ever get anything done?—poured two cups of tea, and handed one to Mateo.

It was the new Soul cup.

Mateo sat reluctantly on the bench on the other side of the tray, grateful for the small buffer. He took a sip, and wrinkled his nose. The herbs were bitter under the honey, and he was used to that, but tonight the tisane was acrid, thick and sour on his tongue.

'Anika's trying another new herb.' Elias took his own sip.

'I wish she wouldn't,' Mateo said, aware of how grouchy and ungrateful he sounded; Elias hadn't blinked at the flavour, after all. 'That's undrinkable.'

'I wouldn't go asking her for another tisane, she's quite distracted right now, cleaning up the mess that Imperial left behind him.' When Mateo winced, he added, 'I'd just drink it, if I were you.'

Mateo choked it down with three large swallows. It left an oily after-taste, and he took his cup over to scoop up some clean water. The water was warm, but at least it took the lingering unpleasant tang from his mouth, and he could look forwards to ginger tea later.

Except when he sat down, Elias poured him another cup. 'You drink *two* cups, twice a day, don't you? And you missed your dose this morning.'

Mateo picked it up but did not yet have the fortitude to drink again. 'What did you want to talk about?'

'To apologise,' Elias said. 'I came on too strong last night.'

'It's forgotten.'

Mateo set down his cup, picked it up again, restless. This was an unnecessary conversation. Bedding Jonas had driven any thought of Elias out of his head, and then, of course, Jonas's betrayal had wiped away any other concern.

'I just… I saw you again, and I—'

'Elias, you know better than that,' Mateo snapped. 'That's you seeing a Soul for the first time in weeks. That's all it is.'

'—I want to tell you how much I regret how things ended between us.'

'You did not appear to regret it at the time. I do not regret it at *this* time.'

'My father did truly intend to make alliance with Taurasi until Anika's interference,' Elias insisted over him. He stretched an arm over the tray, taking Mateo's hand. 'I always thought we'd end up together under an alliance bond. And we were good together, weren't we?'

'We weren't,' Mateo said, pulling away. 'Even before you stood smirking beside your father while he publicly announced Gallasi was rejecting the alliance.'

'You can't hold a grudge forever, Teo.'

'I think you'll find I can, *Elias*.' Mateo rose. 'If not forever, at least until you're officially Taurasi and I'm untouchable to you. Which will frankly be a relief—'

Elias grabbed his wrist. His tolerant smile had faded. 'Sit down. Drink your second cup.'

'Let go of me,' Mateo said, tone lethal. 'I am not the auxiliary Soul of the smallest Kindred anymore, Elias. I am the last Shard of the Divine in all the world, and I will *not* countenance being treated how you once thought you could treat me.'

Elias held the shreds of his fraying temper together to say, with the faded ghost of his usual smooth manner, 'Please accept the reminder that I gifted you this Soul cup.' He released Mateo's wrist and gestured at the seat. 'I petition you to abide my company long enough to drink a cup of tea so that I may see that my Soul appreciates its value.'

It was all very Ystheran. Mateo resisted the impulse to smash two Soul cups in one day. Instead, still standing, he picked up the cup, swallowed the contents in one convulsive grimacing gulp, and clinked the cup back down before refraining from offering Elias a nasty little bow.

The performance, as scaldingly parodic as it had been, satisfied Elias enough that he coughed and said, less formally, 'If I treated you badly, I apologise. I was young and stupid.'

'And so was I, and now I'm not.'

'Are you positive you are not stupid for a particular Imperial?' Elias enquired silkily. 'You were countenancing a particular treatment from him, were you not?'

Mateo translated that readily enough. *You let him get between your thighs*. He exploded, '*I* fucked *him*, you presumptuous shit.'

Elias sneered, all pretence abruptly dropped. 'Look at the trouble you brought down on us because you couldn't keep your legs closed. No wonder Anika's sick of you.'

Turning on his heel, Mateo tried to stride for the door. His hip, so loose a moment ago, had seized up as his muscles tensed. It felt like the floor tilted; he wobbled, then stumbled.

Elias caught him. Mateo elbowed him away, seething. The shock of the raid, the humiliation and fear of the interrogation room, the humid heat of the bathhouse, the white-hot heat of his anger at Elias and Jonas and himself… His head spun, and he staggered again. This time, when Elias put a supporting arm around his waist, Mateo had to let him.

'Shh, shh.' Elias's breath was harsh against his ear. 'Sit down. You're overwrought.'

'I am not,' Mateo mumbled, engulfed in thick fog.

Elias kept murmuring into his ear. After a moment, Mateo came far enough out of his befuddlement to realise that the tone was soothing, but the words were definitely not. 'This is why she sent you away to the bathhouse. She didn't need you making a spectacle of yourself as usual. You're just so very fragile, sweetling. Everyone knows it. You make for such a heavy burden.'

Mateo shook his head. He wasn't fragile. Anika didn't think he was a burden. He tried to say that. But all he could hear now was Jonas casually commenting on how overprotective the Taurasi were. They were over-protective because they knew the truth: *Just because it's fragile doesn't mean it shouldn't be allowed to fulfil its proper function before it breaks*, and they desperately needed him not to break before the goddess whispered Her name in Nikiti's ear.

The insidious murmur went on, echoes of every what-if he had ever had, and below it and over it and through it came a buzzing, bees pouring out of his head and all through his body now, crawling under his skin, blocking his throat, choking his lungs, closing his eyes, and he was lost.

CHAPTER 20

Mateo awoke the next morning in his own chamber, with no memory of leaving the bathhouse or what had happened after Elias had called in the Soul cup debt.

For a moment, it was a blessed relief. He didn't want to have to remember. He suspected that in his morass of guilt and obligation, he'd capitulated to something he'd not wanted to capitulate to. His stomach ached.

But when he pushed away the blankets and slid off the sleeping platform, he discovered that he was still fully dressed, including the bandeau, and that his hair, though disarrayed, was still loosely tied back. Elias would not have stood for that.

Then what, Mateo wondered uneasily as he dressed in fresh clothes, had his campaign in the bathhouse actually been about, if not asserting a claim over Mateo before he became untouchable?

Madam Kerling was in the vestibule of the lodging house, wiping the dust off the large green leaves on one of the shade-tolerant plants the Taurasi had potted. She tsked when she saw him. Mateo supposed she'd been loitering for the opportunity to do so.

'Two men in as many days? Young man, you have rooms here at my sufferance.'

'Elias came back with me?'

At the note of dismay underlying his genuine surprise, Madam Kerling's already-sharp gaze sharpened further. 'I did think you were in your cups,' she said severely.

'I was…?'

'Drunk, you reprobate. I sent your companion off with a flea in his ear.' She intensified her outraged expression. 'He dared argue! That nice boy came over to help me.'

That nice boy, Mateo knew from prior conversations, was, unfathomably, Timon. Now that Madam Kerling had jostled his memory loose from the fog, he did recall a quiet but heated argument happening over his dazed and sagging head while Madam Kerling stood bristling like an angry cat and blocking the hallway down to her and Mateo's apartments.

'I was meant to bring that tray to the teahouse, not you,' Timon had said, 'and that's too close, given he's untouchable.'

'He made himself dizzy from staying in the water too long.' Elias had sounded injured. Mateo well remembered that tone of offended innocence. 'Was I meant to just let him fall over and crawl home, was I? Is that how you treat your Soul? Are you deliberately trying to harm him?'

'Excuse me?' Timon demanded. 'What are you implying?'

'You were one of the Taurasi who wanted to stay and use wild magic with us, weren't you? And now wild magic is here…'

'Careful,' Timon said. 'So's Gallasi.'

'Were we here seven weeks ago?'

'You were here last night.'

'So were *you.*'

And then Madam Kerling had dismissed both men from the lodging house with some very strong words before taking Mateo's elbow and walking him to his quarters herself.

Mateo took a couple of hesitant steps and put his arms awkwardly around Madam Kerling.

'Away with you, you dissolute miscreant,' she said, before giving him an awkward pat of her own. 'I did prefer the first one, lad.'

He released her. 'Me too, Madam Kerling.'

'Though I shall give him a clip over the ear next time I see him for inflicting the Vigile on us.' When Mateo raised his eyebrows at that "us", she added, 'They left a right mess.'

'We'll help clean it up, Madam Kerling.'

She sniffed disdainfully. 'And where's my favourite nailbinder? A job lot of thieves, you are.'

'Have a nice day, Madam Kerling.'

Over in the teahouse, most of the Taurasi were gathered on their cushions, talking in low voices over sips of herbal tea from guest cups, if not merchandise—he winced to see it.

Those assigned to prepare the light morning meal moved quietly about the fragrant kitchen, or slipped into garden clogs and out to the herbs, or along the back path between the workshops and the narrow field full of Penelope's tempering clay to the bakehouse. The children were playing, running in and out through both doors, bare soles flashing, bright voices a balm.

Anika was in the kitchen, absently chopping herbs. No one was bothering her, which was a bad sign. She hadn't had any squabbles to arbitrate in the aftermath of the exile either, nor immediately after the news of the island sinking. It meant tension was subsuming petty grievances but heralding deeper cracks.

The seated Taurasi were, notably, very much in their factions, Penelope and her traditionalists on one side, Andrea and her city workers and younger Taurasi on the other, the parents of young children in the centre, the Gallasi nine, Elias among them, keeping to themselves near the back door to the herb garden. Timon was sitting in the very middle of the arrayed cushions.

Mateo walked over and offered him both hands. Timon, looking puzzled, rose in unthinking obedience to his Soul's silent command. Mateo hugged him—over his shoulder, he saw Elias scowl to Timon's pleased laugh—before he joined Anika behind the counter.

She was looking out over the crowded teahouse with a pained expression. 'A touch of disunity growing today,' she said, scooping a blend of dried herbs into his brewpot.

'Because of me,' Mateo said.

'I think we can put it squarely on Jonas's shoulders.' Anika poured hot water over the tisane leaves and put the lid back on the brewpot. 'Well. It'd be nice if they would.'

'They really are blaming you for the raid?'

'Some are,' Anika said mutedly. 'It's not so much the raid, as what it portends, I'm afraid. Even if we give Henrike want she wants, the path beyond that seems…perilous.'

Mateo nodded his understanding. The raid was done, but so was Jonas's fictitious trade deal. Now they could only hope to be granted the reprieve of exile and somehow survive a trek west or south beyond the borders of the vast empire, abandoning the value tied up in their Anceran mortgages and carrying the last pitiful remnants of their material wealth to barter for food.

And yet Kindred Taurasi had held firm under heavier burdens than that. They could sell the ceremonial robes and the last of the status markers, for starters.

Mateo took Anika's hand and squeezed. He felt useless, perhaps even more so than usual, but he did have one way he could help her. 'Shall we do the ritual first, then? The meeting might be less…fraught.'

'Excellent idea, my sweet. I think everyone will feel a lot better once they have the dose of magic they missed yesterday. But will you be all right? Timon had some things to say, regarding last night.'

She sent a cold glance Elias's way as she poured Mateo's tea into the gifted Soul cup. Mateo refused to look. He picked up the Soul cup like it was just a piece of pottery and not a heavy obligation, and took his first sip. It was, thanks be to the Remnants, the usual recipe, bitter but not acrid. Anika pushed a plate of nuts and fruit towards him as well, which he ignored. He wasn't hungry.

'I want to turn Gallasi away, Mateo.'

Mateo jerked his head up. 'We can't!'

'Can't we?'

He raised the cup tellingly. 'Merely because we dislike Elias?'

'I don't blame you for turning to him for comfort.' Mateo's choke of outrage was lost as she added, 'But Timon said you were in no state to say no, and I won't have that.'

Vexation flared. His mind was suddenly clear, smooth and clean as silk. They were always overprotecting him, because they thought he was weak.

'There's too few Ystherans left to play politics, Anika,' he said flatly. She looked both indignant and slightly wounded. Since she tried to hide it, he felt able to ignore it. 'And as soon as the morning meeting is done, I'm untouchable to him. If he wants to make alliance with any other Taurasi, he must get permission from you first. We're all safer if we absorb Gallasi into Taurasi. We already agreed that.'

He tried not to add, but did anyway, 'And if I could put personal apathy aside to make alliance with the man—if you hadn't interfered—then you can bear merely ruling him. Get on with it.'

With hurt now ascendant over indignation, Anika stepped away from him and tapped the counter with a spoon.

'Morning ritual first, Taurasi,' she called brightly, her frown of a moment ago tucked out of sight but her face turned away from Mateo.

Elias murmured, audibly enough, 'The *dawn* ritual would have seen us ready when the Vigile came yesterday.'

Timon turned. 'Ready to do what, Elias?'

Anika lifted her open hands, adding a meaningful look at Timon, and both men subsided. Mateo, back straight, jaw clenched, swallowed the rest of his tea and went among his kneeling people.

The moment he began to let the magic flow, he knew something was wrong. If his conception of his magic was a deep lake, it felt difficult to draw water through the tap that plumbed it today. It felt like the lake had drained away into fens. It felt like—

He fell to his knees, a shocked gasp rising in unison as he went down. Drops of blood plinked to the floor before him, and he touched his philtrum. His trembling fingers came away smeared bright red.

He made a surprised, confused sound, and tipped forwards, only barely catching himself, the parquetry cool and slightly gritty against the soft skin of his palms.

His thoughts vanished into fog then, and he was only passingly aware of chaos erupting around him, shouts of fear and worry, shouts of anger and accusation, the Coterie rushing to his side, Elias there too, speaking in a low hiss.

And then a familiar voice, unfamiliarly raised.

Jonas.

'Everyone, step back,' Mateo heard him shout. 'I'm a physician, let me through. Step back. Give him some air, would you, Taurasi?'

Anika said, sharp as a knife, 'Let him through.' But as Mateo felt his solid presence beside him, he heard her whisper, 'You were meant to wait at the bottom of the hill.'

Jonas said back, low and furious, 'What is this? Are you punishing him, after all?'

'Of course not!'

'Aniketa, this Imperial should not be here. What are you thinking?' That was Elias. He wasn't bothering to keep his voice down.

Mateo shook his head to clear it. He felt more blood slip free. He found Jonas by his side, hand warm on his face as he gently tipped his chin to look into his eyes. 'You with m— Are you with us, Mattias?'

'Yes,' Mateo said, and was surprised by how dazed his voice sounded. 'Yes,' he said, firmer, and got up in a single surge, Jonas's hand on his elbow. 'I'm fine. It's just a nosebleed. I didn't eat, last night and this morning, that's all.'

He received a round of incredulous looks from just about everyone in the teahouse. Jonas, meanwhile, said, 'You're better off sitting down, Mateo. Pinch just here.' He demonstrated on his own nose.

'You look wretched,' Mateo informed him. He did, grey smudges under his eyes, his ready smile strained.

'Thanks. Not the best night's sleep.'

'Guilty conscience.'

Jonas snorted. 'Guilt's a pointless emotion. Cold cloth, please, someone.'

Anika proved unwilling to move from Mateo's side. It was Niki who soaked a cloth under the kitchen basin and carried it dripping to Jonas.

A few moments later, Jonas had stopped both the bleeding and the ritual, because, of course, they could not resume in his presence. This was to Mateo's great relief. He could safely insist that this was merely a badly timed nosebleed even while he hid how shaky he was, how weak, how deprived of the blessed magic that was meant to flow inside him always.

Something was very wrong, and he could not let the Taurasi know it, not until he had a chance to talk to Anika privately. Thus, when Jonas murmured, 'Do you need me to go?' Mateo shook his head, barely restraining himself from clutching at the man's sleeve.

He was, however, still angry at Jonas, as were the Taurasi. It was against the low rumble of that anger that Anika said, 'Let us then open the meeting by welcoming our new kith.'

She indicated the Gallasi, clustered by the garden door. But it was Elias, hovering protectively near Mateo, steely gaze on Jonas, who answered the welcome, in a most unexpected, and yet eminently typical, fashion.

'If we are to join Taurasi, we must express our reservations about your Heart.'

The susurration of the Taurasi complaining about Jonas—and, no doubt, complaining about the Heart, expressing their own reservations, the hypocrites—dropped off a cliff into a shocked silence.

'It gives me no pleasure to do this,' Elias added.

Mateo huffed. It had given Elias's father no pleasure to publicly renounce the incipient alliance between Mateo and Elias, too, all those years ago. It had probably given him no pleasure to attack Taurasi with wild magic and murder its Heart, Coterie, and guardians in one fell swoop either.

He forced himself to stop. He was being unfair to Elias, again. He had to stop blaming him for what his father had done. And any kith had the right to raise concerns about the decisions made by the Kindred Heart and Coterie. The Soul could not dispute that.

Anika coolly said, 'Very well. Express them.'

'There has been a great many missteps, it seems. The greatest of which is still standing among us.' He pointed at Jonas. 'Behold the spy. For some unfathomable reason, he is allowed to stand beside our Soul.'

'Get your finger out of my face, friend,' Jonas said, subtly shifting his stance into the piratical one that somehow made him seem so much less agreeable.

'What did he say?' Elias demanded, usurped from his speech.

'He said he'll punch you in the face if you don't back off.'

Jonas cast Mateo a mild look for that blatant mistranslation, and then made one of his *sure-why-not* shrugs. 'Should I go?'

Mateo was sorely tempted, but for Jonas to slink out now would merely highlight his trespass. 'Brazen it out, you've plenty of practice.'

'The reason is not unfathomable,' Anika said tiredly. 'We are beholden to give Jonas Nebrija assistance.'

'Indeed. We are under threat of execution unless we scapegoat a compatriot. We are facing, at the very least, exile. Aniketa has taken loans against the apartment block and this very teahouse that cannot be repaid. We will shortly be homeless and destitute, at best. And now. Now. We all saw what happened during the ritual. Our Soul, forcibly taken from us into the dangers of the city, alone and afraid. Left so bereft by the treachery of the spy that he cannot perform his one single function.'

And there went any chance of Mateo staying out of Kindred politics. 'I am not!' He turned to Jonas, switching to Imperial. 'I am not bereft.'

'I can't follow fast High Ystheran as well as you assume,' Jonas said. 'I get the impression that one's being a dick again, but I otherwise don't know what's going on.'

'Liar,' Mateo snapped, his anger at Jonas abruptly igniting again. His attention was arrested, however, by Elias's next words.

'I had a dream, the first night we arrived here.' An awed whisper arose from Penelope's side, a more sustained response than the sceptical scoffing from Andrea's side. Elias raised his voice. 'We all know that some Ystherans have prophetic dreams when they return into the ambit of a Soul—'

'That is a *myth*,' Mateo said, flaring up into full outrage. 'Taurasi! It's a myth. He—'

He cut himself off only because Anika had put her hand on his arm. 'Let him speak,' she said. She was looking sickly. 'I see where he's going, and we just have to hope he's overstepped himself. You can't take sides.'

'My dream was of our fate,' Elias said humbly. 'A nightmare, truly, Taurasi. Our prospects are poor, if we continue under the guidance of Aniketa. I therefore feel it is my duty to stand for Heart.'

Anika couldn't have been the only Taurasi who had recognised the path Elias was striding down, but the teahouse erupted into shouts and exclamations, and then noisy discussion among the smaller groups within the factions.

'What's going on?' Jonas asked, looking about at the unaccustomed noise, loud even for the most contentious of their usual morning meetings.

'Taurasi business,' Mateo said flatly.

'I really am going to wait outside, I think.'

Arms folded, head down, Mateo said, 'It hardly matters now.'

'I don't think this one's on me, Mateo.' Jonas twirled a finger, apparently to indicate the general thickly tense atmosphere, ending with a flick towards Elias.

'You don't think your deception has anything to do with an erosion of support drastic enough that there is a real chance Anika is about to lose her position as Heart?' Mateo said, so infuriated he was hitting every second or third word with an emphasis like the beat of a war drum.

'Ah,' Jonas said slowly. 'Right. Understood. I'll be outside.'

In the wake of his departure, Anika raised her hands. 'Very well,' she said over the noise, and Mateo could only admire the cool steadiness of her voice as she called for, and received, silence. 'Who supports the challenge?' The Gallasi rose in one smooth motion. No one else moved. Anika nodded. 'That is eight, and the challenger makes nine. Under Ystheran law, the challenge needs ten to proceed. Is there a tenth?'

No one responded. Anika had been right, Elias had overstepped himself. If he'd thought it would be so simple to shift Taurasi, even a discontented and frightened Taurasi, away from its Aniketa the Unconquerable—

Penelope stood. 'I am the tenth.'

Mateo heard Anika's short exhale. 'Very well,' she said again, as calmly as if they'd just finalised their feast menu to celebrate the end of winter. 'The challenge proceeds.' For the first time, she hesitated. 'The vote…'

'The challenger chooses when the vote is held,' Elias said. 'I choose tonight.'

That was the minimum allowable interlude between the acceptance of a challenge and the vote on it. Mateo was surprised; Elias would need longer to garner enough support to win this challenge. Unless he didn't want to win it, merely strew discontent about like prickle seeds? But then—

'And, in case Anika forgets to, I remind you all that our Soul plays no part in this procedure.'

Mateo contained himself to a scowl at the floor, since openly glaring daggers at the challenger probably counted as interference. He felt a nudge on his elbow, and came back to awareness to find Anika and Andrea consulting.

'I can't miss another day of work after yesterday,' Andrea was saying. 'I have to go see if I've still got a job, really. I don't even know if they're going to be sympathetic or suspicious about the raid.' She winced. 'We need every scrap of income, Ana, now the trade deal's fallen apart and we've got those extra loans plus travel plans to make. I have to go.'

Anika nodded. 'I know. But...' She took a deep breath. 'Will Timon stand by me, do you think?'

'What a question!' Timon appeared at his sister's side. 'I am with you, Aniketa Taurasi, how dare you doubt me.'

She sighed and gripped his hand. 'Sorry,' she said, her voice so meek Mateo wanted to weep. 'I'm a touch shaken, I think. Will you go with Jonas today, then?'

Oh. Oh, Elias, that clever *shit*. Anika was meant to leave Ravenser Odd today, to accompany Jonas on the ridiculous investigation of sorcery in the city. If she went, she'd return to a vote in which she'd had no time whatsoever to shore up her support.

Timon said, 'Blight on it. I *can't*, Anika, I'm your voice among the traditionalists. We can't stand back and let Penelope have at them all day with no counter. They can fairly well carry the challenge if they vote as a bloc.'

'Anika can't go either,' Andrea said.

'We'll ask Jonas for a day's reprieve,' Timon said, adding, 'He'll be reasonable,' in a tone that suggested there might be trouble if he wasn't.

Anika said, 'It leaves the matter hanging over us. It would be nice to resolve it before the vote. It would help, I think.'

Andrea tsked. 'Is there someone else who could go with him, then?

Timon was firm in his shake of the head. 'We risk too much there, Dee. It's too easy to let things slip around him. He...'

'Invites trust,' his sister finished, an unusually grim note to her voice.

'And Henrike was quite clear that she expects Taurasi to take the investigation seriously,' Anika said. 'Fobbing Jonas off with anyone who isn't senior is not going to sit well with her, and it's her who decides if we live in exile or die on the scaffold.'

'Or fight our way out of the city,' Timon muttered.

Andrea elbowed him. 'We could send Penelope. She's senior,' she offered with a faint grin.

'I mean, he's fucked us over, but does he truly deserve that?' mused her brother.

The three of them ducked their heads, chortling. The lady herself glanced over disapprovingly at the sound of their soft laughter.

Mateo had been considering the problem from all angles. Now he said, 'I have the solution. Please contain your kneejerk response. I will go.'

'No!' the Coterie chorused in horrified unison.

'What did I just say?' he said, glowering. 'Listen. I will leave the street, so no accusation of interference can be made. I will go voluntarily, therefore my absence yesterday can't have been so terribly dangerous. I will go in the company of Jonas, therefore I can't have been so very afraid and *bereft.*' He said that last with a snarl to it.

And it would stop the Taurasi expecting a resumption of the morning ritual. Mateo could feel his magic trickling back within him, but it still felt too shallow to risk trying to gift to the entire Kindred.

Here was something he could do for Anika—he had a lingering conviction he'd been leaning on her too much—help her win her vote, and not bother her over a trivial stutter in the magic…which, actually, probably *had* been caused by the stress of the raid yesterday, and he absolutely could not let anyone discover that titbit before the vote.

'Holy Remnants, for you to leave the street for the second day in a row…' Anika said worriedly. 'It could make everything worse.' Before Mateo could bolster his own argument, she said, 'What if there really is wild magic out there? What if the shadow-dogs attack again?'

'You sound like me,' he said quellingly.

'It feels risky.'

'*Everything's risky,*' he parroted to her with nasty pleasure, before checking himself. 'Sorry, Ana. I'll take Darius. He only has a pocket but you know he holds a strong shield when I flow magic through him. And because it's a pocket, it'll be hard for Jonas to make out what's happening. Under the slightest chance of even having to use magic, that is.'

'I think Mateo might be on to something,' Timon admitted.

'There is no call whatsoever to sound surprised about that,' Mateo said haughtily.

The others sniggered again. That was too much for Penelope. She glided over.

'Best to get these things out in the open, dear,' she said to Anika with neither preamble nor shame. 'But now you really cannot be standing here colluding with the Soul with a vote on the line.'

'We were discussing how best I can recuse myself.' Mateo, taking one of Elias's tactics, let his voice ring out to where Taurasi gathered in clusters that coalesced and broke apart as the threads of discussion spread. 'I am sequestering myself from Ravenser Odd for the day, under the care of my guardian.'

There was the same immediate reactionary response as Anika and the twins had shown. 'It is, after all, perfectly safe,' he went on loudly. 'Andrea and the others go into the city. We send our children into the city.' Neither of those points gained ground with Penelope, as her narrowed eyes and thinned lips showed. 'I will spend the day safely in the city.'

He marched out the door, ignoring the protest of his hip at his dramatics, to find Jonas sitting on the porch steps, whittling at a small piece of driftwood with his seax. He'd never done that before. But he'd never been idle on the street before, even when he'd seemed so. He'd always had a job to do.

Mateo bit his tongue on a curse—*a blight upon thee, spying Imperial dog.* 'Anika is indisposed. I am coming with you.'

'Is that so?' Jonas said, pausing mid-stroke. 'I'd prefer the reasonable one.'

'You have no say in the matter.'

The others had followed him out, still discussing a foregone conclusion in low tones. Jonas stood up.

'*Anika,*' he said. 'Yesterday, you all lost your minds when Henrike's people removed him from the street and today you're just, what, going to let him—'

'They have no say in the matter, *either.*' Mateo snapped around to face his Coterie. 'This is the decision of your Soul. A few hundred years ago, you'd've been executed for arguing.'

'Wishful thinking,' Timon proclaimed, though he did look questioningly at his twin, who shrugged.

Anika stepped close, sliding her hand over Mateo's elbow when he tried to storm away. 'Teo, my sweet, it's not that I truly think it's too dangerous for you out there. It's that he hurt you and you shouldn't have to spend time with him.'

'He hurt all of us and none of us should have to.'

She nodded but insisted, 'He hurt *you.*'

'Please let me do this for you, Ana,' Mateo whispered intensely, all the dudgeon he was using to carry him through this awful morning compressed into a fervent plea. 'Please.'

Anika's nod this time was slower, but more accepting. She released him and presented him with a bow. 'This is the decision of our Soul.'

Mateo veered back to Jonas and Imperial. 'Wait while I dress.' He glanced around and whiplashed to Ystheran again. 'Danae, if you will assist?'

The Taurasi in earshot all made identical 'Oh!' sounds; they all knew what it meant if their Soul needed assistance dressing.

'*That* bodes well,' Jonas muttered, and split the little chunk of wood he'd been working.

CHAPTER 21

I T WAS WELL OVER AN HOUR before Mateo returned, fully made up into the ritual outfit of the Soul—layers of painted silken robes, gold and silver and red, face powered, eyes outlined with kohl and finely crushed malachite, lips rubied with ground ochre slicked with beeswax, ears and neck bedecked with jewels, hair in intricate looping braids fastened with Mateo's favoured emerald-green butterfly pins, a gift from Anika's mother.

Danae had also, gently, persuaded him to eat despite his lack of appetite, and he couldn't deny he felt better for it, and stronger. He could feel the slow replenishment of his magic, a disconcerting sensation, because he'd never felt it before—by the time he'd awoken after his long sleep after the day of the exile, his depleted magic had already returned, the deep lake of his goddess's gift refilled.

A subtle survey of the street showed him that it had settled into its usual business for the day. The city workers and the school-aged children would have departed while Danae had been making him eat and helping him struggle into the robes. The rest were about their chores and various industries; those on the street paused long enough to bow deeply as he stalked past them. The face paint lent itself to scowling, which was lucky.

The politicking would happen casually throughout the day. Anika would be in the teahouse, as ever, harvesting her herbs, making her tisanes and balms, arranging the surviving merchandise on the honeycomb shelves, preparing for her Imperial clientele. She had to open the teahouse today, just as Andrea had to go to the brewery, to monitor sentiment after the raid. She would wait for the Taurasi to come to her, reassuring them, calming them, weighing the promises she could make and those she could not. Timon would be conducting repairs and maintenance near Penelope, soothing the worms of worry and fear she'd be letting loose to gnaw among her own faction.

And Elias would be walking about, free of any other chore but sowing discord.

Jonas was leaning on the covered and curtained cart he'd ridden up the hill, chatting to the driver, possibly bribing her to hold for longer. Once again, he had no difficulty recognising Mateo in the switch between his day-to-day and formal aspects; that should have been the first clue he could see the subtle magical aura that shimmered about a Soul.

He swept an upheld palm from Mateo's head to his toes and back up again. 'No.'

'Excuse me?' Mateo said, with exquisitely raised eyebrows.

'No, you are not going down to Anceral dressed like that. You're wearing someone's yearly income on your ears, for starters. And it's incredibly impractical, and you'll get cold.'

'You said it was an Ystheran who was murdered last night? So we will be visiting my compatriots, yes? Who were raided yesterday morning. Who had an allegedly sorcerous encounter the night before that. They will be frightened, and angry. And you are suggesting I cannot go amongst them in the ceremonial accoutrements of my people to ensure their compliance? Do you wish this investigation to fail before we even get started? May we inform Henrike that her agent thwarted us when we tried to—'

'Yes, all right,' Jonas said, holding his palms up in surrender. 'Wear it, then, if you must.'

'I did not need your permission.'

'I know you're angry with me and you've every right,' Jonas said, fighting a smile. 'But, *fuck*, it does something for me when you're like this.'

Mateo stared at him. 'Get in the cart, Jonas.'

'Yeah, keep right on issuing those orders, honey, I'm loving it,' Jonas said cheerily as he scrambled into the back of the cart.

'You don't get to love it, you…you… Oh, I'm too angry to even think of an insult!'

This was then perfect timing for Elias to come striding over. 'Mateo, you cannot go with this man.'

Anyone would think he'd been in the empire for months, with that kind of directness rolling off his tongue; it was so very direct that it rang strangely in Ystheran. Mateo rotated to face him with the small steps the robes and ornate sandals forced on him, the movement made stately by the outfit.

He presented him with a filthy look and another pointed, '*Excuse me?*', this time in frigid High Ystheran.

Elias flinched, visibly taken aback. 'My Soul,' he said in silken tones, with far more circumspection and a good deal more Ystheran-esque courtesy. 'I have grave fears for your safety, should you depart Ravenser Odd in the company of this man.' Once again, he let his voice carry. 'I believe the Heart is taking an unconscionable risk in allowing this.'

Mateo smiled, which was a savage affair in the formal makeup of blood-red lips in a dead pale face. He, too, did not shrink to let the nearby Taurasi pretending to be deaf hear his reply, though he did carefully keep his glee at the sprung trap well-hidden under his perfectly excusable outrage.

In the most flowery, archaic version of High Ystheran he could muster, he said, 'Are you implying that the Heart has any right to forbid the Shard of the Divine from fulfilling his goddess-gifted role to act on behalf of his people in any way he sees fit? Is that the sort of Heart you're intending to attempt to be, Elias Gallasi?'

He'd apparently been speaking slowly and clearly enough for even Jonas to get the gist. From his perch in the cart, the Imperial laughed, not kindly.

Elias's face darkened. He offered a stiff bow and turned on his heel, almost colliding with Darius. The guardian, dressed in his own pre-scribed clothes—less silk and more metal-studded leather—presented himself to Mateo with a bow of his head and his hands clasped around the hilt of his sheathed sword, held upright before his chest.

It was the formal ritual of a guardian reporting for duty, as bruised and stiff as he still was, and it was just as much a show for the Taurasi as Elias's and Mateo's words had been. Darius was conspicuously reminding them that Mateo would be protected, wherever he went— that the Heart was not taking a dramatic risk with their Soul at all, even if it had been her risk to take.

Well, guardians weren't beholden to stay neutral during the voting procedure. Darius offered Mateo a tiny, smug smile.

And, *actually*, if Penelope had taught them anything, it was expert passive-aggressiveness. 'Thank you, Darius,' Mateo proclaimed. 'Since I must recuse myself from the street today *entirely due to Elias's challenge*, it is good to have you at my side.'

Darius's smile widened.

Mateo clasped his elbow and gently trickled a minuscule allotment of his gradually-returning magic into his small receptacle, for the unlikely what-if of needing it out in the city. As he'd suspected, Jonas noticed nothing; all he could have seen was Mateo shining infinitesimally brighter, and that would be hard enough to spot in sunlight unless you knew to look for it.

Darius then offered his leather-clad hand. Mateo contemplated the step up into the cart and his own excessive and, yes, exceedingly impractical robes. Jonas mutely held out his own hand, implying that he and Darius between them would hoist Mateo into the cart.

Mateo huffed a furious breath and flung himself up and onto the cushioned bench opposite Jonas, making it graceful through the power of indignation alone. Darius went around to ride beside the driver, shaking his head. He was assuming the high lookout position, then, which meant he was leaving Jonas to do the close guarding, and that was so much irony it could outfit a smithy.

The hired cart set off, both wheels and hooves louder than Mateo was used to. The cushions would at least make it a more comfortable ride than the Taurasi market cart. He glanced up to see the eternal light wink out. *A blight on Penelope*, he thought savagely, and immediately felt guilty.

'Hurt yourself?' Jonas shifted his weight as if intending to move across to sit next to Mateo and massage his twinged hip.

Mateo threw up a hand, denying him. 'You do not get to do this,' he said. 'You don't get to, to, *flirt* with me and *fuss over* me like nothing's changed.'

Jonas sighed. 'I am also trying to cope with what's happened, Mateo. This is how I do it.'

'With what's happened?' Mateo echoed derisively. 'How unlike an Imperial, to discover the passive voice. With what *you made happen*.'

Folding his arms, Jonas eyed him for a long moment before saying, 'I'm not going to apologise.'

'Did I *ask* you to?'

Jonas ignored the hostile interjection, as he so often did. 'I've lost too many to sit back and let Taurasi turn a blind eye to sorcery showing up in Anceral—'

'*It's not sorcery.*' He was, again, ignoring the hunting pack of shadow-dogs, but that was a single incident solved with a needle through the eye. It didn't count, compared to these supposed murders.

'—and I won't apologise for coming in and making sure a Taurasi wasn't the source of it. I don't like that Henrike used my report to force you to help, but if that was the only way to get your heads out of the sand, then fine, I won't apologise for that either.' He held up a firm finger as Mateo opened his mouth. 'I *will* apologise for not coming clean before I went to bed with you. I thought it was done with and…no longer relevant.'

'Your deception and espionage weren't relevant to whether or not I let you fuck me?' Mateo was suddenly grateful their rattling progress made it too loud for Darius and the driver to eavesdrop. 'Do you hear yourself?'

'I did intend—' Jonas cut himself off and raised spread hands. 'No. I recognise the error of judgement and offer no further excuses. I know it speaks to poor character on my part, and I am sorry for it.' He paused. 'You're not obliged to accept the apology.'

'Thank you, I won't,' Mateo said, all acid. 'You're just sorry it blew up unexpectedly and you got exposed.'

Jonas sat back, wearing an uncharacteristically severe expression. 'That's a bold attitude from someone who must have *strongly* suspected his people foundered my family ship before *he* went to bed with *me*.'

This punctured Mateo's self-righteousness as neatly as a nailbinder hammered through the eye. He shuddered in a breath, and his voice was tiny when he said, 'I wasn't thinking about that, that night.'

'And I wasn't thinking about *this*, that night,' Jonas retorted. 'I was thinking about…'

He held his palm out flat and tilted towards Mateo, as if that explained all. And it did, because Mateo could have made the same encompassing gesture towards Jonas. He stared back, abruptly overtaken by the memory of Jonas's hands on his skin, Jonas's voice murmuring in his ear, Jonas's mouth…

He resisted the urge to drop his face into his hands. It wasn't as if any of the attraction, the prickling response of his body to Jonas's mere presence, had gone away. It had just been tainted, like a Soul loosing wild magic would taint the pure gift of their goddess's harnessed power.

He managed to give a shake of his head, his earrings rippling musically in response. 'I'm sorry, Jonas. It's no excuse, is it?'

'No. No, it's not,' Jonas said slowly. 'Not for either of us.'

Mateo bit his lip. *He* didn't have the excuse. It wasn't even as if he'd remembered about the ship and dismissed the idea of confessing his fears. A simple lie of omission would have been bad enough. *But it hadn't even occurred to him*. He'd looked right at the wayfinder sigil and the libation coin lying on Jonas's chest and still hadn't thought of it, not then, and not the next morning.

But it *was* an excuse for Jonas. He'd been bamboozled by the aura of the Soul—and how much harder must that overwhelming wave have hit someone like him, cheerfully raised to moderation in all things, never greatly challenged by temptation, and utterly unprepared for the pure and shining lure that was an Ystheran Soul. As selfish as it might seem, when he said he wasn't thinking about the morality of bedding the man he'd informed on, it was true.

For all the trouble Jonas had landed them in, and for all that sleeping with Mateo was the one part of it he was prepared to apologise for, Mateo found it was the one part he could not quite blame him for, after all.

Jonas leaned towards him again. 'Ah, Teo… If there's something you're not telling us, I suggest you spill it now.'

'My name is Mattias to Imperials,' Mateo said by rote, without looking at him, and with guilt weighing far heavier on the scales than anger at that particular instant.

The snub effectively silenced Jonas, who turned away with a single shake of his head. Mateo peeked past the curtain on his side. He had been too miserable the day before to pay much attention to the city. His few weeks down there after awakening—miserable then, too—had been enough to tell him it was noisy, smelly, crowded and prone to random domesticated animals blocking traffic.

But he had to admit, even in his stubborn umbrage, that there was a pleasantness in the industry of the people about their business for the day, the elegant lines and bright paints of the buildings, even the domestic clutter of the chickens scattering along the narrow, though pin-straight, thoroughfare. People stared when they caught sight of his painted face, but they also smiled. Some waved. Mateo waved solemnly back.

Jonas muttered something under his breath, and Mateo glanced back at him. He'd shaken off his brooding—of course he had—and produced his small note-taking tablet and stylus. He carved marks into the wax, still murmuring to himself, a stutter of syllables that, after a moment, Mateo recognised the shape of.

Jonas was sounding out Mateo's archaic title. *Heirankidos Zokyntos.* Shard of the Divine.

Jonas had overheard the Ystheran words at least three times now, the last from Mateo himself when he'd been officiously reminding Elias that the Soul was not to be presumed upon. Now he was writing down the first few syllables, repeating them to himself under his breath.

Translating them.

He said it to himself again, faster. 'Splinter? But sacred? Sacred fragments…' He looked past Mateo distractedly, head on one side, musing aloud. 'Oh, of course, the Holy Remnants…but how did that next bit go…?'

Anger displaced guilt, propelled by fear. 'Where are we going?'

Jolted from his study by what amounted to a snarl, Jonas said, 'I thought it best to start with the second murder, since the evidence there is still fresh. The victim was a coppersmith, portside.'

'You said it was an Ystheran.' He was barely able to keep the accusation from his tone, and then wondered why he was bothering and added a suspicious glare.

'He was. He shared a workspace with an ironsmith. Also an Ystheran.'

'There wasn't any copper on Ysthera,' Mateo said, hiding the relief of finding something to prevent Jonas from returning to his academic exercise. 'Bog iron, yes. And we imported silver and gold for setting gemstones.' He absently fingered one of his earrings. 'But we didn't work with copper, or any of its alloys.'

'If he had a passion for copperwork, maybe that's why he left Ysthera,' Jonas suggested mildly, like the easy-going bastard of an Imperial spy that he was.

Mateo demanded, 'And how would he know if he had a passion for copper if he'd never even seen it before he came to Anceral?'

'You normally pick arguments with a bit more substance than this,' Jonas said, making a pained face. 'I know you're annoyed with me, you don't have to keep proving it.'

He'd realised Mateo was being petty on purpose, but thankfully had missed the real reason—or at least, the more urgent reason. Mateo dug in. 'I'm a bit more than *annoyed*, Jonas.'

It wasn't even the betrayal anymore, or not just the betrayal, but the weeds it had rooted through the garden of his life. It was worrying less, and being roundly punished for the lapse. It was his magic, failing this morning because he'd been *bereft*. It was Anika, facing an undeserved challenge. It was Darius, bruised and stiff and still resolutely on duty. It was Kindred Taurasi, contemplating another mortal threat to their well-earned peaceful life.

'I did think you were being strangely calm yesterday.' Jonas winced again. 'Up to a point, anyway. You were in shock, I suppose. Can we just try to get through the day as pleasantly as possible, please, and then you'll never have to see me again.'

It wasn't fair that the thought of never seeing Jonas again still hurt. 'That might be a relief to you, but it'll fix nothing for my people.'

'Neither will acting like this.'

Mateo's fists clenched, the ends of his long, draping sleeves crumpling into his palms as he squeezed tight. 'I'll act as I like, and you'll sit there and *take it*.'

Jonas shut his eyes. He murmured, 'I certainly will, honey.'

'Be serious,' Mateo hissed.

'Half my family was murdered by sorcery, Mattias. I *am* serious.'

It stopped Mateo in the full flight of his seething resentment. His sense of outrage, his fear for his people, kept wiping from his mind that Jonas had all the justification in the world for moving against Taurasi. The guilt rose again, as sure as the pendulum on the water-clock as the reservoir dripped away.

They marinated in a simmering silence as the cart creaked down through the winding streets of the old city. Jonas stared into space, as absorbed in his thoughts as Mateo had ever been. He showed no inclination to resume his translation efforts, which was just as well, since Mateo couldn't have mustered enough self-righteous fury to distract him again.

At last, he couldn't stand the weight of the quiet any longer. 'You must hate us.'

Jonas stirred from the depths of his reverie. 'No. No, actually. I don't.' Mateo's scepticism had to be writ large; Jonas added, 'Wouldn't have let you fuck me if I hated you, honey.'

Mateo worried at his bottom lip again, tasting the earthy flavour of the ochre. He wondered if the effect of the Soul's aura on an unprepared mind was strong enough to drown hatred.

'We made our choice,' Jonas said, sounding just as mellow as ever, but watching him sombrely. 'I was stood right beside my mother when we saw you falling down the mountainside and my sister said, we should cast the fuck off, and my mother said, not with an empty hold, because she was brave and bold and also not an idiot when it came to how the crew would react if we ran the Ystheran blockade with nothing to show for it, right? But we didn't have to hold at the dock, and we didn't have to fire our ballista either.' He rubbed his right bicep absently. '*That's* what made us a target for vengeance, I suppose.'

When Mateo still said nothing—he didn't know what had made *Steadfast* a target but he thought it was more likely spite for assisting Taurasi than retaliation for the big harpoon—Jonas repeated, 'We made our choices. I don't blame Taurasi for what our choices brought down on us.'

'You didn't know the risks,' Mateo whispered. 'A trading ship calculates its risks, but you couldn't have calculated these ones.'

'I was there. I *saw* the chaos in which you escaped. You didn't know the risks either, honey.'

Mateo bowed his head. He was suddenly close to tears, because Jonas was being Jonas.

'But I do need you all to not stand back pretending your hands are clean while the same hammer comes down on my city.' He cleared his throat. So softly that Mateo wouldn't have heard him if the cart hadn't rolled to a stop just then, he asked, 'Do *you* hate *me*?'

Mateo rubbed his hip as he tried to consider this question fairly. The pain there was an echo of the roil of his emotions: fear a constant dull ache, guilt an intermittent throb on top, and when he moved the wrong way, anger like a sharp spike piercing right through everything else.

'Yes,' he said, riding one of those sudden stabs of rage. He hugged his arms tight to his body. 'Yes, a little. The weight we carry, it doesn't go away, it stays and it stays, and then you came and you made it better, and then you made it so much worse. You went out of your way to nudge me from catastrophic thinking and encourage us to move towards our future, and then you visited the same old catastrophe on us and took our future from us.'

Jonas made a jerky movement with his head that was not quite a nod. 'I know. But it's like your hip—'

He said, bitter, 'Don't even try to metaphor your way out of this. We were safe, and now we're not, and you did that.'

Briefly shutting his eyes, Jonas said, 'I'll own to everything else, but you only ever thought you were safe. You never really were, not with sorcery on the loose. We're here.'

CHAPTER 22

Tʜᴇʏ ʜᴀᴅ ᴀʀʀɪᴠᴇᴅ ᴀᴛ ᴀ ʟᴀʀɢᴇ workshop a few streets away from the shore, and a few blocks from the heart of the port. The street was busy, but not in the same way as Low back on Ysthera. There, Mateo had mostly seen mercantile foreigners, the settled merchants and itinerant ship-based traders; crews stayed shipboard. Here, however, was the industrial side of Anceral's port, and sailors and dockhands and stevedores walked purposefully about, dodging women working over sails and nets and men in scale-smeared aprons carrying the scent of fish and harsh salt. There were others he guessed were carpenters or coopers, judging by their tools.

Shipwrights and their helpers, he realised, when he turned to the workshop and noted the iron rivets hammered into a decorative display by its door, an advertisement for the services of the ironsmith within.

They weren't the only people on the street; soldiers were walking about in small groups, idle. Their uniforms were different from that of the Vigiles, which were a traditional local style. These were men of the Imperial garrisons, Mateo realised.

When they slowed and turned about to stare at him, he made the additional, sinking, connection. They were the soldiers who had been mustering to invade Ysthera, and the marines who had been maintaining the now-defunct blockade, all waiting to be demobbed, all openly interested in Mateo and his distinctively Ystheran regalia.

Jonas turned from paying the cartier to wait, noted the burgeoning interest, and refrained from verbalising his told-you-so. He stepped to block the soldiers' view, ushered Mateo and a glowering Darius inside, and, after a thoughtful pause, bolted the door.

'Not,' he said over his shoulder, 'so much against hostility, as against rampant curiosity.'

The heat of the forge had immediately enveloped them. Mateo blotted his face with the back of his fingers, but the powder was made to withstand the summer heat on Ysthera, so he was unscathed so far. He looked around, nostrils burning at the unfamiliar tang of hot metal and coaldust.

The left side of the space belonged to the ironworker. The Taurasi were not metalworkers but the set-up was familiar from visits to Kindreds who were: a simple firepot forge, anvil, leather bellows, quench barrel, coal bin, smithing hammers and tongs arrayed on hooks on the wall, other more esoteric tools laid out precisely on a workbench.

Dressed in a heavy leather coverall-style apron and long thick gloves, face obscured by large goggles of copper and thick glass held about their head with leather straps, hair in a short plait, the Ystheran was welding chain, ever useful onboard, holding steady glowing iron links on the anvil with a long-armed pair of tongs, hammer raised to strike.

'Heilsa, Alessandra Caprinasi,' Jonas called.

She glanced up in response to the call and saw Mateo. Instantly, she dropped everything and pitched into a full prostration, forehead to the sawdust-layered floor. Then she was leaping back up, ripping the goggles off to glare at him.

'Holy fucking Remnants,' she said, in Imperial-tinged Ystheran. 'Fifteen years since I've been in the presence of a Soul. Forgot how hard it hits. You might have warned me, Shard of the Divine.'

That last was said with a decidedly sarcastic bent. 'I'm not *your* Soul,' he told her.

'You know that doesn't matter,' Alessandra said. 'I suppose I have the blighted Taurasi to thank for the raid yesterday morning.'

Mateo declined to take offence at the extreme provocation of the slur flung at his Kindred. He indicated the other side of the workshop, where copperwork accruements were scattered across every surface. 'We have a lost compatriot to thank for the raid.'

He spoke with some delicacy. She did not act as if she were grieving, but she had shared a space with the murdered coppersmith, and may have shared more.

She half-groaned. 'That poor little fool,' she said, suddenly softer. 'Go and have a look around, I have to finish this chain before it cools. Then I'll come and talk to you, and then you can fuck off back up your hill.'

With only the slightest flicker of acknowledgement towards Mateo's Imperial companion, she returned to her anvil, pulling her goggles on and collecting her tongs. Her rhythmic hammering rang out as Mateo, shadowed by Darius and followed in a somewhat less intense fashion by Jonas, crossed the workshop floor to the copperworking side.

There were no immediate signs of disturbance, which was to say that the murdered Ystheran had not been a tidy man and it was difficult to decide if any of the disarray counted as a clue. Mateo trailed along the long bench with no real idea of what he was about.

'So,' Jonas said, 'Ystherans are just going to fling themselves to the ground in obeisance every time they see you, are they?'

'Something like that.'

'And that title. *Heirankidos Zokyntos*. What does it mean?'

Blight the man, he'd heard it one too many times. 'It's the Soul's archaic title,' Mateo said dismissively. 'It translates the same.'

'Does it, though?' Jonas said. 'Because—'

'What exactly am I meant to be doing for you here, Jonas?'

Jonas paused. Then he smiled. He knew Mateo was changing the subject. Mateo maintained his imperious head tilt and impatiently expectant air.

Jonas relented. 'His name was Solon Caballasi. He was killed back here, at the rear of the workshop.' He moved to put his hand on Mateo's lower back to guide him, but gave ground as Darius crowded in. 'Yes, all right, uncle, you know I'll never hurt him.'

Mateo huffed in disbelief but allowed himself to be escorted. At the end of the long bench, Solon's half of the workshop gave way to a storage room, walled off from the larger space with long, pale planks which resembled nothing so much as shipbuilding material. The planks were riveted together in a classic hull pattern even Mateo could recognise.

Jonas lit a small copper lamp and hung it on a hook just inside the door. The mess here was exponentially worse, with tables overturned, tools and copper ingots and sheets strewn about the floor, and a great deal of copperwork scattered, splintered and broken. There were dark marks splattered about, too, and a larger patch which must have been where the body had fallen.

It appeared it was easy to tell when the disarray was a clue, after all.

Mateo looked it all over from the threshold. He was reluctant to walk inside. 'Are you…Do you expect me to announce that I can sense the lingering presence of sorcery?'

'That'd be handy,' Jonas said agreeably. 'Can you?'

'*No.*'

Darius stalked inside and used his sword to shift the debris aside. The guardian poked about, examining the stains and peering up into the dim corners of the ceiling. He cast Mateo a look he couldn't interpret.

'I think he's found the claw marks,' Jonas said.

'There's a lot of them,' the ironsmith agreed from behind them.

Mateo jumped and Darius moved abruptly to his side, levelling his severest mien at her. She remained resolutely unimpressed. She'd taken off her goggles, apron and gloves. Out from under the all-enveloping apron, she wore plain clothes, just as practical and workaday as Ystheran garb but in one of the local styles, a simple sleeveless smock. Though as petite as any Ystheran, her arms, shoulders and legs were tanned and muscular; she must have been immensely strong, given her work. Her hair in its plait only just reached past her shoulders. It was the shortest hair Mateo had ever seen on any Ystheran. For all that, she did have a narrow band of cloth around her waist, tied in an approximation of the feminine arrangement of the traditional Ystheran sash.

He found himself staring quite openly. Alessandra smiled, cocking a hip under his appraisal. 'Why is only one of your guardians in uniform?'

'That's an Imperial,' Mateo said. 'He's a guard, not a guardian.' He felt Jonas shift his weight beside him, but didn't look at him.

'Got yourselves in strife, didn't you, Taurasi?' she said, now speaking Ystheran. 'I knew you lot'd be trouble when you showed up three years ago.'

'Would you just tell me why the Imperials are convinced this was wild magic so we can set their minds at ease and go home?' Mateo said coldly.

'They're convinced it was wild magic because it was wild magic,' she replied, just as coldly.

There was not much Mateo could say to this except to subtly scoop a hand at himself in violent yet silent communication.

'You think it can't be, since you're the only Soul about,' she interpreted, and Mateo wished he'd warned her his Imperial guard understood Ystheran. 'But you don't know how it works because you've never used it. *I* don't know how it works because *I've* never used it.' She switched back to Imperial, including Jonas in the testimony she must have already provided to Henrike's men. 'All I know was that he was in here working on his pet project and I heard an awful noise and came running, and found him being torn apart by a…'

Here her voice failed, and she half-turned from them, wiping her eyes.

Mateo put his hand on her bare arm, purely for comfort, but she said, 'Oh, for fuck's sake,' even as she went to her knees again. She shoved back to her feet, expression furious. 'It's like an avalanche, you know that? Don't touch me again.'

'Sorry.' He really did forget what it was like for Ystherans who had not been exposed to a Soul for a while, and she'd said it had been a decade and a half for her, which was a phenomenally long time.

Jonas, not a man given to fidgeting, was almost bouncing on his toes at this latest performance. 'Someone should really tell me what that is.'

Mateo resolutely ignored him. 'Torn apart?' he picked up. 'By a beast made of mist?'

'Yes. They call them wish hounds here. Well. They have mythical creatures of the storm that they call wish hounds.'

'We call them shadow-dogs. From the old tales.'

'There you are,' she said. 'And all I could do was run away.'

'You'd be dead if you hadn't,' Mateo said quietly. 'Two nights ago. When, exactly?'

'After the last bell—city gates were locked—but not so very long after.'

Mateo thought back. Elias had been with him, but he didn't know where the rest of the Gallasi were—they'd left the teahouse early with the Taurasi, escorted to their temporary insula accommodations. He couldn't guarantee they'd stayed there, he supposed.

But they had no magic; recovering from their travails, they'd slept through the morning ritual that day, only appearing for the evening meal. The Taurasi had had the ritual, of course, filled to the brim with Mateo's magic.

It felt disloyal to have to realise he couldn't personally attest to where every Taurasi was that night. Some might have gone out to the city, after their early departure from the teahouse. Timon had said he was going, hadn't he, and that couldn't have been long before last bell.

He and Anika could ask, true. But none of it mattered, because he surely, *surely*, would have noticed someone taking magic from him in that twisted sort of way, whether it had been within the ritual or on some other occasion.

'Was Solon… Could he…' He had nowhere to go with that line of questioning. Solon could not have called on wild magic without a Soul to supply it. And Mateo would know if another Soul was in the city.

'He had a prophetic dream,' Alessandra announced. 'When you first arrived. You know how that works.'

'I know it *doesn't* work,' Mateo said frostily. 'It's a myth.'

Jonas made a frustrated noise under his breath and started to rummage through the debris, possibly to stop himself from asking more questions Mateo was absolutely not going to answer.

'He had a dream,' she repeated sternly, 'and he immediately abandoned all his projects.' She waved an arm about the workshop. 'We used to have a profitable partnership, you know. I'd make the iron rivets and spikes and roves and all sorts of iron bound for the ships, and he'd coat them in copper, in between art commissions.' To Mateo's blank look, she explained, 'Copper stops salt corrosion. Shipwrights love it. Then he had his dream, and he broke every contract, stopped paying his half of the rent, and spent three years learning how to make—that.'

She pointed to where Jonas had just pulled out something both heavy and fluid, that shone in ripples of foxy red-gold in the low lamplight.

He held it up. 'Copper armour?' he said, looking doubtful.

'A full coat of scale armour,' she agreed. 'And skirt, gauntlets, and greaves. Helmet, too. *And* a sword and shield. Most of it's stored out back, actually. It was taking up too much space in here, and it's weird, and use- less. No one uses copper armour, or copper weapons. It's technology from hundreds of years ago. Worse! Not even bronze. I had to help him put iron into the sword blade, it would have been unusable if I hadn't, too soft.'

Darius, in his fossicking in the chaos of the storeroom, picked up a knife, hilt and blade all made from the same red-gold metal, and raised it questioningly. It was an admirable display of craft, given no magic could have been involved.

'That one's not so bad,' Alessandra admitted. 'The blade's short enough. It won't hold its edge, though. It's not shoddy workmanship, it's just the nature of copper.' She jerked her chin at the scales draped over Jonas's fists. 'He'd only just started on the second set. That's half a skirt, as far as he got. The coat itself takes thousands and thousands of tiny plates, every one beaten thin and meticulously sewn in overlapping rows onto a leather backing. It's not a quick process without—' She coughed. 'I think he was finally losing momentum on his obsession. He said it was enough. It was right. More wouldn't get used.'

Jonas turned his handful, watching the play of light. 'Because of a prophetic dream he had when Taurasi arrived in the city? Or when Mattias Taurasi, the *Heirankidos Zokyntos,* arrived in the city?'

Alessandra finally remembered that Imperials were unaware of a series of interrelated facts about how Ystheran society functioned, or perhaps she decided she was still just loyal enough to her compatriots to not give them away.

'Oh, it's all a myth,' she said. 'He had a dream with coincidental timing and went haring off on a wild hunt.' Turning back to Mateo, she said casually, 'Can I sell you what he made, though? Like I said, he didn't contribute to the rent for years.'

This was a clever way to say, *He made it for you, so fucking take it,* without putting the Imperial on even higher alert.

Mateo slowly unclipped two sets of earrings, and placed both pairs on the bench near the storeroom door. He heard Darius hiss through his teeth. 'I trust this compensates for both the armour and the rent.'

'Just a tad,' she said, looking at them, one silver studded with rubies and worked in the intricate design unique to her own Kindred, the other the enamelled specialty of Leporasi, both inherited via alliances. 'Ystheran jewellery these days…'

She shook her head, mouth downturned, then added, with a glossy sort of insouciance, 'It's so profitable, yet so hard to replicate.'

Ah. 'You can stop that,' Mateo said. 'We have a hallmark now, you won't be able to pass off your fakes anymore.'

'Fakes!' she cried. 'It's Caprinasi's style!'

'But it's not Ystheran technique!'

'Could we perhaps argue about this another day?' Jonas enquired with polite pointedness.

Scowling to match Mateo, Alessandra turned back towards the iron side of the workshop, mouth tight, that downturn at the edges of her lips once again apparent.

Mateo paused. 'I am sorry for your loss.'

'We weren't kith,' she said, giving him a harshly defensive look. 'We just shared space.'

He hadn't been quite sure if he was offering condolences on the loss of whoever she'd left behind on Ysthera, or on the loss of Solon, but he knew now.

'Yet you paid his rent for three years,' he pointed out. She looked briefly flummoxed before regaining her nonchalant mask. 'You know you are welcome to come to our morning ritual. Our Heart would like to meet you.'

Her, or her tanned and muscular forearms, and, in fact, tanned and muscular everything.

'I left Ysthera for a reason, Taurasi,' she told him scornfully. 'Kindred life is not for me and never will be.'

'I didn't invite you into an alliance,' Mateo said, matching her tone. 'I suggested you could occasionally come up for a visit, should you want what the ritual offers.'

She looked him up and down. 'Offering without insisting on formal alliance? That's a very modern attitude for an Ystheran Soul dressed so very traditionally.'

'Oh, this?' Mateo said, waving a hand up and down himself, very much like Jonas had done that morning. 'Malicious compliance.'

Jonas, holding the half-made skirt against his chest while he watched the interplay with an attention he was no longer even trying to disguise, stifled a groan. Mateo didn't let himself smile, but he did exude a great deal of self-satisfaction nonetheless. Jonas closed his eyes, shaking his head and fighting off his own reluctant smile.

Meanwhile, under the force of Mateo's radiating pleasure, Alessandra dipped at the knees before beating back the impulse to bow down all the way.

'Maybe,' she said. 'I'm used to going without, now, and absolutely no longer used to this ridiculous forced reverence.' She pointed at the door. 'Off you go, Soul of Taurasi, and take the copperwork with you.'

CHAPTER 23

THE SOLDIERS HAD MOVED ON. Jonas hired a couple of dockworkers lingering at a makeshift bar further down the street, and they helped him load the copper pieces into crates and stack them behind the driver's bench. It did not leave a lot of room. Darius had kept the copper dagger, and sat revolving it in his hands, making light glimmer across its blade. The driver looked justifiably nervous but also fascinated.

'We're going to the site of the second incident now,' Jonas told Mateo as he sat opposite him; he'd ducked into the local messenger depot and returned with blank wax tablets. 'Or, the first incident. The one that happened seven weeks ago.'

Mateo hesitated. 'If it's another reliable eyewitness to tell me it was sorcery, I promise to believe your account without having to be told firsthand. I don't think I can gain much by looking at the place so long after it happened. You've…you've proved sorcery is out there, yes.'

'And do we have a theory as to who might be responsible?'

Mateo was still, and supposed he would remain, at a loss. Alessandra had been correct when she had said that anyone innocent of wild magic was also generally innocent of knowledge of its workings. Perhaps Elias, then, could tell them more.

It was stronger and longer-lasting than their domesticated magic, that had been made clear on the day of the exile, but it still came from a Soul, and the Ystheran wielders still had to be nearby; he shivered as he remembered the Gallasi *phalaros* chasing the Taurasi down the mountain, soaring on the invisible updraft of unleashed power.

He wished he could point the finger at the Gallasi now, but it seemed a callous act when these escapees had spent weeks desperately seeking refuge and had in all probability been in Ravenser Odd under the care, and therefore supervision, of the Taurasi at the time of this most recent murder. He at least had to check if any might have left the street before laying the blame at their feet.

Again, it occurred to him that Timon had gone out of Ravenser Odd on the night of the murder, and in an oddly guilty fashion. And had been in the city seven weeks ago, when Gallasi were not. And had voted for using wild magic against the empire three years ago, and not much wavered in that opinion even after Ysthera had paid the price for it. And received a daily dose of tame magic from his unsuspecting Soul which perhaps he had worked out how to free from its constraints.

He shook his head, hating the sick feeling of mingled suspicion and disloyalty. 'Perhaps if you tell me more about what happened seven weeks ago?'

Jonas hummed a few notes in a considering sort of way, then said, 'It's different, that one. I think you do need to talk to the person who saw it happen.'

The lading work had evidently made him hot; he took off his cloak and rolled up his sleeves. Mateo, on the other hand, had been sitting uselessly in the cart. The mist had lifted, and the day was clear, but the cart was moving along in the shade of the workshops lining the streets. He was in layers of silk, but the traditional loose weave was meant for the sun-drenched slopes of Ysthera. He began to shiver.

Jonas held his cloak out to him.

Mateo felt his breath hitch. 'Stop it.' When Jonas merely looked mildly puzzled, he said, 'Stop being Jonas. It's not fair.'

'I *am*—' His expression closed as he understood. 'I was never pretending to be other than who I am, Mateo.'

'You were doing nothing *but* pretending,' Mateo snapped.

Except, of course, his pretence of liking Mateo had been helped along by the blinkers created by the Soul's aura. At that thought, Mateo's flash of anger was smothered by guilt again, and then a sudden existential fear, very clear and cool, like water dripping in hidden caverns, accreting rock as it went: did anyone like him for who he was, tetchy and contrary and anxious and crippled, or only for what the remnant of divinity he bore could do for them?

Both chagrined and confused—did he not have enough conflicting emotions to choke down without having to also season the meal with this smoothly bitter flavour?—Mateo lowered his face to his knees.

'Go ahead and cope how you're going to cope, honey,' Jonas murmured as he tucked the cloak around Mateo's bowed shoulders. 'Have to say, though, the mood swings are a wild ride.'

By the time Mateo composed himself and sat up, Jonas was employing a message tablet. He wasn't translating snippets of archaic Ystheran this time. Brow crinkled in concentration, he wrote for what seemed a long time. The Imperial penchant for making marks on wax and papyrus to note and record things was baffling, but it was hardly unpleasant to watch Jonas carve the wax. He had the thin sleeves of his shirt rolled up and his strong forearms on display, the snake tattoo writhing as his tendons flexed in time to the movements of the stylus.

But that led to flashes of their night together—his forearms caging Mateo's head on the pillow as he smiled affectionately down at him, about to slide his mouth all the way down Mateo's body—which Mateo did not want intruding. Especially not on the way to another murder, no doubt as brutal, or more so, as the one he'd already confronted this morning.

He closed his eyes. Holy Remnants, if the Imperials had an empire-assimilated Ystheran telling them straight out that it was sorcery, no wonder they'd had no patience with Taurasi denials. No wonder Henrike'd had no compunction about deploying her friend's personable son as spy. No wonder Jonas'd had no compunction in following his orders to the letter. No wonder both of them thought the whole Kindred deserved exile at a minimum.

Jonas nudged him. 'You with us, Mattias?' he asked. 'We're almost there.'

Mateo looked around. They were, unexpectedly, moving along a broad street, a tree-lined avenue of villas, somewhere to the northeast of and above the broad docks of the port. It was not as high as Ravenser Odd, but unlike that lonely perch, had an unobscured view of the little harbour, its many trading ships and fishing vessels riding peaceably at anchor within the safe arms of the twin headlands.

'The old man we're going to see will get a real kick out of meeting an Ystheran,' Jonas said. 'Do you mind… You've been biting your lower lip, taking the colour off. Can I…' He half-lifted a hand towards Mateo's face. '…fix it for you?'

Mateo gave a silent nod. Jonas swiped his thumb over Mateo's top lip. Mateo felt his lips part without volition under the assured touch. Jonas gently blotted the ochre-tinged balm he'd collected along Mateo's lower lip and then brushed his thumb back and forth to smooth it out.

'That's better,' he murmured, hand lightly cupping Mateo's face, thumb resting against his mouth.

The cart jolted to a halt, and Mateo started, jerked out of staring fixedly at Jonas's lovely, intent eyes. Jonas, too, blinked and dropped his hand. His thumb was still tinged red, and he licked it clean with a single swipe of his tongue while Mateo helplessly watched.

'Teo…'

Tearing his gaze away, Mateo was deeply mortified by his own blatant yearning, which transmuted immediately into dudgeon of the highest sort. '*Mattias.*'

'Honey, it doesn't have to be like this,' Jonas said. 'We can… Look, I cannot tell you how much I regret—'

'Regret's a pointless emotion.' Mateo flung himself out of the cart.

Then he had to pause to press the ball of his fist against his aching hip. He stood catching his breath and looking about. They'd come to a stop in front of a plastered and painted villa in the local style, of the type the previous owner of Ravenser Odd had been hoping to build up there before Madam Kerling thwarted him. It struck Mateo that this must be quite a wealthy area of Anceral.

Jonas followed him out of the cart. 'Sorry, Mattias,' he said quietly. 'It's not… I don't… I know what I've thrown away, all right?'

'You can't throw away what you didn't have.'

Jonas, abashed, ducked his head to collect his cloak out of the cart. He went to speak to the driver, handing her up the tabulae he'd inscribed his long note on. This time, the cart rattled away after the application of coins, the driver giving Darius a last wave and smile. Some people liked quiet men, even, or especially, when they were conspicuously grim.

Jonas had by now recovered enough to once again take refuge in pretending all was well between them. 'She's taking my notes to Heiko and then delivering those crates up to Ravenser Odd,' he explained conversationally when he caught Mateo looking after the cart. 'We're going to stay for lunch here. I'll send for another cart when we're done.'

He started up a path made of crushed seashells, through a verdant garden and past a large aviary of brightly-feathered and twittering birds towards the villa's main courtyard.

Mateo followed, Darius a stolid presence at his side. 'I thought we were going to…'

'This *is* the site of the other murder,' Jonas said, in the slightly distant way he had when he was touching on something he didn't really want to discuss.

'Oh. And the old man we're going to see?'

The old man, who Jonas knew well enough to know he'd like to meet an Ystheran.

The old man, who Jonas knew well enough to assume they'd be welcome to stay for a meal.

Mateo had the sickly sense that his swing back to umbrage had been poorly timed.

'Don't think about it too much,' Jonas advised, which did not help the oily feeling of anticipatory guilt in Mateo's stomach.

They walked into the large courtyard. It had a mosaic tile floor, and a rectangular pond that reflected the sky and the villa at the end. A small herb garden, composed of square beds rather than the Ystheran curving style, took up one side, under espaliered fruit trees. On the other, a covered colonnade led to a separate structure which would be a plumbed bathing room. That was traditional to Anceral, as far as Mateo understood, but it also featured an ash tree by the bathing room, which must be acting as stand-in for the Vaeringan sacred well.

Jonas knocked on the brightly painted door under the small porch. It was flung open instantly, and two little girls piled into his arms.

'Heilsa, my darlings!' Jonas said, kneeling to further haul them into his embrace. 'I didn't know you were visiting Papi today. How remarkably inconvenient.'

Jonas's nieces. And…

'He's a relative of yours, then?' Mateo asked with dread.

Jonas paused before shrugging and saying, in his easy way, 'My grandfather.'

Mateo surrendered and put his face in his hands.

'I told you not to think about it.' Jonas rose and took each niece's hand in his, letting them lead him across the mosaics of the small atrium. 'Papi? It's Jonas.'

'Jiji, my boy!' came a cry from further inside. 'Come to me. I don't move these old bones so well anymore.'

They entered the main living space of the villa. One of the nieces—the younger, Hilda—had turned about to look at Mateo, mouth agape, hand lax in her uncle's as she lagged to stare.

Her sister nudged her. 'Uncle Jiji says that's rude,' she hissed.

Well, of course he'd told them it was rude to stare; otherwise they'd've given away that their branch of the family could see the Soul's aura, and hadn't Jonas been so boldly complacent to risk that visit.

'He's shiny like a flower,' Hilda said.

'Flowers aren't shiny,' said Asta, which was what Mateo was thinking.

'Flowers with lightning bugs inside them are,' the younger girl announced triumphantly.

Which…inarguable, really.

Jonas, without looking around, snorted and tugged on his girls' hands. There was a large window on the far side of the next chamber, with its shutters flung wide. A fresh breeze was rippling in. An old man, unbent but grey-haired, sat on the divan by the window, looking out to sea. Mateo saw that while Jonas might have inherited his height, or lack thereof, from his half-Ystheran grandmother, he'd gotten his complexion, easy smile, and breadth from his grandfather's side.

'Papi, you'll catch your death,' Jonas scolded him.

'My boy, I spent forty years before the mast, a limp breeze is not going to hurt me,' his grandfather said. 'You know I like to watch the ships come in.'

Jonas kissed him on his lined forehead while tucking in the blanket draped over his lap. 'I know,' he said softly, and Mateo immediately understood that the old man once habitually sat at this window watching for *Steadfast* to return to harbour and three years ago she had not.

The old man gave his great-grandchildren a goofy smile before finally spotting Mateo, Darius at his shoulder. He lit up. 'Oh my, Ystherans!'

Jonas looked up from fussing over his grandfather and a look of true trepidation flashed across his face. Here was a decided opportunity to sink the boot into the conniving shit…by being obnoxious towards a friendly old man who had sat waiting for his daughters' ship to come home carrying half his family.

How many days had he sat here, calculating routes and weather and other reasons for a late return, until the news came about a white storm from clear southern skies?

Mateo wondered if Jonas had been the one to kneel before his grandfather's chair and take his hand and tell him.

Instinctively grasping that the man was hoping for a certain performance, Mateo slid his hands up his copious sleeves and presented to him a deep and formal greeting bow of the most traditional sort, making his looped braids swing.

He straightened, set his hands over his heart and said, 'Mattias Taurasi. My guardian, Darius Taurasi.'

Darius, scowling, dutifully bowed, in the stringently proper fashion of around fifty years before, because he, too, could see what was wanted here.

The old man put a gnarled hand on his own chest and made a fist of bowing from his seat. 'Thorstin Velasco,' he told them. 'How wonderful to meet you. My wife Cynisca was half-Ystheran. Her father was Kindred Serpasi, he met her mother in the Low village and joined the crew for a while. I always wanted to bring her up to meet the Taurasi, but…' A darkness crossed his face. 'She'd been poorly for so long by the time you arrived in the city. It never seemed a good time to take her up the hill. And then…' He shrugged, very much like his grandson.

'We're here to talk about Noni, actually,' Jonas said, still in quiet, respectful tones. 'About what happened, at the end.'

Thorstin's shoulders slumped. 'She always wanted to do magic, when she was a little girl.'

Mateo had a moment in which to consider exactly how much her Ystheran father had told her about where the magic came from, before the old man went on, as wistful as if recalling his own childish longings, 'She never had the knack, though. Not enough Ystheran blood. Though, she looked quite a bit like you. Lovely soft hair. Flew like a flag when she loosed it shipboard, black as the colours we flew. Gods, she was beautiful with a sword in her hand.'

Mateo became distracted by that casual diagnosis, not enough Ystheran blood. How much Ystheran blood did it take to hold within oneself the blessing of the goddess? He did what it had never occurred to him to do to an Imperial. He made the tiniest of forays towards Jonas, grandchild of a half-Ystheran. And sure enough, Jonas contained the *scaphosieros*, the sacred receptacle, the tiniest of pockets.

The girls had been very quiet. Hilda now said, 'See? Shiny like a lightning bug.'

'You with us, Mateo?' Jonas asked, even as he brushed a hand over his chest, frowning.

Mateo, alarmed, desisted. Luckily, Thorstin was still dreamily reminiscing. 'She never even really saw magic. Her father couldn't live without his Kindred, in the end, but they wouldn't accept a foreigner, so her mother couldn't go with him back to Ysthera, and Cyn stayed aboard with her.'

'I'm sorry,' Mateo said. 'We can be…parochial like that.'

'No people is perfect,' the old man said mildly. 'Could I… Could you show me magic?'

Mateo blinked. 'You don't fear it?'

'We only fear what we don't know. Please?'

'I don't do magic.' At the disappointment in Thorstin's face, Mateo glanced helplessly at Jonas, who was apparently making an effort to *not* look pleading. 'But Darius here doesn't mind breaking the rules.'

Darius let all his air out in an audible sigh, which was fairly close to the first noise Mateo had heard him make for years. Then he held out his hands and created from thin air a solid ball of glowing amber. Since Taurasi magic was invisible to those without Ystheran blood, and since most of the Taurasi's magic was directed towards the quiet completion of domestic chores, this simple shield-adjacent manifestation was about the only thing he could do that would look mildly impressive; there was nothing particularly striking about pointing out that Mateo's silk robes were still pristine because they were coated in magic, for example.

Mateo put his hand on Darius's back and subtly flowed more magic into him while the Imperials were distracted by the radiant ball he'd set to float; Darius obligingly sent not just the ball but the contents of the entire room wafting upwards. Thorstin beamed in delight, and his great-grandchildren crowed and clambered up over the levitating furniture to chase the ball on its gentle arc to the ceiling.

But when Darius made the table they balanced on begin to swoop about like a bird, Jonas called a halt. Darius tipped the table so they slid down into their uncle's arms with squeals of sheer ecstasy, quickly followed by wails of disappointment that Uncle Jiji wasn't going to let them do it again.

He soothed them, sent them off to play in the larger garden beyond the courtyard, and turned back to Thorstin, kneeling to take the old man's hand. 'I know it's hard, Papi. But Mattias needs to hear about how Noni died.'

Again, Mateo put a hand over his eyes. This man's daughters and grandchildren, and this man's wife, lost to sorcery, and still he smiled to see Ystherans, even smiled to see magic.

Thorstin said, abruptly, 'It was not merciful, but it was a blessing nonetheless.' Mateo dropped his hand and openly stared. 'Cyn had been ill for such a very long time. There was…' He pressed his free hand to his stomach illustratively. '…something eating away her insides that could not be removed. Koriad tried.'

'My father,' Jonas murmured without looking up.

'She was in agony. Towards the end, she could not sleep nor eat nor *think* for the agony gnawing at her bones and nothing worked to help her.' Thorstin's brow was furrowed, an echo of remembered pain on his face. 'She wanted to die. She asked to die. And where our moral courage failed her, magic answered instead.'

Now his hand shifted from his stomach to his throat, and he closed his eyes. Tears began to leak down his weathered face.

Jonas rested his hand on his grandfather's shoulder. 'What's done is done, Papi,' he murmured. He turned to Mateo. 'Something grew in her throat, in an instant.'

Thorstin's voice was hoarse as he went on with the tale, squeezing his grandson's hand. 'It choked her. It was stuck in her throat and she couldn't cough it out, she couldn't swallow it. She was gasping for air, clawing at her throat. Ashore after years on *Steadfast*, and it was like she was drowning.'

He coughed convulsively as he relived his wife's torment. Mateo had unconsciously moved both hands to his own throat, feeling his own air effortfully whistling in and out of his chest.

'We should have let her float away on poppy milk but she drowned on dry land with a solid mass of magic trapped in her throat.' His eyes popped open and he looked fiercely at Mateo. 'But it was quick, and then it was over, and she was finally at peace.'

'By the time my father and I got up here, she was long gone,' Jonas added quietly.

Mateo tried a few times to get the words out. He had to press his forehead against Darius's stalwart shoulder before he finally managed it. 'How do you know,' he whispered, 'it was magic?'

'My father sliced open her throat to see what killed her.' Mateo must have looked even more appalled at this matter-of-fact pronouncement. 'Autopsies are normal in such circumstances, Mateo. And he was not happy to lose her like that.'

Mateo again took a moment to find his thoughts. 'Your father is not of Ystheran heritage himself? Then he couldn't have seen…'

He made a helpless gesture at his own throat, appalled by the gruesome image of slicing open dead flesh. Mere contact with a dead body was pollution, requiring long rituals of purification; he couldn't imagine cutting into it.

Jonas rose, giving his grandfather one last comforting pat, and took Mateo's elbow. He walked him back out to the atrium, Darius on his heels.

'She wasn't choked by magic in her throat,' he said when they were far enough away. 'She was choked by an item that magic lodged into her throat. That is what my father removed from her.' He paused, looking at Mateo as he struggled to contain his revulsion at the thought. 'Since it was plainly of Ystheran design and there was no earthly explanation for its manifestation, my father reported it to Heiko as a case of sorcery.'

'So Henrike has the…item?'

'She returned it to us when her people couldn't discover anything about it and after Anika refused to examine it.' He gave a hurt-sounding half-laugh. 'It's hidden on one of his shelves. You better come see it.'

Darius at his shoulder, Mateo dismally followed Jonas down a hallway to a room of memories. It was lined with cabinets and shelves housing the exotic mementos of lives lived at sea. One of the cabinets was dedicated to Ysthera, its treasures shining through the large diamonds of a lattice-fronted door. Jonas opened the cabinet for them.

Mateo ran his hand over a fine-toothed bone comb, inlaid with pearl in the familiar curling pattern traditionally associated with Kindred Serpasi. It was not all purely family memorabilia. There was a Kindred cup of the Caballasi. Glass and amber beads, flashes of colour trapped inside, a specialty of Suinasi, and their delicate blown glass bottles, pale green. A jumbled collection of ear and finger rings, in every Kindred style, including the Taurasi's favoured jade and silver. Darius picked up a jade clip, and set it back down, face especially blank. Charion had commonly worn a very similar style.

The cabinet also held, in profusion, the beautiful artistry of the elaborate enamel hairpins made by Kindred Leporasi, Anika's mother's people. One was a stunning jade-coloured dragonfly, gleaming, inviting touch with its creamy smooth enamel.

His heart panged. Anika had kept a set made by her mother, dragon-flies like the one in the cabinet. They hadn't survived the journey, or she'd sold them without a single ounce of mercy for herself while her Soul lay unforgivably unconscious in the first days of landfall.

He'd tried to gift her the ones he wore now, hairpins also made by the hands of her lost mother, and she had waved them away, saying, 'They're butterflies, Teo, they're for you.' He'd gift them to Niki one day, instead— if they didn't sell them to fund their next exile, and then they would never have anything like them again.

Mateo had clung to the notion that while he still existed, the Taurasi still existed, and while that had been a pressure so heavy it sometimes felt crushing, it had also been solace. But the neglected treasure of this dusty cabinet writ large how much had been lost.

Taurasi would endure, but Ysthera was gone.

No one would ever again stand on the sun-drenched shores, or walk about the pretty cottages of the villages, or visit Low to trade for rubies and sapphires, or attend the Klados hall in the ancient hollow high on the sacred mountain. Souls would never again pilgrimage to the very peak and kneel at the mouth of the sacrosanct cave where the goddess was said to sleep.

No one would ever again work enamel like Kindred Leporasi had known how to, magic and craft irrevocably entwined. No one would ever again distil apricot liquor exactly to Kindred Caprinasi's lost recipe, which may or may not include a hint of hazelnut. No one would ever again make glass beads with a magic swirl of fire and ice caught within.

Elias was right. They were diminished, and they would continue to diminish in each generation until they were like Jonas, carrying a tiny pocket that bespoke the gift of their goddess, but blind to it, and not at all Ystheran.

All that was left was detritus, divorced from all meaning, souvenirs to wonder over for a scant moment before moving on to the next fleeting diversion, locked up in a display case for future generations to stare at, with no appreciation for all that had been lost.

He felt then a wave of grief as strong as in that very first moment, not when they'd chosen exile, not when they'd lost Sabine and so many others, not when they'd heard of the destruction of their Sunlit Isle, but the moment that presaged all that.

The moment at Klados when the other Kindreds had announced their decision to forsake their goddess.

That had been the first and deepest cut, because that had been when part of him had known that this was where it would lead: nothing left of Ysthera but dusty relics.

He turned away, fighting his own breath. Darius was stiff beside him, eyes lowered, hands clenched. They were both trapped under the weight, unable to offer each other comfort. Jonas stepped between them. He put a hand to Darius's shoulder, Darius stiffening further, but not fighting it. He slid his other hand around the bare nape of Mateo's neck, under the loops of braids.

'I'm sorry, little elves,' he murmured. 'I should have brought the ball to you instead of making you look at all this.'

Mateo, eyes tight shut, let himself hold there, under the steady, *treacherous*, warmth of Jonas's palm, for one long moment before gathering himself.

Then he shook off the touch and stepped away, mirrored by Darius. 'Show me now.'

Secreted in an engraved box at the back of the shelf lay a silver ball on a fine chain, about the size of an apple. It resembled nothing so much as the censers Mateo had seen temple priests swinging on the steps of their temples on holy days to waft scented smoke about, before Ravenser Odd. It was smaller than those, however, and was etched all over with the same serpentine pattern as on the comb.

Mateo reached for it, and Darius shot out a hand and grabbed his wrist.

'Be careful, friend,' Jonas said, which was directed towards that hard grip but could have been a warning for either of them.

Darius let Mateo go, and picked up the silver ball himself. He weighed it testingly, rolled it about his gloved palm, poked it, sniffed it.

'It's safe to touch,' Jonas said patiently. 'It's been in plenty of hands.'

'It hasn't been in an Ystheran's hands,' Mateo explained circumspectly. He meant it hadn't been in a Soul's hands, but Jonas didn't need any extra clues regarding the nature of the Shard of the Divine.

Darius carried the silver ball with them as Jonas ushered them to the triclinium, the table laid for a meal by a couple of young servants, the only helpers here apart from the cook. Frowning, the guardian kept it held low while they sat on divans and ate salted fish and beans and a dense, nutty bread. This was partly, Mateo guessed, to keep it out of the sightline of the old man in case it distressed him, and partly so he could conduct experiments on it with quick jabs of magic while the heedless chatter of the two little girls on either side of him covered the brief hum.

Meanwhile, Mateo listened to Jonas and his grandfather reminisce about their days at sea.

'Some of these stories make *Steadfast* sound like a pirate ship,' he said at last, as they pushed their plates away.

'That's how we started,' Thorstin said, and cackled with wicked pleasure. 'My father stole that ship off a corsair off the south coast. We were pirates in my day.'

'We were only just on the legal side of privateering in mine,' Jonas added. He, too, laughed at Mateo's indignant look. 'Oh, honey, you are so naïve. No aboveboard trading ship is ever going to risk crossing an Imperial blockade.'

'No, no, I knew that,' Mateo said, because he had. 'I just didn't know I was talking to an out-and-out pirate.' He bowed in his seat to Thorstin, who cackled again.

'What did you think the ballista was for, if not a relic of the days of running down other ships?' Jonas asked, still looking insufferably amused.

Mateo thought about it, and then said, 'Walruses?' sending both men off into roars of laughter.

Afterwards, out in the sunshine of the courtyard, Darius placed the silver ball into Mateo's bare hand. He'd found nothing odd about it after repeatedly poking it physically and magically, and ceded it with an almost philosophical shrug—and yet watched intently as Mateo's hand closed over it, hand on his sword hilt, magic shield ready to fling up.

But when it made no sudden sorcerous moves, he let himself be led away by the girls, apparently for a game of hide-and-seek in the garden.

'So…' Jonas said from behind Mateo. He'd returned from taking his grandfather for a lie-down, and was trying on the innocently amiable manner he employed when worming information from his unsuspecting victims. 'What's different about when the Soul touches it, then?'

'Nothing, obviously,' Mateo said, showing him the silver ball remaining stubbornly inert in the centre of his palm. It felt heavy, and unexpectedly warm. 'If it's a trap, it's either very bad or very, very g—'

He stopped. The silver ball had heated beyond warm, towards burning. The giggles of the girls as Darius stalked about with great dignity pretending he couldn't find them faded away. Suddenly stiff and static, the only motion he could manage was to begin to tip his palm to make the ball roll off.

It was too late. The world flashed white.

Apparently, the sorcerous silver ball had required not only the touch of the Soul to activate itself, but his voice.

CHAPTER 24

Mateo stands at the mouth of a shallow cave high atop Ysthera's mountain.

He knows this cave. It is, it was, like the peak itself, sacred to Ystherans, all of them, not just Taurasi. Their stories say the goddess lived here, or had once, or would visit here. Ystherans do not worship their goddess, not since She shattered and fell into eternal sleep, but if they did, this is where the centre of their worship would be.

Souls came here. Mateo came here, when he was late ascending to his gift. No one else crossed its threshold.

Below him, the mountain falls away into the scrubby grey-green trees of the foothills, a glimpse of golden beaches beyond. It is a familiar sight, and a lost one, and it should tear at him, but he feels nothing.

Light glints over all the edges he can see. The sun is rising over the Sunlit Isle for the last time.

Mateo isn't sure how he knows that. He turns.

Sabine stands quietly in the centre of the cave. There is a small fire lit in a pit behind her, and its play of shadows is cast eerily over her. Her face seems cracked in that weird light, like crazed glaze on a porcelain cup, like metaphorical blight made literal. She wears the robes of a Soul, but they are torn and dirty. Her hair falls in a tangle. She looks gaunt, and unutterably weary.

'This is a sending to the Soul of Taurasi,' she says, and Mateo has the impression it is the third or fourth time she has said it, the building of a scaffold of ritual. Her voice sounds raspy-whispery. She stares past him; she can't see him.

She glances over her shoulder, and back to the mouth of the cave, staring out over the eastern foothills of Ysthera. 'I do not know if this will work,' she says. 'We are using the unbound magic to send this message across the sea. It will kill the Ystheran who takes the message, and desecrate their body. Their throat will be burst open.' This death sentence and defilement is pronounced with neither distress nor regret. 'It must be done.'

Now Mateo can see behind her another six Ystherans, all in the same state of miserable disarray, torn clothes, hollowed cheeks, despairing eyes. There is debris about them, of bedding and food preparation, which suggests they have been living in the sacred cave.

'They broke us,' Sabine whispers. 'They broke the Souls one by one and made our breaking our own blighted choice. I gave them magic freely, and they used it. They used it so much that they now turn their eyes outwards, desiring to introduce the rest of the world to it. But I escaped. *We* escaped. This is our choice now.'

Slowly she draws herself up. The cracks across her cheeks deepen, but she pulls about herself something of her usual cloak of serenity as she says, 'I was Soul of Kindred Taurasi, and this is my choice.'

One of the others takes her hand. 'I was Heart of Kindred Suinasi, and this is my choice.'

A younger Ystheran, about Mateo's age, stands erect on her other side, face also wearing thin fractures across its surface. 'I was auxiliary Soul of Kindred Serpasi, and this is my choice.'

Like Sabine, and unlike the others, the auxiliary Soul's voice is remote, emotionless.

A child now, voice wavering. 'I was neophyte of Kindred Caprinasi, and this is—' He chokes back a sob. '—this is my choice.'

An older woman, her face bearing a badly healed gash, a sleeve dangling empty. 'I was guardian of Kindred Leporasi, and this is my choice.'

Setting a hand to her shoulder, the man beside her says, 'I was Coterie of Kindred Caballasi, and this is my choice.'

The last Ystheran speaks. 'I was… I was just me, of Kindred Gallasi, and this is my choice.'

Sabine begins to glow, and the younger Soul beside her. It is not the pure amber glow of domesticated magic. It is blighted, shot through with white, like mould blooming over something rotten, like a spill of poppy milk spreading in ginger tea, like infection creeping through a vein. Mateo feels the flow of the taint out of the Souls and into the Heart and Coterie and the other two adults. Only the little neophyte does not partake, kneeling and covering his head.

The magic—strong, wild, boundless—seems to tear out of Sabine and the young Suinasi and pierce the wielders. It is not a gentle or easy process, but there is no doubt that it is powerful. The contained magic within Mateo flutters and pulses, responding yearningly to its wild and free kin.

Under Mateo's feet, the floor of the cave trembles, and then comes a deep shudder and crack.

'It is begun,' Sabine says hoarsely. 'They cannot turn it aside now.'

Dust and little stones drift down around the Ystherans. Soon the cave will collapse, but they make no effort to escape. They kneel and hold hands, except that the little neophyte huddles against the guardian until she changes to a cross-legged seat and gathers him close into her lap.

Sabine crosses to the threshold of the cave. Side by side, the ghost of the past and the Soul of Taurasi look out over Ysthera. Above them, Mateo can see dark smoke billowing into the lightening sky, blown eastwards from the peak of the mountain.

'Mateo.' She still stares blankly past him. 'I can only hope this message reaches you.' She gives a laugh, humourless. 'Perhaps I am talking to the Soul of Taurasi another five hundred years from now and this can serve as the warning we ourselves failed to heed. But I hope…' She bows her head. Some emotion seems to finally break through her blank dispassion. 'I am sorry, Mateo. I tried to hold out. But they played on my vanity. I thought I could avert the worst of it if I gave in. They made me—' She frowns. Her voice loses its despairing edge, roughens into alertness. 'Is there something on the water?'

Mateo turns back to the vista of lost Ysthera, and the vast ocean to the east. He can make out nothing amid the expanse of waves, their white caps catching the first dawn light.

'See, there, the—'

THE WORLD EXPLODED in a blinding flash. Mateo recoiled and gasped in a breath as if surfacing from a deep dive. His cheek smarted. Jonas had judiciously backhanded him, and brought him out of the trance.

Jonas pointed upwards. Three shadow-dogs circled overhead. The activation of Sabine's sending, throbbing with wild magic, must have drawn them.

Mateo stared up at them without emotion, dropping the silver ball into the capacious pocket of his outer robe. He turned towards Darius, who was crouched on the far side of the garden, holding the Taurasi shield over the heads of Jonas's nieces, who huddled together under a bush.

Mateo thought, *The guardian must leave the humans and protect me.*

The pain in his hip lanced through him, far sharper than the slap across the face had been. He properly jerked awake, shaking away the terrible frost Sabine's sending had infested him with.

He was still preternaturally calm, but aware enough that this was not like him that he spared a thought to wonder if this was how Anika felt when she faced down crises without flinching. He flowed magic out to Darius, fast but narrow, to not overwhelm his guardian's small receptacle. Hooking onto the flow, Darius immediately expanded the shield so that it came down over Mateo and Jonas as well.

Mateo would be shining bright to Jonas now. 'I admire your moral commitment to obeying the empire's rules, I really do,' he said, 'but maybe you could *use* your magic now, rather than just bolstering Darius's with it.'

He sounded, as usual, perfectly unflappable. Mateo could finally appreciate the man's stubborn determination to take just about anything in stride. He could also finally see what it cost him to do so. He'd lost most of his family to wild magic, and his two nieces were now cowering under threat of more, and still he stood unwaveringly beside Mateo and made the mildest of suggestions, trusting Darius to keep them safe.

The shadow-dogs swooped claws-first onto Darius's shield, and it shuddered. It would be stronger if he'd left it small and protected only the girls. Or protected only Mateo. It would also be stronger if they had more than one magic-wielder holding it up.

It was barely even a decision.

Mateo lunged at Jonas, startling the man into almost taking a step back. He let Mateo set hands to his chest, one deliberately over the wayfinder sigil tattoo showed faintly through the rough weave of his shirt. Mateo flowed magic into him.

He had to be immensely careful. Jonas's receptacle was tiny, the smallest pocket he'd ever encountered, and he was also in the same position as an Ystheran child, taking in magic for the very first time. If Mateo had been in any way panicking, he would never have dared try this. Without precise control, he'd stop Jonas's heart instantly.

But he was still eerily calm, the remote detachment of his brush with wild magic carrying through, without, thanks be to the Shattered One, the cold cruelty of it. The physical touch helped his control too. His metaphor was the lake, and the turning of a tap, but, for Jonas, what came to his mind was pouring a thin stream of ginger tea from the tiny spout of Anika's smallest brewpot into one of the smallest Kindred cups. He gave Jonas exactly the amount of magic as he could hold, hands spread wide on his chest, even while he continued to feed Darius too.

He wouldn't be able to flow more in until Jonas started to flow some out. But Jonas, of course, had no idea how to use magic—if he even understood what the warm glow suffusing him was. His eyes wide, his hands scrabbled at his chest around Mateo's own firm hands, evidently trying to find and swipe away a physical cause of what must be a very strange feeling.

Mateo had been teaching Taurasi children how to first find the flow of magic for years now. He caught Jonas's wrists, stopping the fretful fidgeting. 'Jonas, pay attention.'

Jonas's eyes locked to his, and he fixated there. He'd gone still, but Mateo could feel tension thrumming through him, feel his heart beating fast when he spread his palms on his chest again. 'Good. Can you sense that warmth? That's magic, Jonas. You have Ystheran blood, and you can use magic.'

'You,' Jonas said. 'From you?'

'I'm sharing mine,' Mateo took the time to say; even this risk need not give away the function of the Soul, if Jonas was distracted enough, and he should be. 'I need you to help Darius hold up the shield. I'm going to tell you how. Close your eyes.' Jonas obeyed. 'Good. Look within.'

'Not helpful, honey,' Jonas murmured, eyes still closed.

Mateo took Jonas's wrist and moved his hand so his fingers pressed against his own pectoral where the wayfinder sigil lay. 'You can feel your breath, and you can choose to hold it. You can feel your heartbeat, and you can choose to slow it. You can feel the magic, and you can choose to wield it. Focus your mind on the warmth. Reach into it. Take hold of it. It wants you. Find it.'

Taking the hint, Jonas traced symbols, presumably the familiar runes of the wayfinder sigil, over the cloth of his shirt. It seemed to take forever —it was only a few moments—and then Mateo felt something change in him, some hitch in his chest or shiver across his skin. He had hold of the magic.

That had been the easy part. Mateo put his hand to Jonas's shoulder, garnering his attention again.

'Good. Now. You want to protect us. All you want is to protect us. You want to raise the shield because that will keep us safe. You know what the shield looks like. You can sense what it *feels* like. Fix your mind on that and push *out* with the magic, Jonas. Your body knows how to do it. It just needs to know you want it.'

Jonas shook his head, frowning. Mateo frowned to match. He couldn't use magic; he couldn't tell another Ystheran how to use it. Older children taught younger, at the practice. Jonas would need to be shown this by Darius, who was definitely not available.

Mateo risked a glance. The shadow-dogs were hitting the shield repeatedly now, clawing and biting at it. Darius crouched over the girls, eyes narrowed in concentration.

Jonas had followed his glance. Still resting his fingers on the wayfinder sigil, he dropped his other hand to the hilt of his seax.

'Don't,' Mateo said, tightening his grip on his shoulder. 'The only thing that can protect them now is that shield. You have to find a way to help Darius hold it.'

Jonas drew the knife.

'Jonas, please—'

He inscribed invisible staves into the air with its point, rapid repeated lines and angles in a circular pattern. Around those, he slashed letter-runes. Then he swooped his hand in one big enclosing circle, and shining amber followed in the blade's wake. When the circle closed, the whole sigil lit into being, glowing strong and bright.

He'd drawn the helm of awe, the strongest protection sigil he knew, and now he had an amber shield made of magic. He eyed it with some satisfaction.

'That's beautiful,' Mateo breathed. 'You're doing so well.'

Jonas's eyes snapped to his. Mateo, still marooned in unsettling tranquillity like a ship in the doldrums, wished with great clarity that he'd thought to moan that sort of praise when he'd had his hand locked around his cock, because the look Jonas was giving him suggested he'd have received a highly positive response.

Mateo's tranquillity shivered.

The sigil-shield wavered too, then steadied as Jonas understood that he had to keep flowing magic into it to hold it in existence. Mateo began to trickle more magic into him to match the outwards flow.

'Lend your shield to Darius,' he ordered.

It took another few moments before Jonas worked out how to do it.

Frowning at the sigil-shield didn't work; commanding it aloud to move didn't work; wafting his hands towards it didn't work; but taking hold of it like an actual shield did. Jonas's grip on its solid rim rapidly tightened from tentative to firm, and he tossed it like a discus with a mighty jerk of his shoulder and arm.

It spun through the air and hit Darius's high, wide, thin shield, dissolving into it. The hum of magic all around them increased in intensity, and the shield overhead thickened. Jonas, a sheen of sweat across his face, spared himself a smile.

Looking back to Darius, Mateo saw the guardian was caught in a frustrating bind. Now the shield was reinforced, he wanted to fight back, but he also didn't want to leave the frightened children. Jonas, still holding the seax, shifted his own focus through the translucent shield to the overhead threat.

'You can't,' Mateo said, hand still firm on his shoulder. 'You have to concentrate on holding the shield.' At the obvious protest, he added, 'Darius has had thirty years' practice wielding magic and a sword at the same time. You've had thirty heartbeats. Look after your nieces.'

They crossed to the others. Darius looked Jonas up and down, shrugged, and pressed the dagger he'd taken from the coppersmith's on him. As soon as he was confident their new guardian was holding fast, physically and metaphysically, Darius prowled forwards, measuring the underbelly of the closest shadow-dog.

The day of the exile had taught them that the things were not vulnerable in the usual soft spots, so Darius did not lunge out of safety to try to cut into its intestines. Instead he made himself bait, bringing the shield lower and lower until the shadow-dog was hurling itself over and over again against the glowing barrier just above his head.

And then, scowling as he calculated the timing of it, Darius spiked his sword up just as the creature's head flailed downwards, and stabbed it in the eye.

When Madam Kerling had done that, it had killed the shadow-dog instantly. This one merely howled a high-pitched protest and wrenched away, taking the sword with it.

Darius glanced over towards Mateo, but it was Jonas's eye he seemed to want. He pulled Madam Kerling's nailbinder from his sash and held the ridiculous, flimsy weapon in one fist. The shield flickered, another shadow-dog barrelled down at him, and Darius plunged the nailbinder into its eye, his fist sinking deep.

This time, it worked; the very narrowness of the nailbinder must've allowed it to pierce some vitality the wider sword could not. Head nailed to Darius's fist, the thing's body crashed onto the shield, leaking white mist.

Jonas waded on in when the third one swooped while Darius was still trying to pull his hand free from the twitching creature he'd just felled. Jonas had his seax in one hand, Darius's knife in the other; it was this latter weapon that he jerked upwards. He might have been trying for the eye, too, but the shadow-dog lurched and the knife and much of his arm rammed down its throat instead.

Before its teeth could close on him, Jonas, face screwed up in pain or concentration, twisted, shoulder flexing. The blade punctured the shadow-dog's neck from the inside, and Jonas ripped it out in one long stroke, mist billowing about him.

'Gutting a fish,' he muttered, staggering back as it thrashed in its death throes.

It fell still and evaporated. Jonas dropped the knife, breathing hard. His hand and forearm were reddened and blistering.

Darius finally yanked free of the other one, and it too spun into mist. The half-blinded one turned writhing circles in the air like an eel caught in a trap before rising up and vanishing. Darius's sword fell out of mid-air where its eye socket had been, clanging onto the courtyard tiles and making both girls cry out.

Jonas turned to them, dropping to his knees as he tucked his seax away so he could gather them both into his arms. Their distress sundered his attention to the shield as effectively as anything could, and it thinned. Mateo cut off the flow of magic to his receptacle now he wasn't using it. Jonas touched his chest again but didn't look away from his nieces.

Darius released the shield. He retrieved his sword, cleaned it off as if tendrils of mist still clung to it, and sheathed it. He retrieved the knife he'd lent to Jonas. Weapons seen to, he stood before Mateo and made him a deep bow with his hands fisted together, very formally.

Over his guardian's lowered head, Mateo saw that Jonas had turned to stare at him, hand still pressed against his chest.

CHAPTER 25

Never had Mateo been more grateful for Jonas's stalwart ability to continue on as if nothing too out of the ordinary had happened. Within moments, it seemed, he had comforted his nieces, checked on his grandfather, and set the appeased staff as lookouts in case the shadow-dogs came back.

Meanwhile, the last of Mateo's eerie calm cracked and fell inexorably away, and he began to shiver in the aftershock and the renewed grief of witnessing Sabine's end. He wiped at his eyes, covering his fingers with powder and kohl. He felt unclean. He could remember himself coolly decreeing that Darius should abandon children. He could remember himself thinking of them as human, as if he wasn't. Even the calm that had been so useful during the attack was suspect now.

What had he become, after the merest brush with enough magic to make anyone a god in truth? Perhaps he preferred the fallible human with the bees in his head after all.

Signalling Darius to stay with the girls, he followed the colonnade past the herb beds to the small bathing room. He soaked a linen cloth and started to scrub at his face.

Jonas came to bathe his arm, setting a small clay pot of some sort of salve on the tiles nearby. Darius's fist was unaffected; he'd known how to magically shield his skin. Mateo wasn't sure if Darius had offered to take the worst of the blistering away and Jonas had refused, or whether the guardian was not confident enough to try. Healing was a speciality, needing a skilful, delicate, and trained touch.

Jonas didn't speak as he rolled his sleeve up and ran cold water over the scald-like injury. The blistering was worst around his wrist and forearm, but the rash went up past his elbow.

'Are you all right?' Mateo said after bearing the silence for a few moments. He looked at the damp, stained cloth in his hands.

'Hale and hearty,' Jonas said, turning his wrist and watching the play of the water over his skin. 'I've sent for carts to evacuate the villa. I can't guarantee the wish hounds won't chase the traces of magic even once you're not here.'

'Sorry,' Mateo whispered. 'I'm sorry your family got dragged into this.' He grimaced. 'Again.'

'It's just bad luck the girls were visiting today.' But Jonas still wasn't looking at him.

'You're angry with me.'

Jonas finally met his eye; Mateo had the strong impression he had to force himself to do it. 'No. Just thinking things through.'

'Oh, don't do that,' Mateo said. The man was far too clever for thinking things through to be anything other than dangerous.

Jonas smiled suddenly. 'I've already figured it out, honey. You know, when that big storm hit us after we'd taken you off Ysthera, we couldn't understand why you wouldn't use magic to quell the wind and waves—'

'Because we can't control the weather.' His heart was beating too hard in his chest.

'—*or* help hold the ship together, but I understand now. *You* were sick.'

Biting his tongue, Mateo turned back to the tap to rinse his cloth. Jonas did not need a single extra clue at this point.

It didn't matter. 'All the Taurasi magic is *your* magic, isn't it? You gave it to me, like you gave it to Darius, like you give it to everyone. That's what the Soul is. That's why you shine. That's why the Taurasi are reluctant to let you out of their sight.'

Mateo wiped at his face again, getting the last traces of powder off his skin. Jonas liked to make fishing sound like certainty. Mateo wasn't going to confirm anything for him this time.

'I know I'm right,' Jonas said. 'I'm really just reasoning out the right thing to do about it.' He shook his head. 'I thought you were the only Taurasi too virtuous to break Imperial law, but instead you're the one enabling everyone else to do it.'

Carefully, Mateo put down his cloth. He slowly removed the status markers, earring by earring, ring by ring.

Stepping back from the water, Jonas dried off his arm and began to rub the salve into it. 'Is it always there, inside you? Does it hurt you, to hold it without sharing it? Tell me it's painful to not use it.'

Mateo hesitated, fingers at his ear. That would be a very neat, reasonable, helpful excuse.

'You don't know,' Jonas said. 'Because you've never even tried not using it.'

'We wouldn't be Ystheran anymore, if we didn't use our magic,' Mateo said. He looked down at the jewellery he was holding, remnants of a vanished world. 'We're already diminished, but that would extinguish us.'

They were still Ystheran, as long as they had a Soul and the threefold gifts of their goddess. Mateo tucked the jewellery into his robes.

'You're not the first people to face extinction and have to change to save themselves,' Jonas told him. 'You undoubtedly won't be the last.'

He left unsaid the simple fact that their stubborn use of magic was now threatening them with extinction far more imminently than turning from it was.

'I wouldn't be useful,' Mateo blurted.

Jonas melted. 'Oh, honey.'

'If we can't do magic, it takes away my reason for being,' Mateo said, crushing his sleeves into his hands. 'I wouldn't … I wouldn't have a use in the Kindred anymore.'

'Do you really believe you have to be useful to be loved? Did Elias teach you that one, too?'

'I think this might be my foible, not his. And it's not that I don't feel loved.'

Even as he said it, though, he felt the intrusion of that silky thought again, cold water dripping in a secret cavern: he only felt loved because people had to love him, because the Soul's aura forced them to. He shook his head; he already had perfectly good worries, he didn't need to add more.

He went on, 'It's that I've felt useless all my life, except in this one thing.' And now one of his usual passing worries did try to catch him, unusually clear and fast as it whispered, *Including in this one thing.* Again, he faltered; again, he rallied. 'I can't—I can't not do it for my people.'

Jonas looked at him with quiet affection, almost but not quite shaking his head. 'That day, coming down the mountain, the great blaze of light that we, that some of us, could see shining bright in the middle of the glowing Taurasi. That was you, then, wasn't it, giving your magic to them so they could protect themselves?'

'Yes.'

'Gods.' The single word held an uncomfortable note of awe.

'People died because of me that day,' Mateo said in the teeth of that awe; too late, he realised he was not making Taurasi's case as well as he could be.

'People died because it was an awful day and people died,' Jonas said. 'I'm guessing people lived because of you too, yes?'

Mateo, after a moment in which Jonas waited him out, nodded.

'Say it aloud, then,' Jonas said, very softly.

He took a breath. 'People…' A second breath. 'My people lived, because of me.' His third breath was easier, as if a load of bricks had been lifted off his chest.

'All right. The light went out just about when you collapsed. I'm assuming a connection?'

Another nod, and a reluctant, 'The drain was too much.'

'And that caused your "seasickness". You were recovering.' Jonas tugged his sleeve down over his arm. 'Right. So the Taurasi are as unlikely as ever to give up magic, and it has its benefits as well as its risks, like everything else in life. But if I report the truth about the Soul to Heiko—'

Sucking in a breath, Mateo held his hands out towards Jonas. He only barely stopped himself from going to his knees. 'Jonas, please don't tell her. The empire will murder me.'

'Yes, I know,' Jonas said. 'And Niki, right?'

Mateo's hands were shaking. He clasped them together, stepping backwards, cursing the robes and the sandals and his hip, because he couldn't run and he had to, he had to get to Darius, he had to get back to Ravenser Odd, he had to warn Anika, he had to save Niki, Taurasi had to *run*—

Jonas went on blithely. 'That's if they don't decide to go the other way and force you to feed magic into any impeachably loyal Imperial with Ystheran ancestors so they can recreate the battle wizards.' He shrugged. 'They wouldn't even need to intend harm. My father alone, tempted by magical healing, wouldn't be able to resist trying to put you to work if he knew.'

Mateo, still edging backwards, froze as Jonas lifted his gaze and stared at him gravely, pinning him. 'That's why I've decided it's wrong to tell Heiko, or anyone. I will never, ever, tell.'

'Holy Remnants, say that *first*,' Mateo said, clutching his stomach. 'I mean—thank you, Jonas.'

Again, he won one of Jonas's rueful smiles. 'Of course, all that's just to justify my choice to stay silent solely to keep *you* safe. It's very shaky, morally speaking. Because there's still the matter of the sorcery, isn't there? That must come from Souls, too. And you're the only Soul in all the world. Or no?'

'I am. I'd know if I wasn't. But I would never give anyone sorcery. I don't even know how.'

He did, though, if he would let himself think about it. In the same way that his metaphor of a tap to flow magic to the Taurasi had become a thin brewpot spout for Jonas, he sensed he could visualise instead a wide-mouthed pipe, a sluice-gate, a great egress from the still lake within him. He sensed that it was somehow his choice, as Sabine had said it was hers.

'I would never give anyone sorcery,' he repeated firmly.

Jonas, as if in answer, wrote in the air with a forefinger, the rune lighting up as he finished the last stroke; because of the constant flow of magic until the moment the shield was dropped, Mateo had left his receptacle filled. The rune flashed once, and a golden raven blossomed to slowly flap about their heads.

Jonas looked up at it. His fascination was exactly that of Ystheran children achieving their first magical workings.

'I'm aware that I very much forced it on you,' Mateo said slowly, also watching the raven, 'but you do understand that that doesn't make it sorcery?'

'I know. This—this does not feel bad. It feels beautiful and clean and…holy.'

Mateo opened his mouth to point out that the sheer glamour of magic could very well impart a false sense of righteousness. Jonas headed him off. 'Really? Even this, your self-proclaimed reason for being, you're going to be obstreperous about?'

Mateo managed a very meek, 'No.'

Jonas abruptly swiped his hand through the rune, making it and its raven vanish. 'I know I should be troubled anyway. If I was properly Imperial, I'd be terrified I was infected with sorcery. If I was properly Chalcadean, I'd be furious that my chance at a peaceful afterlife has been ripped from me through no sin of my own. And if I was all Anceran, I'd be wondering what price to sell it at.' He smiled. 'As it is, I'm an empire mongrel, and—' His smile became a brilliant grin. '—*and*, it turns out, an actual fucking wizard.'

Concentrating, Jonas drew the raven rune again, followed quickly by a second that Mateo recognised, from the children's excited demonstrations, as a number. This time nine golden ravens circled Jonas. He smiled in satisfaction.

'Let's not get carried away,' Mateo said. 'Right now, you're like a toddler with a new toy.'

The nine ravens winked out as the magic in Jonas's receptacle ran out; he made a disappointed face, touching his chest, and sent a rather plaintively hopeful look Mateo's way.

'Are you seriously asking me to fill you with more heresy?' Mateo demanded.

Jonas gave his unrestrained laugh—Mateo had never been so glad to hear it—but before he could answer, a rumble from outside signified a new arrival.

It was Jonas's father, Koriad, coming to escort his father-in-law and granddaughters away to safe refuge. He hadn't gifted Jonas much in the way of looks, or demeanour. He was a tall man, of an age with Darius, his fine, straight hair entirely white where Darius's merely bore the first threads of silver around the patch of white where the shadow-dog had gashed his scalp on the day of the exile.

He was also spittingly enraged.

'Right,' he said, once his family and the house servants were loaded into the cart and he had assured himself they were safe and well. He stormed over to Mateo and towered over him, hands on hips. 'The mercantile side of the family might be philosophical about this kind of shit—'

Jonas muttered a pained, 'Da,' and Darius stepped between Mateo and the shouting healer.

'Let him yell,' Mateo murmured; he was relieved that *someone* in Jonas's brutally pruned family was expressing the appropriate level of rage about it.

His guardian—his guardians—reluctantly stepped aside. Koriad hadn't even paused for breath during the interruption.

'—they might have a tradition of accepting unexpected death as the risk of doing business at sea, but I'm from the medicinal side of the family and we don't accept unnecessary death for *nothing*. And I tell you, you sorcerous shit, I've lost the mother and grandmother of my children, my daughter, several nephews, a niece, and some very good friends, and now you've put an old man and my grandchildren at risk, and if I fucking lose *any* of them now, or, so help me, *my only son*—'

At this point, he made the error of poking Mateo in the chest. Darius stepped smartly forwards and grasped the offending finger. Koriad stopped mid-diatribe, looking down at the much shorter man with a fist wrapped around his index finger. Darius, unsmilingly holding his gaze, gently shifted Koriad's whole hand so it was pressed to the other man's chest, and then left it there with a final pat.

'Right,' Koriad said again, now sounding uncertain. Short and round, Darius was not exactly an overtly menacing man among Imperials, but he did carry that aura of grimness that bespoke the need for caution.

Koriad looked back to Mateo but was unable to regain momentum. 'I love my son,' he said in more reasonable tones. 'If anything happens to him—anything else, because don't think I don't see you've hurt your hand, Jiji—I will see that Heiko crushes you. You know you're dangerous, or you wouldn't need a guard.'

Mateo silently bowed to acknowledge this; it was somewhat illogical, which suited an Ystheran perfectly well. By now, a second cart, to take Mateo and Darius back to Ravenser Odd, had pulled up in front of the villa, the driver watching the interaction with consummate disinterest.

'I'm fine,' Jonas told his father. 'None of this is their fault.'

'They brought wish hounds down on you and my granddaughters!'

'Trust me that they didn't,' Jonas said gently. 'I'm escorting them home; we have some things to discuss.' His father opened his mouth, the vein in his forehead suggesting a return to volume. 'Go ahead and yell at me, and then I'm getting in the cart with them.'

'Oh, you're as stubborn as your mother was,' his father said, and here in his tone of mingled frustration and fondness was an echo of his son. 'You just smile more, so it's harder to tell. Be safe, Jonas, and *come home*.'

They all set off, Jonas with Mateo in one cart, Darius once again keeping watch beside the driver, and Jonas's remaining family and villa staff in the other, headed for Koriad's residence, closer to the water.

'Bye, lightning bug man,' Hilda yelled. Mateo waved her farewell.

Jonas waved too. He said, 'Sorry about my father. He means well. He just expresses it loudly.'

'Oh, I imagine Darius would shout at me quite a lot, if he hadn't taken a vow of silence.'

'You know it's not a vow of silence, right? You know it's an expression of deep trauma?'

'You would know,' Mateo said, unable to hide the thickening despondency in his voice.

Their affable spy shook his head, smiling. 'What's the matter, honey?'

Mateo took a deep breath. 'I'm so sorry,' he said. 'I've been doing my best to ignore the fact that you lost as much to sorcery as we did. I see why you felt like you owed it to your family and your city to help Henrike. I understand why your first loyalty was never going to be to Ystherans. I've been selfish, acting like I don't. You never deserved my anger, and my…mood swings.'

Jonas watched him, wearing a peculiar expression. 'That's all right,' he said eventually. Again, he hesitated, before saying, 'Gods do tend towards the capricious, don't they, Shard of the Divine?'

Mateo froze. He felt a cold burn start low in his stomach. 'That's a funny thing to say.'

'I *was* hoping you'd laugh in my face. But, Mateo…you're not laughing.'

'I'm not a god, Jonas. That's ridiculous.'

'I already told you I won't be telling Heiko anything,' Jonas said calmly. 'I sent her an update, but I didn't mention anything about that archaic title of yours. I understand why you must keep the Soul's role hidden. I understand why you were so convinced these murders couldn't be sorcery. But I need you to tell me the whole truth now. I need some reassurance that my trust in you is not misplaced.'

'It's not misplaced,' Mateo said. 'I'm not a god.'

Jonas didn't shift his steady gaze. It was Mateo who squirmed, looking away.

He blurted, 'I'm what you'd probably call a demigod.'

CHAPTER 26

To Mateo's great surprise, Jonas looked not pleased but shocked to have his last suspicion confirmed.

'Oh my fucking *gods*,' he swore, clapping his hands over his face. 'I was really, really hoping you'd laugh in my face.'

'Jonas—'

'No, I need a moment. I was not as prepared for this as I thought I was.' He breathed into his hands.

'You *asked*,' Mateo snapped. 'Should I have lied, then, straight after you demanded I tell you the truth?'

'Possibly that would have been better for my peace of mind. Shit, and you were pissed I didn't tell you I was a spy before we fucked, and meanwhile, you were hiding *this*! A god. I took a *god* to bed.'

'Demigod!' Mateo moved then, ignoring the growing ache in his hip to slide off his seat and to his knees on the cartbed in front of Jonas. He clasped his hands to the other man's knees. 'Please, Jonas, you can't tell Henrike.'

The response was immediate, and immediately calm. 'I already said I wouldn't, this doesn't change that.'

Mateo sagged against him in relief. Jonas gently drew him to sit beside him…and then shuffled away so they weren't touching, very much in the manner of a younger Taurasi. Mateo glared until his trepidatious expression dissolved into amusement.

'It was Hilda, you know. She kept saying you were like a firefly inside a flower, and eventually I put that together with the archaic title. The divine shard is what makes you shine like you do, yes?'

'Do *not* tell me a half-millennia secret was outed by a child.'

Jonas's smile widened. Mateo could see him adjusting, absorbing the revelation; yes, Mateo was, by some definitions, a demigod, but he was also still just awkward, tetchy Mateo.

'Can I ask you some questions?'

'Can I stop you?'

'Well put. Who, actually, are you?'

Mateo sighed. 'We don't really know. It's not as if the goddess sat us down and explained it all. We have a story. Five hundred years ago, Meredonia shattered—yes, sorcery, and did we learn our lesson?—and our goddess shattered with it, into twelve shards.'

'The Holy Remnants.'

'It's said the Souls each carry one of those remnants within them. Five were lost as we fled Meredonia, and the surviving seven guided us to Ysthera, Her gift. It's mostly just a story, though. There's more than seven Souls...' Mateo stopped, and started again. 'There *were* more than seven Souls at any given time on Ysthera. But only seven Kindreds and we know we were divided into twelve on Meredonia. So, perhaps, some truth to it.'

'And the remnant of your goddess inside the Soul gives the Ystherans magic,' Jonas said slowly. Mateo nodded. 'It already makes no sense, because if sorcery existed to shatter your goddess, then you can't have had magic only *after* She was destroyed.'

'Firstly, it's just a story, and secondly, it's said that on Meredonia, they drank a thick, bitter, frothing brew to unleash their magic. Everyone could do this as they liked, and the magic was powerful but also wild and dangerous. The remnant within the Souls contains it. Domesticates it. Makes it safe for us to share. *That* is the true gift of our goddess, not the magic itself. The Soul, the divine and the human together, is the gift.'

'And then the prayers of your people—'

'No!' Mateo said sharply. 'No one prays to me. We haven't prayed to anyone since we lost our goddess.'

'They ask for the magic and you give it to them? Sounds very much like praying to me. Oh, all right, no need to scowl at me like that. Not praying.' Jonas looked lost in thought. He nodded to himself. 'Are you...born?'

'We manifest.'

'That's why you all got a bit tense when I was asking about your and Niki's parents. You don't have them.'

'Quite a few of our children don't have parents now,' Mateo pointed out. 'But, yes. That is the case. It's said... Some people on Ysthera used to say that Souls are children who were lost before they could be born, and the goddess holds our spirits in Her hands and breathes part of Herself into us so that we can live the life we had no chance to have.'

Again, Jonas took some time to turn this over. 'That…may be a recipe for a highly unpleasant and unscrupulous methodology.'

Mateo blinked a few times, realised what Jonas was implying, was duly horrified, then said, '*Pacifists.*'

'Sure. I'm just quietly doubling down on my vow to keep this secret, that's all.' He touched Mateo's hand. 'Do you die?'

'I am still just human,' Mateo said. 'I know technically I'm a demigod, but I'm not a very good one.'

A rather insulting nod of agreement from Jonas, followed up with, 'Bit of a rude question now. Were you born—manifested—into a female body because your goddess wished it so? If She's female…'

'No, there are, *were*, male Souls with male bodies. This is… Remember when you talked about letting go of weight? That's what this is. I let go of a weight.' He resisted returning Jonas's responsive smile. He was fretting too much for that nicety. 'The Shattered One is only traditionally a goddess, anyway.' To the puzzled look he received, he said, 'Deities aren't human. They have their masculine and feminine avatars, but the deity themselves aren't either.'

Jonas snorted. 'We've got twelve gods and thirteen goddesses who would vehemently disagree with you.'

'But…' Mateo frowned, his turn for puzzlement. 'They're all aspects of a single amorphous divinity, aren't they?'

'What? No,' Jonas said, very firmly, and even with a slightly nervous glance around him. 'They're twenty-five separate deities with actual bodies and appallingly bad tempers who aren't going to like some uppity foreign godling—'

'Uppity foreign godling!'

'—telling them they're actually some sort of amalgamated blob, thanks.' Jonas sat back and looked about again. 'I was just wondering if your goddess ever manifested Herself at all. Not to smite the impious, plainly.'

'You could have just asked! Count yourself lucky She doesn't.'

'Ever? All right, is She even still alive, then, if She shattered?'

'Where do you think the magic comes from if She's dead?' Mateo said moodily. 'She's sleeping.'

Clasping his hands in a conspicuously sanctimonious display, Jonas said, 'You'd know, O Shard of the Divine.'

'Stop that!' Mateo cried, mortified.

Jonas stopped sniggering and pulled himself together. 'All right. Thank you, Mateo. I'll have more questions later, I think.'

'Um,' Mateo said. 'I think there's probably a very obvious question you're missing right now.'

'And what question would that be, honey?' Jonas asked, with his rueful smile, so that Mateo knew he'd been avoiding thinking about it just as much as Mateo had been.

Mateo squared his shoulders. 'The answer is yes. Sorry.'

'Why are you apologising? You know I love it when your answer's yes.'

'Stop,' Mateo said again, soft and serious. 'Yes, you took a god, of sorts, to bed. And yes, that's because you had the same reaction Alessandra had when she first saw me in the smithy.'

He saw Jonas bite down on some reflexively flippant response, the amusement draining from his face. 'She…got over that reaction fairly quickly?'

'That's because she grew up around Souls. You didn't. It would have hit you even harder than it hit her, and taken longer to shake off.'

'I was around you for near-on seven weeks. Surely I shook it off.'

Mateo had hoped that too, in weaker moments, but there was an obvious counter.

'You were coming and going, Jonas. What you call the shine would have caught you again every time you came back. Don't worry,' he added to Jonas's pensive expression. 'It really does wear off. And in the meantime, I can only apologise for taking advantage. I didn't do it on purpose. I didn't know you could see me like that.'

'That's on me,' Jonas said gravely. He touched Mateo's hand again, even more tentatively. 'And what if I don't want it to wear off?'

Mateo let out a bitter laugh. 'Of course you don't want it to. That's the nature of it. But it will. I'm surprised it hasn't already.'

'All right,' Jonas said. 'But, for the record, honey—I do see you. *You*, Mattias Taurasi, not some divine shard.'

'You think you do,' Mateo said. 'Ask yourself if you'd really tolerate someone like me, though, otherwise.'

'Ah, *yes*,' Jonas said. 'Hold on, no. Not tolerate. Enjoy. Have I not told you that repeatedly?'

When Mateo just shook his head—explaining this to Jonas was hurting more than he'd expected, and he'd expected it to hurt—Jonas said, 'Alessandra wanted you in bed, did she?'

'No!' Mateo said, his voice squeaking in his horror. 'Well. I certainly assume not.'

'There, then.'

'That is not the point you think it is. She had a brief and superficial impulse to worship me. You took me to bed and…worshipped me.' After a beat, he burst out, 'Jonas! That should dismay you, not make you look smug.'

'Oh, I'm dismayed,' Jonas said, still smirking. 'Look at me, truly dismayed. And are you a god who demands a regular schedule of worship, by any chance?'

'I'm a *demigod*, and *no*.' Mateo tugged agitatedly at his robes until Jonas stopped chuckling to himself and sobered.

'Sorry, honey,' he said. 'I'm trying to take this in stride, that's all.' He shrugged. 'And I'm going to say it. I don't believe you when you tell me I only want the divine in you. I have a goddess. I'm not looking for another one.'

'I know.'

Jonas pointed an irreverent finger at him. 'I see what you did there. Not looking for a new goddess. *Very much* in the market for a grouchy sweetheart with a penchant for control, if he ever feels inclined to forgive me.'

Mateo wiped a hand across his eyes and looked down at the remnant smears of kohl he'd left on his fingers so he didn't have to look up. 'Jonas…'

'One day,' Jonas said, the slightest edge of a question to it. 'Not any time soon, I know.'

'I can forgive you, if you can forgive me,' Mateo said, but shaking his head at the same time so that Jonas would not raise hopes for the inevitable dashing. 'Taurasi won't. How could I possibly bring you back amongst my people after you had their Soul dragged off in chains?'

'All right, it wasn't literally in chains, you bunch of overdramatic magic elves,' Jonas said. 'How do I put this nicely? My father is unlikely to ever truly warm to you and you don't see that stopping me.'

'I am the centre of their world,' Mateo said, finally meeting his eyes, 'and you hurt me. They will never accept that you were justified.'

Jonas's mouth pressed thin. Sombrely, he gave Mateo a nod.

'Don't worry, though,' Mateo added. 'You won't even want it, soon enough.'

And Taurasi wouldn't even be here, soon enough, one way or the other.

This time, Mateo could almost see the wrench it took Jonas to act like nothing was different. 'Seems grossly unfair of your goddess,' he said in typically amiable fashion. 'To give you a shine that makes people desire you, and then stick you with a tradition that makes you untouchable.'

'I'd say that that was on purpose, to protect them from themselves,' Mateo said, 'but it doesn't normally make people desire me. It makes them want to follow me about, and protect me, and coddle me, and serve me, and worship me.'

'Ah,' Jonas said, smiling. 'Like the Taurasi do?'

'To an excessive degree,' Mateo clarified, scowling. 'It's quite trying. Thank the Remnants it wears off fast.'

'Does it?' Jonas said, looking over Mateo's head. 'I feel none of that for you.'

Mateo pushed down the pang ruthlessly and said, 'Good. That's it wearing off.'

'No, listen properly. I've never felt that for you,' Jonas said. He thought about it with his head on one side. 'Niki.'

Blankly, Mateo said, 'Nikiti?'

'I felt that for Nikiti when I first met them. On *Steadfast*. They were in a bad way, but you all were, and they were the only one I felt drawn to…coddle and protect. I thought it was because they reminded me of my nieces.'

To Mateo's silence, he ventured, 'Does that mean anything?'

'No,' Mateo said. 'Nothing important.'

He rubbed his hip.

CHAPTER 27

'**I**'M GLAD TO HAVE YOU HOME,' Anika said, after their cart had rolled past the sign at the bottom of the hill, today announcing an early rather than complete closure, and up the slope to the mouth of Ravenser Odd.

This was quite probably an understatement, given how quickly she had come from the Imperial-free teahouse to greet them.

Mateo said, 'So. It really was wild magic that killed the Ystheran, and it was a different sort of wild magic seven weeks ago, and I saw the destruction of Ysthera and I have to finish seeing it so I can hear all of Sabine's message to me—oh, no, wait, Anika, there's *more*—then we were attacked by shadow-dogs and I had to give Jonas magic and now he knows the Souls are the ones with the gift of the goddess within them, but he says he won't tell anyone, though now that I think about it, we should probably be quite careful about not annoying him, and I probably did annoy him by telling him the Taurasi will never forgive him and what he feels for me isn't real anyway.'

'Well,' Anika said, when it was apparent that Mateo had finally come to the end of his long blurt. '*You* had a day.'

'Hey,' said Jonas, returning from paying the driver and seeing the cart on its way. 'I got the gist of that last bit. When I said I'd keep your secret, it wasn't dependent on my good opinion. It's a promise.'

Anika and Mateo both presented him with ceremonial Ystheran bows for that; it was the only way to indicate both their trust—much abused, it had to be said—and their gratitude.

Mateo fed magic into Anika, at the same time pulling back Jonas's sleeve to expose the blistered skin. With a quick glance to check for permission, she smoothed both hands down his arm, trailing the amber glow of magic in her wake.

Darius, meanwhile, offered only a grim stare before striding off to examine the boxes from the coppersmith that had been stacked down the side of the teahouse, probably for lack of other ideas. Overhead, the eternal light began to glow as word spread that Mateo was safely returned.

'And what is it you feel for Mateo?' Anika asked carefully as the glow of her healing faded.

'Superficial reverence,' Mateo said. 'You know.'

Jonas stopped running fingers over his unblemished arm. 'Deep admiration and abiding attraction that might very well go somewhere if Mateo stops being obstinate about it.' Mateo glared. 'Weren't you trying to be nice to me less than a heartbeat ago?'

Anika nodded. 'You understand that he is correct that we will not forgive you, and that you will never be welcome on this street again?' When Jonas looked taken aback, she said, 'Please do not mistake my forced courtesy for acceptance of what you have done to us, Jonas.'

'Anika—' Mateo started, thinking of a lost ship and an old woman and a furious father and an ancestral philosophy that taught Jonas to accept that which he could neither change nor control.

'All right,' Jonas said. 'And how goes your challenge, then, Anika?'

'I am about to be voted out as Heart,' Anika said. She sounded calm, but she also only answered after a lingering look over her shoulder at the teahouse, face turned away from them.

'No,' Mateo said, shocked; he'd known the Coterie were concerned this morning—*he* had been concerned this morning—but he hadn't believed Anika's position could truly be in danger, that the Taurasi would turn from her so resolutely.

'Penelope's bloc is against me, and carries a good deal of the vote. The rest… Apart from everything else, many noticed that I encouraged Jonas in his pursuit of you and are unhappy that you are now wounded of it.'

Jonas sighed but said nothing to defend himself or Anika. Mateo frowned. 'None of that is true.' To two identically blank looks, he added, '*I* didn't notice you encouraging him.'

They made their respective sounds of disbelief, and Jonas said, 'You wouldn't have noticed if I'd danced naked in front of you—'

'I really think I would have noticed that,' Mateo said, as his treacherous brain presented him with the vision of a mid-thigh sky-blue sleeveless tunic and an expanse of smoothly muscular skin.

'—so your obliviousness isn't a testament in Anika's favour, I'm afraid.'

Mateo turned abruptly to Anika. 'I won't serve Elias. If they vote you out, they don't get to vote him in.'

'And there is the great irony of this situation.' Anika held up her hands in helpless surrender. 'The Soul does not serve the Heart, the Heart serves the Soul. And yet the Soul has no say in who the Heart shall be.'

'That's how it was on Ysthera,' Mateo said. 'Not here, Anika.'

It was empty defiance—not even the Soul could change ancient traditions overnight—but it made Anika venture a small smile, which only served to highlight to Mateo that he had failed to notice that she had not been smiling. 'Then this shall be a very interesting meeting, indeed. And dare I ask if we can now point the finger at Elias and eliminate him as prospective Heart altogether?'

'The first case must be laid at the feet of Sabine,' Mateo said reluctantly, touching the hard lump the silver Serpasi ball made under his robes.

Later, he would have to show it to Anika. She would see for herself how careless Sabine had been of the life she knew it would cost, the violation and desecration it would cause, to send the message to Mateo.

Anika squeezed his hand. He coughed and resumed, 'The victim was Jonas's grandmother, Anika.'

She wrapped her arms about herself, face suddenly drawn. She offered another bow to Jonas. 'It is very difficult to be angry with you and beholden to you and yet sympathetic towards you all at once.'

'Yes, Mattias has demonstrated that fairly effectively today.'

Mateo went doggedly on. 'But the one from a few nights ago, that was real sorcery and I do not know where to put the blame.'

'Gods,' Jonas muttered. 'Your way of life—your pacifism—is so ingrained in you that I didn't feel the slightest bit concerned about standing in front of an incipient mob in the teahouse. And it's so ingrained in you that you won't even suspect *actual sorcerers escaped from an actual sorcerous island*—'

Anika turned to Mateo with raised eyebrows. 'Did you tell him about the Gal—'

'He's very good at guessing.' He raised an admonitory finger to Jonas. 'It's not as if I don't want to suspect them. It would be convenient to set it all at their feet and be rid of Elias in one stroke, but they were on the street and I hadn't given them any magic regardless. And as far as we know, the sorcerer has to be close by their shadow-dog, and they were outside the city when those things swooped on Ravenser Odd.'

'As far as we know,' Anika repeated.

'Did any of them leave the street today?'

Anika indicated a silent no. Mateo couldn't ask his next question, and then he was asking it. 'Did Timon?'

Anika looked shocked, but she answered in her usual thoughtful way. 'He was here this morning. I haven't seen him at all this afternoon, whereas the Gallasi have been in and out of the teahouse.' She hesitated. 'He was absent but nearby, when the shadow-dogs came last time.'

'And,' Mateo said dismally, 'I gave him magic the morning of the murder, and he was not on the street that evening. He left us early, remember, to go down the hill, and he was odd about it.'

She glanced at the quietly listening Jonas and back to Mateo. 'Let's set aside the obvious point that Timon would never do such a thing. You gave him your usual tame magic, Mateo.'

'Can the wielder turn magic into sorcery without the complicity of the Soul?' Jonas asked.

'No!' Mateo said, and Anika said, 'Absolutely not.'

'And you know that for sure?'

Mateo and Anika exchanged looks. Jonas nodded as if they'd confirmed something for him. 'Alessandra—the Ystheran witness to the murder, Anika—said you couldn't know how sorcery worked unless you'd actually used sorcery.'

'I can't really follow Ystheran,' Mateo mocked in a voice meant to be Jonas's. 'I don't know what's going on, I'm just innocently standing here pretending not to listen to everything you say.'

Jonas looked only mildly chastened. 'She speaks with an Anceran accent, it's easier to understand.'

Anika straightened, capturing their attention. She clasped her hands over her forearms, a formal stance, and addressed Jonas gravely.

'The murderer of your grandmother has already met justice, of sorts. We will present to you the name of the culprit for the more recent murder as soon as we have uncovered it, and will further undertake to subdue them so that no further harm can be done. Will this suffice for Henrike?'

'More than enough, Anika,' Jonas said.

She addressed Mateo. 'We go, then, to the teahouse. Now, do you want the makeup back on, or the robes off? Because the mismatch is disconcerting.'

'What best helps you?'

'As you so desire, *melimou*.'

'Costume off, then. I'll…I'll see you in my apartment, Anika.'

She offered a shallow bow and tactfully withdrew. Mateo turned to Jonas, but promptly discovered refuge in practicalities. 'Henrike will hear from Anika within the next few days, I suppose.' He held out his hand, Imperial style. 'Goodbye, Jonas.'

Jonas neglected to accept the proffered hand. 'You know, if you were to kiss me fare-thee-well, it would go a long way to reassuring your people that you are not so very wounded, which can only help Anika.'

'*Or*,' Mateo said, 'they would assume I am obliged to submit myself to you to preserve our good standing while you hold our fate in your hands, and you can *fare-thee-well* to the last of Anika's chances, and, indeed, pacifists or not, your skin.'

He pulled a face. 'That's the second time in almost as many moments that you've implied you're obligated to keep me sweet. Do you really feel that?'

'I suppose I don't,' Mateo said reluctantly. 'But it's very unfair to ask that we merely trust your word after the trick you pulled on us. I'd almost be relieved if you exacted a price for your silence.' When Jonas seemed to be struggling to know what to say to that, Mateo unbent enough to add, 'I wouldn't actually be relieved.'

Still, Jonas looked at him with unquiet regard. Mateo shook his head. He had sent Anika on ahead so he could have a last private word with Jonas, but there was nothing more to be said here.

He offered his hand again. 'Goodbye, Jonas.'

Now, finally, Jonas regained equilibrium. 'Does it have to be, though?'

'What is it that you hope for?' Mateo asked coldly, tucking his hand away into his draping sleeve. 'That I will undertake a brief fraternisation with you in secret, away from Ravenser Odd? You know my life. Do you have the wherewithal to fuck me with Darius standing guard at the door of some grimy lovers' nest?'

'I'm not asking for sex! I'm asking for…'

But here Jonas ran out of words himself, because, really, what *could* he ask for? That Mateo demand his kith simply ignore their righteous anger as they prepared for an exile that very well might be the final stone that broke them?

He suddenly put his hand over his eyes. 'Oh, Teo, I fucked this up so badly.'

Mateo began to point out that it could be argued that Jonas had in fact performed his job entirely too well and that regret was a pointless emotion anyway. He didn't have the heart for it, the guttering flame of his anger finally drowned by the very same regret.

He said, merely, 'Jiji,' returning familial sobriquet for familial sobriquet to stand in for all the words they could not find and the embrace they could not take.

Jonas nodded behind the shelter of his hand. After a long moment in which he must have been calling on his upbringing, he managed a second nod, firmer.

He dropped his arm and looked Mateo in the eye. 'You can't cherish a memory you've turned into a woe.' It sounded like an axiom of sorts; it was definitely a bolster: he even managed a smile. 'So, mutual secrets notwithstanding, I don't regret the night we had together. I hope you don't.'

And Mateo discovered he could say, 'I don't,' and have it be true.

'Then—'

'Please make this easy,' Mateo whispered. 'You make everything easy, so please…*please*, Jonas, make this last thing easy.'

Jonas smiled, eyes bright. 'Then, I will shake your hand, Mattias Taurasi, and wish only to meet again in better days.'

They clasped hands in the Imperial way, and Mateo bowed over their joined fingers in the Ystheran way. Then he limped over to the lodging house without a glance back, listening to the sound of Jonas's slow footsteps moving away, down the hill for the last time.

Madame Kerling was on the stoop, and opened her mouth to say something, no doubt caustic.

'Not now, Madame Kerling.'

He'd pay for that later. He was wet-eyed by the time he reached his apartment, and very much tempted to cry when Anika greeted him with a soft, 'Oh, my sweet,' and her open arms.

He wiped at his eyes, holding on to his control. 'It was just a dalliance, Anika.'

She murmured, 'My sweet,' again. But, after her calm practicality in helping him out of the heavy, ornate robes was complete, she pushed. 'Is there anything I can do for you, Teo?'

Mateo started to say no, and paused in the middle of securing his sash around the soft wrap-tunic. 'Yes, actually there is, Ana.' He smoothed his palms over the sash. 'You can lose your shit for me.'

'I can what?' Anika said, floored either by the sudden Imperial slang from the mouth of the Soul, or the very idea.

'Those ungrateful shits'—Mateo pointed in the direction of the tea-house—'are about to turn on you, and you intend to simply smile your way through it. So I think I need you to lose your shit.'

Anika laughed. 'I'm fine, this is just…' And she stopped. She nodded, one brisk jerk of her chin. She said, 'Those absolute shits.'

'*Absolute* shits,' Mateo echoed.

'I brought them down that fucking mountain,' she said, voice rising, 'and got them on board that fucking ship.'

'That's right!'

'Everyone else got to come tell me about their family who died when the island sank, and my mother died too, and no one helped *me* grieve.'

She hadn't let them, but that didn't stop Mateo from chiming in with, 'Unforgivable.'

'I've walked the line between Taurasi and empire for *years* and none of them have done anything to help and actually, they've only made it harder.' She was shouting now. 'And then they're just going to turn around and vote me out because some glib arsehole with his pretty words comes along?'

'Those *shits*,' agreed Mateo.

'And you! You've been so mean to me the last few days, Teo!'

'I have and I'm sorry.'

'I know I've messed up, but—'

'You don't deserve it, you've never deserved it.' Mateo caught her by the arms, speaking earnestly. 'Don't worry, Ana, from now on, you'll get to spend your days brewing up new tisanes in whatever new teahouse we open in whatever new place we fetch up in, and you can laugh and laugh and *laugh* while I torment Elias instead of you.'

'Oh, you never have,' Anika said, and burst into tears.

They were, as far as Mateo knew, the only proper tears she had let herself shed since the day of the exile. She sobbed on his shoulder, rage and grief and stress and hiccupping relief, for a very long time.

'That,' she said, when she'd subsided at last. 'That— Thank you, my sweet, I didn't know how much I needed that.'

'Any time, Heart of my heart,' Mateo said. 'Schedule it in for feast days.'

Anika laughed at that; there were *so many* feast days. She had to wash her face with magic to remove the traces of the emotional storm, and then they walked together over to the teahouse, hand in hand.

They weren't late, but most of the Taurasi were already gathered, and the rest came in on their heels. They knelt in neat rows on their cushions, a very formal arrangement compared to the usual crooked lines of the morning meetings and comfortable circles and clumps of the evening social gatherings. The children, the eldest shepherding the youngest, romped unsupervised in the garden, a rare treat for them amid the rampant assault on Anika's herbage.

Anika stood before her kitchen bench, Timon and Andrea on one side of her, Mateo on the other but a few steps away. Niki, looking unusually overwhelmed, crowded right up against him as if needing comfort. Mateo put an arm around them, hoping it would indeed feel comforting.

On Niki's far side, again a few steps away, stood Elias and two other Gallasi, who would petition Mateo to join Timon, Andrea, and a demoted Anika as Coterie if the vote went Elias's way.

Mateo was confident Anika would put aside personal dislike to stay with him, but wondered if the twins would deign to work with Elias; unlike Mateo, they had a choice. He wondered if it would be safe for Andrea to work with such haters of the empire, or if it would be appropriate for Timon to work with people too likely to reinforce his own antipathy.

He wondered, wincing, if it would be too tempting for reformed *phalaros* to work with *Timon*.

'Are all here who intend to be here?' Anika asked the crowd. 'Check for your friends and neighbours, please.' After the brief stir as everyone looked about and confirmed each other's presence, Anika said, 'We shall proceed. Does anyone wish to make any final comments before the vote?'

Penelope, of course, rose.

'Speak,' Anika said, the very slightest of crisp notes entering her voice.

'I think we can all agree our Heart has made a great many mistakes recently,' Penelope told the meeting, looking benignly about, and Taurasi mostly murmured its concurrence. 'Our future is now at great risk, and we must therefore consider most carefully how to walk onwards into that future. Our Soul has been hurt, and we must therefore consider most tenderly how to assure his wellbeing.'

'Thank you, Penelope,' Anika began. Mateo glanced aside and saw that Elias was smiling.

Penelope held up a regal hand. 'I have more to say.'

'Of course you do,' Timon murmured.

'Taurasi, when we consider those things that we must consider as we go into this vote, there are only two facts that are truly relevant.' She curled her upheld hand into a single finger to count the first fact. 'Aniketa led us down the mountainside and has never since failed us at the crunch.' She presented a second finger. 'Aniketa is the Heart to whom our Soul is cleaved.'

Into rapt silence, Penelope made her raised hand into a fist. 'Aniketa the Unconquerable.'

She said it mildly; the Taurasi punched the air and roared, 'Aniketa the Unconquerable!'

'Indeed,' Penelope said. 'I believe the vote is carried.'

She sat.

Anika turned her back and hissed savagely into her hands, in Imperial no less, 'What the *fuck*?' before rapidly cloaking herself in her usual calm authority and walking out amongst her cheering people to accept their felicitations, flanked by her Coterie pair.

Penelope, meanwhile, approached Elias. She collected the Soul cup he had gifted to Mateo from its nook and handed it to him.

'Mattias does not need this from you,' she informed him. 'I am perfectly capable of making our Soul a new Taurasi cup. It may not be as pretty as one made from superior Ystheran clay, but it will suffice. It will be symbolic of our new lives within the empire, in fact.'

Elias cast Mateo a dark look before tossing the cup disdainfully down onto the counter. It chipped and rolled towards the edge, but Penelope caught it before it could fall. Elias shouldered Mateo aside to stalk off to sulk with the Gallasi near the rear of the teahouse.

Penelope turned the rescued cup upside down and showed Mateo and Niki the underside where the ox horns had been on the Taurasi Soul cup. It did not bear the stylised coxcomb of Gallasi, but rather the long ears of Leporasi. Mateo frowned.

As Niki, irrepressible again, raced to join the other children playing outside, the swirl of the crowd washed Anika back over. She bowed to Penelope, her eyebrows crooked interrogatively.

'Why, then, did you support his challenge?' she asked bluntly.

'Oh, my dear, I was Heart almost longer than you've been alive. I've seen it all before. Elias would have spent months undermining you if he hadn't been tempted into making his play prematurely. Now his teeth are pulled, the boil is lanced, and the Taurasi have cause to remember that their Heart bears a heavy burden and the occasional stumble under its weight is much to be expected.'

Anika linked her hands and made another bow, very deep, and had to wipe at her eyes when she came upright again.

'Perhaps,' and now Penelope was speaking with the delicate tones that normally bespoke one of her subtle digs, 'you would consider hearing my advice a *touch* more often. I was, after all, Heart for many years before my Soul crossed the eternal bridge and Sabine chose Charion—'

'The Soul has no part in—'

'Twaddle,' Penelope said severely. 'The Soul has no official part in a challenge, but the good of the Soul is paramount. Do you truly think any vote would be cast without thinking foremost of our most precious Shard of the Divine?' She patted Mateo's hand. 'We were never going to make you work with that utter arsehole, dear.'

'Penelope!' Anika said.

'You've heard worse, I presume.'

CHAPTER 28

THE TAURASI SETTLED INTO THE EVENING, passing around trays of food and cups of wine. The nine Gallasi stayed clumped near the back door, but partook peacefully enough, hiding any lingering resentment. Outside in the cool evening air, the calls of the playing children, Niki loud among them, were like the cries of nightbirds. They were all making the most of being forgotten for the evening. Not a one had come in with any sort of complaint to remind the adults they were still out there.

The atmosphere was warm and relaxed, as if their troubles had been lessened merely by the act of facing them square. Mateo joined in as far as he was able. As ever, he eschewed the wine and sipped ginger tea, from a normal Taurasi guest cup for now—and the nice thing about *that* was that he could fidget with it as much as he liked without inviting glares.

But when the celebration finally wound down, adults gathering over-tired toddlers and overexcited children and heading out, Mateo withdrew to his usual position by the stove, nodding absently to farewells.

'You're pensive,' Anika said to him as she came to kneel on the cushion by his stool. 'Is your hip hurting you?'

Jonas had warned him it would, set off into inflammation by the travails of the last few days. He nodded.

'...Remember when I suggested it might sometimes ache as a symptom of a less physical sort of pain?'

'Let's say it's aching, and leave it at that.'

'Ah,' Anika said. 'And this tourmaline pillow that J— that was mentioned?'

'You can say his name,' Mateo said grouchily, before catching his breath. 'Sorry, Ana, Heart of my heart. I really been horrible to you lately. I just... I don't need to be your burden. Please, let me have that.'

She looked eminently confused. 'How, by the Remnants, could you ever be a burden?'

'Aren't I, though?' he asked.

'Whoever put that buzzing thought in your head?' she asked. 'Jonas, calling us overprotective?'

'No,' he said slowly. 'Not Jonas. I came up with it all by myself, I suppose.'

But the thought was clear, not like his usual murky worries at all, that sometimes buzzed like bees in his head, but didn't linger, smooth and silky.

Anika sighed. She leaned her shoulder against his legs. 'My sweet. Please tell me you know it's not true. You are not a stone upon us. You are the foundation *under* us.'

These were pretty words, but comforting. He ran his fingers over her topknot, touching the simple silver pinheads that should have sported the enamelled decorations of her mother's Kindred.

'The tourmaline pillow is in my room,' he conceded. 'Jonas is right, I should use it.'

Anika tipped her head up questioningly. She had caught something in his tone. After examining his face closely, she gestured about the last few Taurasi, some still quietly chatting, some half-asleep on their cushions.

'They are more forgiving than we expected them to be. Perhaps...'

'Perhaps the blighted Imperial can show his face on this street without them wanting to tear him to pieces?' Mateo asked sceptically.

'We didn't have the day you had with him, Mateo. There is still anger. But you are not the only one who had grown to like him. Perhaps, with time...'

'Don't give me false hope, Anika. If things go as they should, we're leaving Anceral. Do we drag the man with us, away from the tatters of his family? And to earn our exile, we must hand over an Ystheran, likely a Taurasi, to Imperial justice. Will they forgive Jonas then, and make a space for him on the carts? What if it's Timon?'

'What if it's me what?' Timon asked cheerfully, flinging himself down beside Anika.

His cheeks were flushed with the wine; Andrea had also tapped a keg of the beer from the brewery she worked at, so there would be sore heads in the morning. He was possibly unprepared for the appalled silence the other two presented him with. His smile slowly faded.

Anika took a very deep breath. 'We're wondering... We were just wondering where you go at night, Timon, when you leave Ravenser Odd and go out into the city?'

Timon stared. 'And might I politely enquire as to why you would ask me such a question about business I clearly want kept private?'

'Of course, of course,' Anika said soothingly. 'It's your private business. But perhaps…where you went, night before last?'

'Oh.' Timon pushed himself to his knees and then to his feet. 'Aniketa,' he said. 'First you question whether I will support you in the vote. Now you—' His voice cracked. He heaved in a gulp of air. 'You ask me whether I've turned to wild magic? If you don't trust me, why am I part of the Coterie?'

'It's not that we don't trust you,' Anika said urgently, also rising to her feet. 'You are, of course, most trusted. But…'

'But where was I on the night of the sorcerous murder?'

His raised voice was beginning to penetrate the cosy atmosphere of the teahouse. The last few Taurasi were glancing about, murmuring. Andrea and Penelope were strolling casually towards the tableau, Darius marching over with only the amount of subtlety required to have not already drawn his sword.

'It's a fair question.' That was Elias, blight him, walking up behind Timon. 'You wanted to stay on Ysthera and fight with freed magic. You voted for it. You even suggested you wouldn't have changed your vote, knowing the Sunlit Isle would be lost. You don't sound like someone averse to using wild magic now.'

'Neither do you,' Timon said flatly. 'Difference is, I've never actually done it. You have.'

'I merely foolishly held to the decision of my Kindred.'

'So did I!'

'Foolishly?' Elias smiled. 'We were in our quarters here two nights ago, Timon. Why won't you tell us where you were?'

As Penelope and Andrea joined them, Timon turned to Mateo, hands open in appeal. 'Teo, you are our Soul. You know you haven't given me—anyone!—unbound magic.'

'I know,' Mateo said.

'Oh, dear,' Elias said. 'You're playing on their ignorance of how it works with that argument. You know very well that under certain circumstances you can take domesticated magic from a Soul and turn it wild with neither their permission nor their knowledge.'

'Goodness,' Penelope said. 'You learn something new every day.'

Andrea took her brother's hand. 'It doesn't matter where Timon was,' she said loyally. 'We all know who the more likely culprit is, don't we?'

'Is that an accusation?' Elias said.

'You just told us you know how to steal magic from Mateo, idiot,' Andrea snapped, all forbearance gone.

Elias arched his brows at that Imperial-influenced unsubtlety. 'I said it was possible under certain circumstances. But not circumstances where the Soul can't produce any magic at all. I mean, Shattered One bless the poor little sweetling, I'm sure he does his best, but Mateo hasn't successfully completed a ritual since we've been here.'

The Taurasi were abruptly united in indignation. 'You were asleep the first morning!' Andrea said.

'I fail to see how our Soul could have conducted the morning ritual amid an Imperial raid, dear,' said Penelope.

'And this morning was an aberration,' Anika finished. She raised her voice. 'We are not accusing anybody.'

'Except me,' Timon said, arms folded, posture stiff.

'We are not accusing *anybody*,' Anika repeated. 'We trust you, Timon, absolutely.'

'I'm going to bed,' he said sourly. 'Feel free to have me escorted by Darius.'

'Ti...'

'I bid you good night.'

Andrea looked reproachfully at Anika as she took her brother's arm and went out with him.

'That quite ruined the conviviality,' Penelope commented, and took her leave as well, joining the final exodus, along with Elias and his people. Darius melted away, but only to lurk in the shadows on guard as usual.

Anika knelt back beside Mateo with a heartfelt sigh. 'Indeed, a poor ending to a pleasant evening.'

'Anika,' Mateo said fretfully.

'I know. He didn't tell us where he was, did he?' Anika brooded momentarily. 'But you have more to tell me about your day, and we've had barely a moment. You said you saw the destruction of Ysthera?'

Mateo had been careful to transfer the silver ball from his robes to his sash, keeping his mouth shut and a fold of silken sleeve between the metal and his skin. Now he drew it out and placed it on the floor before them.

'It's a message from Sabine to the Taurasi Soul, but I think you should see it,' he said. 'It's not… It is exceedingly unpleasant, even beyond having to watch the end of the Sunlit Isle and witness Sabine's fate. It will make you feel contaminated.'

'I'm not afraid,' Anika said quietly.

'That's one of us.'

He took her hand. With the other, he picked up the ball.

'Sabine,' he said. 'I am here.'

AND AGAIN, MATEO stands at the mouth of the sacred cave. Anika is not with him.

Again, he sees the despair of the small band of rebels. Again, he watches them pledge their choice. Again, he hears Sabine's rambling message. Again, it all comes to him as if he were lost within a frozen casing; he feels nothing beyond cold, cruel dispassion.

Sabine says, 'Is there something on the water? See, there, the boat.'

She does not point or change the direction of her gaze, and Mateo, as before, cannot see what she can see. 'Some of them are leaving the island, as rats leave a sinking ship. They have guessed our intention and believe their Kindreds will not stop us in time and they are *correct*.'

She summons the others with an arrogant abruptness utterly unlike her usual manner. Her manner when she had been Soul of Taurasi, not *phalaros*.

'We must not allow any to escape,' she tells them. 'Sink it.'

Her magic, wild and tainted, floods into the magic-wielders. Mateo sees again how much more powerful wild magic is. She is only gifting four of them, and those four have set into train the sinking of Ysthera. She is only gifting four of them, and they strike out over the water, to a speck on the horizon which Sabine insists is a small boat.

But the occupants of the boat are resisting. A great boiling of water and thrashing of air comes, the boat cradled safely within the eye of the storm and speeding ever further away.

Sabine hisses. 'They carry the magic they have taken from the other surviving Souls, and we alone cannot defeat them. And they will not give it up now they have tasted of its bitter fruits. They are—'

From the maelstrom out to sea rises a single massive shadow-dog, and it arrows at them, following the path laid by their magical attack. Mateo stands unmoving as the battle rages about him, the shadow-dog plunging right into the sacred cave on a gush of wild magic that batters the renegades. It lashes about with claws and teeth and spiked tail, writhing through loops of sorcerous retaliation.

Then it snatches the little Caprinasi neophyte, and whisks him away in a single shocking instant.

'No,' Sabine cries. 'Kallias!'

The Leporasi guardian plunges out of the cave and slides down the mountain as if she can somehow catch the lost child. She stumbles and falls, and a crack, blasting heat and steam, opens and swallows her. The crack grows and lances up towards the cave.

'Oh, Teo, Teo,' Sabine wails, all remote calm gone. 'They will come for you. They will come. They have Kallo and they know how to break a Soul. You must—'

The cave collapses.

MATEO JERKED AWAKE. He had brought back none of the icy tranquillity of last time, just as Sabine had lost all of hers in those final awful moments. He gasped for air, feeling dust choking his lungs and superheated air burning his throat, the scorching smell of stone on fire lingering in his nostrils, the dreadful weight of rocks and dirt crushing him.

The weight of the water, the weight of the wall; the wall had cracked, it would crush the Taurasi before they had time to drown.

He flailed, fighting it, fighting for calm, reaching inwards to reassure himself that he still held the great lake of power safely behind its mighty, unbroken wall.

He had one hand still around Anika's, the other around the orb, and he clenched both tight compulsively. 'Did you see?' he got out. 'Did you see? Elias!'

He convulsively tossed the orb away. Its message had been delivered; it rolled to a corner and withered inwards like an apple with a rotten core.

'I wasn't taken in with you,' Anika said calmly. 'It must have been meant just for Souls. Yes, Elias is here. He has requested a meeting of the Coterie. Take a breath for me, Mateo, that's it.'

Elias was there. Two other Gallasi were there. Andrea was there. Timon was there, arms folded. Darius was there, standing back in his unassuming and yet vaguely threatening way.

Mateo's thoughts were a swarming hive caught in a wildfire and he barely heard Elias say, 'We have a proposal for the good of all people of once-Ysthera. We decline to be absorbed into the Taurasi. We will continue as Kindred Gallasi, and merely take some of your women, and your neophyte.'

Andrea and Timon drew closer to Anika and Mateo; Darius drew closer to all four of them. Anika held on to Mateo where he knelt on the floor, desperately fighting his way from a dense terror that had collapsed on his head like half a mountainside. It crushed the air from his lungs, as his kith would be crushed by the weight of the water if he let his walls crack.

Calm, he tried to tell himself. *That is not what's happening here.* But his body would not stop reacting, shaking down to his very bones, destroying any attempt to centre himself.

Anika said, 'No.'

'So abrupt, we learn such bad habits from our Imperial neighbours,' Elias said. 'Will you not at least think on it? How much stronger we will be, with more than a single Kindred.'

'I do not disagree,' Anika said, modulating her tone back to a sharp sort of politeness. 'I, too, wish for the strength of more than one Kindred. However, we cannot contemplate any such endeavour until Nikiti ascends to be our auxiliary Soul and we have a new neophyte manifested as well.'

'That might be years,' Elias said.

'Then it will be years.'

Elias began to pace. 'The threat is now.'

His words echoed dimly in Mateo's ears. *The threat is now. The threat is now.* Panicking, flailing, he struggled for enough air to make words, to cry a warning. He could not suck enough into his throat, which was the thinnest of straws, which was a collapsing cave full of burning dust and scalding ash and melted rocks flowing like a red-hot mudslide.

'You are harbouring traitors in your midst,' Elias went on.

'By the Remnants,' Timon said. 'I was at the theatre, all right? I saw a play when I was down there getting the bandeaux for Mateo, and the songs were stupidly catchy and I wanted to go see more performances. I felt like a bloody hypocrite so I didn't want to talk about it.'

'You didn't have to tell us,' Anika said.

'Yes, I did,' he said bitterly. 'Will I spend the rest of my life being held to account for voting yes back on Ysthera? Maybe I should join Gallasi, then.'

'You would be welcome, Timon,' Elias said.

Timon looked appalled and edged closer to Anika. 'I don't actually want to leave you,' he whispered. 'I was just being dramatic.' She squeezed his arm.

'However, your assumptions are wrong. The traitors are not the so-called blighted.' Elias swept back and forth over the wide space of the teahouse, his pacing gaining a slow momentum. He pointed at Andrea. 'The traitors are those who will collude with the empire.'

'Go find yourself a new island and stay there, if living in Anceral is so distasteful to you,' Anika said impatiently. 'Taurasi will have none of this. We made our decision years ago.'

A cold expression flashed across Elias's face. 'You made your compromise years ago. You make new compromises every day. You are *diminished*.'

'That is the nature of living under Imperial rule. That is the nature of surviving.'

'We can do better than survive!' Elias cried. 'Great power is within your very grasp and you are too cowardly to grasp it for fear it might sting. You know more than one Kindred makes us stronger, because you know more than one Soul giving us magic makes us stronger. You know more magic makes us stronger.'

Darius came closer, and Anika waved him back, wary of letting things escalate further.

Just as Charion had waved Darius back, on the day of the exile.

Mateo's hip throbbed, pulsing pain through his body but paradoxically calling him back from panic. As solidly as if the man himself was there, Mateo felt Jonas's warm, imperturbable presence, and then, too, Sabine's serenity, as if she was holding his hand with Anika.

Be here, Jonas said, and *All will be well*, Sabine said.

Mateo's breathing settled. His thoughts marched into order.

Whoever had been on that boat had been able to send a shadow-dog over a vast distance—he and Anika had been wrong, wrong, wrong, to assume the magic-wielder had to be close by their servant just because that was how it had been on the day of the exile. The other Ystherans had only just started using unbound magic then. They had had three years to learn better.

Whoever had been on that boat had snatched a nascent Soul, which meant they'd had a source of magic they could corrupt. He and Anika had been wrong, to assume that only Mateo could have been the source, at least at first.

The first attack, against Ravenser Odd, had come from the last of poor Kallo's fragile, burgeoning magic, but by then—it was horrible to contemplate—by then, they must have drained the child to the quick, because that attack had been an attempt to take either Niki or Mateo, or both.

They'd had just enough wild magic remaining to summon one last shadow-dog to kill the coppersmith, for who knew what reason.

And then…and then, the magic used for the attack on Jonas's grandfather's villa today, that had to have come from Mateo, because poor Kallias was dead or Mateo would have sensed him, and wild magic was powerful and enduring but it ran out eventually, just like the domesticated magic did.

Mateo had given Elias and the Gallasi no magic.

Not voluntarily. Not knowingly. But somehow, he must have. Elias had outright told him he could steal his magic when he'd been gloating at Timon.

He rose to his feet. 'They are the *phalaros*.'

'Obviously,' Elias said scornfully.

Anika stepped between him and Mateo, though she didn't let go of Mateo's hand. 'Taurasi will not join you in betraying our goddess, Elias,' she said. 'And our Soul will not help you.'

The teahouse door opened, and another Gallasi pair came in, herding a few Taurasi children—Helena's children—blinking sleepily, rugged up in their nightclothes, the youngest whining for her blankets. Niki was in their midst, a head taller, looking just as dozily confused as their foster-siblings.

The children had to have been taken from their communal sleeping platform, from within Helena's shared apartment, and past others. The Gallasi could have only done that with magic, but not Mateo's magic. Or, not his *domesticated* magic.

The Taurasi had no magic left, because Mateo had failed to complete the morning ritual today, and been taken in the raid the day before, and it had not occurred to him to give them any outside the ritual, nor had it occurred to them to ask for any.

Because they were trusting pacifists of the most idiotic kind, who had learned nothing from the treachery of the other Ystherans on the day of the exile, and their Soul was weak, and a burden, and a failure.

Mateo belatedly extended his magic, beginning to feed it to his Coterie. But as soon as he did, he felt invasive tendrils like the creep of unwanted fingers over his skin—the Gallasi, snatching the magic in a way that should have been impossible without his permission. He cut off the magic and cast a desperate look at Anika, at Darius, at Timon and Andrea, at Nikiti and the other children.

Anika had some magic, from when Mateo had filled her receptacle so she could heal Jonas. She formed the shield over the children. Niki had moved to the front of the little group, tall and serious, watching with intent eyes. Darius came to Niki's side, hand on his hilt.

'Oh, don't be so suspicious,' Elias said. 'We just wanted the neophyte here for these discussions and we couldn't have their foster-siblings waking Helena. We don't want to have to hurt anyone. Especially not a mother.'

He could sound as mild and reasonable as he liked; the unexpected presence of the children was a silent threat. Anika took a few moments to answer, a few moments in which Timon and Andrea began to shift over towards the children too.

Elias smirked at this. 'If you're really that attached to Niki, we'll take Mateo. That's fine. He'll do.'

Anika's hand clenched tight on Mateo's, but when she spoke, her voice was as calm as Elias's. She looked about at Elias's silent comrades. 'Elias, Gallasi, all of you, we do understand your fear. We do understand the temptation to reach for the power to keep yourself safe. But we lost Meredonia through wild magic. We lost Ysthera through wild magic. No good ever comes of it.'

'Ysthera did not sink through magic, but through the actions of a small group of discontents,' Elias said. 'All the evil that you ascribe to it truly comes only from the actions of a few ill-advised people wielding it.'

'Like attacking people with shadow-dogs?' Andrea said, voice low.

She and Darius together had gathered the sleepy, confused children, and started back towards the door. A Gallasi blocked them, swiping casually at the shield. It didn't fall, but it would take Anika more magic to maintain it; she'd run out if Mateo couldn't flow more to her.

'Quite. But won't you listen? Mateo will keep us in check, just as a Soul should do. In check, but less contained. Able to withstand the might of an entire empire.'

'Sabine showed me it,' Mateo said. 'The wild magic. And you're right, it's not evil.' Anika sucked in an audible breath; Elias smiled brilliantly. 'It's just…more. But, Elias, it is not meant for humans to wield. It's too much. It makes us cruel. It makes other people too small in our minds.

It…it makes it too easy to justify defilement and murder, to kill an old woman just to pass on a message. *That* is the blight of it.'

Elias, sighing, resumed his pacing, bringing him arcing back towards them. Anika kept herself between him and Mateo.

'I should have known you would be obstinate, Teo,' he said musingly. 'I suppose we must use other tactics.'

He smiled his silky smile. 'Sabine got a message out. I should have expected it. *She* was strong. And yet all she achieved was to teach us how to best break a Soul.'

Anika stiffened. She pulled hard on Mateo's hand, trying to tuck him further behind her, protecting him as she always did.

Something was gleaming dully in Elias's hand. He said, 'The first and simplest step is to sunder you from your Heart.'

And he stabbed Anika in the stomach.

CHAPTER 29

ANIKA MADE A PUNCHED NOISE AND fell over.

Her shield winked out. The Gallasi, glowing with their own shields, were on Andrea and Timon even as they lunged, trying to catch their fallen Heart, trying to grab hold of Elias to wrestle the knife from him. They were borne to the ground and held there, wrapped in sorcerous chains and knelt on by a Gallasi each.

Timon was cursing and Andrea was grimly silent and they struggled and writhed and were punched in the face and head and squeezed tight by their bonds.

The other two Gallasi grabbed Mateo, wrenching his shoulders as they forced him to his knees. The angle they held his arms at should have been excruciating but he didn't feel it. His lips moved as he said Anika's name over and over, but he couldn't hear himself.

Darius, on guard before the cowering children—Darius looked at Anika, and looked at the twins, and looked at Elias, and looked at Mateo.

And he turned and ran from the teahouse.

Mateo whispered his name, drowned out by the noise of a scuffle from outside, a few thuds and a shout. Two more Gallasi came in, latching the door behind the fleeing guardian.

One gave Elias a small shake of the head. Elias laughed delightedly anyway. 'Not even your own guardian will stand by you.'

'He's gone for help,' Andrea shouted. 'The Taurasi are coming.'

'No one will come. Even if they heard something, even if they've fought off the fog we put them in, my people have sealed both apartment blocks. The whole street's locked in.'

The children had made no sound. The day of the exile had taught them not to scream. Nikiti crouched by Anika and brushed her hair from her eyes. She had fallen on her side, one arm trapped under her. Blood was spreading in a pool across the polished wood floor of the teahouse. She stared at the wall, gaze blank.

She was so quiet. She was dying on the floor, and it was so quiet.

Mateo started the flood of magic that would signal to the rest of Taurasi that their Soul was in trouble, that would fill them and help them escape out of magical sleep and through magical barriers, that would fill Timon and Andrea and let them break free and help Anika.

Again, the Gallasi snatched at his magic greedily, clawing it out of him like tearing pieces of his very flesh. He fought them off, drew it all back into himself and locked it down tight.

Unworthy, flashed nonsensically through his mind.

Elias went behind the counter into the little kitchen. He pulled a vial from his sash, uncorked it, and tapped its opened mouth over a brewpot, sprinkling dark grains into the rounded belly. He took the ever-present kettle from the back of the stove and poured boiling water into the brewpot.

He worked one-handed. The other hand still held the bloodied knife.

He chatted as he worked, an insufferable parody of the true Heart of Taurasi. 'Timon. There's no need to fight so. You wanted your magic set free, and you can have it. Why not join us? You were never a traitor. Not like your sister.'

'If you think a misunderstanding among friends is enough to make me turn to your side, you know little of me and nothing of Taurasi,' Timon said hoarsely. His magical binds were tight, his chest barely able to move to take in air. His face was already swelling. He added, 'And if you *touch* my sister—'

A Gallasi kicked him in the face, splitting his lip. 'Stop,' Mateo cried.

'Ah, well.' Elias swirled the brewpot. An acrid scent began to rise; it was the same as had been in the pot he had brought to the bathhouse. 'You'll drink this, Mateo.'

Mateo finally realised where Elias had obtained his last draw of magic—with a secret potion smuggled from sorcerous Ysthera, he'd poisoned Mateo's tisane and then forcibly drawn out tainted magic as he'd crouched beside him in the bathhouse, whispering dark half-truths, twisting Mateo's mind even as he twisted his magic. Those were the certain conditions that let Elias pull magic from the Soul and set it loose.

But it couldn't have been so very satisfactory a method, not to keep nine *phalaros* properly fed. Elias gestured at him nonchalantly with the knife. 'You will drink, Mateo, like you drank it before, but this time you'll drink it knowing it'll set your magic free.'

Sabine had said, *They made me—* and hadn't had the chance to finish her sentence, but Elias's actions finished it for her. They had made her *choose*. Elias could very well hold Mateo down and pour the bitter scalding brew down his throat, but he wouldn't. Because Mateo had to choose it.

If the only way to stop Gallasi from turning Mateo's gift into untrammelled magic was to refuse the choice, then Mateo would refuse the choice.

'I won't,' he said.

Elias strolled over to look down at him, knife in his hand, expression sickeningly affectionate.

'I don't want hurt you, Teo,' he said. 'You know you were my first love, right? Oh, don't give me that look, you disagreeable creature. Just drink the potion, and this all goes away. I'll heal Anika. I'll let your Coterie live. I'll let you choose whether it's you or Nikiti who joins Gallasi. I wanted Nikiti, so I could make alliance with you. But you'll keep us on the righteous path, at least. You're strong enough for that, aren't you?'

'You tricked Sabine by playing on her pride,' Mateo said. 'I won't fall for that.'

Elias's fond gaze didn't falter. 'Oh, you're simpler to get at through your silly little fears. You hardly have any pride to play on, do you?'

'I probably don't,' Mateo said. 'I do have obstreperousness, apparently. I will not drink.'

'You won't even take a sip for Anika's sake? She's still alive. Barely.'

'I won't.' He tried to say it firmly, but his voice cracked and shattered into a pitiful whisper.

Sheathing the knife, Elias knelt. He waved off Mateo's captors and tucked him under his own arm, ignoring his stiff resistance. 'Come on, sweetling. Will you so easily give up the one person who actually loves you? Everyone else loves the Soul, but Anika loves *you*, Mattias. And yet, you so readily sacrifice her, just to be difficult. It's sad, Teo, it really is.'

His voice was as silky as ever, dripping cold cavern water into Mateo's ear. It was a wise play for Elias, an obvious fear with which to prey on Mateo. But it was also the one fear he'd never had, until Elias had goaded him into drinking two cups of doctored tea and then whispered soft lies as he fell into fog.

He had Sabine to thank for that, and Anika, and Timon and Andrea, and Talia, and everyone they'd lost on the day of the exile, and everyone they'd safely brought here to Ravenser Odd, and even…and, yes, even Jonas.

And Anika's love for him, and his for her, told him she would rather die than live by betraying her promise to the Sleeping One.

'I won't.'

Elias put his free hand over his heart and glanced over to where the children had followed Nikiti to cluster sombrely around their fallen Heart. 'Oh, Anika,' he said, sounding shocked. 'Hear how he values you.'

Restoring Mateo to the tight hold of the two Gallasi guards, Elias returned to the kitchen. He collected the brewpot and the Leporasi Soul cup, and knelt back by Mateo. He slowly poured the cup full of thick, acrid liquid. Setting the pot down, he held the cup towards Mateo so that the bitter scent of it was unavoidable.

'One little drink.' Mateo shook his head. Elias said, 'Don't you want to be strong? You're so weak, sweetling. Unfetter yourself. It will make you strong, strong enough to protect the Taurasi from anything. Don't you want to be strong for them, as they are strong for you?'

Elias had hit on Mateo's true fear now. *Just because it's fragile doesn't mean it shouldn't be allowed to fulfil its proper function before it breaks.* He shivered, resistance eroding, and Elias, smiling, held the cup towards his mouth.

The two Gallasi guards were holding Mateo as tightly as ever. To choose to take the drink, he would have to nod and allow Elias to hold the cup to his lips and tip the liquid into his mouth.

He heard Anika say, *You are the foundation under us.*

He heard Andrea say, *The whole Kindred is his Coterie.*

He heard Sabine say, *They broke the Souls one by one and made our breaking our own blighted choice.*

It had cost Jonas's grandmother the last days of her life and a horrid choking death to give Mateo that warning. It would cost Mateo's Kindred even more for him to refuse to heed it.

He turned his face from the cup. 'I won't.'

Elias tsked. 'It's pointless to resist. We can still draw magic from you if we force you to drink it.'

Mateo half-remembered, half-saw within himself, the tap, the brewpot spout, the sluice-gate.

'But not enough,' he said, and saw from Elias's momentary flash of fury that he had the right of it.

Elias got himself under control quickly, tipping the cup and smiling invitingly. 'Last chance, sweetling.'

'I won't.'

Elias rose smoothly to his feet. He held the Soul cup pensively, and then flung it across the room so that it smashed against the wall, the dark liquid spattering the plaster and the honeycomb shelves.

He kicked Mateo savagely in his bad hip.

Mateo yelped and sagged helplessly against the hold on his arms. At a brusque command from Elias, his guards let him drop face-first to the floor. Elias kicked him again, not being overly nice about whether he connected with hip or stomach.

Elias landed more quick blows into Mateo's side, rolling him across the floor and pacing after him. Mateo was sobbing by now, unable to help it. Agony was radiating from his hip, and throbbing in his ribs and thigh. He could hear the shouted protests of Timon and Andrea, and silence from Anika.

'Every bite of food and every sip of water will taste of this,' Elias told him conversationally. 'You'll choose to eat eventually.'

Somewhere behind him, Nikiti was saying something, to Anika, or to the other children, he couldn't tell.

'I'll choose to starve,' Mateo gasped out between screaming waves of pain.

He flinched as Elias drew his foot back, but the other man checked the blow. He smiled down at Mateo before strolling over to where four of his people gathered about the twins. He bent over Timon, drawing the bloody blade again.

'I was always going to cut your throat, Timon. I just hoped to see you betray Mateo first. Never mind.'

He tugged on Timon's hair, drawing his head back so his throat lay bared and taut. Timon struggled and Andrea thrashed in an attempt to reach him, but their bonds were as of iron.

Elias stomped a foot on Timon's chest. 'Drink it.'

'I won't,' Mateo whispered. 'I'm sorry, Ti.'

'Don't be,' Timon croaked, and shut his eyes.

Elias bent over him. 'Don't worry, Andrea,' he said as she cried her brother's name. 'Your turn's coming.'

Just as the blade touched Timon's throat, the shutters of the teahouse smashed inwards, and Darius careened through them to land square on the teahouse floor.

He was dressed fully in the copper armour, the laced-up scale coat, the thigh-length skirt, the elbow-length gauntlets, the knee-length greaves and even the rounded helmet. He ran the nearest Gallasi through with the matching blade, burnished in the lamplight, punching it straight through the sorcerous shield protecting him.

He was followed by Jonas.

Mateo shook his head in the haze of pain to dispel the vision, but Jonas was really there. He, too, won an easy strike in the surprise of their arrival, felling the other Gallasi door guard with a hard blow across the throat with the same copper knife Darius had given him once before, to face the shadow-dog. Its edge would be dulled now.

He took it all in, Mateo huddled on the floor on one side of the teahouse, the twins bound and overpowered on the other. Anika in the middle, surrounded by children and a pool of her own blood. He might have been taking an instinctive half-step towards Mateo, but as soon as he understood what he was seeing, he was over to Anika's side even before Mateo had to point that way.

Darius, meanwhile, ran at the Gallasi bunched about Timon and Andrea. Elias struck out with wild magic, the strong flash of power that Mateo had seen his father use to fell Charion, and Sabine's rebel group employ when they were trying to sink Elias's boat.

It rippled harmlessly over Darius, and then he was on them, striking with three years of righteous fury. He'd cut down one of them and knocked another over before they finally understood their sorcerous shields were useless. One called up a shadow-dog, the mist rapidly coalescing from thin air, roaring out from a smoky smudge. It lunged at Darius and caught him around the waist in its needle-sharp teeth, but then spasmed and spat him out.

He crashed to the ground and got back up bleeding, the small overlapping plates of his armour dented. His eyes flicked from threat to threat—shadow-dog, Elias, two uninjured Gallasi, the third slowly getting up.

Elias issued sharp orders and his Coterie lunged at Darius, battering at him with wild magic that he somehow seemed to slide around but which kept him fully occupied. Elias himself stalked furiously over to Mateo.

Mateo had rolled to hands and knees and begun to try to get up despite the lance of pain every time he moved. Elias simply planted a fist into his hair, yanked him upright, and then punched the same fist into his stomach, flattening him again and taking every inch of air left to him.

Elias kicked him in the hip, flipping him onto his back. Mateo tried to curl into a defensive ball, and Elias kicked him again before picking up the brewpot from the floor, where it had miraculously remained unscathed.

'Drink, or I'll pour it on your face.'

Mateo looked desperately about. Darius was backed into a corner, the *phalaros* unremitting in their attack, the shadow-dog coiling and darting overhead. The Gallasi appeared to be armed with something like invisible whips. Where Darius blocked their slashes with a copper gauntlet, he remained unharmed but if the lash touched his bare skin, it gashed it open. He was bleeding freely, and looked exhausted, but fought on grimly, pressing hard, trying to slip past them.

Andrea and Timon seemed to be pointlessly thrashing about, but after a moment Mateo recognised the coppery gleam of a blade, propped up by Timon's awkwardly bent hand; Darius must have found it in the crates with the sword, and dropped it for them in the few frenetic seconds available before the Gallasi onslaught. Andrea was rolling against it with furious rhythm, making it slice the sorcerous bond strand by strand. Like Jonas's weapon, the edge would be rapidly dulling.

Elias is desperate, Mateo told himself. *That's why there's only one shadow-dog. They're running out of the magic he stole from me last night. We just have to hold out a little longer.*

Jonas was kneeling with the children, tending to Anika, listening intently to Nikiti. Nikiti shone with warm amber light. The murmur of their voice carried over to Mateo. They were reciting one of the chore routines from the children's practice ritual, the one used for mending.

'We clean up the mess.' It must have been very comforting; the children looked composed and resolute. 'We sew up the tear.'

'Do you think your Imperial's going to help you?' Elias said. 'He's watching me kick you and doing nothing. He's watching your guardian fail and doing nothing.'

'Now we make sure it's right inside,' said Nikiti dreamily, and the other children echoed it. The whole group was glowing now.

Mateo said, 'Oh,' and felt an overwhelming burst of pride cut through the fear and pain.

Nikiti was ascending. The Shattered One was here, whispering Her true name in their ear.

But the amber shine of the new auxiliary Soul's magic coming in strong at last caught Elias's attention. He gestured and the shadow-dog left off harassing Darius and swooped down on the children. Jonas immediately leapt up and fended it off with a ringing blow from the copper knife. That was the last straw for the soft blade; it bent in his hand.

Jonas shrugged, tossed it aside, and sketched the major stave from the helm of awe, making a quick circle about it. Niki had to be feeding him their magic—his shield shimmered into being. He hadn't even had to form the whole sigil, just that single instance of its central motif.

He tugged and stretched at the shield so it spread like a thin sheet over himself and the children and Anika.

'*What?*' Elias howled. Mateo had never heard him give way to such rage. 'He's a fucking Imperial!'

'I'm a fucking Imperial wizard,' Jonas answered back in accented Low Ystheran, eyeing off his fragile shield with misplaced pride.

'You weren't content with just spreading your thighs for him, you had to despoil your magic like this?' Elias sneered at Mateo. He called to Jonas, speaking Low. 'That shield is too weak and you have too little skill to hold against the shadow-dog for long. Stand aside.'

'I'm not going to do that,' Jonas told him comfortably.

'You don't want to die for some dirty little foreigners, do you?'

Jonas shot him a look from the corner of his eye, most of his attention on the shadow-dog. He drew in the air again, a different rune, and grasped the glowing sword that appeared before him. Elias blinked— but, of course, Jonas was not bound by any vow of peace to keep his use of magic harmless.

Elias had to be mindful of what the *phalaros* used their limited magic for. He modulated his tone, all silk again. 'Look around. Their Heart lies dying. Their guardian is about to fall. Their Soul cowers on the floor. This is over. We'll let you walk out of here.'

'I can't control what you do,' Jonas said. 'I can't control how this turns out. But I *can* control what *I* do. And what *I* do is not step aside and let children come to harm.'

'We're not going to harm them,' Elias said soothingly. 'And it's no shame to your Imperial honour. No one will ever know you left them.'

Jonas returned Elias's attempt at a reassuring smile with a sardonic twist to his lips. He said, '*I'll* know, you dick.'

Elias snarled and gestured. The shadow-dog reared back into tight coils before springing unstoppably forwards. Its claws ripped through the sigils Jonas had drawn. The sword vanished and the shield shivered. Jonas patted it back into place with both hands in a terribly amateurish fashion.

Elias cast Mateo a contemptuous look—Jonas really had no idea what he was doing and they both knew it—and the shadow-dog hurled itself at the barrier. It tore through it and struck Jonas's chest so hard he was knocked flying. Lunging and snapping with its teeth, spiked tail whipping wildly, it set about trying to rend him. The struggling pair rolled out of sight behind the counter, grim thumps and clawing scrapes continuing unabated. Mateo cried out helplessly.

Elias pushed him onto his back again and knelt on his chest. He held the pot over Mateo's face. 'Drink, or burn.'

Mateo stared at the steam coiling from the spout. He forced himself to look away, shutting his eyes, bracing for the scald of the thick liquid on his bare cheeks and in his eyes. It wouldn't hurt more than knowing Anika was dead, Darius was dead, Jonas was dead, the twins would soon be dead, Niki would be taken and drained, the Taurasi would be enslaved, if the Gallasi even left them alive.

Ystherans did not pray; they did not call on their shattered deity, and they did not treat the magic that was Her final gift as the holy benediction it was perhaps intended to be. They used it for domestic chores, by all the Remnants, about the least sacred use possible.

But in that desperate, terrified moment, Mateo felt the prayer rise without choice or logic: *Goddess protect and shield me, I shall never grant Your magic to the unworthy.*

Something inside him stirred, like he had imagined it had stirred on the day of the exile. If his magic was contained within the metaphor of a lake, the wall that dammed the lake shuddered and began to crack, threatening to break and let the water crush all in its path.

This, Mateo supposed, was what Elias was torturing him for, to transform his contained magic into a limitless expanse, whether Mateo allowed the sluice-gate or not.

Except Elias was still trying to make him drink, and this was happening without a drop of the bitter brew crossing his lips.

Mateo opened his eyes and looked up at Elias. Elias jerked backwards, face slackening into shock.

Mateo rolled over and got to his knees. He ached all over, a duller but more pervasive kind of pain than from Elias's blows. His limbs felt odd, as if his joints were dislocated.

Wild magic raged like an ocean through every part of him.

A voice spoke in Mateo's head, in chiming and archaic cadences he could only half-translate. The meaning bypassed such mundane things as words. *Those who keep their promise in the face of certain destruction shalt be rewarded. What wilt thou, mine last and loyal Shard? Shred thy enemies, heal thyself, change thy form.*

Mateo considered it. His magic had become an ocean, wild and stormy, but he stood becalmed on an island of his own making, still himself, still human, still fallible and awkward and full of what-ifs.

I want my people to be safe, he told the ocean.

Mateo looked at the cluster of children.

Anika clambered to her feet, hissing through her teeth. Her sash and tunic were bloodied and rent, but she was touching the whole, clean skin underneath. Aniketa the Unconquerable. Nikiti and their new Coterie had healed her with small tame magic, their domestic routine, and Jonas's guidance. Niki lifted their hand to hers, and they clasped, palm to palm, prime Heart to auxiliary Soul.

Mateo looked at the twins.

Andrea rolled free, ripping the last of the invisible bonds from her arms. She snatched the knife, cut Timon's bonds with three precise slashes, and ran on silent feet up behind the Gallasi holding Darius penned. By the time Timon had raced to the wall and ripped a copper pipe and half the mechanism off the water-clock, she had incapacitated one of the Gallasi with another slash. Even as Darius lunged and pierced the second through the heart, Timon swung and dropped the third with a ringing blow to the head.

Mateo looked at the kitchen.

Jonas walked out from behind the counter. He was bleeding from a great slash on his forehead and many deep scratches on his forearms. He dragged the body of the shadow-dog behind him.

'Glad that worked,' he said cheerfully as he pulled free his seax, dripping with thick white mist; the body dissolved immediately. 'Given it's bronze, not pure copper.'

He caught Elias's eye. 'Ooh, I hope no one finds out our weakness,' he mocked, tugging his shirt aside to show the half-made scale skirt tied on underneath, protecting his entrails. 'We'll just sink the ship that used a copper ballista against us and kill the only Ystheran coppersmith in Anceral, that'll stop anyone from figuring it out.'

He drew another rune in the air; the dragon from his helm of awe emerged thin and sinuous as a snake, but with a mighty toothed head. It began to circle his body like a whip made of lightning. He gestured and it expanded to wrap the children, thin and quick and wicked.

Having achieved this minor wizardry, he smiled at Mateo. 'You with us, Mateo?' Then he paused. 'No, you're not quite Mateo, are you?'

Yes, of course I am, Mateo tried to say, but couldn't.

Elias, gaining spirit from Mateo's apparent abstraction, visibly girded himself. 'I knew you'd give in,' he said. He touched Mateo's wild magic, and drew it in to himself. 'You were always weak.'

'Stop your nonsense,' Anika said, as calm as ever, hand still clasping Niki, the Soul she had almost destroyed, the Soul now flowing a tiny rush of magic into her, the sundered trust between them restored. 'Mateo is stronger than you will ever know.'

Andrea and Timon, supporting Darius, weak and sallow from blood loss, joined her. Jonas shifted carefully to stand with them, seax still in his hand, the children huddled behind him. Niki held his hand too. The shield shimmered into being, and Jonas's dragon writhed over its surface, leaving ripples in its wake as the Imperial form of the magic reinforced the Ystheran with its sheer unpredictability.

Wild magic whirled around Elias. A rictus smile of triumph distorted his face. He floated up, and began to fly towards the door. Two, no, three shadow-dogs, small and savage, coagulated into being at his back.

'I like this not,' Mateo said, or at least, his mouth said it. 'This maketh not fair reward for one who lays hands on mine servant. I abjure thee.'

Mateo raised his hands. No. Something raised his hands. 'Only the worthy may taste of mine gift.'

Elias spun in the air and tried to throw wild magic at Mateo.

He turned to ash.

The Gallasi strewn about, dead or wounded, turned to ash.

The power flooded harmlessly through the Taurasi and Jonas—they dropped to their knees as it passed over, and the shield thickened, the dragon lengthened, as they all utilised the magic to prevent the overflow—and rippled out, extinguishing the shadow-dogs and expanding ever onwards.

It would, Mateo knew, wash over the street, over the city, perhaps even beyond the city, filling the receptacles of the worthy and turning all the unrighteous to ash. It wouldn't be just the Taurasi and the Anceran Ystherans, but their children, their toddlers and babies, and any Imperial with a tiny pocket from Ystheran ancestors—and even if the goddess judged them worthy, the rush of power would stop their hearts.

'Stop,' Mateo said, his voice harsh as he fought the shape of his own throat. 'This is not fair reward for me. This cannot be for any human.

Take it back. Please.'

The cresting roll of power ceased. Divinity was all about him, a storm that blotted out the teahouse. Despite its words and actions, he could not call it a benevolent presence. It was, rather, benign, only incidentally kind because they were all too small for it to know the difference between kind and cruel.

But now he had the sense of being looked at with an almost-human curiosity. 'Thou want naught?'

His friends were damaged and bleeding and in pain. His hip when he shifted his weight felt like it might have shattered as comprehensively as the Ystheran goddess. His body was wrong in a way that only didn't bother him because his friends were determined to not let it bother him. Their time within the safe bounds of the empire was ending, and his time with Jonas had already ended.

There were certainly many things Mateo could want.

Anything he asked of the deity awakened inside him would make him take a fatal step off his island and into the shallows of the ocean of wild magic, and then he would be lost.

'I want naught,' he answered himself.

He felt, then, the full weight of divinity upon him, a demand for truth. 'Thou want—'

He *did* want; the desire was pulled out of him, past any denial made of weak words. He wanted to look after his people. He wanted to feel this strong for them forever. Jonas was correct when he said they couldn't control the future but Mateo, with this power, could have full control of the Taurasi response to it. He could control—

He could control *everything*, and nothing bad would ever happen to the Taurasi ever again and all his little buzzy worries and what-ifs would go away.

The waves of wild magic, freely offered by his goddess well beyond the bounds of Her promise, were lapping at his feet, washing over his toes. He just had to take the tiniest of steps. He wanted to control—

Jonas said, *It's not given to humans to control everything, as much as you might like it otherwise* and he could not tell if he'd heard it inside his own head, or aloud.

'But I'm not human,' he replied anyway.

Somewhere in the far, far distance, people were shouting a name, but that didn't matter, because it was his human name, and he wasn't human.

The Shard of the Divine made to step into the waves.

And then he felt a hand in his. He looked down with a feeling like opening his eyes. Nikiti was standing beside him, holding his hand.

'Greetings,' they said, faltering. 'Greetings from your humble auxiliary, you horrible adult.'

Mateo blinked down at their linked fingers. He wasn't sure if Niki was standing with him in the teahouse, or if they had joined him on his crumbling mental refuge in the wild ocean, or if some part of him had merely conjured a psychopomp in its own defence.

He whispered, 'Greetings from your venerable elder, you horrible child.'

Niki's hand was hot in his and his goddess's attention was poised over them both like an axe. He raised his face to Her.

'I want naught,' he said again, firmly.

The weight lifted, his goddess's attention drifting, Niki's hand releasing from his as the mystic vision wafted away. The divine left him, or rather, it folded itself up small into the confines of his usual domesticated magic. He sagged, once again merely the Taurasi Soul, too human, rather than the divine's omnipotent avatar.

His friends moved to catch him in a babble of concern and exclamations and affection and mutual gratitude. As their hands touched him, he gave them his magic, so small and safe, displacing the last vibrating shiver of the divine wave of power.

Anika kissed his forehead and his palms, murmuring his name, and then, ever the Heart, she turned to her kith as the hum of her healing magic rose.

Jonas, taking the cue, gently peeled back Mateo's sash to open his tunic and lift his undershirt, and hissed air through his teeth. Bruising had already begun to bloom from hip to ribs, livid. The mere sight of it should have redoubled his pain, but he was too numb inside to really feel anything more than a vague throb.

'Anika can't heal this, right?' Jonas asked. He turned to Anika, who'd paused in tending the others to touch her own healed stomach with professional interest. 'It'll have to be salve and tisanes and rest.'

Mateo rediscovered his first human emotion. He threw his arms around Anika. 'So sorry, so sorry, I didn't know how to save you.' She gathered him up, and then Andrea and Timon were there. Mateo held as much of them as he could reach, too. 'Not any of you.'

'He only went for us so hard because he was jealous of how much you love us,' Timon told him.

They hugged until Mateo was wincing and still unprepared to let go. Jonas gently rescued him and his sore ribs, and his Coterie turned to reassuring the children. Niki escaped the rampant concern and wriggled in for their own hug, softer.

Heedless, Mateo squeezed them tight. 'Greetings to the auxiliary Soul, marvellous child, sibling of my heart.'

'She told me Her name,' Niki whispered, thrilled, and Mateo silently thanked his goddess for not terrifying them with the full alien enormity She had shown him.

They dashed back to the other children, their nascent Coterie. Mateo became aware that Jonas was holding him firmly about the waist, half-support, half-embrace.

'Why are you even here?' He knew he was sounding quite indignant; it was another safely human emotion.

'Here's the thing. I'm coming up the hill, and suddenly, Uncle Darius bursts out of the teahouse and, to my surprise and alarm, exchanges some unheard-of blows with other Ystherans. Then he runs off around the corner to those crates full of armour. I figured he was going to need some help getting squired into it, and afterwards.'

Mateo glanced at Darius, standing sentinel by his side, and found that, while Anika had already healed his physical wounds, he was silently weeping.

'What is it?' he asked stupidly. 'We knew you weren't running away, and I'm safe now thanks to you.'

Darius spoke in a rasp. 'You said, *Only the worthy may taste of mine gift*, and I felt it here.'

He touched a fist over his heart. Mateo was too surprised at hearing his voice for the first time in years to reassure him of the sentiment.

His guardian repeated, wonderingly, 'I'm worthy.'

That jolted Mateo from his stupefaction. 'Uncle of my— *Father* of my heart, you always were.'

Darius's whole face constricted, and he lowered it to rest on Mateo's shoulder, but straightened before Mateo could hug him too. He wiped at his eyes, and glared at Jonas, who held out a hand.

'Help you get the armour off, uncle?'

'Go home.'

'You've been wanting to say that for *weeks*, haven't you?'

Darius glowered and marched sternly away to inspect the broken shutter.

Mateo finally turned back to Jonas. 'But why did you even come up the hill?'

'My father sent me up to invite Darius to dinner.'

'Oh,' Mateo said. 'How's that going to go, your father yelling and my—mine glaring?'

'Probably,' Jonas said. 'Should be delightful.'

He flashed a sudden smile, and understanding dawned. 'Are you *teasing* me?' Mateo burst out. 'That's not fair, I've had an awful evening! Just tell me why you came.'

Jonas started to laugh. 'Teo, honey. Either obstreperous or oblivious and only your goddess knows which. Could there be *any* reason for me to come back up that hill other than you?'

He checked. 'I—'

Both doors, front and rear, simultaneously slammed open in a shower of splinters. They all ducked on traumatised instinct, except Darius and Jonas, who positioned themselves between the others and each door, Jonas's slinky dragon already circling about him.

The Coterie's shield rose, only to meet and merge into the shield held by the Taurasi arriving in force through both doors and the broken-shuttered window, the Imperial dragon swimming through it all with joyous disregard. Penelope led the front force, wearing a rigidly outraged expression on her face, Selia at her shoulder. The rear guard was spear-headed by a startlingly fierce-miened Danae and Helena, who both had children inside the teahouse.

Penelope looked about. 'Ah. Taken care of, I see?'

She frowned up at the sinuous disturbance frolicking across the communal shield, before Anika signalled and both shield and dragon shimmered out of existence.

'Indeed,' she said, only slightly smugly.

'We were locked in. There was a wave of power which filled our recept-acles and released the bonds,' Penelope explained. 'And turned the blighted on guard at the door into ash.' She nodded towards the piles of ash about the teahouse. 'And you?'

'About the same.'

Anika turned, then, and bowed to Mateo, deeply, in the respectful way that would warm Penelope's heart. The rest of Taurasi followed suit, except Selia, who was too busy running to throw her arms around Andrea.

'Oh, stop that,' Mateo told the Taurasi, effectively giving permission for Danae and Helena to follow Selia's example and gather their own loved ones into their arms and reassure themselves they were truly safe.

'Why is he here?' Penelope suddenly demanded, pointing at Jonas, by which Mateo understood she was not going to forgive that Imperial dragon swimming through the Taurasi shield any time soon.

The tension in the Taurasi shifted, came to bear. Mateo straightened, not without difficulty. He held up his outspread hands, and, as he done for the Coterie, gently dislodged the fierce, wild power of the goddess and replaced it with his own tame magic, not thinking too hard about how he was doing it.

Some Taurasi, it had to be said, looked disappointed, which only went to show just how dangerous untrammelled magic was.

Anika, meanwhile, murmured to Jonas, 'I know it's not fair, but I think you better go. I'll send word when you're welcome back.'

Jonas hesitated, then nodded. He touched Mateo's arm in a muted farewell, and was carefully making his way through the mass of tense, uncertain people clogging the front of the teahouse when another disturbance sounded at the door—a querulous voice announcing the arrival of Madam Kerling.

Mateo's landlady was accompanied by the Imperial occupants of the lodging house. They were all dressed for bed, in intimate apparel covered with thin robes, their hair pinned and covered with cloth. They were carrying various implements pressed into service as weapons.

Finding no immediate threat, they looked around curiously; they worked long hours during the day and had intuited that they weren't welcome in the early morning or late evening, so this was the first time most had been inside.

Madam Kerling stared about the crowd in sanctimonious confusion before pointing crossly at Mateo. 'What is going on, you silly boy?'

'Did you all…come to help us?' Mateo asked, in a confusion of his own.

She put her hands on her hips. 'What sort of hour of the night do you call this?' she demanded. 'Go to bed, you reprobate, you are past curfew.'

'Yes, Madam Kerling,' said Mateo meekly.

CHAPTER 30

Mateo limped over to the teahouse earlier than usual the next morning; pain had awoken him. The entire side of his body was mottled with bruises, and he could barely move from the wretched agony of his hip, swamping the ache of the muscles in the rest of his body. He carried the tourmaline pillow with him.

The teahouse was already busy with Taurasi, Andrea and the other city workers finishing their morning meals, the children, Niki among them, gathering to walk to school with Helena, others just pouring their first tisanes, all of them awaiting their Soul as always. Despite his pain, he made a circuit through them, touching shoulders, murmuring greetings and reassurances, a morning ritual without the magic.

It wasn't just Taurasi here, though. The Anceran Ystherans arrived just after Mateo did, as a cautious but determined group. Mateo had stopped the gush of the goddess's overwhelming magic before it reached them, but they'd still sensed the immense disturbance at the top of the hill and joined together to face the trouble in admirable, if prudently delayed, fashion.

The meeting between Anika and Alessandra was everything Mateo had hoped it would be. Anika was enraptured the moment Alessandra marched up to her with her confident long-legged, and bare-legged, stride and taken her hand in the Imperial way, biceps flexing.

They were still flirting glances at each other while Alessandra indulged herself with a tisane, kneeling by Helena to discuss metalworking and Andrea to discuss distilling. Partnerships were brewing. She managed to be relatively polite to Mateo as he paused by them.

But that was not all. A second high table was by the little ceramic stove, and Penelope and Madam Kerling—her gifted name, it turned out, was Breone—played Lithos on the Imperial set presented by Freydis, Anika's sympathetic regular customer.

They had all been, in the end, too worked up to dissipate immediately last night, and Madam Kerling had been mollified into accepting a tisane on a proper seat. Her giggling lodgers had knelt on the cushions amid the Taurasi to accept their own cups of herbal tea. She had, it seemed, found the teahouse acceptable.

Mateo cast his eye over the game as he ensconced himself at his own table. Penelope was perhaps being kind; Madam Kerling was not losing too badly.

'Natural friends,' Anika murmured in greeting.

'I am honestly terrified,' Mateo whispered back.

Smiling, she set his brewpot down and collected the bead-filled pillow. 'Just a small dose. It won't affect tomorrow's ritual.'

He'd allowed Anika to dose him with infused poppy last night, after persuasion from both her and Jonas. They were reluctant to insist—someone standing over Mateo demanding he drink an unwanted potion was not entirely appropriate right then—but Anika very gently reminded him that Taurasi wouldn't need more magic the next day, and Jonas reassured him he could get the dosing precise enough that unintended ill effects were unlikely.

He'd fallen asleep resting on Jonas's shoulder. No one had dared again demand the Imperial leave, not after Anika had had time to make it clear what he had done for their children, not after they had all seen their Soul wrap his hand about Jonas's wrist and refuse to let go, which was embarrassing to think about, but not very, because eventually he'd had Anika's hand in his other hand, and the twins leaning against his back, with Danae and Selia leaning on them, and Niki at his feet surrounded by the other children, and all the other Taurasi finding ways to cluster in and touch their loved ones too.

He had been the grit in the centre of an accretion of nacre, and if that was not the most flattering of metaphors…they still altogether made a pearl.

Mateo sat and drank, warmed pillow moulded about his hip, and watched the Taurasi, the endless ebb and flow of a busy and contented people. Andrea and the city workers and the children and the visitors departed for their days in Anceral, but the eldest, the infirm, the heavily pregnant gathered to handweave and chop herbs and painstakingly paint gilt touches on Penelope's pottery, and Lucius brought in the toddlers for their midmorning snack. Helena and Danae and others flowed in and out as they organised themselves for their own work for the day.

Soon it would be as if the struggle had never been. Timon and his team already had the damage to the teahouse under repair. Penelope had been particularly strident about the water-clock, and loudly horrified when Timon had questioned whether it was worth repairing just to dismantle it when they closed up the teahouse for the last time.

Others had cleaned away the blood on the floor and the noxious splatter on the walls using magic, but they gravely swept up the piles of ash inside, plus the two in the insula foyer, with a proper broom. They'd taken the ashes away to be poured into a pottery urn out of sight of the rest of the Taurasi, because, Mateo supposed, there was no way to make it not look like tipping dust into a bin. Once his hip was better, he would consecrate the sealed urn and they would take it out to sea and let the last of the Gallasi join the other Kindreds under the endless waves.

It would never have been Mateo's choice, to kill Elias, to destroy one of the last two Kindreds, especially knowing that his goddess, vast and benignly amoral, had barely noticed the human lives she had snuffed out with the cleansing burn of her remorseless blessing. He found he could think of good memories, both of his once-lover and of the largest Kindred, and thus mourn their loss in appropriately sombre fashion.

Others were more sanguine. 'Darius, did you really have to come through the window?' Timon asked.

He and his team were working together to reverse the damage to the splintered shutters. The door had been an easier repair.

'Yes,' Darius said, glowering from behind his cup.

He'd evidently fulfilled the terms of his oath of silence, not that he was bestirring himself to explain as much. He wasn't saying much at all; it appeared a severe expression still communicated most of his thoughts on any given topic.

Anika squeezed her uncle's free hand as she passed him. She was carrying her own cup, contents steaming. Despite a full healing, the Taurasi had insisted on taking over a good portion of her duties in the teahouse today, so she was indulging in a rare pause.

As soon as Timon had a moment, Mateo intended to tell him that Anika was to have every market day as a *scheduled* rare pause. She loved running the teahouse, but that didn't mean she should have to do it every single day without rest.

The Taurasi had been—Mateo had been—terribly complacent about their Heart.

She stopped to check on the shutters. The renovation team was taking the opportunity to paint them a shade of blue close to the sash colour she favoured. Timon sat back from his work to acknowledge her.

'Perhaps you could take us to your favourite theatre show soon?' Anika said. 'Before we leave.'

Timon smiled, a little fraught, but mostly genuine. 'How about I don't have to spend the rest of my life being held to account, and you don't have to spend the rest of yours making amends?'

She paused. 'Take us anyway?'

At his nod, she patted his shoulder and continued over to Mateo's table, while the team lifted the new shutters into place and secured them. She kissed Mateo on the top of his head and moved about to sit opposite him. He could feel the warmth of the poppy-dosed tisane she had made him coursing through him with each sip.

Even amid the soothing hum of the teahouse returning to its normal safe and cosy atmosphere, his feelings were conflicted. The teahouse had been his sanctuary, and he wasn't sure yet if he would manage to restore that feeling of haven, in their last days on Ravenser Odd.

And yet, it was warm, and his people were calm and comfortable, reflecting his own equilibrium back to him, and the lamps were glowing, and…

And two Imperials were walking in the door.

The Taurasi, kneeling about the room on their cushions, fell silent.

'Oh.' Anika rose mid-sip. 'I really thought they'd give us more time than this.'

The Taurasi, except Mateo, rose with her. In unison, they bowed deeply to Jonas and Henrike, and then knelt again, and watched them intently.

This only gave the unflappable Jonas the briefest of pauses. Carrying a thin rectangular box, he led Henrike to their table, where Anika again bowed to them ceremoniously and invited them to sit.

Henrike, large even by local standards, towered over the small-statured Ystherans, and eased down quite gingerly as if she wasn't sure the bench would hold her. Jonas set his box on the table and sat next to her, smiling at Mateo.

Gradually, the quiet conversations of the Taurasi resumed, and the soft click of the Lithos game between the two elders.

'I must beg of you leeway,' Anika said, placing her hands together and making yet another small bow over them. 'Our wealth is tied up in the mortgages. We need time to sell the properties and as many of our assets as we can before we go into exile. Otherwise we will starve, and you might as well just execute us and save us the misery.'

'They are overdramatic little elves, aren't they?' Henrike said to Jonas. 'What are you talking about, Aniketa?'

'Exile,' Anika repeated blankly. 'You said execution if we don't help, transmuted to exile if we do. I am requesting time to—'

'Oh, tish tosh, lot of bosh,' Henrike said. 'Jonas told me all about it.'

'*All* about it?' Mateo darted a glance up at Jonas, who looked innocent.

Henrike narrowed her eyes at this exchange. 'He hit the high points and went conspicuously quiet about certain questions, so it'll have to do. That's not to mention the waist-high stack of tablets I've received from every wealthy wife in the city, threatening to wield their husbands at me if I cause the Come-by-Chance to close, or harm their favourite magic elves in any way. Not least, I should add, from the wife of the governor himself. You know her as Freydis, I believe.'

Anika shaped 'Oh,' with her mouth but didn't manage to make the corresponding sound.

'Thus, you've been found "not as guilty as you could've been" with a "don't let us catch you doing it again" thrown in. Consider yourself both reprieved and protected.'

Anika rested her forehead on her hands; it could have been taken as a very deep bow from a seated position but was more a complete slump of relief.

'Thank you,' she said as she straightened. 'We'll still need to sell off some of our equipment but we are deeply grateful for your mercy.'

'Why would you sell off equipment? Won't you need it?' Jonas asked.

With brittle care, Anika said, 'We need the funds. We're rather over-capitalised at the moment, Jonas, thanks to the false trade deal you encouraged us to invest in.'

Jonas said, 'That deal wasn't false.'

They stared at him.

'I assumed you'd check my credentials,' he said. 'So I set it up properly with some trading friends of my mother's. I didn't know you're an aston-ishingly trusting people and wouldn't even send a single note of enquiry.'

'We signed a real contract?' Anika said slowly.

'You've got a merchant consortium expecting the first consignment any day now, Taurasi.'

'Oh, shit,' Anika said. 'I mean, good! But—'

She looked about; the potters were already stacking their cushions to the side and heading out with some haste, and others, contracted for the other artisan goods, were not far behind.

'Timon!' Jonas shouted across the teahouse, startling the remaining Taurasi and causing some of them to spill their tisanes. 'You're still building Andrea a distillery up here, right?'

'When I get to it,' Timon called back. 'Have to build Teo's cottage first.'

'The clock first,' Penelope interjected sternly.

Mateo gave his friend a small bow in grateful acceptance while Jonas saluted in cheery acknowledgement.

He undid the latches on the box he'd carried in. 'My grandfather wishes to give you a gift.'

He flipped the lid. Inside, neatly laid across velvet, was jewellery from Thorstin's cabinet: combs from Kindred Serpasi and earrings from Caprinasi and bracelets from Caballasi and rings from Gallasi and beads from Suinasi and those stunning hairpins from Leporasi.

Mateo and Anika stared at the bounty in silence. Penelope turned from the gameplay to stare. Helena, bringing a tray of food for the guests, stopped and stared.

'The Ystheran collection of Cynisca Velasco, of Serpasi,' Jonas said. 'There's quite a bit more. Ah.' He looked around at the silent Taurasi. 'Try not to let it make you think of what you've lost. Try to think of it as…possibility.'

Mateo picked up the dragonfly hairpin. 'You can't cherish a memory you've turned into a woe,' he said, repeating Jonas's axiom.

Jonas smiled, obviously relieved the gift had not been taken awry. 'I'd like to wrangle him an invitation up here to present the rest of it, if I can?'

'Yes, of course.' Anika rose and bowed. 'Thank you, Jonas. You cannot know what this means to us.'

'I think I probably can,' he said. 'A bit.'

Mateo, still holding the hairpin, touched his Heart gently, and she lowered her head. As he slid the pin into her topknot, where it shone against the inky strands, he had almost the opposite sensation to the feeling he'd had seeing that lost relic jumbled amid the rest.

Their people, diminished, forever sundered, way of life slowly drowned by this empire or the next one, forgetting they'd ever carried the gift of the Shattered One—and yet, they would still carry Her gift. They would always carry Her gift.

Perhaps one day, a thousand and more years in the future, there would be no more Taurasi, but part of Ysthera would yet abide. Perhaps instead of the great burning sun of a single Soul, there would be pinpricks of endless stars in a dark sky, unknowingly connected by a sleeping goddess who cared little for any individual but who would always gift Her Soul-touched children with what they most needed in the worst moment of their lives, the blessing of domesticated magic, one way or another. And that was hope.

He adjusted the pin one last time, and smiled at Anika. That was hope.

Helena unfroze and set the tray before Henrike. But then their jeweller couldn't help lifting from the velvet one of the bracelets, its links twisted, amethyst winking from inside the twists. 'Kindred Suinasi. We lost this technique when we lost Ysthera.'

She set it back down and bowed to Jonas, wiping her eyes. Others were beginning to rise from their cushions, jostling to take their turn to see and touch the salvaged treasures of the Sunlit Isle. Anika took Mateo's hand and kissed it, nodding for Helena to take the box to show the others. Helena wasn't the only one giving way to tears.

'Overdramatic little elves,' Henrike whispered to Jonas, but she sounded fond.

Anika turned to the Vigile commander. 'Care for an authentic Ystheran tisane, Henrike?'

Henrike brightened. 'Can I try the spice tea?'

'That's for afternoons,' Jonas said. He flashed his teasing smile. 'And it takes an hour.'

'Well, it *does*,' Mateo said. 'I don't see what's so hard to grasp about it.'

'Teo,' Anika said, 'as a gesture of good faith, I think it's time to come clean on that one.'

Mateo sulked for a moment. 'Fine,' he said. 'It does take an hour, but it doesn't have to be in the afternoon. We created a new "ancient" tradition so Imperials wouldn't bother us in the mornings.'

Jonas covered his face with one hand. 'Oh my *gods*.'

'You really were the worst spy, Jiji,' Heiko informed her honorary nephew.

Anika smiled at Mateo. 'If you can manage it, *melimou*, why don't you take Jonas for a walk while Henrike waits for her tea?'

As Anika summoned a brew and a Lithos set for Henrike, Mateo slipped into garden clogs and slowly led Jonas into the curving paths of the garden. He was moving at the barest of shuffles; only his need for a private conversation with Jonas had got him off his stool, though the poppy seed infusion in his tisane had dulled the edge.

By the garden bed with twelve types of lavender, bees busy amid the fragrant blossom, he turned to inflict a scowl on Jonas. 'I can feel your intense desire to physick me from over here.'

'Intense desire to do something to you, anyway,' Jonas said cheerfully, before swooping to his side and brushing a careful hand against his aching hip. 'But, yes, please let me reassure myself.'

Mateo unwrapped the sash from around his hips, and let his tunic fall open, pushing his jacket back and his undershirt up. Jonas made the same noise he'd made the night before when he saw the progress of the bruising, but his hands were cool and competent as he gently felt over Mateo's ribs and down his side.

'Everything's swollen, but nothing's broken,' he diagnosed eventually, just as he'd done the night before. 'Rest and use the tourmaline pillow, and whichever salve Anika thinks best.'

He traced over the scars on Mateo's hip. 'You can see them?' Mateo asked. 'I thought you should be able to, the wounds were as real as Timon's and Andrea's, but you…'

'I couldn't tell if someone who couldn't see magic would be able to see them, so I thought it safest to ignore them.'

Mateo tsked. 'You gave yourself away so many times.'

'Only in retrospect,' Jonas said with a grin. But he sobered, rapidly. He straightened and faced Mateo square. 'I'm sorry, Mattias. And I'll stand in front of your Kindred and say it too.'

'I'm not entirely convinced you have to,' Mateo said.

'But is Kith Penelope entirely convinced I don't have to?' Jonas countered. 'Aside from anything else, I was insultingly dismissive of the damage I did, to you and to Taurasi. Dismissive of the damage the empire did, too.'

'We were dismissive of the threat of sorcery, to you, your family, your city. We owe you an apology ourselves.'

'I don't expect it.'

Nodding mechanically, Mateo said, 'I know. Jonas, I didn't have a chance to thank you last night. Well. I did have the chance, I just didn't.'

'You were distracted, honey, that's natural. And I don't need it either way. I'm proud of how I conducted myself there, at least. It—it let me put down a weight.'

'Then…tell me why you came back last night? Properly. No teasing.'

'To beg,' Jonas said. 'Can I?'

'If you must,' Mateo said with as little graciousness as he could muster while actually meaning, *Please do*.

Jonas's amber eyes were as intent as he'd ever seen them. 'You know I've been raised a certain way in regard to losses. We mourn them, and we accept them, and we move on. But the reason we can do that in any functional way is to always make the best of what we have before we lose it.' He waggled a finger between the two of them. 'We didn't get to do that, Mateo. We got barely a taste of what the best could be. And the more I sat down there thinking about it, the more I couldn't let it go. Couldn't let *you* go. I didn't, I *don't*, want to mourn it and accept it and move on. So I came back up here to beg you to help us find a way to be together that won't upset your people but won't require you to sacrifice something that could be so, *so*, good.'

'That good?' Mateo asked.

Jonas smiled then. 'Oh, I think you know it would be, honey.'

'I do, Jiji, I really do.'

'I know you took against the idea of a love nest, but it doesn't have to be some sordid, grimy thing. I'm not talking about sex. Ah, not *just* sex, I'm not taking it off the table. It should definitely be on the table.'

'Are you getting distracted, or am I?' Mateo asked innocently.

Jonas smiled. 'I am blathering and trying to say we can rent an apartment to meet at, just down the hill, with big bright windows and views of the sea and a balcony for sharing meals and the children will visit too, and—'

Mateo held up a hand, and Jonas fell silent, shoulders bowing, tension thrumming through him in a way it hadn't even as he'd faced shadow-dogs.

'Jonas,' Mateo said. 'This may be the only time I ever get to say this. *Now* who's being oblivious?'

'All right, but there must be *some* way to make it work. Don't give up on us, Teo, we—'

'Jonas!' Mateo pointed back at the teahouse. 'Did you, or did you not, stand in front of our children at risk of your very life last night?'

'I like knowing for sure I'm not the sort of person who lets children get threatened.'

'Are you, or are you not, called to be a guardian of the Taurasi auxiliary Soul?'

'Is that what that was? I—'

'Of course, that means I'm untouchable to you now.'

Jonas went still. '*What?*' He sounded more alarmed than Mateo had ever heard him. Then, when Mateo could not keep a straight face, he said, 'Hold on. What is happening here?'

'I'm teasing you,' Mateo confirmed.

'Oh my gods, you're *teasing me.*'

'You're Kindred Serpasi, not Taurasi, so perfectly…'

'Touchable,' Jonas supplied, with a sly shift of his stance to invite just that.

Mateo valiantly ignored it. 'You could even ally into Taurasi, if you wanted.'

'Could I?' he asked testingly, not because the idea of anything more than a temporary dalliance repelled him, Mateo thought, but because he was still unsure of his standing.

Mateo thus resumed his rhetoric. 'Did the Taurasi, or did they not, bow to you en masse when you walked in just then?'

Jonas raised his eyebrows. 'And frankly I can see why it disconcerts you.'

'And did the Heart of Taurasi, or did she not, invite me to take you for a walk?'

'She more *ordered* you to take me for a walk…'

'Then are you, or are you not, once more welcome in Ravenser Odd?'

'Gods, I love it when you're this stern,' Jonas said. 'I'm welcome here?'

'Yes.'

'By you?'

'By everyone.'

'Not so much with the worrying about *everyone*,' Jonas said, shaping an invisible circle with his hands, and then shaping a second smaller circle within it as he went on, 'Very much with the caring about *you*.' He paused. 'I am in love with you, Teo, you do get that, right? I want to make sure you know that, whatever the outcome here.'

'Yes,' Mateo said. 'Yes, I do know that. I, um… Yes, you are welcome here by me. I… Yes.'

Only as Jonas relaxed into a bright smile did Mateo truly realise how tense he'd been. 'And are we going to finish that sentence, honey?'

'Not if you're going to be smug about it, Jonas.'

'It's not every day a demigod tells you he loves you.'

'*So* presumptuous.'

Jonas drew Mateo closer. 'I don't expect you to say it, honey.'

'I'd like to say it,' Mateo said, 'but I'm me, so I have to work myself into a fret about it first, and then blurt it out at an inopportune moment.'

'I wouldn't have it any other way.'

Mateo looked down. 'You're not scared off by seeing the divine manifest within me?'

'She was wearing you like a theatre mask for a bit there, wasn't She?'

Mateo nodded, unable to speak, feeling again the alien surge of some other entity's power controlling him as an echo along his skin.

Jonas touched gentle fingers to Mateo's jaw, brushing a thumb over a graze on his cheek he hadn't noticed until he felt the light sting. 'Oh, honey. Not scared off, no. And, you know…' He narrowed his eyes, then shrugged and committed heresy. 'You know She didn't actually do anything, right? I'd already stabbed the wish hound, the children had already healed Anika, the twins had already got themselves loose. And you and Darius had held fast and given us the time to do all that.'

'Um,' Mateo said. 'Respectfully disagree?'

With his usual easy grace and an amused bow of his head, Jonas ceded the point.

'And you're not…' Mateo made himself stand straighter. 'Not disappointed?' Jonas looked blank. 'That I'm just human?'

He gave his unrestrained bark of amusement. 'You think I wanted for a single moment to trade up from demigod to amorphous deity?'

'I'm not a very good demigod…' Mateo said.

'Yeah,' Jonas said. 'And you'd be, ironically, a gods-awful deity.'

He put his hands on his hips. 'I'd be an excell—'

'Oh, there he is. A perfectly human person. My very favourite sort of person,' Jonas said.

'I love you,' Mateo blurted, and kissed his mouth as it blossomed into the most magnificent smile Mateo had yet had from him.

Then he got both hands into Jonas's hair and kissed him harder, the scent of lavender and the buzzing of the bees rising up all around them, Jonas's arms locked around him, one around his waist, the other lower, supporting his hip.

'I want to prop you against the wall and worship you with my tongue until you moan my name like a benediction and you can't stand up,' Jonas murmured eventually.

The wall was the *teahouse* wall; Mateo, blushing at Jonas's frank and enticing words, blushed hotter to think of his people just on the other side and what they might be able to hear should Jonas decide to push him against the—

Jonas, chuckling, tucked an arm around him and turned them both towards the teahouse door. 'Except, I think you already can't stand up. So, unless you want to gift me some magic and tell me how to make myself invisible so I can sneak into your apartment—'

'You're going to be so disappointed,' Mateo said. 'Our magic can't do invisibility. Or teleporting. Or even flying. It really just does chores.'

'—we should head back inside so you can rest that hip where it's warm.'

Mateo patted at his cheeks, willing the heat away. 'We have to wait until I look less ravished. Madam Kerling is going to have *words* if I go in looking like this, Jonas.'

'She and Penelope both will gang up on you,' Jonas agreed. 'I've got another idea for when your hip's feeling better, though. Give me your magic, and show me how to make a phallus out of it, and then you can...' He waggled his eyebrows with cheery lechery. '...give me your magic, nice and hard.'

Which did not help with the blushing but did help with absolutely everything else.

BONUS

If you want more in this world, here's a bonus short story (it was originally written to a strict word limit, which is why Darius gets such short thrift— apologies to the surprising number of readers who like quiet and conspicuously grim men).

ON THE EVENING OF THE ANNIVERSARY of the death of the old Soul, a Taurasi unwrapped a feminine-folded sash and took down long inky-black hair from a feminine-styled topknot.

The next morning, Mattias Taurasi tried to work out how to fold the sash into its masculine configuration. Anika, his dearest friend, who had already helped him bind his breasts and pin his hair into a low bun, stepped back to examine their latest attempt critically.

'I don't know, Mateo, it still looks wrong,' she told him.

He looked down at the familiar sash, bright green with pips of gold. Running his thumbs anxiously along its crooked top edge, he asked, 'Because it's the fold-and-twist on a girl?'

'*Because,*' Anika said, 'neither of us have ever had to do the fold-and-twist before, and it's blighted troublesome compared to the treble-wrap.' She patted her own woven blue sash, with its simple triplicated wrapping style. 'If only one of us had a brother to show us how to do it right. Are you sure you won't ask Timon? He's your friend as much as I am.'

Mateo shook his head. He hadn't told a single other person in Kindred Taurasi about this. He hadn't even told Sabine, his foster-mother and mentor, and the Taurasi Soul, their spiritual guide, the exact person he should have been able to tell.

'I know you're nervous,' Anika said. 'And I can't tell you how honoured I am that you've trusted me to help you. But are you truly convinced this is the best way to announce it to the rest of the Kindred?'

His stomach was in knots, his mind abuzz like a hive of angry bees. This was the sort of jittery mood that usually drove Sabine to gently prod him to run up the mountain trails, calming his miserably circular thoughts with the steady exertion, the rise and fall of his feet, the ache and release of his thighs, the suck and release of air into his labouring lungs.

But he couldn't run up the mountain until he'd first stepped out into the village square, dressed, finally, as he truly was.

'I can't stand the thought of telling everyone bit by bit,' he said. 'Having to explain it again and again. Asking me if I'm sure, over and over. I just want to go out there and have it seen and talked about and over with within a single morning.'

'You know it'll take more than a morning, Mateo,' Anika said. 'Penelope alone…'

She smiled, and Mateo smiled, and they chorused together in adolescent disdain, 'Penelope.'

Penelope had been the Heart partnered with Lucius, the Soul who had stood with the six other Kindred Souls as they gifted the magic that had held back an invasion, and she was only slowly adjusting to the change in her leadership role and relative status. Now Sabine was Taurasi Soul, paired with Charion the Heart.

And Mateo—Mateo was meant to have ascended to be Sabine's heir by now. He was almost fifteen, which meant he was months, if not years, late in receiving the Shattered One's blessing. Sabine had to be worried, as little as she showed it.

His thumbs ran faster along the edge of the sash. Anika took his wrists, stopping the motion before it became frantic. 'Let's give it another try,' she said. 'I think I see the step we're missing.'

She undid the sash, smoothed it out, and began to twist it again, fine dark brows furrowed in concentration. Mateo held his tunic, a drape of folded knotweed-blue cotton, closed left side over right, while she worked.

Everyone wore the same style of simple wraparound tunic here on the island of Ysthera. He'd worn it yesterday, when he'd still been pretending to be what his body told everyone he was. But it felt different today. His breasts, firmly bound flat against his chest, made the tunic sit differently, so he could wrap it tighter around his torso. His hair, gathered low on his nape, made his neck sit differently, and so made him stand differently, which changed the fall of the tunic, too. And when Anika wrapped the twisted sash about him this time, securing the tunic firmly over his loose trousers, it changed how his waistline and hips looked.

Anika nodded, satisfied; or, at least, she was able to control her somewhat perfectionistic tendencies and acknowledge that it passed muster, after one last tweak to make it sit straight.

Mateo spread his hands over his hips, looking between himself and Anika. He'd always looked different to her, of course, tall and gangly in the manner of Souls among a people that were uniformly short and round, but between the binding and the sash, he looked down at his body and felt *correctly* different.

His friend made an aborted gesture towards his hair, loosely massed in the bun at the nape of his neck. 'I'd like to have another try at that, too, it's already coming undone. Topknots are easy!' She touched the tail of silken hair cascading from her own topknot. 'No wonder Andrea says Timon always takes twice as long as her to get dressed.'

'I think I—' Mateo's hands had begun to shake. He clasped them together. 'I think I just need to do it now, Ana.'

'All right, Teo,' Anika said soothingly. She stepped neatly to his side, and took his arm. 'I'll be right with you the whole time.'

'Are you sure you want to be Heart one day,' he asked her as she walked him towards the front door of the cottage, 'if I'm the Soul you'll be stuck with?'

'I know you're very good at your what-ifs,' she said. 'And so, what if one day I'm the best Heart the Taurasi have had in all our five hundred years on Ysthera, and you're the best Soul we've ever had?'

'You're doing it wrong,' Mateo said, ever grateful for her lightness. 'What-ifs must be inexorably horrible. I'll have none of your relentless cheer, thank you.'

Anika, smiling fondly, opened the door. They paused for one last moment on the worn stoop. Mateo took a deep breath. He had a sickening feeling of momentousness, a daydream ending, a journey about to begin. The bees threatened to swarm from his head and invade his throat, his chest, his lungs.

'Everything's going to be fine,' Anika whispered, and they stepped together off the stoop and into the square of the Taurasi village.

The morning, as befitted a place known widely throughout the empire as the Sunlit Isle, was bright and clear, the sky a broad swath as blue as Anika's sash above the scrubby olive trees. All around, the people of Kindred Taurasi bustled about their daily chores among the well-tended cottages, artisan workshops and cultivated plots of the little village perched halfway up the sacred mountain.

The quiet hum and glow of their gentle domesticated magic accompanied everything they did. From the steady low thump of the weavers at the looms, to the workers pulling weeds in the vegetable beds, to the pickers in the olive grove, to the potters in their shed, the young workers chasing the toddlers who were chasing the geese, and the beekeepers checking on the skeps at the outskirts, the Taurasi drew on the magic gifted to them by their Soul, enveloping the village in an aura as thick as honey.

It was the same gentle magic that had thrummed around the whole island a generation ago, shielding Ysthera from an Imperial invasion force that could not gain a single foothold beyond the mystical wall.

With a last squeeze of Anika's hand, Mateo let go and began to walk with her across the square. The paving was sundrenched and warm already through the thin soles of his sandals. He could feel every uneven pitch of the worn stones underfoot, every kiss of the breeze on his bare arms, every touch of sunshine over his face, every murmur of conversation.

Every pause in the murmur of conversation. Every glance. The hum and glow of the magic faltered in a ripple as he walked past his people in their small groups of chores and errands and gossip.

The heat prickled over his hairline. Anika took his hand again.

Outside the meeting hall, Timon and Andrea and the rest of Mateo's cohort, sixteen or seventeen adolescents, were waiting for the daily lesson. It wasn't just Mateo and Anika who were late; Sabine wasn't there yet either. Mateo winced at the soapy-sick feel of disappointment and relief her absence engendered. He wanted this done with.

Andrea glanced around, probably because the lacuna in the wake of Mateo's stubbornly slow passage across the square was becoming the most ringing of silences. She blinked, and nudged her twin, and they both turned to greet Mateo, the others clustering close behind. It was no secret that Timon and Andrea were the strongest candidates, along with Anika, for forming Mateo's Coterie when he ascended properly into the gift of the goddess. Their reaction was *important*.

Mateo didn't have to turn his head to know that Anika would be levelling her best quelling stare at both twins and, in fact, everyone else.

'This is new,' Timon said at last, friendly but a touch cautious.

'Well,' Mateo said, and then, 'Not really.'

'So, is it Mattias, then?' Andrea asked.

At the note of doubt in her voice, Mateo ducked his head. Of *course* changing how he wore his sash and his hair didn't convince anyone he was truly—

Andrea went on, 'Or have you chosen a new name you'd like us to use?'

He looked up, sucking in a breath. The others were all smiling at him, encouragingly or sympathetically or happily. He helplessly began to smile, too. 'Just the suffix. Mateo, if you like.'

The others chorused, 'Mateo,' and surrounded him with hugs and reassurances and congratulations; behind them, the hum and glow of magic rose again as the rest of the Taurasi placidly turned back to their chores.

'See,' Anika said, nudging her shoulder into his. 'I told you everything would be fine.'

Mateo bit his lip. He was full of baseless worries, it was true, and always ready to share them with the ever-patient Anika. But he had not faced Sabine yet.

And, more significantly, he had not tried to perform the daily ritual yet.

Anika jostled him from his drift into rumination with another nudge, this one a less companionable jab of an elbow. Sabine was strolling towards them now, a full head taller than her petite compatriots, who included Charion, the Heart, most of his Coterie, Penelope, and his husband and head of the guardians, Darius.

It was a large and very senior collection of the Kindred, all told, who had likely been interrupted in preparing Lucius's anniversary death rites by the fleet race of gossip about the village. Mateo braced himself, carefully avoided the automatic reach of Anika's hand, and came forwards alone to meet them.

Anika hummed under her breath at him and made sure she was at his shoulder; Timon and Andrea stepped up with her. The developing junior Coterie faced its senior, silently supporting their nascent Soul.

Mateo breathed, breathed, breathed.

'Good morning, all,' Sabine said in her serene way. 'Morning, Mattias. Are you ready for our lesson?'

'Um. Yes?' Mateo said. He put both hands on his stomach and couldn't help a beseeching look towards his mentor.

'I suppose you've worked yourself up about this,' Sabine said softly. 'The prime Coterie has something to say to you.'

She nodded over her shoulder. The elders of Kindred Taurasi bowed as one, deep and formal, hands folded together, heads inclined. One by one, they took Mateo's hand, or squeezed his shoulder, or patted his back. They looked more neutral than Mateo's agemates, some puzzled, some vaguely pleased, a few blank-faced, but none looked angry or outraged.

Sabine saw the delegation off, then turned to Mateo. 'All is well, my dear,' she said. 'You have no need to explain yourself or justify yourself, not to me, not to anyone. You are Mattias Taurasi, and we all know that now. Understand?'

Mateo, overwhelmed, offered a silent bow of acknowledgement.

'And if you need to talk,' Sabine murmured. 'Or just *want* to talk. About anything. I am always here.'

She led the other young ones into the hall for their daily attempt at the ritual. However, Penelope, as always, had lingered to have the last word, and thus, so did Anika.

'I cannot profess to understand,' Penelope announced. 'However, should you wish a recipe for contraceptive tea to stop your monthly bleed, you may attend me in my cottage.' She jerked her chin. 'Mattias, dear, your teacher is waiting for you.'

At her delicate tone of mild disapprobation, Mateo managed his own nod and a bow of thanks. He followed the others into the hall. Some were flinging open the shutters, Andrea and Timon were sweeping the wooden boards clear of dust, Anika hurrying to help lay out cushions in their wake. He felt a burgeoning of hope. Anika was right, of course; everything was fine, and today, Mattias Taurasi was as he should be, for the first time since his long, gangly body had betrayed him by growing into the wrong shape, which meant that *all* would be as it should be.

Today, the ritual would work, the gift of the goddess would rise within him, and She would whisper Her name in his ear, lost to all but the Souls when She had shattered. He would open himself to Her wild gift, and tame it, and gift it in his turn to his people.

Mateo knelt on a cushion before the arrayed ranks of his cohort, their gazes brighter, expectant, hopeful. Yesterday, he had done this as a different person; his body might be the same, but it felt different. He felt more honest, truer to the sensation at the core of his being. He felt as calm as he ever had.

Sabine knelt with him, and he closed his eyes, feeling the weight of her hands as they settled over his shoulders. Her voice was slow and soft and serene as she began to speak into his ear like the low and soothing hiss of ocean waves on the shore.

'Deep, slow breaths, Mattias. That's it. Now seek within, my dear. Sense within yourself the Shattered One's gift to Her Souls. It is a burning wildfire, an inferno, but you are safe. Reach for it, for it will not harm you. Her gift is threefold. Her gift blesses you with Her power. Her gift protects you from the scorch of Her power. Her gift bestows upon you the strength to contain Her power. Make of Her inferno a kitchen hearth for our people.'

Her soft murmur continued, and the cohort knelt patiently before him and breathed in harmony with each other and him, a single creature of slow inhale and slow exhale like the rush of waves in and out of a sea cave, a loud counterpoint to Sabine's ocean susurration. Mateo searched within himself, and it was the same as ever.

He bowed his head and covered his eyes with his hands without opening them.

'No?' Sabine said, and he heard, in the merest tremor beneath that one mild word, that his momentous step into his true self had raised her expectations too.

The ritual still didn't work.

He had stopped lying to himself, and to the Taurasi, and to the Shattered One, and the ritual still hadn't worked.

Mateo stood up from his cushion. He walked stiffly away as the gift rose in Sabine and she bestowed her magic into the waiting adolescents. His cohort turned to practising managing the ebb and flow of the gift within and through them. They made orbs of glowing amber to toss to each other, and formed their defensive shields, a personal version of the mighty communal wall that had held back an empire. Anika, the most skilful of them, focussed her attention to try to heal a small cut on Timon's forearm.

'I'm trusting you, Ana,' Timon said laughingly, but he really was, holding out his arm in front of her, steady as a rock.

Mateo watched, body tight. It was the same magic he would have given them. It shouldn't feel wrong. It shouldn't feel as bad as having to put the wrong sash wrap on every morning. The bees in his head were back; he was trying to contain them so hard that he tasted blood on his tongue from biting his lip.

He had thought that the walk through the village this morning would be the worst of it. But now that the worst had not come to pass, he could no longer deny the deeper, truer, fear that had underlaid his apprehension all along.

'Mateo, don't worry so.' Sabine had followed him across the hall. 'The gift will come when it comes. Trust our goddess; Her blessing is upon you.'

She was keeping her attention mostly on the others—they were trained from the moment they could start taking in magic as toddlers to never turn it on one another, but it could be intoxicating enough to draw them into trying to outdo each other, a danger in itself—but she still caught Mateo's flinch.

'What is it, my dear?'

He shook his head, wordless.

Sabine laid a hand on his arm. 'Give me some time, after the lesson, won't you?'

So Mateo sat cross-legged on his cushion and mutely waited until the others were finished, Sabine moving gracefully among them, prodding some to take more magic, others to be more cautious in their greedy snatch for it. She talked with Anika about her tiny healing, which Anika had performed with consummate skill, of course.

Eventually, Mateo's cohort gathered themselves up to head back out into the square, chattering and elated. Anika detached herself and held her hand out to Mateo. 'I'll come with you to Penelope's.'

'I need to talk to Mattias, Aniketa,' Sabine said. 'You go ahead. We will see you at the rites for Lucius this afternoon.'

Anika, hearing the smooth dismissal, went, not without a last look and a smile, part reassuring, part concerned.

Sabine stood before Mateo, head cocked. He couldn't meet her eye. 'Your hair is coming loose,' she said eventually, and knelt behind him.

She loosened the pins and combed out his hair with her fingers. She gave a small huff of laughter. 'Neither you nor Aniketa had done one of these before, had you? You more-or-less make a neater, wider, and lower version of the topknot, but without the tail, like we elders do.'

She tied his hair and began to roll it at his nape, adding confidingly, 'Some of the boys when I was growing up used to make their buns around a roll of silk to make them look bigger.'

Mateo blurted, 'What if She's angry with me?'

Her sure hands paused, just for an instant. Then she resumed the careful slide of the little jewelled pins, Soul status markers, into his hair. 'Ours is a benevolent goddess, Mattias. She is not angry with you.'

'But I'm—' He waved his hands up and down his body, which would speak his fear more eloquently than he could manage when he was in this keyed-up state. 'Wrong.'

'Wrong,' she repeated, a flat note entering her serene tones.

It was easy to excavate the words, when he couldn't see her face. 'I tried to make it right, and the ritual still didn't work. So I must still be wrong, in Her eyes. I can't ever be right with a, a *costume* and a suffix change.'

Sabine gave the newly reinforced bun a pat and rose with smooth grace. 'I think it's time to go up the mountain, Mattias.'

Mateo nodded tiredly. She was right. He needed to run the trails, to outrace the circling thoughts, the blackness lying in wait to trip him and drag him down.

But to his surprise, Sabine took his arm as they left the meeting hall together. 'You'll have to help an old woman on the steepest bits, my dear.' When he glanced at her, she smiled. 'We're going all the way to the peak today.'

BEYOND THE LAST of the mountain trails that networked between the seven Kindred villages and the Klados hall lay a neglected path, stony underfoot except where the wild goats had worn a narrow thread up to the very peak of the sacred mountain, where no one but Souls were permitted, and not even they came here often anymore.

Sabine, though she had been mostly joking about needing help up the slopes, was indeed leaning quite heavily on Mateo's arm by the time they made the last clamber across slippery scree. They stood together in the open clearing, breathing hard and sweating in the inevitable sunshine that bathed the Sunlit Isle in every direction.

The sun was high overhead now; if they were not careful, they would be late to the rites to mark the anniversary of Lucius's passing, and if Charion was a mild and forgiving Heart, Penelope would certainly have words to say about the failure of the Soul to properly honour her predecessor.

Sabine did not seem concerned. She waited patiently while Mateo drank his fill of the view, turning a full circle to fully take in a sight that only the chosen of the goddess were blessed to receive: the unbroken vista of their glorious sky, an arched vault of cerulean kissing the unending ocean in every direction, the fall of the grey-green slopes to the seawards cliffs and golden beaches, the little dip that bespoke the trading village at the harbour, the glimpse of the Taurasi rooftops through the scrubby trees far below them, and those of other villages.

It set off in Mateo a yearning like the opposite of homesickness, a sort of anticipatory nostalgia for the very earth under his feet. Some Ystherans left their Kindreds and their island, made their homes on the empire-ruled mainland. The thought of that, the aloneness of it, the exile of it, was dreadful.

His mentor nodded her chin towards a narrow path on the far side. Mateo followed her obediently. His mood was already better, the exertion on the mountain trails capped by the reward of the island vista working its magic, but Sabine would still want to talk to him about his morose outburst; he'd brought it on himself.

They scrabbled around a rocky outcrop, to find a wide mouth yawning on its eastern face. Mateo checked; he hadn't known the sacred peak held what must be an even more sacred cave. The space inside was bare, more a deep, broad nook under an overhanging ledge rather than a true cave. Abstract designs of ochre and soot ringed the rough walls, protected from wind and rain, but Sabine didn't give him time to examine them.

Instructing him to kneel opposite her at the mouth, she said, 'It is said this is where the goddess came to sleep, after She was shattered.'

Mateo resisted the urge to turn to look again at the bare space behind him, small and empty, and smelling vaguely of goat.

Sabine smiled and indicated the designs daubed on the back wall. 'The cave extends deeper, beyond what you can see. But no, we do not find Her here in any literal sense. Nonetheless, Her spirit is here. Close your eyes. You may feel Her breath on your cheeks.'

Mateo obliged, but all he felt was the salt-tinged caress of the breeze from over the ocean. His mood began to falter again, yawing off its even keel. He wondered if he should tell Sabine he felt the goddess. He wondered if this was his last chance. He wondered what happened to nascent Souls who did not ascend, their height and thinness forever marking them out as failures amid the other Ystherans.

His breathing stuttered as the bees began to buzz.

'Now, Mattias, I have a confession to make,' Sabine said. 'I have done poorly by you.'

'No,' Mateo said in alarm, his eyes springing open. 'Sabine, you have been the best, most patient, teacher. It's not your fault I'm—I'm wrong.'

'This whole time,' she went on, as mellowly as if he had not spoken, 'I have been giving you the metaphor that worked for me, that of containing a wildfire. And do you know, I had forgotten, until this very morning, that when Lucius began to train me as his auxiliary, more years ago than you need to think about, he taught me with a different metaphor. It doesn't really matter what it was; what matters is this—Lucius's way of conceptualising the gift of our goddess was different to mine, and it *did not work for me.*'

She took his hand, and held it warmly between both of hers, smooth palms cradling him. 'I've been trying to force you into using what *I* use, doing what *I* do, understanding the way *I* understand. I didn't realise I was doing it, but I was. You are *right*, my dear, and I am the one who was wrong.

'So now we are here, within the nimbus of our shattered and sleeping goddess, for you to find your own way to Her.'

Sabine released his hand, and rose. She bowed formally, and unhurriedly left the little cave, walking out of sight around the outcrop back to the clearing; for all Mateo knew, she was walking back to the village with the implicit injunction that he should not return unless he had ascended.

No. That was the buzz of the bees in his head. He was still a Taurasi, even if he failed at becoming a Soul. His people would not turn him out, no matter how odd and anxious a creature he was. They would still care for him. Pity him. Murmur about him.

Mateo hit the heel of his hand into the side of his head. *Breathe*, he told himself. *Breathe.* It didn't help. The rush of misery was instant and absolute. He lowered his head into his hands.

And then there was rustle and a slide of scree, and Anika was sitting beside him, wrapping her arm about him, out of breath and hot to the touch.

'Anika!' he said. 'You can't be here, this is sacred ground.'

Anika scoffed. 'Sabine *saw* me. Why do you think she left you on your own when she knew your thoughts would start to spiral in on you like that?'

'I am so very useless,' Mateo said bitterly.

'You're not,' she said. 'You've just got your what-ifs. That's all right. One day, I'll be the best Heart on Ysthera, and I'll need the best Soul. That's you, Teo.'

Mateo sighed deeply, both touched and alarmed by her unshakeable faith. He rested his head on her shoulder while she stroked his tense back, safely anchored in her calm, solid presence, and thought about what Sabine had said.

He had to find his own way to the goddess. Closing his eyes and turning inwards inevitably invited the worst of his thoughts to run rampant. He kept his eyes open instead and stared out over the ocean, a deep midnight blue with just the white caps of the wind-driven waves to add texture and endless motion.

He tracked the constant ripple of the waves towards Ysthera across the deep blue, spending long moments tracing his gaze from the horizon to the point where the grey-green slopes blocked his view, and then back out to the horizon to watch a new ingress of waves. The repetitive motion was almost hypnotic, as soothing as Anika's gentle rhythmic stroke over his back.

The waters of the uncharted sea were a vast expanse, untamed, unplumbed, as wild and deadly in storm as any raging wildfire would be in the hot summer amid the groves.

When it happened, it was with an almost audible click. Mateo saw within himself not an inferno, and not even a stormy ocean, but instead the smooth and still surface of a great stretch of water, as grey as the sky it reflected like a mirror. It was not a memory; this was not a place that existed on Ysthera, which was not flat enough to hold a lake the size of this one.

All that water was very deep, and very heavy, so heavy that it would crush his Kindred, crash upon them and drown them all, should he ever let the wall holding it back falter.

He set his hand upon the dam wall. Its height was a hundred of his. It was strong, and it sheltered his people from the water. He could turn away from it now, and know that his was the strength that kept his people safe.

But he wasn't done. He couldn't be done yet, for the gift of the goddess was threefold.

His trance was not gauche enough to give him an actual vision of Her, but he felt Her aura all about as he walked along the wall and found the tap.

For Sabine, it was a kitchen hearth.

Mateo turned the tap, and magic began to flow, and the sound of it was the name of the goddess. It spread through him, blooming from a kernel at his core, spreading across his torso and down into his limbs, transforming every inch of him in its wake.

He blinked awake. He was kneeling in the cave mouth, Anika holding him. So strong was the feeling of transformation that he put a hand to his chest, and was surprised to find the binding still there.

But that wasn't what had changed.

'Teo,' Anika whispered. 'You're *shining*.'

BY THE AUTHOR

Thanks for reading. If you enjoyed this book, check out more titles and bonus material at wendypalmer.au.

The Domain trilogy
Wild Imperative
Cursed Girls
Lost Child

Mosaic Virus duology
Bastard's Grace
Six Feet of Ridiculous
Mosaic Garden: Stories from Aspermonde

Artisans
The Uses of Illicit Art
The Use of Myriad Arts

Standalones
Fair Haven
Domesticated Magic